Saving
Rafael

Saving Rafael

LESLIE WILSON

ANDERSEN PRESS

First published in 2009 by
Andersen Press Limited,
20 Vauxhall Bridge Road, London SW1V 2SA
www.andersenpress.co.uk
www.lesliewilson.co.uk

British Library Cataloguing in Publication Data available

ISBN 978 184 270 918 4

Typeset by FiSH Books, Enfield, Middx.
Printed in the UK by CPI Bookmarque, Croydon CR0 4TD

For Kathy
with love

Acknowledgements

I have been greatly helped in writing this novel by many people who've generously given time, assistance, and information. Special thanks are due to Matthias Brundel, John Yule, Ann Turnbull, Rabbi Dr Charles Middleburgh, Wilma Wilson, Ronnie le Drew of the Little Angel Marionette Theatre, Stig Edner, Elke Asmus, the German Federal Archive, the Imperial War Museum, the Jewish Museum in Berlin, Air Marshal Sir John Cheshire, Sheena Hennessy, Brenda Bailey, Drs Sue and Andy Black, Edward H Milligan, and Jacki Evans of the Hungarian Puli Club of Great Britain.

I also want to thank my husband David, my daughters Kathy and Jo, my brother Phil Baker and all my fellow author friends for their steady encouragement; my agent, Sarah Molloy and editor Liz Maude. Last but not least I should thank my dogs Bramble and Matilda – though they're not Pulis – for providing a model of canine behaviour.

Prologue
Uckermark Girls' Concentration Camp, Spring 1944

We were in a cow byre, ten of us, cleaning out the stalls in our thin striped calico skirts and jackets. We were girls without names and we were cold and hungry and bone-tired every hour of the day.

They'd given us dented old shovels to work with and the muck we had to clear up was runny; it kept trying to slither off before you could get it into the wheelbarrow. As soon as we'd got a barrowload, Kerner picked on a girl to stagger away with it, out to the steaming manure heap in the yard. At least there was some heat coming out of the cow shit.

Then a cow splatted and some of it went in my clog. It was warm and squishy, but I knew it'd be cold soon enough. And the whole trembling lot of muck toppled off my shovel. Oh, God, I thought. *No.* And Kerner lashed out at me. Hard as she could across my back.

'Stupid whore!' she yelled.

Inside I was crying like a hurt kid, but I bit my lip and managed to keep quiet. I knew I'd get another blow if I made a sound. I bent down, I loaded my shovel again, while all the time my back was hurting and I was trembling. Then the door creaked open and the outside air came rushing into the byre. The farmer's wife had come to check how the job was going on. The mess on my foot went cold round the edges and my wet clothes felt like ice.

I knew better than to look at her. I hefted my shovel and tipped the muck into the wheelbarrow. I wished I could throw it into Kerner's face.

'They're doing a wonderful job,' the farmer's wife said to Kerner. 'I don't know what I'd have done if you hadn't been able to help me out, my son's been called up and my Frenchmen went down with the 'flu, both of them, it'll be a few days before they send me any more—'

She broke off. I did raise my eyes then and saw her looking straight at me. My headscarf had slipped and she could see my fuzz of hair, shorter than most boys'. A little shudder went through her.

Kerner said, 'It's a good thing you haven't got any Frenchmen around at the moment, too fond of men, these scum are. That's what most of them were sent here for. Letting themselves down with filthy foreign workers, prostitution – take that one, 610.' She pointed at me.

I dug my shovel into the muck; it scraped on the cement floor and set my teeth on edge. The wind was still sharp coming through the byre door, I hated the farmer's wife for leaving it open. All right for her, with her big thick coat on, and gloves on her hands. Kerner had gloves, too.

'She'd been whoring around with God knows how

2

many men, only to be expected really, her family were a proper nest of delinquents, couldn't be bothered to join Party organisations, never lifted a finger to help the war effort.'

I wanted to hit her over the head with my shovel then, because of my brother Karl. And Dad, in prisoner-of-war camp in America. But she was right, really. None of us had ever wanted to do anything for Hitler's war.

'Degenerates,' Kerner said. 'And they used to be really cosy' – she sank her voice – 'with Jews.'

'She's very thin,' the farmer's wife said doubtfully to Kerner.

'Food's short for everyone,' Kerner said in a hard voice. 'She's up to the job, don't worry. And we give them extra rations for outdoor work.'

I wondered what the farmer's wife thought we'd got. A big glass of milk, maybe, fresh farm bread, jam made from fruit? Oh, we'd had a better breakfast than usual, but that wasn't saying much, it hadn't been enough to fill our starving bellies. Suddenly I was yearning for fat sausages with a heap of fried potatoes. Hot and filling. Real sausage with spice in, and potatoes all brown and crunchy at the edges. And then, while Kerner had her head turned towards the farmer's wife, Erna grabbed her opportunity and grimaced sympathetically at me. Beyond her, Luise clenched an angry fist.

'Oh, of course,' the farmer's wife said quickly. 'I'm

sure you treat them better than they deserve.'

Luise's eyes rolled. I rolled mine back, then looked quickly away before Kerner noticed. I felt a tiny bit better.

'These little trollops are from the reception block,' said Kerner, 'they stay there six months, for assessment. We set the new ones to knitting socks for the troops – first time in their lives most of them have done anything useful.'

She grinned evilly. I saw Luise's fist clench again.

Kerner went on, 'It's not a bad idea for them to get a taste of agricultural labour, that's what we'll put most of them to later, the hopeless types. There are a few that we might make something out of after all. Just a few. We send those to work in the armaments factory – take that barrow out to the muck heap, 610! Jump to it!'

I pulled my scarf back over my head and put my shovel down, got hold of the barrow's handles and started to push it out. It was almost too heavy for me and it wobbled crazily, for a moment I thought the whole lot would spill over, but I just managed.

The farmer's wife gave me a hard look as I went out into the yard. She'd switched off feeling sorry for me. And I was almost glad. I'd hated her saying how thin I was. I knew, of course, I could see my own arms and legs, and I'd seen my face in the mirror two weeks ago, in Grendel's quarters. I'd looked like a ghost, with huge shadowed eyes, a sharp, starved pointed chin and convict-cropped hair that was drab with dirt and grease.

Grendel had laughed when I'd shrunk away from my reflection.

I hated the farmer's wife now, hated Kerner and Grendel. I burned up with hate so fiercely it almost warmed me. I thought: There *is* a girl inside the starved, scared slave those bitches see. Not 610. Jenny Friedemann. I thought how I'd had a family and friends who'd loved me, and a boy who'd loved me, too. Who'd said I was beautiful. Only I pushed that memory out of my mind, it was too dangerous.

All at once I heard an engine coming here. A car by the sound of it. I didn't hang around to find out if I was right, not with Kerner standing on guard at the byre door, stroking her truncheon with her leather-gloved finger. I emptied the wheelbarrow onto the muck heap and trundled it back into the building.

'Don't shut the door, girl,' Kerner said to me.

I picked up my shovel, hearing the car getting closer. It couldn't be anything to do with the farm, because the farmer's wife was looking surprised. I met Luise's eye again, just for a second and we shared our fear. Unusual things were usually bad news for us. I knew everyone was like me, listening, listening as we worked, as the engine stopped and a vehicle door opened, holding their breaths.

I knew Grendel's footsteps as soon as I heard them

tramping across the cobbled yard. You learned the guards by heart here, they were always there, watching us, hitting us, yelling at us. Now she came in through the open door with her truncheon swinging at her belt. Kerner was brown haired, square and raw boned. Grendel had blonde hair and curves inside her uniform, you could call her pretty if you didn't know what we knew about her.

'610!' she barked. 'Put your shovel away in the corner and come with me!'

My throat went tight, as if someone had whipped a noose round it from behind, but I put the shovel away promptly and followed Grendel outside. I just noticed the farmer's wife staring with a blank look, like one of her own cows. There was just a whisper of hope inside me, but I was too afraid to pay much heed to it.

There was a big grey car standing in the yard. Grendel opened the back door and pushed me in there, then she came in beside me. The driver started the engine and we drove off, bouncing over the farm road.

I grabbed the leather strap that hung down from the roof, I held on tight. Grendel was close to me, I could smell her sweat and the cheap scent she put on to mask it. She shot a cold look at me and that tiny hope died inside me.

I stared out of the window. The fields and trees blurred in front of my eyes. I'd been a fool, hadn't I, even thinking I could get her to help me. Just because

6

I'd had an English grandmother, because I'd spun her a line about my family connections, because Germany was losing the war – I'd thought I was being so clever. All the time she must have been laughing at me up her sleeve.

I knew what must have happened when I'd given her that letter to Aunt Grete. She'd handed it straight to the Director, who'd read it. All the things I'd said about the camp. How I'd asked my aunt to help me get out. And it made cold sense that they'd waited till today to pounce. Till I'd done my bit for their marionette show.

The car turned off the farm road. How far was it to the camp? Ten kilometres? They were going to kill me. They liked killing people here. They'd killed a girl last month for trying to escape.

My heels were pressing down inside my clogs as if they could go right through the floor and hold the car back, make it go slower, stop it altogether. My hand cramped on the strap, I thought I'd never be able to let go of it. I was just a skinful of fear, every part of me was sour and on edge with terror. And inside me a voice kept yammering: Help me, please, won't somebody help me? I want my mum.

They were the dead girl's words, that's what she'd screamed out. It'd be me this time. They'd let their dogs savage me and the guards would smash my limbs with their truncheons and then they'd rope me to a post to die slowly, blood trickling off me. Unless the

Director decided to do something different to me. Something worse, maybe.

The car swung round a corner, throwing me against Grendel. She hit out at me, pushing me away with her truncheon. I shrank back towards the car door. It was locked, of course. I couldn't jump out of it. I thought if I could only make myself small, really small and tiny, like a mouse, I could find a hole in the bodywork and she'd never find me, none of them would ever find me. Then I knew what a fool I was to imagine something impossible like that. I was a fool in every way. And I needed to pee, any minute now I was going to wet myself.

I heard Dad's voice, as if he was here. 'Jenny, it was worth trying.'

I'd never see Dad again, not even to say goodbye to him, or Mum. Or Raf – but no, I mustn't let myself think about Raf.

The car stopped. Grendel came round to the door beside me and unlocked it.

The sky was dark as lead above the squat, ugly camp buildings and the wind blew a spatter of sleet into my face. We were outside the fence. I stumbled in the clumsy wooden clogs.

Grendel whacked the back of my thigh with her truncheon.

'What do you think you're doing?' she snapped. 'Dawdling along like an idiot.'

We went into the block where the Director's office must be. Grendel knocked on the door. No answer. Grendel frowned. Then a woman came out of a side door with a lot of brown paper files. Horn-rimmed glasses on her face, hair scraped back. A secretary.

She didn't seem surprised to see us. 'Oh,' she said. 'She's been called away. You can put the girl in the holding room till she comes back.'

There were bars on the window of the narrow holding room, a wooden bench to put my bum on and a chlorine-stinking bucket that I used at once. I let go of my pee and the memories of Raf came, the ones I'd shut away so they wouldn't spill out of me when the Gestapo interrogated me.

No, I thought. I've got to remember the others. Dad and Mum and Karl and Paula. And Muffi. I summoned up the picture of my dog with her cords of black hair hiding everything except her shiny button nose and her pink tongue, desperate to drive Raf away. But I couldn't, he was right there in front of me now, looking at me questioningly, intently, with his grey-blue eyes. I could feel his fingers playing with mine. I could hear his voice, saying, 'Jenny.'

I couldn't stop myself wanting to be with him, wanting to hold his face in my hands and stroke it. I wanted to kiss him and feel his body pressing against mine. I was answering him in my mind: Oh, Raf, Raf. *Raf*.

Chapter One
Charlottenburg, Berlin:
October–November 1935

It was a blowy afternoon in October when I was a little kid of eight with bright carroty hair and Raf was ten. I was going down the back staircase into the yard behind our apartment block and I was fed up. Karl was out with his friend Fritz. Mum was downstairs in the shop helping Dad, and Kattrin, our maid, wouldn't let me make a cake because she wanted to clean out the kitchen.

But I stopped being fed up when I saw Raf in the yard and he gave me his grin. If Raf grinned at you, you had to laugh, even if you'd just been wanting to hit him. He said it even worked with angry teachers, and I believed him.

'Are you coming for a bike ride?' he said.

We fetched our bikes out from the shed in the yard where they lived, and wheeled them through the passage between our parents' two shops and onto the street.

In those days Charlottenburg was all clean and there was bright, pale paint on the big five-storey apartment houses, and that day the street had just been swept and washed. The wind was pulling the yellow leaves off the trees and making them sail down slantwise till they hit the wet road surface and stuck there. The tram ran along with all its windows clear; there wasn't any need to black them out because we weren't at war.

Raf cycled away, his white-blond hair shining in the sunlight, and his jacket flying open and flapping like a pair of grey cloth wings. 'Come on!' he shouted. 'This is the All-Germany bike race and we're the frontrunners!'

I put my foot down on the ground and pushed off, pedalling as hard as I could to catch up with him. We went up and down the street, aiming for the tidy heaps of leaves that the street sweepers had left to be collected, making them crackle and fly dustily up round us.

Then Raf stopped his bike so suddenly I almost fell off mine, braking. He said, 'Mum was making apple cake. It must be ready by now. Let's go and eat it.'

We were back in the yard behind the house and I was putting my bike away when he came up to me and said, 'Have you ever kissed a boy?'

I felt shy all of a sudden. I said, 'I've kissed Karl.'

'Not like that,' he said scornfully. 'He's your brother.'

I knew what he meant, really.

'Do you want to kiss me?' he asked. 'See what it's like?'

I didn't say anything, but I put my face up and he put his arms round me and squeezed me so that I could hardly breathe and pushed a kiss onto my screwed-shut lips.

'Did you like that?' he asked, letting go of me.

'Not much,' I said. That was a lie. I had liked it, and now I was confused with the feeling of his lips on mine, and of his dusty, pushy boy-body all warm against me. I wanted to run away and think about it.

I said, 'Maybe you ought to practise some more.'

'Oh,' he said, and he sounded so downcast I opened my mouth to say all right, I had liked it. Only I could hear someone coming. Kattrin.

'Come inside,' she said. 'You've got to see your parents.'

She was scared. She was shaking, I couldn't understand it. She didn't say a word to Raf, who stood there staring. She pulled me towards the shop.

They weren't angry but Dad was miserable. He looked as if he'd gone all frayed at the edges.

'Jenny,' he said. 'I have to explain something to you.'

I looked down and saw the new marionette he'd started, lying on his work table. A wolf. Its mouth was snarling. Snarling at me, I thought. And I didn't want to be there. My feet fidgeted under me, they so much wanted to take me away. I'd been caught kissing Raf, and somehow that was naughty – or why would Dad be looking like that? I didn't want to think about kissing him now. I never wanted to think about it again.

Dad put his hands on my shoulders. 'Jenny,' he said. 'Raf and Uncle Markus and Aunty Edith are our special friends, like family. But – they're Jewish.'

13

'I know,' I said, wishing he'd let go of me.

'Jenny,' Mum said, and there was an edge to her voice. 'Listen to your father.'

Dad said, 'The trouble is, the people who are in power now and make the laws – they hate Jews, and of course it can't last, but in the meantime – Jenny,' he said all in a rush, 'they've made a law that means you can't kiss Raf.'

My skin prickled with fright and I started crying. I already knew how bad it was to break the law. I said, 'You won't let the police take me away to prison, will you?'

Dad put his arms round me and held me tight. '*No*,' he said, 'but they might do something to Raf and Uncle Markus and Aunty Edith. Or even to Mum and me for letting it happen. And, Jenny, we have to be especially careful, with me being a Quaker.'

The wolf puppet snarled at me again. Suddenly everything in the world seemed to have grown sharp, savage edges. I knew Dad was a Quaker. He went to meetings in a shabby house in the centre of Berlin; they sat quiet and still and every now and again someone stood up and said something. Dad called that 'ministry'; it wasn't planned in advance, people just felt they had to speak. He said it was different from other churches where people said prayers out of a book, but we didn't go to other churches. None of the rest of us went to the Quaker Meeting much either. When I did, I was bored a lot of the time, but

14

there was something about the silence, it wasn't ordinary silence, if you let yourself go into it you felt as if you were wading into cool water.

'Why?' I asked – and I could hear how shrill and scared my voice sounded. 'Why do you have to be careful because you're a Quaker?'

Dad said, 'Because we care about people the Nazis don't like.'

I'd had enough of hearing bad things. I said, 'I'll be good, Dad, I promise.'

And Dad said, in a voice that shook, 'Not good, Jenny. You haven't been bad. It's the times we live in.'

I didn't want to speak to Raf after that, and he was shy of me, but then one day he grinned at me, and I had to be friends with him again. We didn't try any more kissing, though. We'd learned our lesson.

Chapter Two
1938

Three years later it was five thirty in the morning and Raf and I were side by side on our sitting-room sofa, listening to a group of Nazi thugs wrecking the Jakobys' apartment. Uncle Markus was holding Aunty Edith in his arms. She was trembling violently, as if someone else was shaking her. 'Our home, Markus,' she kept saying. 'Our home.'

Raf stood up, clenching his fists.

'I want to kill them,' he said.

Uncle Markus nodded.

They were wearing the things they'd managed to scramble together when the men had smashed the glass in the shop and our dog had started barking. Raf was wearing a pair of trousers and a jumper, but his feet were bare. Uncle Markus had shoes on, but no socks, and a shirt without a collar under his jacket. Aunty Edith was in her dressing gown. Her big black shiny handbag huddled at her slippered feet.

And I was so scared. I said, 'Mightn't they come here, Dad?'

'If they do,' Dad said to Uncle Markus, 'we'll get the three of you out down the back staircase.'

He was only thinking about our friends' safety: it

hadn't occurred to him that they might come and destroy our home too. I was ashamed of being scared, but my belly went on cramping up inside me. I wanted Mum, but she'd gone to look after Grandma, who had 'flu. Karl was sleeping over at Fritz's house.

There was a helter-skelter of smashes next door and a picture flashed into my mind's eye of a man sweeping all the best cups and saucers out of Aunty Edith's china cupboard. It didn't make sense to me. Oh, I'd heard it in the classroom – 'The Jews are your misfortune': that was what the teachers said. But I knew Uncle Markus and Aunty Edith were our good fortune, they were wonderful friends, and it was all horrible.

Muffi growled at my feet. I wanted to cry, but we had to be quiet, and I said, 'No, Muffi,' to her and put my hand over her nose and mouth. And I kept thinking: Why? and it felt as if my skull was an echo chamber, yelling back at me, Why, why, why? and it hurt.

'She might as well bark,' Kattrin said. 'They'll never hear her, with the racket they're making.' She was twisting nervously at the rags she put in her hair every night to make it curl. I wanted her to stop.

Uncle Markus said, 'I've fought for Germany, I've spilled my blood for my country, and if fellows who call themselves patriots come to destroy my livelihood—'

'*No*, Markus!' Aunty Edith said in a high, terrified voice.

Dad said, 'You can't fight them, Markus.'

Raf was still standing in the middle of the floor. Furiously, he said, 'We're helpless, aren't we? I can't stand it.'

'I'll get hot drinks for us all,' Kattrin said, getting up. 'Look at the lad's feet, blue with cold they are. It's a crying shame—'

She swept off to the kitchen and came back after a while with coffee for the grown-ups and hot chocolate for me and Raf. Nobody really wanted to drink, but she made us.

At last the noise stopped and we heard the men tramping away down the stairs. 'I'll go and see if they're really gone,' Dad said. 'If any of them's still there I'll just tell him we heard the noise and wondered—'

Uncle Markus said, 'I ought to be with you—' but Aunty Edith grabbed his arm and held on tight.

'They've gone,' Dad said, coming back. 'You'd better prepare yourselves. It's not a pretty sight. And Jenny, shut Muffi away. She'd cut her paws on the broken glass.'

'Raf—' Aunty Edith said, looking at his bare feet.

'Put a pair of Karl's shoes on,' said Dad.

The apartment door was lying in fragments on the entrance hall floor. Someone had hacked it to bits with an axe. The men had hurled the pictures down and broken them and the chest in the hall was in splinters. I stared at the wall behind where it had stood; my eyes were still expecting to see it, and the owl I always saw in the grain of the right-hand door. They'd smashed the china cabinet in the sitting room and there were shards of china and glass everywhere. The sofa was just a mess of distorted springs, chunks of horsehair and cotton wadding, rags of brocade. The apartment wasn't a home any longer and the worst thing was the rank, sharp smell in the air and the trails of wet all over the sitting-room carpet. I couldn't believe it, the men had pissed on the carpet as if they'd been dogs in the street.

'Oh God,' Aunty Edith said. 'Oh God.'

'I want to kill them,' Raf said again. His voice was shaking.

I saw an arm sticking out from behind the remains of the sofa. It's a child, I thought, they've killed a child and left it there – but then I realised.

'Theresia,' I said. She'd been a big china doll that Aunty Edith had had when she was a girl. I'd loved playing with her. That was over now, though. Someone had stamped on her head. There was a tangle of brown hair with sharp fragments of porcelain all through it.

When I saw that, I started to sob, because Theresia had been a person to me, with her big brown eyes and her soft real hair and her small, shy smile. I'd loved her and the men had killed her. Aunty Edith put her arms round me. She was crying too. A tram went past in the road outside. I wondered how trams could run, just as usual.

'The swine,' Raf said. 'The filthy, filthy swine.'

We went down to the shop. They'd taken an axe to the bookshelves and hacked at the leather-bound books. Uncle Markus picked the wreck of a book off the floor. Its spine was broken. A few pages flew away from it like scared birds, but they fell on the ground.

'Goethe,' Uncle Markus said. The morning stubble on his cheeks made his face look thinner, grimmer. 'Germany's greatest writer. German men did this, Dietrich. And I've been proud to call myself a German.'

Dad put his hand on Uncle Markus's shoulder. '*I'm* proud to have you as my countryman.'

'But I'm not your countryman, Dietrich,' Uncle Markus said. 'Not any more. The Nazi laws have made me into a subject, not a citizen. They threw me out of the chess club because I'm a Jew. We had to get rid of the maid because she was an *Aryan* and I might force my filthy Jewish attentions on her—'

'Markus!' Edith said. 'The children!'

'I'm sorry, Edith. But I've swallowed insult after insult, hoping things would get better. I've been a fool, Dietrich.'

I felt as if he was angry with us. Aunty Edith put her arm round me again and I huddled up to her.

Raf said, 'You're right, Dad. We'll have to emigrate.'

I clutched at Aunty Edith's hand then. I wanted to stop her leaving us. I was still such a kid. She kept hold of me, but she said, 'Jenny. You ought to get dressed. You should be going to school, you and Raf—'

'No,' we said together.

The grown-ups didn't argue, I think they were still too shocked. Dad said, 'We'll need everyone's help to put the shop back together again. I wish Karl hadn't stayed out, he'll just go straight on to school—'

I said, 'Dad, Fritz has a telephone at his house, you can ring there, Karl won't have gone out yet.'

He went to use the telephone in our shop, but he came back quickly.

'It's not working,' he said. 'They must have cut off the wires when they broke in.'

I offered to go to Fritz's and get Karl, and Raf said he'd go with me.

'Should we tell Mum?' I asked.

'Later,' Dad said. 'She's worried about your grandmother, this news can wait.'

We'd no idea, any of us, what was going on.

Chapter Three

When Raf and I went out onto the street, we saw a crowd outside the Silbermanns' antique shop. There were gaping jagged holes in the shop window.

'They've been there too,' Raf said, walking up the street so fast I had to scuttle to keep up with him. The sweet taste of the chocolate I'd drunk hung around in my throat, it made me feel sick. Then an ambulance came along with its bell jangling. It pulled up outside the shop, two men jumped out and unloaded a stretcher. The crowd parted to let them go to the door.

The ambulance was from the Jewish hospital.

Raf pointed at the crowd. 'There's Frau Janke.' We pushed and shoved our way through the crowd and fetched up next to the caretaker's wife.

'Rafael,' she said. 'Jenny. Old Herr Silbermann's had a heart attack, and no wonder, after what they've done here – and what are the pair of you doing out in all this?' But she didn't give us time to tell her. She leaned close to Raf and whispered, 'Don't let anyone know you're Jewish.'

'Why not?' he demanded aloud.

She shook her head at him and went on whispering.

I could only just hear her. 'You know how a Jew's shot an official at our Embassy in Paris?'

I didn't, but Raf seemed to.

'Well, I don't see why that should be poor Herr Silbermann's fault or your family's, but they're saying all the Jews in Germany were behind it—'

'What?' Raf hissed.

She said, 'They're raiding all the Jewish businesses. It's dreadful on the Kurfürstendamm.'

Raf and I stared at one another, then we just turned and ran up the street. I didn't believe what was happening, maybe he didn't either.

There was plenty to see. As soon as we turned the corner we almost ran into a grinning gang of men coming out of a wrecked jeweller's shop with their pockets bulging. There was a smash of glass and I saw a lot of tough-looking types breaking a shoe shop window with a sledgehammer; a high-class shop, like all the ones round here. The men were in civvies but you could see they were storm troopers, the kind you saw marching round the streets singing songs with catchy tunes and Nazi words. One of them reached gingerly in past the shards of broken glass and fetched out a pair of crocodile-skin pumps without scratching himself. He wanted them for his girlfriend, maybe, or his wife. I hoped he'd got the size wrong and she'd smack him round the head with them. And suddenly something big was hurtling down from above. Raf grabbed me and pulled me out of the way.

A hand clutched my shoulder as the thing went down. Not Raf's hand.

Raf's grip tightened on my arm. 'He's dead,' he said. His voice was very quiet.

I said, 'What? Who touched me?'

Then I looked. There was a man lying like an unstrung marionette on the pavement right beside me. His face was bruised on one side and his skull was an odd shape. There was blood running out of his mouth and making a little red stream across the pavement, steaming slightly in the cold air.

Raf said, 'He reached out to try and hold onto you. He was still alive till—'

'No,' I said. 'Don't.'

There was a shouting from the second-floor balcony. We looked up and saw a thickset man giving the Hitler salute.

'Another filthy Jew croaks!' he barked out. 'This is the spontaneous revenge of the German people! '

A smartly dressed man walked past the corpse and the shouting and his whole body said: I'm not paying attention to all this. I've got my work to go to. But a wiry chap in spattered painter's overalls stopped and said, 'Spontaneous as kissing your arse, mate.' He didn't say it loudly, and when another group of roughs came towards us he moved on fast. Raf towed me away, too.

When we'd got out of earshot of the Brown Shirts, he said, 'That could had been Dad.'

I started to cry. I couldn't help myself.

'How could we have gone to school?' Raf demanded. 'What would have been the point?'

He let go of me. I wished he hadn't. I put my sleeve up and wiped my eyes and nose on it. 'Raf, it's like a nightmare,' I said.

'Yes,' Raf said. His face was grim. 'It's a nightmare that someone else has dreamed and now they're making us live it.'

I said, 'Let's go and find Karl.'

We had to turn off the Kurfürstendamm to get to Fritz's place; that was when we saw the synagogue burning. The flames were leaping and roaring at the windows and there was a plume of smoke going up into the morning sky. The Brown Shirts had got a bonfire on the pavement outside. Jewish sacred things: I could see the end of a scroll poking out of the flames. There were firemen there, but they were only spraying the nextdoor buildings, not the synagogue.

I wasn't surprised. It was too late to be surprised.

An elderly man in an overcoat said, 'At least they're making sure the Aryan property doesn't get damaged.' He sounded relieved, or even satisfied.

Then I saw my big brother. He was a metre or so away from us, in his school clothes with his leather schoolbag in his hand and he was scowling at the man who'd just spoken.

'Karl!' I said. I went to him and he put his arms

round me, but he couldn't drive the crazy nightmare feeling away.

When we got home Karl and Raf went straight to the bookshop. I went upstairs to the Jakobys' apartment. Kattrin was there already, scrubbing away at the carpet, muttering to herself.

'They've smashed the beds to bits,' Kattrin said to me, 'but I've told Frau Jakoby they can all sleep at our place. And have you seen the wallpaper? They've relieved themselves there, too. It's disgusting. Did you find Karl?'

I said, 'They've been to all the Jewish homes and shops to wreck them.'

Aunty Edith came in with her hands all black. 'They put my best coat in the kitchen heating stove,' she said. 'I was trying to get it out, but it's ruined already. It might as well burn. At least they left me something to wear. I suppose it wouldn't do to have a Jewess walking naked round the streets.'

It hurt me to hear the hard bitterness in her voice.

Kattrin said, 'It looks like it's not just you, Frau Jakoby. Jenny says—'

I told them what Raf and I had seen – except about the man falling out of the window. I couldn't make myself talk about that.

'They set the synagogue on fire?' Aunty Edith asked. 'And the fire brigade just stood by?'

'Dear God, dear God,' Kattrin said, and started to

scrub the carpet again. I watched the lather come out from under her brush. 'I'd like to go and see that Hitler hanged,' she muttered. 'Never liked him, the disgusting rabble-rousing...'

Aunty Edith said, 'Jenny, I don't know what to do with Theresia.' Her voice was trembling. 'I've gathered the pieces of her up, but I don't want to put her in the rubbish bin.'

'No, of course not,' I said, feeling my own throat knot up. 'You know, Dad could probably use her hair for a marionette. Then a bit of her would be alive still.'

'That would be good,' Aunty Edith said.

I said, 'Dad could think of something to do with the rest of her, maybe.'

'We'll ask him. I'd better get on.'

I worked alongside her, clearing up, filling a bucket with the fragments of her best cups and saucers and plates, taking them down to the big bins in the yard. The storm troopers had stolen the silver teapot and milk jug. Janke was out there, and he frowned at the bucket. 'Filthy beasts,' he said, and I was glad there were some people around who thought the way we did.

When I went upstairs, Frau Janke had arrived. She was doing what she could with the stains on the wallpaper. A few minutes later there was a ring at the doorbell. It was Frau Tillmann, who kept the chinaware shop next to ours and lived upstairs. She had a basket in her hand.

'Give me a job, Frau Jakoby,' she said. 'And – I worked out you'd need some cups and saucers—'

Aunty Edith burst into tears. I put my arms round her. Frau Tillmann made soothing noises. Frau Janke threw her cloth down and muttered against the storm troopers. Kattrin went off to make coffee for Aunty Edith.

'Thank you all,' Aunty Edith said. She took my hand in hers. 'You're so kind.'

'Kind?' Frau Janke snorted. 'A lot of thugs have disgraced our country, and you talk about kindness? You're owed the help, Frau Jakoby.'

'What's a bit of china?' Frau Tillmann said.

I stroked her hand. I knew it almost as well as I knew Mum's. The fine fingers, the little topaz ring she always wore. It was a hand that had always patted me, comforted me, loved me. She'd never got impatient with me, the way Mum sometimes did. She'd used to bring Theresia out for me to play with; we'd made sticky poppy-seed candy together and Raf had helped me eat it. She'd shown me the photographs on the big sideboard and told me stories about them.

I said, 'Aunty Edith, your photographs!'

Her face tightened. 'Oh God, how could I have forgotten about them?'

They were lying scattered on the hard floor beside the stove-in sideboard. Aunty Edith and I got down on our knees to pick them up. I fished her mother's photograph out of its broken frame.

'Careful, Jenny,' she said. 'That glass is sharp.'

I said, 'It's only in two halves. Look, they haven't ruined the photograph.'

Aunty Edith was grieving over the photograph of Uncle Markus's parents on their wedding day. The glass was in smithereens and there was a boot mark on the picture. Uncle Markus's parents were dead and Raf had never seen them. I couldn't remember Dad's parents, either, or my mother's father. There was only my Grandma, who'd been born in England, but now she was a Berliner.

I found the picture of Raf's Uncle Herbert. It was messily torn, there'd be no repairing that. Then I saw Aunty Edith reach for another photograph. I knew whose it was. Ursula. I thought: Please, please.

She lifted it and I let my breath go. It was all right, there was only a crack across its glass. I looked at the little girl with Aunty Edith's wavy brown hair and big pretty eyes, Raf's elder sister, who'd died of scarlet fever just before I'd been born. She'd been six. I'd always wished she'd lived, so we could have been like sisters.

I said, 'All it needs is a new glass.' I handed her the other photographs. 'Are the albums all right?'

'Yes,' she said. 'They didn't have time to destroy everything; I suppose they had a schedule.'

I tried for a moment to imagine someone drawing up the list; then I didn't want to. Kattrin came back.

'You have a rest and drink your coffee, Frau Jakoby,' she said. 'You can bring those photographs over to our place.' She looked at Ursula. 'Lovely lass she was, and clever! I can still hearing her calling out to me, clear as you like, and she can't have been more than a year and a half. "Good morning, Tattrin! How are you today?"'

Aunty Edith smiled shakily at Kattrin. I hugged her again and kissed her cheek, and I hated the men who'd hurt her so much.

Later, Kattrin went to get lunch for us. She invited Frau Tillmann and Frau Janke too, but they said they had to feed their husbands. She sent me down to the shop to get Dad and Uncle Markus and the boys.

Dad looked round from the bookcase he was working on. 'We can put this one together, at least,' he said, 'and there are quite a few books in good condition.'

I said, 'Kattrin's making soup and Aunty Edith says you're to come up and have it.'

'In a minute,' Dad said. 'We'll get this shelf glued in first.'

Uncle Markus said, 'Raf, this job only needs two people. You go up. Make Kattrin happy. I don't know when Karl will be back, Jenny, he went out for more screws.'

Raf came upstairs with me. 'Herr Tillmann's going to come and help when he closes the shop up.'

I said, 'There are some good people left.'

'Not enough,' Raf said.

I said suddenly, 'I wish I could wake up.'

He knew what I meant. 'So do I. Jenny, have you heard any news about Grandma?'

She'd been like a grandmother to Raf, too. We had been each other's families and now they were going to have to go away because the Nazis didn't want them.

'Yes,' I said. 'Her maid came over. She's better, but not well enough for Mum to leave her.' But I was suddenly terribly scared Grandma might die.

'I wonder what she thinks of all this?' Raf's fists clenched. 'It wouldn't happen in England, would it?'

I shook my head, thinking about England, where I'd never been because we weren't rich enough to travel abroad. Where Raf might go. I wished we all lived there, then things would be all right.

There was chicken soup on our dining table with egg dumplings in it.

'I wish the men would come up,' Aunty Edith muttered.

I said, 'I don't think they'll be long.'

'The soup will be cold,' Kattrin complained. Then: 'Frau Jakoby, did those scum steal your jewellery?'

'Some of it,' Aunty Edith said. 'But we've got a place under the floorboards for the best pieces. They didn't find those.'

'Well, thank God for that—' Kattrin began.

Then we heard it. A big vehicle, like a truck,

coming fast down the street. It screeched to a halt outside. Muffi started to bark.

'What—' Raf demanded. A minute later we were all at the window, pushing it open, looking out.

It was a truck – the kind that carries coal sacks. Three men got out of it and went into the shop. They were wearing leather coats, peaked hats and long shiny boots.

Aunty Edith gasped as if she'd been stabbed. 'Gestapo,' she said.

I stared at the prisoners huddled on the flat bed at the rear, about ten of them, all ashy-faced, several bruised and smeared with their own blood. My heart started to thump.

And now one of the Gestapo men was hustling Uncle Markus out. Dad was coming after them in his shirtsleeves, protesting, trying to get hold of the Gestapo man, saying, 'What's my friend done wrong? He's been a good citizen all his life, he's fought for Germany. He's got the Iron Cross, do you hear? You can't arrest him.' I caught my breath and held it, terrified. You didn't argue with the Gestapo.

I saw the second Gestapo man step casually behind Dad and kick the back of his knees, knocking Dad onto the pavement. I saw him spit on Dad and start kicking him in the ribs and it felt as if every kick was landing on me. I saw Dad curling round, trying to protect himself, I heard his gasping yells of pain. I opened my mouth but before I could make a sound Kattrin's hand came over it. I screamed all the same, 'Leave my dad alone! Don't hurt him!' Kattrin's hard, soap-smelling palm muffled it all.

'Jennychen,' Kattrin hissed in my ear. 'Keep quiet, you can only make it worse.'

I saw Uncle Markus try to fight loose, maybe to protect Dad, and the brute who had hold of him punched him in the face. He staggered, blood streaming from his nose.

Aunty Edith whispered in anguish, 'Why didn't they come up to lunch when they were called?'

Raf said, 'I'm going down there!'

'No,' Aunty Edith said. 'No, Raf, for God's sake, aren't things bad enough?'

The men heard that. They glanced up and then they all three of them started laughing at us. And I saw other people crossing the street so as not to get involved with what was going on and for a moment I saw it the way they must see it, like a tiny, tiny moving picture: the two men and the Gestapo laying into them, our chalk-white, watching faces at the window. A picture they'd want to forget, for fear it put them off their dinner tonight.

They heaved Dad onto the truck like a sack of potatoes and dropped him. I whimpered into Kattrin's palm. They shoved Uncle Markus up after him. As they drove away I saw Karl come down the street with a paper bag in his hand.

I ran out into our hallway and into Karl's arms. He held me so tightly his fingers dug into my back, but I didn't tell him he was hurting me. It didn't seem to matter.

'*Bastards*,' Karl said. 'Filthy stinking *bastards*.' He let go of me and we went into the dining room together.

Aunty Edith was still by the window, rigid and white in the face. Raf was stroking her back. His jaw was set tight.

'What can we do?' I asked Karl.

'There's Uncle Hartmut,' he said.

I couldn't see it. 'He's a Nazi.'

But Kattrin nodded approvingly. 'One of their rich backers,' she said. 'You've got a good head on you, Karlchen.'

'He's got connections,' Karl told me. 'Maybe he can get them set free.'

'I'll go too,' I said.

'So will I,' Raf put in at once.

'We'll all go,' Aunty Edith said. 'No, don't tell me I mustn't, Karl. If I have to stay here and wait for you, I'll go mad.'

Chapter Four

Aunty Edith made us all change into good clothes. 'It might make a difference,' she said. Kattrin gave her Mum's coat with the fur collar to wear. Raf put on his best blue suit which the storm troopers hadn't destroyed. I had to wear my new Sunday dress. I hated dressing up, it felt like a waste of precious time.

We caught the light railway out to Wannsee, where my rich Uncle Hartmut and Dad's sister, Aunt Grete, lived on the lake shore. We walked along the tree-lined road to their garden gate and made our way down the drive between two lines of little blue Christmassy-looking trees to the big showy villa with its half-timbered gable end. Karl rang the polished brass cowbell that hung there. I heard barking from Schnucki, their dog. She sounded just like Muffi; that wasn't surprising because she was Muffi's mother.

Minna, the maid, opened the door. Her eyes widened when she saw us, but she dropped a curtsey and ushered us into the house. Aunt Grete came out in a waft of over-strong, musky perfume, Schnucki running at her heels. She raised her plucked eyebrows at the sight of two Jews in her entrance hall.

'Where's your mother?' she asked Karl. He said she was with Grandma, who was ill.

'I see,' she said, as if being ill was something Grandma had done to spite her. She and Uncle Hartmut didn't like Grandma – and Grandma didn't like them – because Grandma came from England and believed in democracy.

'Aunt Grete,' Karl said, 'Dad's been arrested. And Uncle Markus, and we were hoping—'

She let out a little wail. 'Arrested? Oh no.' That got her moving. She went to the telephone and I heard her tell Uncle Hartmut's secretary he had to come home at once. It was urgent, I heard her say.

Then we had to sit in the salon, as Aunt Grete called it, waiting for my uncle. Another age. The fear and impatience kept gnawing inside my belly. I heard the big walnut grandfather clock going tick, tick, tick, booming at the half hour. The furniture was massive, rearing up from the parquet floor like a lot of cliff-fronted islands in a yellow sea. Schnucki lay down on a huge Turkish rug and her black cords of hair splayed round her like the edges of another much smaller rug. She didn't pay any attention to us. She never did.

Raf looked at her. 'She's bigger than Muffi.'

Aunt Grete raised her eyebrows as if he shouldn't have spoken, but she said, 'That's because she's a pure-bred Hungarian Puli. We don't know who

Muffi's father was. It's amazing that Muffi turned out so like her mother.'

She always let us know how much better Schnucki was than her cross-bred daughter, but it didn't matter today. Nothing mattered except Dad and Uncle Markus. The clock went on ticking.

Suddenly Schnucki scrabbled to her feet and ran to the door, barking again. A moment later we heard the bell ring. My cousins Hildegarde and Kunigunde were home from school as if it was a quite ordinary day.

'What are they doing here?' Hildegarde demanded, standing in the door and staring at me and Karl, and at Raf. 'Who are these people? Oh no, Mum, it's their Jewish friends.'

She was a year older than me, with fair Aryan plaits hanging down her back. She'd always jeered at me for having red hair. That was another thing that didn't matter today.

'Hush,' Aunt Grete told her. 'They've got troubles.'

'Troubles?' Hildegarde said in a high-pitched, sneering voice. 'The Jews deserved what's happened to them. We had to go to the gym this morning and the Head explained it all to us.'

Aunty Edith closed her eyes and Raf gave Hildegarde a bad look. She narrowed her eyes and stared back at him. Kunigunde picked Schnucki up and started twisting her head-hair upwards so her eyes showed for once. Schnucki put up with it for a while, then she struggled loose and ran away. Kunigunde was two years younger than me, a little blonde-pigtailed monster.

'Did they come to your house and break all the windows?' she asked Aunty Edith with an evil grin.

'Hush,' Aunt Grete said again. 'You don't say things like that, Kunigunde.'

'Yes, I do,' Kunigunde said. And even the gloating note in her voice was nothing compared to what the Gestapo might be doing to Dad and Uncle Markus.

Minna came in with a silver tray, coffee and chocolate and a lot of biscuits. I didn't want anything. It'd taste of Aunt Grete's vile perfume. Kunigunde held a lemon wafer biscuit out to Schnucki, who came, snatched it, and backed away. Aunt Grete tapped her platform soles on the floor and fiddled with her pearl earclips. Then we heard a big car pull up outside. Uncle Hartmut had come home.

He told us to come into his study. He didn't ask any of us to sit down. He said to Karl, 'What do you expect *me* to do? Your father's been digging a pit for himself and now he's fallen into it. Anybody could have seen it coming. As for the Jew—'

He said that. 'The Jew.' With Aunty Edith and Raf standing beside us.

He was a broad, angry man sitting at his huge polished desk in his business suit. He said to Aunt Grete, 'I can't believe that you've dragged me home from the office for this.'

Hildegarde and Kunigunde loitered against the

door frame. Hildegarde had picked Schnucki up and was clutching her.

Karl said, 'Uncle Markus is Dad's best friend, of course he tried to stop them arresting him.'

'Your father's a disgrace to me,' Uncle Hartmut said. 'His best friend is a Jew, he's a *Quaker* – a huddle of troublemakers – how many of them are there? A couple of hundred in Germany? Have you any idea of the atrocity stories they spread about us to other countries?'

I did have an idea. Dad hadn't told Karl and me outright, he tried to shield us from the dangerous things he did. But he and Mum said things, quietly, when they thought we weren't listening, things we knew better than to repeat outside. I'd heard about the Quakers who came to Berlin from Britain and America to find things out.

Karl opened his mouth, I was sure he was going to say that they weren't atrocity stories, we knew that after all the things that had happened today. I felt the man's hand brush my shoulder again, I saw his dead body lying on the pavement, and I saw them kicking Dad. I clutched my arms round myself, I was freezing cold, all of a sudden. But Uncle Hartmut went on talking at us. 'The Führer's doing the right thing by this country, do you hear, Karl, Jenny? Everyone who's in a concentration camp deserves to be there, and the worst thing that happens to them is a bit of hard work. Whatever you've heard from your fool of

39

a father. What does a marionette-maker know about it, anyway? As for the Jews – in the future, people all over the world will thank us for what we've done today. But I know those Quaker scum will be sending letters out about it right now, calling us brutal – a surgeon's brutal when he cuts into a patient to get a cancer out, I tell you.'

Aunty Edith turned her face away from him. I reached my cold hand out to hers and felt it just as cold. We'd come here for nothing.

He said, 'The Jews' whole agenda is to bring Germany down, either by spreading Communist unrest or by playing the financial markets in America – we're beleaguered on both fronts—'

Raf burst out, 'My father went into No-Man's-Land with his company in 1917, by the end of an hour there were only ten of them left alive, but they captured a French machine-gun emplacement. He got the Iron Cross for that. Does that sound like a man who wants to bring his country down?'

Uncle Hartmut didn't even seem to hear. But Hildegarde whispered to Kunigunde, 'He's quite cute, isn't he? I could fancy him if he wasn't a Jew.'

Uncle Hartmut heard that. He got up from his desk, strode over to her, and slapped her hard in the face. She let out a whimper.

That was horrible.

Aunt Grete didn't seem to care that he'd hit Hildegarde, but she said, 'Hartmut, Dietrich is my brother.'

'What good's a brother like that to you?' Uncle Hartmut asked her – and I felt as if something broke inside me. I started to wail, tears and snot dribbling down my face. I was terribly ashamed of myself, but I couldn't help it, and I almost shouted at Uncle Hartmut, about the men kicking Dad and punching Uncle Markus and why wouldn't he help them?

Aunt Grete took hold of my hand and pushed a little silk handkerchief into it. I tried to use it, but it was too shiny, so I wiped my nose on my sleeve instead.

'Please, Hartmut—' Aunt Grete said. Now *she* was in tears.

'Women,' he snarled, sweeping a bad look round every female in the room, even Schnucki inside her mop of hair. 'You can turn it on and off like a tap, can't you? A man can't call his soul his own. All right, Grete, I'll see what I can do for your brother. I can't and I won't help the Jew.'

We shivered on the platform till the train came. Nobody said anything.

We got seats facing each other, Raf sitting next to Aunty Edith, holding her hand, Karl next to me. The train rattled onwards. Outside the windows the afternoon sun shone through the last rusty leaves of the trees in the Grunewald.

'Well, *I* think it's outrageous,' a thin elderly woman across the aisle said to a young woman with a toddler. 'And they had lists. It was all organised in advance.'

41

'Now they're taking the Jewish men off to concentration camps,' the young mother said, clutching her handbag and shuddering. 'They're not criminals.'

I remembered what Uncle Hartmut had said about the camps. 'The worst thing that happens is a bit of hard work.' If that was true, why was everyone terrified of them? Anyway, I knew the truth from Dad and Mum. People died there.

I felt sore and hollowed-out inside from crying, and desperately tired. Raf was stroking Aunty Edith's hand and she was staring at the frivolous little bows on her best black patent leather shoes. They hadn't been any good to her, had they? We might as well have gone in our ordinary clothes to Uncle Hartmut.

I shut my eyes and dozed, hoping I'd wake up in bed and it'd all have been a nightmare. Only when I woke I was still in the train, just nearer home.

From the window I could see the grubby backs of trackside buildings, then glimpses of the streets where people were shopping and waiting for trams and walking their dogs and getting on with their ordinary lives. We weren't those people now, not since Dad had been arrested. We were the others. The ones respectable, Heil Hitler-ing citizens didn't want to know about. I saw the smoke from the burned synagogue like a smear over the blue sky, and then we passed a building site with a large sign up saying:

IT IS THANKS TO OUR FÜHRER THAT WE
CAN WORK HERE.

The elderly woman started to tell the young mother about a wonderful cake recipe she'd just found in a magazine.

When we came back home, Mum was there. Karl had to tell her that Uncle Hartmut was doing something for Dad but not for Uncle Markus. He hated that. But Mum made Raf and Aunty Edith sit down and she persuaded them to stay with us, in case the storm troopers came back. That was good.

'They might come here,' Raf said, standing in Karl's room, looking at the camp bed Kattrin had just made up for him. 'You're in danger now, because of us.'

Karl sat down on his own bed, looking at Raf. Even when he was upset, there was a quietness about Karl.

'We've always been in danger,' he said. 'It's not just you, it's Dad and his views.'

'You could change,' Raf said. He was taut as steel wire. 'Uncle Dietrich could give up being a Quaker.'

I saw it, then. There was a door open for us to bring us back among respectable people if we left our friends outside and shut it behind us. The idea jangled inside me. Then I was sure Uncle Hartmut had always really meant to help Dad, but not Uncle Markus. He'd maybe meant Aunty Edith and Raf to be angry with us so we'd fall out with them.

'He might as well give up being himself,' Karl said. That made me feel a bit better. He went on, 'I've got views, too. One of my views is, I'd like to punch Uncle Hartmut.'

Savagely Raf said, 'I want to kick *his* ribs to smithereens. He's a big man, though, he'd be hard to knock over.'

'He's overweight,' Karl said. 'Stuffs himself at banquets with Hitler, he'll be out of condition. I should learn ju-jitsu and fell him with a chop to his neck. Anyway, I'm going to get some weights. Work on my body. Then maybe I can do something against some of the bastards. You can work with them too, Raf.'

Raf grinned suddenly, the old cheeky grin. 'Body building? So I can go out and smash a storm trooper's face in?'

'Take it gradually,' Karl said. 'Start with a Hitler Youth and work up.'

They were saying it to make themselves feel better, I knew that, but I couldn't bear to hear about people hitting each other. I went out to my own room. Muffi came with me. I shut the door and sat on the bed with her, twisting her thick cords of hair at the base to keep them separate from each other, which you had to do with her kind of hair.

Uncle Hartmut had wanted Muffi to be drowned when she was born because she wasn't pure-bred. He'd been furious with Schnucki, for getting out of the garden and running off with God knew what kind of dog. Maybe he was scared Muffi's father had been a Jewish dog.

44

I thought how Dad had to tell me it was against the law for me to kiss Raf, and the Jakobys had lost their maid in case Uncle Markus forced his Jewish attentions on her – Mum had explained sex to me so I'd understood what that meant. And Uncle Hartmut had hit Hildegarde because she'd said she almost fancied Raf.

Hildegarde and Kunigunde liked to call me a mongrel because I was part English. I was a little bit suspect, but not the way I would have been if I'd been part Jewish because the Nazis had decided that English people were Aryans.

So I was meant to be a pure-bred bitch like Schnucki, I was meant to have an Aryan mate so I'd have the kind of children the Nazis wanted. They kept telling us that at school. They said our bodies belonged to the Aryan race.

I looked at my Pinocchio marionette that Dad had given me for my sixth birthday. He had a set of detachable noses that you could put on for his nose to get longer every time he told a lie. Pinocchio had started off as a wooden puppet who couldn't feel properly, then he'd become a real boy, but the Nazis wanted to do it the other way round.

I held up my hand and arm and imagined it turning into hard wood, with strings attached. You wouldn't know, I thought. All your feelings would be dead and you'd just do as you were told. I shivered, and said to Muffi, 'No, it's my body. It belongs to me. Not to them.'

Chapter Five
July 1939

The tombstones of the Jewish cemetery were tall and crowded together and dank with the rain. The writing on them was in Hebrew, so I couldn't read it, but they seemed to be watching us, looking over each other's shoulders. I couldn't help wondering what they thought.

I walked with Mum behind Aunty Edith. In front of her, Dad, Karl, and Raf were carrying Uncle Markus's coffin, along with three men I recognised because I'd seen them in his shop. Jews didn't let strangers carry their dead to the grave: it was for family and close friends to do that.

They walked slowly, slowly, it almost hurt my legs to follow at that pace. I saw the skullcap Dad had been given slide sideways on his balding head – it was going to fall off, I thought, and I was scared. It'd be horrible if that happened, it'd make things even more wrong than they already were. But he shifted his head and it stayed on. The coffin was staggering a little because Dad and two of the other pallbearers had limps: Dad's was a present from the Gestapo and so were the Jews' limps, probably. But at least they weren't dead like Uncle Markus. The SS had starved him in the Sachsenhausen concentration camp and it had damaged his heart. When they'd let him out he'd needed an ambulance to take him to the Jewish hospital in Berlin.

We'd all gone to visit him there. He'd turned into a fragile, bluish-faced man propped up on a lot of pillows with a cylinder of oxygen beside him. I'd hardly known him the first time. He'd had to fight for breath; he'd been barely able to talk.

If Raf came walking down the ward between the long rows of tidy white beds, giving his father the grin, then Uncle Markus's face lit up and he looked almost like his old self again. But a miserable stiffness seemed to have settled in Raf's shoulders, for all he always worked hard to be cheerful. Uncle Markus didn't want Raf to be in Berlin at all, he and Aunty Edith were trying to send Raf away on one of the Kindertransport trains that were taking Jewish boys and girls to safety in England. Only he wouldn't go. Everyone had tried to persuade him, Dad, Mum, Karl, me. He'd dug his heels in. He wouldn't leave his parents.

Uncle Markus had been ill for five months and now he was dead, gone for ever. They'd murdered him. I still couldn't believe that. He'd always seemed so big and strong. Safe.

Raf had a tear in his jacket. Aunty Edith had one too. Nobody needed to explain that to me. The raw edges of the rents looked like wailing mouths. I wanted to tear my coat too. I kept crying; I just couldn't stop myself. And I was so angry.

Grandma had died last winter and I'd only been terribly sad – but she'd died of old age. Uncle Markus hadn't been old enough to die.

Some of the prayers were in Hebrew, so I couldn't understand them, but some of them were in German, so I understood what the rabbi said at the graveside: that God was in charge of everything and nobody could challenge what he'd done. I heard the way the rabbi's voice shook when he said it, but he said it all the same.

I looked at Raf. He was standing there, clutching his jacket just beside the rent. His eyes were wild with hurt. God? I thought. Is God on the Nazis' side now?

Jews didn't let strangers cover their dead with earth, either, the rabbi had explained that to us before the service began. That was a job for relations and close friends, even non-Jews. It was a job for Raf and Aunty Edith and Dad and Mum and Karl and me.

Raf and Aunty Edith started off. Raf's face twitched and his thin sinewy boy's wrists quivered as the pale sandy soil showered off the shovel. Aunty Edith's face was set and almost severe. I didn't think I'd be able to bear to cover the coffin up but when it came to my turn I was surprised, because I suddenly felt an odd peace. I dug the shovel into the earth and let it spill softly into the grave. I found myself whispering, 'Sleep well, Uncle Markus.' And another spatter of rain came down like tears and pockmarked the soil.

The peace didn't last, though. As soon as I stood up

the rage and grief were burning inside me again.

Mum hugged Aunty Edith and Raf, and Raf buried his head on her shoulder. He held Dad's hand really tight with both his, saying, 'Thank you. Thank you for coming.'

Dad said, 'Of course we came. Markus was like a brother to me, Raf, you know that—' and then he couldn't speak any more. Karl just thumped Raf on the shoulder and swallowed hard. Karl was a Hitler Youth now. He'd got to be; they'd passed a law that said every young person who wasn't Jewish had to belong to the Nazi youth organisations. Uncle Markus had had a member of the Hitler Youth to carry his coffin.

Raf was fourteen, shot-up and skinny, still fair-haired, with a bumpy nose that had started to look almost too big for his face. He held my hands, and I looked into his grey-blue eyes. They were red round the edges and there was a smudge of dirt on his cheek. I squeezed my fingers against his. I wanted to tell him what I felt about the stinking Nazis killing Uncle Markus, but the words caught in my throat and I started sobbing again.

'Thanks, Jenny,' Raf said. His voice was beginning to break and now it went rough and deep. He bent forward and kissed me suddenly on the cheek. 'Just – thanks.'

The next Sunday Mum said she was going to Quaker

Meeting with Dad, and Karl and I said we'd go too. I think none of us wanted to let Dad go on his own.

There was nothing grand about the Quakers' Meeting room; the chairs were scratched, the walls could have done with a coat of paint and the Turkish rug in the middle of the room was faded, but on the table that stood on the rug there was a vase with roses. Their petals were red and yellow together and they flashed like a splash of bright paint in the room. I remember looking at them and knowing they were lovely but I couldn't feel their loveliness, it was cut off from me.

I sat beside Dad, being quiet, waiting. That was what Quakers did. For God. Only I was frightened because there were all those sore, angry feelings inside me and now they flared up like a bonfire. I looked at the flowers again and they seemed to be on fire. I looked round at the Quakers' serious faces. Just by being here they were defying Hitler. And there were probably Jews here and what the Nazis called 'Non-Aryans' which meant they were half Jewish. And maybe Gestapo agents, spying. If anyone felt they had to get up and speak, they'd have to be careful. They had to keep it quiet that they were all really pacifists. Pacifism was against Nazi law; if you said you were a pacifist you'd end up in concentration camp.

I thought about Raf and Aunty Edith. Since Uncle Markus's illness they'd started going to synagogue on Saturdays and had started having special Shabbat meals on Friday evenings. They'd invited us a few times. Aunty Edith had lit candles and then Raf had said a blessing. He'd been a bit nervous and shy but all lit-up with pleasure at doing it, and it had felt special and really important. We'd said a prayer for Uncle Markus, but it hadn't done any good: he'd been murdered. And the rabbi had stood at the graveside and said God wanted us to put up with that.

Angrily, I wondered if there really was a God, wasn't it just a story like Father Christmas? Dad said there was something of God inside everyone – what, I thought, even the Nazis?

A balding man with round glasses stood up to minister. He said something about loving your neighbour, and that your neighbour was anyone who needed you to help them. I knew he meant the Jews. I thought about the times Dad went out and didn't say where he was going. We never asked, we knew it was better if we didn't. Maybe that man was doing the same kind of secret things. When he sat down there was a long silence.

I started wondering if there was going to be a war. Everyone was afraid there would be, because Hitler kept taking more and more territory. He'd had Austria and Czechoslovakia and now Dad was sure he was planning to invade Poland. If he did, and the British and the French declared war on us, each of the Quaker men would have to decide whether he'd go and fight or whether he should refuse and be hanged as a traitor to Germany. Dad wouldn't refuse, I knew that, I'd heard him telling Mum. She'd said, 'Thank God.' I'd been standing in the hall and they'd been in the sitting room. They hadn't known I was there.

Dad had said, 'It's better to be alive and do what I can than be a martyr.' And she'd said, 'What about me and the children? Aren't you staying alive for us, too?' He hadn't said anything else, but I'd known, somehow, that he'd put his arms round her. I'd crept away to my room. I hadn't wanted them to know I'd heard.

Anyway, Dad had been in the Medical Corps in the last war, and that was where they'd send him again, so he wouldn't have to fight, he'd be healing the wounded. Usually I was glad for him, but now I thought: Maybe he should have fought Hitler to stop him taking over Germany. It was a shocking thought, but it wouldn't go away. I thought: Even if he didn't want to fight he could have looked after wounded fighters, couldn't he? And there was Uncle Markus, he'd been so proud of fighting in the World War, but he hadn't done anything against Hitler and now Hitler had killed him.

Then Dad got up. He was going to minister. It'd be the first time, I knew that. He used to say, 'I've never given ministry, but that's all right.' He didn't speak at once. I thought: Supposing he can't say anything? I was scared and embarrassed, then he started to speak after all.

He said, 'Friends, we are living in dark times, and facing deeper darkness. But it is our tradition to look for a way forward, to trust that the way will be shown us. That trust is going to be required of us more and more in the times to come.'

He sat down. His arm was touching mine and he was trembling. From the other side of him, Mum reached out and took his hand. He squeezed it and sighed. The trembling stopped. I knew what he meant about the way forward, he was always talking about it at home. He'd explained to me that when the Quakers didn't know what to do, they asked God to show them and usually they did find the way.

Now I wondered if that just meant that an idea came to them. Maybe it was people who did the good things, and it made them feel better to say it was God. I thought I probably shouldn't have come to the Meeting, I was having bad thoughts that I could just as well have had at home. I hoped Dad hadn't guessed them.

I talked to one of the Quakers afterwards, a middle-aged woman with friendly grey eyes and untidy greying hair. She had a pair of secateurs sticking out of her pocket and a smear of dirt on her coat, so I guessed she'd brought the roses. When I asked her, she said yes, they grew in her garden. She lived in Dahlem Village. 'Fountain Lane,' she said, smiling.

She was called Agnes Hummel. The Quakers didn't call each other 'Herr' and 'Frau'. Or any other titles. If Agnes Hummel had been Countess Agnes von Hummel, as a Quaker she'd have been Agnes Hummel just the same because they believed everyone was equal before God.

I said I wished we had a garden, for our dog. She said she had two rough-haired dachshunds and she had to stop them digging in her flowerbeds. I said Muffi sometimes dug in the flowerbeds in our yard, and it made Janke wild.

I'd no idea how important it was that I'd met Agnes Hummel. I had to be polite but really I just wanted to leave.

We walked along our street and came past the shop front that had once said:

JAKOBY
ANTIQUARIAN BOOKSELLER

Now it said:

MINGERS STATIONERY AND BOOKS.

In the window, underneath a framed picture of Adolf Hitler standing in his brown uniform with an expression on his face that people thought was heroic, was a cardboard sign. It announced to the neighbourhood:

IT IS THANKS TO OUR FÜHRER THAT WE WERE ABLE TO TAKE OVER THESE PREMISES.

Just after Crystal Night – as the Nazis were calling their orgy of vandalism and murder – they'd passed a law that no Jew was allowed to own or manage a business. Aunty Edith had dealt with it because Uncle Markus was still in concentration camp. She'd been given a month to find a purchaser before the government confiscated the shop and left her with nothing.

She'd put the apartment up for sale too, because they all wanted to emigrate and they needed as much money as possible. Our new neighbour, Herr Mingers, had made her a reasonable offer at first, but when it was almost completion time he'd lowered it to a ridiculously small price, which she'd had to accept because she'd never have found another purchaser before the cut-off date.

The sign had been there seven months and it was beginning to fade. I wondered if the Mingers would take it away or just make another sign.

I muttered to Karl, 'It's thanks to Adolf Hitler that we have the foulest neighbours in Berlin.'

'Hush!' Mum said, shooting a quick glance over her shoulder.

Yes, I thought. Keep quiet. Have a tea cosy to put over the telephone when you talk about anything dangerous inside the house, just in case the engineer put a microphone in there when he was servicing it. Don't stick your neck out. And I knew that was sensible, because of staying alive, but it still made me want to spit.

I thought about the big marionette theatre in Dad's shop, a proper one with a hidden standing-place over the stage for the puppeteer. Customers used it to try out the marionettes before they bought them for their shows. It was painted red, carved and gilded, and Mum had made blue velvet curtains for it and put a silver fringe at the bottom of them. Just after Crystal Night it had moved from the wall at the side to stand in front of the door to Dad's stockroom. Dad had hung a rack up in the shop and now all the marionettes dangled there while they waited for someone to buy them.

What we used to call the stockroom was very narrow, tucked away underneath the back stairs from our kitchen down to the yard. Our apartment was the only one to have those back stairs and only Janke apart from us knew there was a space underneath them. He wouldn't have told anyone, though. Dad was keeping something forbidden in the stockroom – Quaker newspapers, maybe? Material about Nazi brutality? Or Aunty Edith's jewellery, that she was supposed to have given up to the authorities, but she'd given to Mum instead and Mum sold pieces for her whenever she needed money. Mum was breaking the law. That was brave of her, I had to admit, but what I wanted them to be keeping in there was guns.

When we got to our apartment door we met the Mingers family, the whole horrible troop of them. Norbert, aged seventeen with his Hitler Youth straps across his chest and his big hairy knees on display. Willi, who was a year older than me, wearing the brown shirt and shorts and black scarf of the Junior Hitler Youth. Herr Mingers with his face that was the same colour as a boiled frankfurter sausage, clutching eight-year-old Siegfried with his huge goblin eyes and thin pale cheeks. And Frau Mingers holding onto the younger little goblin, Adolf – no prizes for guessing who *he'd* been named after. She was a tall skinny woman and her whole body was stiff and hostile, like a broomstick, I thought.

'Good afternoon!' Dad said.

'Heil Hitler!' Frau Broomstick corrected him. Not many people in Berlin greeted you with Heil Hitler – Uncle Hartmut did of course. The Mingers always did. 'Why were you in black the other day?' the Broomstick wanted to know.

Willi Mingers was staring at me. Whenever I saw him, he stared. I hated that, even though he was the only one of them who didn't look like a freak. He was almost good looking in a brutal kind of way.

Dad said, 'A friend's funeral.'

Frau Broomstick pursed her lips but she didn't ask who the friend was. She'd probably guessed. We were a byword among some of our neighbours. Dad had been *in prison*. Only for two days, but Frau Schmid from two floors up always clicked her tongue when she saw us now. At least it had shown us who our friends were: the Tillmanns, the Jankes, and old Herr Berger who lived on the top floor. The Kohls, the Kribs, and Herr Schmid greeted us hastily, if they were feeling brave enough.

Frau Broomstick fingered the bronze cross that she had hanging round her neck, the one the Nazis had given her for producing her four Aryan children. 'A brood mare,' Mum always said. 'That's what she is.'

She demanded, 'Has your daughter joined the Youth Girls' League yet?'

'She's going to,' Mum said. That was a lie. It was easier for girls to forget to join than it was for boys to stay out of the Hitler Youth, and I was going to stay out as long as I could. Always, if it was up to me. My best friend Paula hadn't joined either.

Frau Broomstick clicked her tongue. We had to put up with that, we mustn't tell people like her where they got off, because they might denounce us to the Gestapo. And she hadn't finished. 'Norbert doesn't see this young fellow at Hitler Youth very often,' she said, staring at Karl.

'I've got a lot of homework at the moment,' Karl said.

'Homework!' Frau Broomstick almost spat it out. 'You think homework's more important than working for the German people? You've no idea, have you, any of you? Let me tell you, we've had the Jewish yoke across our shoulders. All the years we've worked hard, saved up—'

'I've never smoked,' Herr Mingers chipped in, giving Dad a bad look. 'Never even allowed myself a glass of beer, always putting money by – and then the Jews in New York brought the mark crashing down and destroyed our savings. Our son had to leave school at fifteen and help in the shop, no chance of grammar school for *him*. But the Jew-boys can always get an education. Even now.'

Raf had been thrown out of his state school and

now he was at a Jewish school. His school fees were one of the things Mum had been selling Aunty Edith's jewellery for.

Our front door opened and Kattrin came out with Muffi at her heels. 'I've got lunch ready,' she said.

Frau Broomstick gave Muffi a filthy look. 'That foreign thing covered in germ-ridden strings of hair—'

We escaped inside.

'I heard her,' Kattrin said as soon as the door was safely closed. 'I thought you needed rescuing.'

She'd put the tea cosy on top of the phone. I saw it and felt as if it was over my mouth, suffocating me. If we'd been English we could have said exactly what we thought anywhere, Grandma had told me.

Dad said sadly, 'They're like too many people in Germany, they've had a hard time in the past, and they blame the Jews for everything. They've been led astray.' He bent down and played with Muffi's coat. His pipe fell out of his pocket. I imagined him smoking it in the shop and Herr Mingers glowering through the window at him.

'You're too generous,' Mum said. 'They're just poison.'

Muffi picked Dad's pipe up and held it out to Dad – picking dropped things up was a trick I'd taught her. It had been very useful when it had hurt him to bend after his arrest – the Gestapo had broken three of his ribs when they'd kicked him. He took it from her, wiping it off on his trousers. 'Thank you, Muffi,' he said. I wondered if he'd remember to wash it before he put it back in his mouth.

Karl said, 'Listen, one evening Herr Mingers goes out to his Party meeting, and leaves a note on the table telling the rest where he's gone. Then Frau Broomstick goes out, leaving a note saying: "Heil Hitler! I'm at the Nazi Women's Association"and Norbert goes out and leaves a note saying: "Heil *Hitler!* I'm at the Hitler Youth," and Willi —'

'OK,' I said, 'they all go out to their different Nazi groups. What about the goblins?'

'They're at their grandparents',' Karl said. 'Now let me get on with the joke.'

In a rush, I said, 'And then some burglars come in and clear the apartment and they leave a note saying: "It is thanks to our Führer that we were able to carry out this robbery."'

Karl shook a fist at me. 'Where did you hear it?'

'Paula told me,' I said. I started laughing, but then I put the back of my hand to my mouth and bit my knuckles hard, so it hurt.

I said, 'We shouldn't be telling jokes. Not with Uncle Markus dead.'

Karl looked worried, but Dad said, 'It's all right, Jenny. Markus would have loved that one, anyway.'

I wouldn't listen to him. I went and shut myself in my room.

Chapter Six

Now that Uncle Markus was dead, Raf and Aunty Edith were free to try and leave Germany. Aunty Edith's day started early, when she began queuing up at some embassy with hundreds of other Jews. None of them had much chance, but Aunty Edith kept trying. The school holidays had just begun, so Raf went with her.

But the best way to get a visa was to find someone who'd guarantee to keep you when you arrived, so you wouldn't become a burden on the state you wanted to move to. Ages ago, Aunty Edith had written to her brother in South Africa and to Uncle Markus's brother in New York. Only none of them had enough spare money to guarantee the whole family. They'd all offered to take Raf on his own, but of course he wouldn't go. Now Mum wrote to her cousins, the Montgomerys, in England, in case they'd help.

We all went to visit Raf and Aunty Edith shortly after the funeral. To the flat they'd moved to, at the top of an ugly tenement in Moabit. I'd baked them a chocolate cake – Raf adored chocolate – and I'd bought them a bunch of roses from a street stall. I'd chosen bright red ones because they looked defiant, though they didn't burn like the roses in the Quaker Meeting House. It had been hot all day, and the heat had built up inside the walls of the house. We were all gasping for breath by the time we got to the top of the smelly stone staircase.

Aunty Edith opened the door and brought us into their little living room. She had company: the rabbi was sitting on the battered sofa. He stood up, looking pleased to see us and smiled when I gave the roses to Aunty Edith. I'd been too upset to really notice him at the funeral, now I saw a dark-haired, thin-faced man with a beard and intelligent eyes behind his round glasses. I dropped him a curtsey, all very proper, but I remembered his prayer at the graveside and I didn't like him.

He was saying he had to go, but Dad started to ask him questions about Judaism – that was Dad all over, always wanting to learn about other religions. So the two men sat down on the sofa to talk and Aunty Edith took the cake into the kitchen to put it on a plate. Mum went after her.

'Come into my bedroom,' Raf said to Karl and me.

It was more like a cupboard, there was just room for a bed and a desk and chair. Karl and Raf sat down on the bed, I perched on the desk between Raf's schoolbooks and put my feet on the chair. The walls were dingy brown; Aunty Edith couldn't spare money for paint. The window was wide open but it was a still day and only the smell of the hot dusty streets came in through it.

'How's it going?' Karl asked Raf. Karl was seventeen, tall, with brown hair and big hands. He and Raf both looked too big for the little room.

'Badly,' Raf said. 'Listen to Mum now.'

The walls were really thin so you could hear Aunty Edith in the kitchen, talking to Mum and crying. Mum was saying soothing things: I knew she'd have her arms round Aunty Edith.

I said, 'It stinks. I wanted to tell you that at the funeral, Raf, only I couldn't.'

'I knew you were thinking that,' Raf said. 'That rabbi's a good man. He's been round here a lot. He used to buy books from Dad, you know, he really liked him. It helps Mum to talk to him.'

If it helped Aunty Edith I wouldn't say how angry I felt with the rabbi, but it burned inside me like a stomach upset. I rubbed my forefinger over the desktop and a splinter of wood went into it. It hurt, but I was almost glad, I didn't know why.

'It does stink,' Karl said. 'But listen, our English cousins might help.'

Raf ran his hand through his hair. 'I'm tired of hoping. You only get disappointed.'

Karl said, 'They're good people, Mum says. And well off. They've got a big house in Oxford with a huge garden.'

Raf said, 'Maybe Mum could be their maid and I could be their gardener's boy. We don't want to scrounge.'

'I know,' Karl said.

Raf pulled his knees up to his chest, locked his hands round them and stared down at them. 'You've no idea what it's like in those queues. The day before yesterday – it was boiling hot and a swine of a man came and threw a couple of rotten tomatoes. One of them hit Mum in the face. I wanted to go and punch him and she wouldn't let me. She just stood there, wiping it off with her handkerchief. And he was laughing.' His voice went squeaky and his hands cramped with frustration. 'When we did get to the end of the queue it was the usual story. They don't any of them want us because we don't have enough money. We might have had enough if that lousy Mingers hadn't cheated Mum.'

'It stinks,' I said again, trying to get the splinter out. 'Why has nobody ever fought the Nazis?'

'The British and the French?' Raf asked, sitting back against the wall now and running his hands through his hair. 'If we – if Germany invades Poland?'

He hadn't wanted to include himself in Germany. He was separate now because he was a Jew.

I opened my mouth to say that hadn't been what I'd meant, but Karl got in before me.

'We had to go to Wannsee this afternoon. Uncle Hartmut was going on about the Poles. They're supposed to be setting German farmhouses on fire and shooting at German passenger planes – I think that's all propaganda, Hitler just wants to be able to say he was provoked into attacking them. And why's he signed that non-agression pact with Stalin?'

'Because they both think they've got a right to divide Poland between them,' Raf agreed, 'the way it was split up before the World War.'

Karl grinned suddenly. 'Dad asked Uncle Hartmut if he was happy that his Führer had signed a pact with a Communist leader.' He imitated Uncle Hartmut's irritated growl. 'Don't push your luck, Dietrich.'

I didn't laugh because I'd been saying something else, something important, and they hadn't paid attention. I tried to say it again, but this time Raf wouldn't let me speak.

He said, 'I don't think the British and the French would do anything to save Poland. They let Hitler take Czechoslovakia last year. Daladier and Chamberlain are scared of war.'

Boys, I thought, why do they always think what they say is most important? I went for the splinter again. This time I managed it.

Karl said, 'Poland might be going too far for them. Plus, they've had extra time to build up their armaments.'

'Even if they do declare war, they won't be fighting for us. Nobody's on the Jews' side,' Raf said.

He looked terribly lonely all of a sudden and I forgot to be annoyed with him. I gave him a pat on the arm.

Aunty Edith came to the door. 'Come and have the cake.'

I saw her face all blotchy from her tears even though she'd mopped it up. I went to her and gave her a kiss. She said, 'You're sweet, Jenny,' but sadly. I was just a kid, the youngest. I couldn't change anything for her.

We went back into the living room.

The cups and saucers and plates Frau Tillmann had given Aunty Edith were sitting out on the ridged shabby table. They had a thin silver edging round them, otherwise they were just white. The cake was on a plate with pink roses and the coffee pot was steaming. Mum had brought apple juice. The rabbi was standing up ready to go, but he was still talking to Dad.

'Hope,' he said. 'We have to keep hold of hope, Herr Friedemann.'

'I think so,' Dad said very seriously, and he came out with one of the Quakers' sayings. 'There's an ocean of darkness, but we have to remember that beyond it there's an ocean of light and love.'

But the anger flared up in me like a torch, and I was turning to the rabbi and demanding, 'How could you say that prayer at Uncle Markus's funeral, about it being God's will that the Nazis killed him?'

'Jenny!' Mum said, but the rabbi turned to me. I saw the tired lines round his dark eyes and the sadness round his mouth. For a moment I imagined him walking along a hot dusty road all on his own. He wasn't angry. He spoke to me as if I was an adult.

'Jenny, these are hideous days, I know. I go from house to suffering house, I see terrible things happening to my people – and to anyone else who opposes the Nazis.' Almost to himself, he said, 'We are become a taunt to our neighbours, a scorn and derision to those around us.' I guessed that was something from the Bible. He sighed, and added, 'All I can do is remind myself of what my people Israel have endured in the past and how our trust in God has brought us through the darkest days.'

Mum said, 'That was rude, Jenny.'

'No,' the rabbi said. 'Jenny had a right to ask the question.'

I liked him now, because he'd taken me seriously, but I thought: If all you can do is hope, what good is that?

He smiled at us, sadly, and went. We sat down at the table and ate the cake I'd made. I didn't enjoy it.

And Aunty Edith put her coffee cup down and burst out, 'Raf, why won't you go on a Kindertransport? Or to your uncle in New York, or to South Africa?'

'*No, Mum*,' Raf said, sitting up very straight in his chair. 'I'm not running off to England on my own. Or anywhere else.'

'Dad wanted you to go,' Aunty Edith said angrily. 'It made him worse, worrying because you were so obstinate—'

Raf went white. I couldn't believe what I'd just heard. It felt as if everything was tearing apart.

He demanded, 'Are you saying I killed Dad?'

My dad said quickly, 'The concentration camp killed your father.'

Aunty Edith said, 'No, I don't think that, Raf. Of course I don't. Only...' She put her hands over her face. 'Raf, I'm going crazy. If I only knew you were safe...'

Raf stood up and put his arms round her. 'Listen,' he said, holding her tight. 'It's going to be all right, do you hear? We'll get a visa for both of us together and we'll be on a ship, waving goodbye to Germany, we'll have a new life somewhere else and the only bad thing will be leaving our friends behind. Look at me, Mum.'

He gave her his grin. She had to smile back then.

'Raf,' she said, laughing and crying together. 'You're *meshugge*.'

That was Yiddish, but I knew what it meant. Crazy.

'So I'm a *meshuggene*,' he said, 'and you know you can't do without me.'

Ten days later I came home from a trip to the lake beach at Wannsee with Muffi and Paula and Mum called me into the sitting room. She was hemming a skirt for one of her dressmaking clients, but Muffi came snuffling at it and she put it up on the back of the sofa.

'Jenny, the Montgomerys are going to guarantee Aunty Edith and Raf. They can stay with them in Oxford till they find a place to live, even.'

It was what we'd been hoping for. I stared out at the geraniums on the balcony and said the first thing that came into my head. 'Raf'll work as their gardener's boy to repay them.'

'That's nonsense,' Mum said impatiently. 'Of course he'll go to school. They'll be the Montgomerys' guests.'

The red geraniums were flowering so cheerfully, I hated them, they had no hearts. I thought: Raf and Aunty Edith are going away.

I said, 'Raf doesn't want to depend on anyone.'

'He'll do as he's told, for once,' Mum said. She snatched up a stray pin that had fallen onto the sofa and snapped the pin box lid shut on it.

'So when will they go?' I asked.

Mum sighed. 'The sponsors have to write to the Home Office, that's the British Ministry of the Interior, and certify that their Jewish visitors will never become a burden on the state. Then they issue an immigration visa, I don't know how long that'll take. And Aunty Edith and Raf'll have to get an exit visa from Germany as well and that takes time.'

I said, 'But the Nazis want Jews to leave Germany.'

Mum fetched the dress off the sofa back and inspected the hem as if she didn't like it. 'They do, but they want to torment them, too. I just hope the war doesn't break out before all that stuff's done.'

The war, she'd said. As if it was bound to happen. And we'd be on the opposite side to Aunty Edith and Raf. I couldn't stand it. I shouted at Mum.

'Why didn't you stop Hitler before he could make all these horrible things happen?'

I felt churned-up and frightened, that was why I'd said it, but she was furious. 'Jenny! I've had enough of your rudeness, I can't believe I've heard you speaking to me like that—'

I stormed out, slamming the sitting-room door. I heard Mum shouting at me about that and Muffi barking because I'd shut her in. I didn't care. I went into Karl's room and said to him, 'They should have done something, all the grown-ups, before it got to this.'

He was squatting on the floor, hoicking up a pair of the weights he'd got a year ago. Now he put them down again and looked up at me. 'Is that what all the noise was about?'

I said, 'Doesn't it make you angry?'

He stood up. 'I don't like getting angry.'

He didn't. Nor did Dad. Mum and I were the ones who lost our tempers, it was supposed to be because of our red hair.

He said, 'I know things are bad, little sister—'

I said, 'You got those weights so you could be strong enough to beat up the Nazis, now you're a Hitler Youth. And I hate you talking to me in that condescending way.'

He frowned. 'I'm not a Nazi, Jenny. And I don't try to condescend to you—'

'You don't have to try,' I snapped. 'It just comes naturally.'

That night Mum sent me down to the shop to take a cup of coffee to Dad. He was putting in long hours making marionettes for Mum to sell in case he had to go away to war. Sometimes he was at it till nine or ten at night. I'd taken him coffee before, but the way she told me to go, I knew they'd arranged it between them so he could talk to me. I stamped down the back staircase to the yard, splashing the coffee into the saucer so I had to stop before I went indoors to tip it into the cup again.

There were squirly shavings everywhere and the air was full of the grassy smell of fresh-cut lime wood. The puppet theatre stood with its back to the wall, shielding the stockroom and whatever was inside it.

Dad was working on a man marionette's head; it had a big nose that bent slightly sideways. Its face was sad and comic and dreamy all at the same time.

'Who is it?' I asked, giving him his coffee.

He put the head down on his workbench. 'Don Quixote.'

Dad's workroom had been my playroom and my kindergarten. He'd made me marionettes for birthday and Christmas, told me their stories, and taught me how to manipulate them. Some of the marionettes he made were meant to entertain kids, but a lot of them were for adult performances. Plays and opera. I'd learned about Romeo and Juliet when I was five.

'Don Quixote's the one who tried to fight a lot of windmills, isn't he? The mad one?'

71

'He tried to make the world a better place,' Dad said, 'only he didn't know how to set about it.'

I knew that had something to do with what I'd said to Mum. I picked up a bit of shaving and let it curl round my finger.

Dad pulled his handkerchief out of his pocket and wiped his damp face and his bald patch. He said, 'You're upset about Raf and Aunty Edith going.'

I threw the curl of shaving down on the floor. 'You're going to try and be understanding, aren't you, Dad? Only it's no good, because you understanding things doesn't make them better.'

He said, 'You asked Mum a question.'

'She said I was being rude.'

'She's upset, like you. About everything. Sometimes the two of you just rub each other up the wrong way.'

I said, 'I do love her.'

'I know you do. But this isn't about you and Mum getting annoyed with each other. It's about why we didn't stop Hitler. And I can't give you an easy answer.'

He drank some of the coffee. I stood there and waited. I couldn't run away from Dad, he'd be hurt and I loved him too much.

'Jenny, we never thought he'd last, that's the truth. We talked about it, Markus and I. I don't believe in fighting, but we did think about it. Only none of the other political parties did anything. Hitler had been invited to form a government by President Hindenburg, after all. He was legitimate. And fighting him

72

would have meant civil war. Maybe civil war would have been better than what's happened. I'll never know. I wish we had found some way to stop the Nazis, I wish Markus had taken his family out as soon as they came to power, then he'd still be alive. Maybe we should have gone, too. And now...' he stopped.

I said, 'Is there going to be a war?' And it was stupid, I knew it was stupid, but I wanted him to say no, there wasn't going to be. I wanted it so much.

'I'm afraid there is.' His voice was bleak. 'And I'll have to be part of it.'

My belly was cold and tight with fear, but I said, 'At least you won't have to kill anyone, Dad. You'll be in the Medical Corps again.'

He laughed the bitterest laugh I'd ever heard from him. 'I'll see a lot of men die.' I stared at him, suddenly he didn't sound like my dad. In the same harsh voice, he said, 'Three years of it I had last time. I thought I'd got used to it, but it came back at me afterwards. I still dream about those wounded men coming in howling with pain – and the stink of blood and filth, and the surgeon's bone-saw going, hour after hour. And the gassed men choking—' He shuddered. 'And all for fifty metres of soil that we lost the next day. What am I doing, telling you about these things? I'm sorry.'

Now I was ashamed of what I'd said. And shaken, because I'd never had any idea how bad the war had been for him. I asked, 'Do you often have those nightmares?'

He pushed his glasses down his nose and looked at me over the top of them. He was his usual kind self, all of a sudden. 'What do you have nightmares about, Jenny?'

Oh, he saw things, my dad. He noticed people, that was why his marionettes were so alive, why puppeteers were so keen to buy them.

I hesitated, then, all in a rush, I said, 'I dream about gas bombs falling on us. The air gets all thick and I'm choking.' I stopped because I didn't want to cry.

He put his arms round me and held me close. He said, 'Jenny, there'll be a way forward.'

'Through the war?' I asked. I couldn't stop my voice wobbling.

'Even through the war,' he said. He stroked my hair. 'Listen, Jenny. As long as we love each other and hold onto that, we'll find it.'

The Poles had attacked a German broadcasting station at Gleiwitz. They'd been beaten off, and they were all dead. That was what the Nazi news programmes told us.

Grimly, Dad said, 'I'd like to know what really happened there.'

The next day, German troops went roaring into Poland. Dad's call-up papers arrived the day after that. This time the British and the French decided to fight.

Mum sat and cried in the kitchen, saying, 'I went

through the last war with people spitting at us on the street because Grandma was born British – and this time Dad's going to be out there, and – and Karl – and what have the Poles done to have us overrun them and bomb their cities?' She wiped her eyes. 'There's something else, Jenny. Aunty Edith just telephoned. Their visa came today, and it's too late. They can't go. It's so cruel.'

Chapter Seven
1939–1940

We were at war, but nothing was happening. Our troops were in Poland – Dad was in Poland – but we weren't fighting the British or the French. And there hadn't been any air raids yet. Air Marshal Goering had said no bombers would ever reach Berlin; he'd said he'd change his name to Meyer if they did. Meyer was a Jewish name. That was his idea of a joke.

But I kept thinking: If that's true, why did they give us gas masks? So I went on being scared. I was sure I'd never be able to breathe in my mask, anyway.

It was a bitterly cold winter, harsh dry freezing winds howling down our wide Berlin streets, getting to my skin through however many warm things I had on, numbing my cheeks and my nose. Whenever I came home I raced straight to the sitting room without taking my coat off, and huddled against the tiled stove there. I was desperate for the warmth, but then the numbness went off in a fury of pins and needles, and my cheeks went flaming red – as red as my hair, Karl said, so then I tried to hit him, but he held me off.

We couldn't heat any rooms except the sitting room and the kitchen because there was a fuel shortage. There was no black coal from England any more and our own brown coal was needed to make weapons. We had to make sacrifices, that was what our teachers said as we all sat in our overcoats in the classrooms.

Karl and I did our homework at the table in the sitting room – we ate there, too. Mum sewed at the other side of the table. Karl couldn't be there when her clients came for fittings, so he had to move to the kitchen. He didn't like that, he said Kattrin kept talking to him and he couldn't concentrate, but it wasn't easy for me to work when the clients were there, because they talked too.

At the start of December, Frau Tillmann was trying on her new suit, standing right beside the stove so she didn't catch cold when she took her things off, and saying the British and the French were going to make peace.

'And Herr Friedemann will come home.' She smiled at Mum and me. 'Then you'll be happy.'

Herr Tillmann wasn't in the army, he was too old.

It was a beautiful idea, the war ending now, before anything bad happened, but Karl kept saying the British and the French would never leave Poland to Hitler. Especially not the French, because they knew the next place Hitler would march into would be France.

Mum didn't answer because her mouth full of pins. She was crouched down beside Frau Tillmann, pinning the half-sewn blue skirt tighter. She was wearing a pair of old gloves with the fingers cut off. Karl and I had them too. Mum complained about having to wear them, she said they made her clumsy. When she'd finished what she was doing she said, 'Frau Tillmann, you've lost weight.'

'Even inside my woolly vest?' Frau Tillmann said, shivering. 'Just when I could do with a layer of fat to keep me warm. It's the rations, isn't it? But it shows every cloud has a silver lining, getting a bit slimmer at my time of life—'

She wasn't fat anyway, just comfortable old-lady-shaped with her grey hair tidied into a bun at the nape of her neck and little pearl clips in her ears. She always looked smart, plump or not, because she got all her clothes from Mum and Mum was couture-trained. Aunt Grete used to say, 'You look so elegant, Sylvia, whatever you've got on.' Aunt Grete spent a fortune on her clothes but she never looked as good as Mum. She had no taste.

I was supposed to be doing a boring translation from English into German. It was easy, English always was, because Grandma had taught me. 'George takes a boat out on the River Thames. It is a delightful sunny day, and the willows trail their leaves in the water.' Only I was thinking about what George would really be doing now. Maybe getting ready to fly a bombing raid against Berlin, maybe he had a hold full of gas canisters to drop on us.

Frau Tillmann said, 'Well, we still have to think about clothes, war or no war.'

How could she? I thought. Wasn't she frightened?

She went on, 'Let's hope it will turn out better than '14–'18. You look tired, Frau Friedemann. In the shop all day, then having to squeeze in the fittings after hours – how is the business, anyway?'

'Lively,' Mum said. 'The old puppeteers are coming out of retirement, and they're off to perform to the troops. And they want new marionettes, we're selling a lot of stock.'

'You should cut down on the dressmaking,' Frau Tillmann said.

Mum shook her head. 'We'll sell out of marionettes in the end, what'll I do then if my clients have gone elsewhere? That's it, Frau Tillmann.'

'They'll come back,' Frau Tillmann said, shrugging the half-made skirt off and grabbing her old one. 'Quality tells, you know.'

I knew Mum wouldn't take her advice. She loved dressmaking too much.

I sat at the dining table that evening and looked at the empty space where Dad's place used to be. I thought: If only he wasn't with the army, if only he'd just got absorbed in his work, and any minute now Mum'd tell me to go down to the shop and fetch him. I thought how much he must be hating it in Poland.

Kattrin came in with the potatoes. 'The grocer says, Frau Friedemann' – she put the dish down in front of Mum and started ladling out the stew of vegetables with a few bits of beef (good stew, still, though we didn't think so then) – 'he's not allowed to sell chocolate or cake to Jews. And the Jews haven't been told officially, the shopkeepers have to let them ask for it, then say they can't have it.'

'What?' Mum said. I saw the horrible picture in my mind's eye. Aunty Edith going in to buy chocolate for Raf for Christmas and the grocer telling her she couldn't have it because she was a Jew. She'd be humiliated. In front of other customers, probably – of course that was why they'd done it that way. I wanted to hit someone for it, but Kattrin had a better idea.

'Well, Frau Friedemann, I thought, we've got plenty...'

Chocolate and sweets were still off-ration for us. Mind, Kattrin had her black-market shopping well organised, so we didn't go short of on-ration things, either.

'Of course,' Mum said.

That was how it started. We took chocolate and stollen and spice cakes when we went to celebrate Christmas with Aunty Edith and Raf. Karl came with a bag of coal for the stove, they had much less fuel than we did, and Mum said she'd sold one of Aunty Edith's rings to pay for everything. That was a lie, but it made Aunty Edith and Raf feel better.

In March the next year Jews were forbidden to buy chicken, fish, smoked meat or milk, so Karl and Mum started to take those to Aunty Edith and Raf. They were breaking the law, giving Jews rations they weren't allowed, so they went at night. Kattrin made a fuss whenever Mum went there on her own. She knew all the stories about how dangerous the black-out was, like one about the girl who'd been murdered and they'd found bits of the body on every railway station in Berlin.

'That was a nice bit of Prussian methodicalness,' Karl said. 'Every railway station.'

'It's no good laughing,' Kattrin said stubbornly, 'those men are out there with their knives, looking for women to butcher. And worse. And people are always breaking their ankles, falling over things...'

'I'll be all right, Kattrin,' Mum said. But I was scared too.

Then one day it was my turn. I was given the shopping bag and told to meet Raf near the zoo and casually pass it to him. That was in the daytime. Mum wasn't scared of the men with knives for herself but she wasn't going to risk them for me.

'We need to do it in different ways all the time,' Mum said. 'But it has to be quick, Jenny. No hanging around or chatting. Just tell Raf I'll be over next Thursday. And make sure there aren't any policemen about.'

*

Raf was getting taller all the time, and he was thin, even with the extra rations. But when we met he gave me the grin.

'No policemen,' he said, 'I've already checked. Listen, you don't have to go straightaway, do you? We can just have a few minutes. I've been missing you.'

'What?' I said. I was so pleased to see him. 'You haven't got anyone to annoy?'

He reached out and twitched my hair. 'Not really.' But that was just joking about, it was a long time since he'd pulled my hair and kidnapped my toys and held them to ransom.

It was a lovely spring day and we strolled down past the zoo. Raf swung the shopping bag and the things bounced around. There were carrots and potatoes in there as well as meat and milk, because Jews were only allowed to go shopping between four and five in the evening and by that time most of the fresh stuff had gone.

I looked at the zoo gate. 'Do you remember how we dared each other to touch the glass in front of the poisonous snakes' mouths?'

Raf's jaw tensed. 'I'm not allowed in there now.'

I'd been stupid and thoughtless. I didn't know what to say.

Raf shrugged his shoulders. 'It's not all bad. We're not allowed to go to the theatre either, but the Jewish organisations put on concerts and shows for us.' He made a face. 'It's the Nazis' loss, we get world-class performers they don't allow themselves to see.'

And then we heard the paperboy yelling down the street.

'Special edition! Read all about it!'

Raf and I looked at each other, then we half-ran towards the man and heard him yell again. 'Our troops go into Norway and Denmark! Special edition! Read all about it!'

I had a bad feeling in my stomach. I said, 'I thought Denmark had a treaty with us, we were supposed to leave them alone?'

Raf said, 'They didn't know Hitler, did they?'

'Maybe they'll send Dad there.'

Raf looked at me. 'Nobody attacks hospitals or ambulances.' I could tell he was only saying that to reassure me. The bad feeling grew, and I knew I had to go home. I hated leaving Raf, it felt all wrong, but we'd already broken the rules and Mum was waiting for me and looking at her watch. When I walked back along the Kurfürstendamm there seemed to be another paperboy yelling about special editions every ten steps I took.

The next morning our geography teacher came marching into the classroom with a rolled-up map in his hand, which he opened and tore in two.

'*That's* the old map of Europe,' Klotz said triumphantly. 'Obsolete. Now look at the new one.' He started to draw on the blackboard. 'History in the making, girls. I wish I hadn't had my knee injured in the last war. I'm on fire to join our lads.'

He had a fat face and wide nostrils like a pig's that spread further sideways when he smiled. I looked at Paula as she sat at the desk beside me. She rolled her eyes to the ceiling.

'I wish he was out there too,' she muttered.

Klotz was quick with the chalk. He had Europe sketched out in ten minutes. 'It's a wonderful thing,' he said, drawing swastikas over Denmark and Norway, 'for a man to fight for his country.'

Paula picked up a pencil and scribbled on her rough book: *And for us to grow up to comfort the victors with our Aryan bodies.* I choked.

Klotz said, 'And of course we need the women and girls at home, supporting their menfolk – Jenny Friedemann, what's that noise?'

'Sorry, Herr Klotz,' I gasped. 'I've got a cough.'

Paula was already rubbing her note out. Klotz sent me off to get a drink of water.

A short time after that the lilac was coming out in our back yard and Klotz was drawing swastikaed tanks heading for France. Travelling through Belgium, Holland, Luxemburg, Hitler didn't care about their neutrality either. Dad was sent to France, with Brigadier Rommel. He was in an ambulance unit, carrying out operations on the edge of the battlefield with shells going off all round him. Even if nobody attacked him he might get killed by accident. I started to jump every time anyone knocked at the door, in case it was a telegram.

Mum hadn't sent me to take groceries to Raf again. I wanted to see him, but I didn't dare ask to go because Mum'd think we'd disobey orders and chat. Which of course was what I wanted to do. And Germany went on winning all the battles. I met Frau Tillmann on the staircase as I came home from school and she said to me, 'Well, things look better now. We've driven the British out of France, now they'll make peace. Your father'll be home really soon, you'll see.'

I went into the house and found Mum crying on the sofa in the sitting room.

'What's wrong?' I said. I was terrified. I looked around; there wasn't a telegram, but maybe she'd dropped it in the hall. I made myself ask, 'Is it Dad, Mum?'

She shook her head. 'It's not Dad.'

I sat down beside her. I needed to, I'd been so scared. 'What is it then?'

'It's the news,' she said. 'It's like dark night falling over Europe. And I don't want Hitler to have Britain – and I keep worrying your father might decide to refuse to serve, Jenny, even in the Medical Corps, because that's part of the war after all, and they'd hang him . . . ' She bit her lip.

'I shouldn't have told you that,' she said. 'You'll worry too.'

I said, 'Mum, I'm not a baby, you know.'

She looked at me, shaking her head. 'He did say he didn't want to be a martyr, he said he'd think about us. And he said he *could* just square it with his conscience if he was looking after the wounded.' She got her handkerchief out and blew her nose. 'I'm all right again now,' she said. 'I just had to have a cry.' But I could hear it in her voice: she wasn't all right.

That night I lay in bed, staring at the blacked-out darkness and trying to send my thoughts to Dad: Don't decide to be a conscientious objector, Dad. Don't do it. Stay alive for us.

And then Hitler came to Berlin to celebrate the fall of France – and the school took us to see him. Paula got a sick note from her mother, but Mum thought it'd look suspicious if she wrote me a sick note, and we needed not to look suspicious, because of taking care of Aunty Edith and Raf.

We stood there for hours, waiting. My legs ached, and I got really thirsty. People were singing and waving flags. We'd had to bring flowers to throw down on the street. I'd brought lilac. Now it lay there in the road, waiting for the Führer's tyres to squash it. That was what I said to myself at first, till the thought came up in me: I'm going to see Hitler! What'll he be like?

Suddenly I was really excited, I wanted to see him.

It was like eating sweets you know are going to make you sick. I wanted to be just like all the other girls, a lot of them in their German Girls' League uniform, which I didn't have, but I was wearing my dirndl, that looked properly German. And we heard a roar coming towards us: *he* was on his way. The Führer, that special He we were all waiting for. And then I didn't think of Aunty Edith and Raf, or of Dad, there was something about that roar, all those people shouting for Hitler – it blew all my thoughts out of my head, everything I knew. Just being part of it, a German, that was what seemed to matter.

There were boys shinning up the lampposts in their Hitler Youth uniforms, to get a better view, and we were all putting our arms up, saluting. I was saluting, shouting, 'Heil!' with the rest of them, I couldn't help it. I was there in my dirndl, saluting, and he came, standing up in his Mercedes wearing a peaked cap and a long coat, saluting back, and when he saw us girls he turned and smiled, specially for us. I thought my eyes met his for a moment, his were very blue, and there was such a kind expression on his face – and then he was gone. And we were all crying, saying, 'He looked at us! The Führer looked at us!'

I didn't want to go home after that. The excitement was still fizzing in me, and I felt strange, as if I'd changed all the way through. I kept remembering the kindness on Hitler's face, and how we'd all shouted for him, and how I'd felt so sure and happy and certain when I'd been shouting and belonging to it all. I didn't want to be an outsider again.

Only home was the only place I had to go, and as I realised that, I felt the happiness drain away, leaving me shivering and scared, the girl I'd been before, who had Jewish friends and loved them – and what chance had we? There were so many people who'd shouted for Hitler. The next thing was the shame because I'd shouted with them. I wondered what Aunty Edith and Raf would feel if they knew. I wondered how I could have done what I'd done. I felt like a traitor.

When I got in, Mum asked me how it had been and was I very tired from all the standing? I ran to my bedroom and shut the door. I was scared she'd come after me, but she didn't. I sat on my bed, all jarred and at odds with myself. Then I looked at Pinocchio and thought how I'd almost turned into a marionette that afternoon, and how lovely it had felt, not needing to think or go against everyone else.

Herr Mingers was in France, too. He sent a fur collar home for Frau Broomstick, who showed it off with a sour, triumphant smile.

'Now,' she said, stroking the sleek fur, 'those Frenchmen are biting the dust. Now they know what defeat tastes like.'

Karl said, 'Who did he steal *that* from? Someone prettier than her, I'll bet.'

I laughed, but I felt really bad inside. It scared me

88

that I understood now what Frau Broomstick got out of being a Nazi.

The first bombs dropped on Berlin. Not on us, yet. But the sirens went and we had to go down to the cellar all the same.

'Our pilots are reducing London to rubble,' Klotz gloated the next day, drawing airfields onto what he was calling his 'dynamic map'. 'Girls, you can see from this that we can reach London in an hour or so, while the British bombers have to struggle to get to Berlin and when they do get here, they're too exhausted to do much damage.'

I thought about those scary nights when we sat there clutching our gas masks along with all our neighbours. It was quiet and still in the cellar, but I was always listening out for the noise of the bombers.

'*I* thought,' Paula muttered, 'fatso Goering reckoned Berlin would never be bombed at all. He was going to change his name, wasn't he?'

'Paula Fischer,' Klotz said menacingly, 'would you mind sharing your thoughts with the rest of the class?'

Paula stood up at once. 'Herr Klotz, I was saying the Luftwaffe pilots are really marvellous. I was saying later, when I'm old enough, I want to have a baby with a Luftwaffe pilot.'

She said it in a stupid, little-innocent's voice, but she stared at Klotz, straight at his piggy little eyes. The other girls put their hands in front of their faces to stifle giggles, and Klotz gulped. Suddenly he was bright red in the face.

'Very praiseworthy,' he said. 'Of course every German girl will be dreaming of marrying a Luftwaffe pilot. And to be the mother of a hero's family – you can sit down, Fischer. Now' – he turned round to the board and found the chalk – 'what do you think this map will look like in six months' time?'

'It's all about sex, really,' Paula said when we were having our second breakfast in the break.

'What is?' I said. It was fun talking to Paula about sex and boys. We got excited and laughed a lot.

'The war is. Klotz wants to be part of the Master Race so he can go to France and have his pick of all the glamorous Frenchwomen.'

I giggled. 'And then we get preached at about Faith and Beauty so we don't misbehave while the soldiers' backs are turned.'

'And get given those pictures of hairy dark Jews with hooked noses,' Paula said in a throaty voice like a sultry film star's, 'so we know who to go with if we want something *really* exciting to happen.'

I had to put my apple down so I wouldn't choke on it. But I hated those pictures, they were like a pair of distorting spectacles the Nazis kept putting in front of my eyes. They made me remember the day I'd shouted for Hitler.

'You know what it really means, don't you, Faith

and Beauty?' Paula asked. 'Keep your mouth shut and your legs open.'

Paula didn't care what she said. Maybe that was because Paula's grandfather had been a baron. Her aunt and uncle lived in a castle on the shore of the Chiemsee in Bavaria.

The newsreaders kept telling us the British couldn't do any real damage to Berlin, but the government started to evacuate children to the country. Six girls went from my class. Then one day Mum and I came home from shopping and Adolf and Siegfried Mingers were standing outside their front door with little suitcases and frightened faces and labels round their necks.

'They're going to Bavaria,' Frau Mingers said, turning the key in the apartment door. 'Because of these unprovoked bombing raids that the British have started. The Jews are behind it all, of course.'

Mum was with me, and I could feel her stiffening, just like me.

I said, 'What about Willi, is he going too?' I hoped so, because he was still staring at me every time he saw me. Paula said that meant he fancied me and I should never let him get within two metres of me, that was a good distance to be safe from creepy boys, she said. 'Any closer and they can grab you.'

'No!' Frau Mingers snapped, jabbing her thin elbows out as if she wanted to hit us with them. 'I'll need Willi to help me in the shop. Norbert's going into the Army like the patriotic boy he is.'

I looked at her and thought how horrible she was, only then I saw a tear run out of her eyes. She put her hand up and rubbed it angrily away. She was having to send her goblins to strangers and her husband was in the war like Dad and now she was going to lose Norbert. I couldn't believe it but for that moment I felt sorry for her.

I said, 'It's nice healthy air in Bavaria.'

'Yes,' Frau Mingers said, pushing the boys towards the staircase. 'No Jews polluting it. Or race-traitors, I hope. Heil Hitler!'

Just after that Mum told me to meet Raf and hand another bag of groceries to him. Just outside City Hall this time. I didn't show how glad I was. I made sure I was there early, though. It was a warm afternoon in October. I walked up and down beside the huge red building and watched a soldier on leave sitting on a park bench with his girlfriend. He kept kissing her with little pecking kisses and then suddenly their mouths seemed to glue themselves together and stay glued for a long time. I stared at them for a moment, then I felt hot and embarrassed, and I looked away, wishing Raf would come. A flock of pigeons settled on the pavement and started strutting around and cooing. And all of a sudden Raf was there, at my elbow.

I said, 'Raf! I've got some money. Let's go to a café and have cake.'

The grin went off his face. 'I can't let you pay for me.'

'Aunt Grete tipped me two marks. It's Nazi money, she'd be furious if she knew I was using it to feed you.' He was still looking obstinate, but I thought of something else to say. 'It was probably stolen from Jews anyway.'

'Oh!' he said, his face lightening. 'All right, Jenny. Only one day, when this is all over, Mum and I'll treat you, and your family, over and over again. Do you hear?'

We found a little café in the square round the corner, with outside tables. We sat down there and the pigeons and sparrows came round our feet looking for crumbs. I put the shopping bag under the table. It was a noisy place, so we could say what we liked without other people hearing. We went inside to choose our cakes from the counter and then sat down to order apple juice to drink with them – restaurant and café food was still off-ration, though people were always complaining about the quality. Raf told me a bit about his school and the other boys, then he said, 'What's in the bag?'

'Smoked ham,' I said, 'and Tilsit cheese and a tin of sardines and a cauliflower and a bar of chocolate.'

His face lit up at the idea of chocolate – and a policeman appeared.

'Identity cards, everyone,' he called out.

*

93

I thought: Please don't let this be happening. Only it was, and it was my fault. Raf shouldn't have been in a café and I'd persuaded him to come. What'd they do to him? Concentration camp, probably. Maybe they'd kill him. I felt cold and sick.

The policeman was beside us now. I saw the green sleeve of his uniform as he held his hand out.

'Come on, you pair.'

He said it quite good-humouredly, that was even more frightening, somehow. A pigeon walked under the table, cooing, it didn't have to worry about anything. I showed my card.

Raf went through a big pantomime of hunting in his jacket pocket. 'Oh, no,' he said. 'I left it at home.' He fixed his blue eyes on the policeman. 'I'm sorry.' He gave the policeman the grin, only he put a scared, sheepish tinge into it.

The policeman shook his head at him, but the corners of his mouth twitched. It's working, I thought. Just as long as it keeps on working. 'I ought to take you to the station and get your parents to bring it there,' he said. 'They wouldn't be pleased, would they?'

Raf hung his head and half stood up to go with him. My hands were in tight fists under the table, I was thinking: Please, please, please.

The policeman put a hand on Raf's shoulder. 'Don't worry, lad,' he said in a friendly voice. 'Just remember next time you go out, all right?'

And it was all right to let my breath out as he left,

and show how relieved I was – after all, I'd have been scared even if Raf hadn't been Jewish. But Raf just let himself down on the seat and gave me the full Rafael grin. 'I should have been an actor,' he whispered.

My heart was still jumping inside my chest. 'You didn't enjoy it, did you?'

'Chutzpah,' he said, still grinning. 'Cheek. That's what it takes. And being a bit crazy, Jenny. Then it's fun.'

And suddenly it was fun. It had worked to be cheeky and crazy, hadn't it? Suddenly everything was exciting, the sky was bluer, and I saw a sparrow hopping round, confident as Raf. I tossed it a bit of cake and watched it eat.

'We'll do it again,' Raf said. 'Next time your Aryan aunt gives you some Nazi money we'll sit down in another Aryan café and eat Aryan cake.'

I said, 'What if another policeman comes?'

'I'll think of something,' he said. 'Do you think I'm not able to?'

'You were a long time,' Mum said when I got home.

I'd already worked out what to say. 'I met Paula and we went to a café and had drinks with the money Aunt Grete gave me.'

Chapter Eight
1940–1941

Uncle Hartmut sat on our sofa in his double-breasted suit and said, 'I'm getting *Jews* to work in my factory.' He fingered the little swastika in his lapel. 'They'd better pull their fingers out, that's all I can say.'

Kunigunde shot a spiteful, grinning look at us and leaned against her father. 'You won't let them slack, will you, Daddy?'

Uncle Hartmut tweaked one of her Aryan plaits. 'They'll find out what hard work is.'

And I couldn't stop myself. I said, 'My friend Paula's father says all the factory owners want to have Jews because they're going to work so hard.'

He'd said they were bribing the Labour office to get Jews, but I had enough sense not to say that. And Karl drew in a quick, worried breath, and Mum, who was sitting beside me on our sofa, put her hand on my arm and gripped me tight and angrily. Uncle Hartmut was staring at me with his hard, bullying eyes. Aunt Grete was looking at the floor, and my cousins' faces, excitedly turned on me, said: Now she's in trouble.

I knew that, but I wouldn't back down yet. I met Uncle Hartmut's eyes and for a moment they flickered aside from mine, as if he didn't want me to know what he was thinking. But he said, 'Little girls should show respect for their elders.'

Mum gave me a little shove, and I said what I had to. 'I'm sorry, Uncle Hartmut.' But I wasn't sorry, even though I had to hear a lecture from him about being spoilt, and how Dad should have spanked me; spanking was good for children, he said, and I remembered how he'd clouted Hildegarde in the face.

All the Jews in Germany were being enlisted for forced labour now, and the worst thing was, Aunty Edith was going to be one of Uncle Hartmut's new slaves. As for Raf, he was going to have to leave school, so that'd be the end of his education – and Raf was really clever, he'd always got top marks in all the class tests. While stupid little Kunigunde was still being educated. She was a lazy little trollop in spite of all the hidings Uncle Hartmut had dealt her, she'd just failed all her end-of-year tests and was going to have to repeat the year.

In March of 1941, when Raf was just fifteen, he was sent to work in a gas works. It was quite near us; if he'd lived in his old home it'd have been convenient, but he had to walk all the way back to Moabit. Jews were only allowed on the tram if they lived some really long distance from their work. He was working twelve-hour shifts, six days a week, and so was Aunty Edith.

Mum sent me to give him some groceries shortly after he'd started – it had to be on a Sunday now, of course. I was shaken to see how he looked, as if a lamp had been put out inside him. There was no chutzpah about him that day.

All I could say was, 'Let's go and have some cake.'

I'd told Mum I was meeting Paula afterwards. I'd told Paula I was meeting a boy. I invented his name, Klaus-Heinrich, and where he came from – Prenzlauer Berg. He was a worker's son, I said.

'Has your aunt tipped you some more Nazi money?' he asked, trying to sound cheerful.

'Yes,' I said, lying. I'd been hoarding my pocket money for weeks. 'And there's chocolate in the bag for you, Raf.'

He made himself smile.

We found another good noisy café where it was all right to talk freely. He let his hands flop on the table and stared down at them. They were stained yellow, as if he'd spent years smoking cigarettes, and on the back of his left hand there was a red gash.

He said, 'We have to crawl into the retorts to clean them out – they're the things they make the coal gas in. They're designed to use black coal from England, and of course there's only brown coal now. They get clogged up with tar. It's like trying to shift treacle and it stinks. I was sick the first few times.' He pulled his hands back off the table. 'I shouldn't be so sorry for myself, should I? I'm not the only Jewish lad at the gas works.'

Angrily, I said, 'They shouldn't be doing it to any of you.' And then a memory flashed into my mind, the

kindness of Hitler's face when he'd looked at us school-
girls. It was horrible to remember that because of what
was happening to Raf.

Raf shrugged his shoulders, then he looked angry.
'The factory's not good for Mum. She keeps coughing,
the fibres get stuck in her throat.'

When we got up to go, he said, 'Do we have to wait
till our mothers arrange something? It could be ages.
Couldn't we meet Sunday after next? I've got a friend
I can tell Mum I'm meeting.'

I said yes at once. I'd tell Mum I was doing something with Paula.

Paula thought my romance with Klaus-Heinrich was
blooming. She wanted to know if my mother would
really mind me meeting him.

'Yes,' I said. 'She'd think I was too young.'

'Oh, I see,' Paula said, grinning. I felt bad about
telling lies to her, really bad. I had to, though.

I didn't have enough money for cake this time, only
for a drink of lemonade, but Raf said that was fine.
We sat down opposite each other, and he said the
foreman at the gas works wasn't a bad sort, not too
hard on them.

'I've decided I'm going to be an architect some day,'
he said. 'You've got to have something to look
forward to, you know?'

I nodded eagerly. I was so glad to see him a bit more
cheerful.

'It's opened my eyes, seeing what life is like for labourers. For one thing, if someone's doing a filthy sweated job, day in, day out, they shouldn't need to trudge up five flights of stairs at the end of it, they need lifts. Listen, do you think I could ask Aunty Sylvia for some paper, Jenny, because I want to sketch out some ideas. I'm sorry, it sounds as if I was always asking for things – and I loved the chocolate, by the way, we both did.'

The grin lit his face up again. I felt as if the sun had come out.

I said, 'Kattrin gets the chocolate for you. She says heavy workers need sugar.'

He laughed. 'Thank her from me. How are things at home?'

'Karl's got his call-up. He's got to go to training camp next week. Mum's really upset, but she's trying not to show it.'

Raf's face hardened. 'I wish I could fight.'

'What?' I said.

'If we'd got to England, I'd have wanted to fight the Nazis. But not in the Air Force. I wouldn't want to drop bombs on you.'

I wanted to cry when he said that, but I managed not to.

It was May time and the lilac was out, just as it had been when we'd invaded France and Klotz had got so excited about it. This year, though, he had to rub out the swastikas he'd hopefully drawn over the British

Isles. 'For the time being,' he said darkly, scowling at the islands for refusing Hitler his victory. He drew a swastika over Crete instead, because that was the latest place we were invading.

Karl had been selected for radio interception work because he was clever and spoke such good English. He'd finished his training and he was already a sub-lieutenant. Now he and Dad came home on leave. They were both going to Rommel's Africa Corps.

Karl sat at the dinner table and said, 'Look, Dad, I know how you feel. And I know we're fighting a bad war. But what I reckon is, if I've got to fight, I'm going to fight properly. The only other option is to say no.'

'Not that!' Dad said quickly.

I saw Mum go white. I felt ill with horror.

'You can't, Karl,' I said. 'You know what they'd do to you.'

'You see?' Karl said. 'There's no way out of this.'

Dad didn't answer.

Later, he sat with Muffi on his lap and played chess with Karl. We went with Dad to the Quaker Meeting. I sat beside Dad, hungrily concentrating on his nearness, as if I could pull that inside me and hoard it up for the time ahead when he wouldn't be there.

I didn't want to go to bed at night because that was another day finished. When I was shooed off, I'd lie there muttering into my pillow: 'They'll be together, that's a good thing, isn't it? And Karl says Rommel's a good commander, he doesn't waste his men's lives. Even Dad admits that.'

And then they were both gone and that was so awful I couldn't let myself think about it.

At midsummer German troops invaded Russia, which was the Russians' fault, that's what we were told. We'd had to do it, to protect ourselves.

Mum laughed angrily, then she said, 'I don't believe the war will ever end.'

I can't explain how desperate and furious that made me feel. 'Yes, it will,' I said. 'Don't be so – I hate it when you make everything seem so—'

And she told me not to talk to her like that and I went to my bedroom and banged the door and when I came out I met her in the hallway and walked past her, still raging against her. She turned her shoulder away, ignoring me. Then I saw Kattrin standing in the kitchen door. She was laughing at us.

'You're too alike,' she said, 'the pair of you.'

We couldn't keep it up after that.

There was a letter from Karl. Mum opened it and grey sand fell out all over the table.

I haven't tried to get rid of it,' he wrote, *because it blows into everything here, so it gives you an idea of how things are. I always thought the desert would be yellow, but it's all grey and chunky rocks underfoot, you have to be careful or you turn your ankle on it and make work*

102

for Dad and his colleagues. The sand drifts, though, like snow, and in the mornings you see little animal tracks in it, but you never see the animals making them. They come out at night. I like being under Rommel's command, he's tough, but fair, and he cares about us. The work's interesting. I see Dad every now and again, that's nice. Hope the air raids aren't too bad.

And that last line meant what our '*Take care of yourself*' meant when we wrote to him and Dad; what Dad meant when he wrote '*Your letters mean a lot to me, my dearest ones*'.

Write to me soon, that was what it meant. Let me know you're still alive.

Neither of them ever asked about the Jakobys. It wasn't because they didn't care. It was because all the letters were read.

In the autumn of 1941 Uncle Hartmut decided Berlin was too dangerous for Hildegarde and Kunigunde, so he sent them to his mother in the country near Heidelberg. I was glad I wouldn't have to see them any longer. Aunt Grete went down one week a month to be with them, but she said Uncle Hartmut needed her to be with him the rest of the time.

I'd stopped being scared during the air raids. They'd happened too many times and we'd never had any bombs. The worst thing was the way Willi Mingers kept staring at me. Once he sat down beside me so I couldn't keep any space between us. He had a wart on the back of his left hand and he kept fingering it. He smelt of carbolic soap.

He jerked his thumb at the patch of rough bricks that covered the escape hatch. 'Norbert and I helped make that,' he said to me, as if I'd been away when it had happened. 'Bet the British don't have anything as clever. If we're trapped in here all we have to do is knock the bricks away and then we go through next door and into the next cellar all the way to the Kurfürstendamm.'

'I know,' I said. 'Karl helped, too.'

His mother said quickly, 'Your brother won't have worked as hard as my boys.'

Mum gave me a look that said: Don't encourage them. Willi started picking at his wart again. I thought about Raf's hands, with the yellow tar stains on them.

Raf had shot up now, he was as tall and fair as a Nazi dream boy. He'd got muscles from labouring at the gas works but he was thin and his nose still seemed on the large side for his face. We were still meeting every other week. I'd got so used to telling lies to Mum and Kattrin and Paula I hardly noticed them.

One afternoon, Mum started to talk about my new winter dress. 'I'm desperately late making it,' she said. 'You know how busy I've been.'

I nodded. She was still selling marionettes as well as making clothes for her clients, and she'd started a new line; making dolls' clothes out of bits of leftover fabric. A lot of people bought them to send to little girls who'd been evacuated.

'You'll have it before Christmas,' she said. 'How about a round collar and smocked gathers? I think that'd be sweet.'

She had her faraway designer's expression on – it was already growing inside her head, that sweet little girl's frock – only I knew what I wanted, I'd seen it in a fashion magazine at Paula's house.

'Mum,' I said, 'can I have a fitted dress, with darts, and a little V neck?'

'That's far too sophisticated for you,' she said at once.

'Paula wears clothes like that.'

Mum frowned. 'I don't know what that girl's mother's thinking of, she'll turn into a proper little spoiled madam—'

I shouted at her, 'I'm fourteen and you're still trying to dress me up like a doll. I wish I could buy my own clothes.'

She was furious. Of course she would be. I'd insulted her Art, but she'd insulted my absolute best friend, how dared she? And nobody knew better than her how important friends were.

'Well,' she said coldly, 'if you earned your own money you could waste it on stuff that was half the quality of the clothes I make you, but you don't, do you? And you needn't think I'll let you leave school yet, because I won't. You've got to get an education.'

'Yes,' I snapped, 'it's really important for me to be stuffed full of Nazi propaganda.'

I went to my bedroom and slammed the door. I thought she'd come after me, but she didn't. There was a long silence and then I heard her going out.

I went to find Kattrin in the kitchen.

'Where's Mum gone?' I asked.

'To Moabit,' Kattrin said. 'I think she wants to talk to Frau Jakoby about you.'

It was after blackout time and Mum was out there in the dark. I thought about some murderer ambushing her. It'd be my fault if anything bad happened to her, I'd driven her out after all.

I worried for two hours, then Mum came home safely. I ran to meet her at the door, and we both started off at the same moment.

'Mum, I'm sorry, only—'

And Mum, 'Your dress – well, you are growing up, after all. Listen, I've got some fabric put by – it's got cashmere in it—'

I was so grateful to Aunty Edith, I knew she'd persuaded Mum to make me the sort of dress I wanted. We put our arms out to each other and hugged. I said, 'Mum, I'm sorry I said I wished I could buy my own clothes, you're a fantastic dress-maker…'

She made a face at me. 'I should listen to my clients, though, shouldn't I?'

She got the fabric out and showed it to me, it was

blue-green crepe and really soft. I could see how good it'd look. I was thrilled.

I came home from school the next day and she called me in. 'I've done the toile, come and see if you like it.'

There was the mock-up of my dress-to-be, cut out of an old sheet. Mum always did it that way, couture-fashion. It had the fitted top, the little V neck in the yoke that I wanted and a full, bias-cut skirt. The best thing was, now Mum was pinning the toile on me, she was as excited as I was.

'That skirt'll hang beautifully,' she said, standing back from it. Then, 'You're getting really pretty, did you know?'

'You're only saying that because you're my mother,' I said. 'Paula's prettier than me.'

Mum gave me a look that said she knew better. I was glad, really. Suddenly she frowned. 'Don't grow up too quickly.'

I didn't like her saying that. She saw it and sighed. 'Never mind. I know you can't be my baby any longer.'

The next time I met Raf, he asked, 'Is your dress almost ready?'

I said, 'I'll have it in a week. I'm glad your mum was on my side about it.'

'She loves you,' he said. 'So – next time we meet you'll be wearing it?'

I felt shy, somehow. I said, 'I don't know if she'll let me.' Best clothes were supposed to *be* for best, maybe going out with Paula wouldn't count.

He looked disappointed. 'I'd like to see you in it.' I saw a flush growing on his cheekbones, and suddenly I realised why I'd wanted that sophisticated dress: it had been for him. I wondered what Mum would say if she knew that and about our secret meetings. Only I felt she mustn't know, it wasn't just for fear she might stop them.

I said I'd try and wear the dress next time.

I told Mum Paula's mother was taking us out and I wanted her to see you didn't need to be rich to be elegant. That did the trick. Mum even agreed to me wearing the string of facet-cut amber beads that I'd inherited from Grandma, and the little amber drop earrings that matched them.

We were meeting by the zoo. I nipped into the ladies' room at the railway station opposite and decorated my mouth with the lipstick I'd bought. I'd practised putting it on with Paula. 'Klaus-Heinrich will love it,' she'd said. 'And the amber beads will be perfect, they match your auburn hair.'

'Red,' I said.

'Auburn,' she said firmly.

For a moment I saw Klaus-Heinrich in my mind's eye, rather shy, with brown wavy hair and soulful brown eyes like a pet spaniel's. Paula thought he sounded sweet. He was still at school, his favourite subject was German literature, and his family didn't understand why. I spent quite a lot of time thinking about new things to tell Paula about Klaus-Heinrich. Sometimes I started to believe he was a real boy and felt bad about neglecting him.

Raf was standing outside the zoo gates with a scarf round his neck and his hands stuck into his pockets. They'd brought in the law that Jews had to wear a yellow star on their clothes, but Raf had his attached with safety-pins and now he'd got it in his pocket. I waved at him and he saw me.

'Are you wearing the dress?'

I nodded.

'Well, I've got my best clothes on,' he said, 'and look...'

He pulled a little roll of Reichsmarks and ration coupons out of his pocket and showed them quickly to me. 'I found a wallet on the street. I suppose I should have handed it in at the police station, but,' he shrugged, 'the owner's a Supporting Member of the SS. I found his card. So I don't care about taking his money.'

I said, 'He'll get the coupons replaced, anyway, if he says he's lost them.'

'So he will. I'm going to give Mum some of the money, but I'm going to treat you, too – don't say no, I really want to – and you know where I'm taking you? To the Kranzler.'

Only the smartest café in Berlin! I let him see I was impressed, I knew how good it made him feel.

We left our coats and hats in the cloakroom. Raf looked at me in my dress, but all he said was, 'Let's go and get a table.'

He sounded awkward, maybe he was nervous because of this being the Kranzler, but I was scared then, I thought he didn't like me in the dress. Or maybe my lipstick was smudged and I looked stupid.

We went into the café. Raf's best jacket and trousers had been Karl's three years ago and they were a little bit worn, though they were good. The waitress looked doubtfully at him, but he gave her the grin and I saw her melt. When she glanced at me she looked approving – and a quick look round the room showed me that none of the rich ladies who were sitting there had better clothes than me. But that didn't make me happy, because I'd put my dress on specially for Raf and he hadn't said he liked me in it.

Chapter Nine

The waitress took us to a table in a corner. At one side of us there was a Luftwaffe officer keeping company with a blonde girl in a red straw hat and a seductive little black net veil, at the other side a middle-aged couple were shouting at a stout deaf old lady with a mink flower brooch on her collar. They made the Kranzler into a safe, noisy café – though if Raf and I couldn't find anything to say to each other, that wouldn't matter.

There was a mirror on the wall beside the table and I glanced sideways at it in case my lipstick had smudged or gone on my teeth, but it hadn't. We went to choose our cakes at the counter. There was more patisserie than I'd seen for ages – rationing was beginning to bite, though Kattrin still had her black-marketeering well organised. Raf chose a piece of lemon cheesecake and I chose a poppy-seed cake. They looked good. Pre-war. Worth the ration coupons he was going to give for them.

We brought back the little tickets that showed which cakes we'd ordered and handed them to our friendly waitress. I ordered lemonade and Raf ordered hot chocolate.

We sat opposite each other. I stared at all the nice things, the white damask tablecloth with its shiny pattern of white roses, the pretty china cup and saucer, the silver cake fork lying beside the plate, the smooth curved fold of the napkin, and I just wanted to run away because he still hadn't said anything.

'Bombed out,' the man at the next table shouted. The old lady crooked her head sideways and said, 'I didn't catch that.'

'Herr Schilf got bombed out,' the man shouted again.

'Oh,' the old lady said loudly. 'Herr Schilf. How is he nowadays?'

'He got bombed out,' the man's wife said just as loudly. 'He's had to find a new place to live.'

The Luftwaffe officer's girlfriend suddenly screeched at them, 'My Gerhardt's risking his life up night after night, fighting those bombers off, we come here for a little peace, and can we have it? For heaven's sake, keep your voices down!'

'And my mother be left out of the conversation?' the man demanded.

The waitress came with our drinks and cakes. I tasted my cake: it was good, black and sticky inside – and I could hardly swallow it. The lemonade set my teeth on edge. I put it down. I didn't know what to do with myself for misery.

A piano started up in the background and a woman singer launched into a schmaltzy song.

> *I'm dancing in your arms*
> *Forgetting grief and harm*
> *When I look deep into your eyes*

My heart flies off to paradise—
And then Raf reached across the table, he took my hand. He did it cautiously, maybe he thought I'd pull away from him, but I didn't and he began stroking my fingers. Shivers of delight went all through me, they started small but they grew so strong I was scared the whole café would feel what was going on inside me. I could feel my cheeks getting hot. 'Jenny,' he said. I looked up and our eyes met. There was an intent, questioning look on his face that I'd never seen there before.

Suddenly, everything was wonderful and exciting, down to the gas works stains on Raf's fingers. Even the clientele having their row in the background.

The Luftwaffe officer was shouting for the bill. He said he'd had enough. The old lady's son got up with his face all red, shoving his hands through his grey brush of hair. 'I flew aeroplanes in the first war, young fellow, I'll tell you, that was real flying – and I'm a personal friend of Reich Air Marshal Goering. We were comrades.'

Raf kept playing with my fingers. I stretched mine out and stroked his hand in return. The sweetness kept fluttering through me, it was almost unbearable. I didn't want it ever to stop.

Now the Luftwaffe officer was sweating slightly, and apologising. The stress, he said, it got to a man sometimes. And of course he didn't want to be offensive to the gentleman's mother. He Heil Hitler-ed, paid the bill and left.

Raf leaned across the table and I felt his breath on my cheek. 'It's who you know that counts,' he whispered. Then he grinned. 'Or who you claim to know.'

He smelt faintly of the gas works; even that made me happy. But I could see the old lady behind him, giving us bad looks, saw her lips go 'tch!' I moved away from him, jerking my head at her, hating her, but we couldn't afford to draw any hostile attention to ourselves. I drank the rest of my lemonade. I was desperate to hold his hand again, all the same, the prickle of the bubbles on my tongue was the feeling of heaven itself.

'Well,' Mr Brush-head shouted to his mother, 'now we can talk in peace.'

'Is that what he calls it?' muttered Raf. I giggled.

The old lady asked, 'And is it true, Martin, that the Russians are absolutely beaten?'

All at once I smelt something that made my heart sink. A rank, musky perfume. I saw the waitress showing another couple to a table. A big man with wide shoulders in a double-breasted grey suit, and a woman in a dark pink costume with a black fur collar and what looked like a window box of silk flowers on top of her hat.

Aunt Grete saw us and she went rigid. Uncle Hartmut noticed and looked where she was looking. I saw his shoulders stiffen; he knew who Raf was, all right. By then it was illegal for Jews and Aryans to socialise, it was illegal for a Jew to be in a café, and illegal for Raf to have taken his yellow star off.

Oh God, I thought. We've had it.

Mr Brush-head yelled, 'Yes, the Russians are finished, that's for sure. The Slav subhumans can't stand up to a real German army.'

Uncle Hartmut stiffened and he looked away from me and Raf. His lips pressed together and his eyes creased as if he was thinking really fast. He sat down at the table, muttering something to Aunt Grete.

'We'd better go,' Raf said.

'Yes,' I said. We got the bill.

'Had a quarrel?' the waitress asked us. 'Make it up, go on.'

If that was all, I thought. But I couldn't tell her we were headed for concentration camp. Raf handed over the notes and the coupons and we left the table.

I had to walk right past my uncle, and as I did, he hissed, 'I haven't seen you. I don't know what you're up to, and I don't want to.'

Raf and I walked quickly away from the café.

'What did he say to you?' Raf asked.

I told him.

'Why?' he asked. 'But maybe it'll be all right.'

I said, 'I'm scared.'

'Cheer up,' he said, and he gave me the grin. 'Look, we'll meet next week, not in two weeks, shall we? In Alexander Square. Promise?'

I promised. Then he said, 'Take your glove off.'

When I did he lifted my fingers to his lips, and kissed them. My head swam. We parted, but I'd only gone a few steps before I turned to look back at him. He was looking at me. He waved. He looked so jaunty and cheerful it made me feel better, only the good feeling drained away as soon as I'd waved back and turned away again. I walked on down the Kurfürstendamm and a stout woman in a fur coat turned away from a display of hats and trod heavily on my foot. She gave me a bad look, as if it was my fault.

I didn't care what she thought, I didn't care that my foot hurt, I had other things to bother about. Because maybe Uncle Hartmut had meant he didn't want to get *me* into trouble because I was his niece. He might inform on Raf, just saying he'd seen him out without his yellow star. He'd certainly think it'd be better for me if Raf got taken away. And I kept thinking how stupid we'd been. The Kranzler was just the kind of place Uncle Hartmut and Aunt Grete would go to on a Sunday.

Suddenly I wanted to tell Mum everything. Even if she was angry with me. I ran up the stairs in our house and pushed the bell, all ready to confess.

The door opened at once. Kattrin was there, in her outdoor things, and there was a suitcase sitting where she must have put it down to answer the door. Mum was standing there with a strained look on her face, I could see she'd been just going to say goodbye. It was like the curtain opening on a play. I stood there and stared at them both.

'Jenny,' Mum said. 'Kattrin's mother's had a stroke.'

'How is she?' I asked Kattrin.

'She's crippled all down her left side,' Kattrin said, starting to cry. 'Poor Mum, she's worked so hard all her life, and now this! I'll have to stay on and take care of her. You do understand, don't you, Jenny? You can't imagine how much I'll miss you.'

I wanted to say, 'No, don't go, you're part of our family,' but I couldn't. After all, her mother was her family and she needed her more than we did. I stood there, trying not to cry and said how much I'd miss her, and we hugged each other.

'I'll be back to see you,' Kattrin said. 'You needn't think you've seen the last of me. And I'll help out with the shopping—'

She tried to wink but that turned into tears. 'It's no good hanging around,' she said. 'I'd better just go.'

When she'd gone, Mum and I cried in each other's arms. Then Mum said, 'We can't have anyone else. We couldn't trust another maid. She'd be asking what was happening to the food. And we'd have to mind every word we said.'

I realised I wasn't going to tell her what had happened at the Kranzler. She'd worry too much – and she'd want to know what was happening between me and Raf. I couldn't bear that. And what could she do to help, really?

The next fortnight was bad in all kinds of ways.

I had to clean the oven. The dirt was tarry and didn't want to shift, but I thought about Raf having to scrape the tar off the insides of the retorts at the gas works. His arms must ache much more than mine were doing, he must feel the way I did, as if the filth was sticking just in order to spite him. The next moment I was stiff with terror in case the police turned up at the gas works and sent him to concentration camp. He might not even be allowed to see Aunty Edith before he went. I certainly wouldn't be able to see him. I started to cry. Muffi came into the kitchen and shoved her nose against my shoulder.

I wiped my face on my sleeve and patted her. I'd had enough of the oven, I must have got as much off it as would shift. And there was a queue of other jobs to do, and my homework. I went to the sink to try and clean out the snarl of steel wool that Kattrin had been using on the cooker for ages, because steel wool was like gold dust, with all metals going to weapons production. It was all sticky with dark brown oven dirt now, it was disgusting.

Muffi lay down underneath the kitchen table, keeping an eye on me in case I started to cry again. I was pretty close to it with the worry and the horrible impossible jobs. Now I had to put black lead on the front of the cooker. I thought: If only we could turn time back to when Raf suggested the Kranzler; say no, let's go somewhere else. And suddenly I had the feel of Raf, close beside me, the sense of him breathing and moving and looking at me, smiling, and I thought: Please, please please, the way I'd done when the policeman had come into the café. Then Hitler's kind, smiling face flashed into my mind again, and I was scared I was going mad.

I had to schlepp the rugs down to the yard to bat the dust out of them. I couldn't complain to Mum because she had the shop to mind as well as her dressmaking and she was going to do the oven the next day, we were taking turns at everything.

'I never realised how much Kattrin did,' she said that evening. 'Thank God we can send the washing and ironing to the laundry.'

And then Mum took all the photographs of the Jakobys out of the albums. 'The way that Mingers woman talks,' she said, 'I keep wondering how long it'll be before she denounces us. And if they came and searched the house—'

I'd been going into the sitting room when she was in the shop to look at Raf. Now I wouldn't be able to. I didn't dare ask her for a photograph to keep.

I knew where she was going to put the pictures. She took me down to the shop and showed me the clever series of catches that Dad had fixed into the carved sides of the marionette theatre. You had to know which gilt leaves to find, which grape in each of three bunches, and then you had to know which way to twist each of them. Then the back swung free and you could push open the door of the stockroom behind it.

She asked me to rearrange the other photographs to hide the blank spaces. I hated that, it felt as if I was wiping Raf and Aunty Edith and Uncle Markus out of our lives.

Raf was waiting for me when I arrived at Alexander Square. It was a freezing cold afternoon but I thought it was beautiful weather when I saw him and knew he was all right after all. We found a shabby clean little café down a side street. The kitchen was close to the tables so even at quiet times there was a constant useful clatter of washing-up.

When we'd stopped saying how much each of us had been thinking about each other – that took quite a while – we talked about Uncle Hartmut.

'I reckon,' Raf said, drinking tea with one hand and holding my hand with the other, 'he's beginning to wonder if Hitler's really such a good bet.'

I was drowning in giddy pleasure to have him holding my hand, but I said, 'He's a really keen Nazi, Raf.'

A couple came in through the door, a soldier on leave and his girlfriend. The cold air shot in and bit right through my stockings to my legs and feet. That was all right, though, it was almost a pleasure, since I was with Raf.

'No,' Raf said. 'He's a businessman. Oh, I know he mouthed all those slogans that day we went to see him. I hated him for it, of course, he *is* a swine, but – Jenny, Mum says there's a new foreman at his place, he's easier than the last one and he talks. The word is, your uncle was looking for a contract for cold-weather combat clothing material as soon as the invasion happened last June. Only he didn't get it because Hitler reckoned the troops would reach Moscow before the winter set in. Your uncle knew they'd start dying of frostbite if they didn't, and of course they got bogged down in all that mud in October so they couldn't move – anyway, they're turning out white uniform fabric now. The kind of thing you need for fighting in the snow. Can't get it made fast enough. Nice for Hansens to get the contract at last. Only maybe your uncle thinks it's too late. The Germans are losing too many men.'

'So we're beginning to lose the war? We haven't conquered the British, either.'

Raf started to play with my hand, then his fingers came creeping up my underarm, up my sleeve. My eyes shut, I couldn't think of anything else but his touch. But he let go of me, sighed, and said, 'I think your uncle's making a little insurance policy for himself. If Hitler loses the war and the Nazis get what they deserve, he'll claim he was nice to Jews. Not denouncing me the week before last will be another feather in his cap. He might as well be kind to his workers, it's no skin off his nose. Jewish workers pull their fingers out all the time. Even if they're ill.'

I knew why. Anyone who slowed down would be added to one of the transports that were leaving Germany now – for resettlement in the East, they said, but there were other stories. Terrifying whispered stories. *No*, I thought. Raf and Aunty Edith have got to be all right.

Raf had kept a bit of money back from his find, so he paid and we went out. It was sleeting now. He took my hand and led me into a little alleyway. He took my bag out of my hand and put it down with his, then he put his arms round me.

After a while, he said, 'You didn't like it the first time I kissed you. You said I needed to practise some more.'

I asked, 'Who've you been practising with, then?'

'Nobody,' he said. 'Did you like it now?'

I laughed. 'I liked it the first time, Raf. I just didn't want to admit it.'

'But did you like it now?' he asked again, rather anxiously.

'*Yes,*' I said, and we kissed again. He kept going all hot and quivery and pulling me really close. My knees all-but gave way and my insides turned to melting sugar-candy.

Only the church clock struck four. Even though they didn't know we were out together, Aunty Edith and Mum would be worrying if we didn't go back soon. We kissed each other one more time, arranged the next meeting – at the Museum Island – and then let go of each other. It hurt, as if I was pulling apart.

I walked towards the tram stop and kept saying to myself: I'll see him again in a fortnight.

Then I wondered if I would.

No, I told myself again. He and Aunty Edith are essential workers, they won't take them away. But it didn't work. The sleet drove into my face and wet my gloves and numbed my fingers and I was imagining waiting for him at the Museum Island. And waiting. And having to realise the awful truth.

He *was* there the next time, but when we'd found a quiet place to kiss I burst into tears.

'What's wrong?' he asked.

I didn't want to say. I told him about something else that bothered me: 'I miss Dad and Karl, and I worry about them. And I miss Aunty Edith. I hate it that I never see her.'

'She misses you,' he said. 'And I miss Uncle Dietrich and Karl.'

I hesitated, then I said, 'I miss your dad, too.'

He ducked his head away.

'I'm sorry,' I said.

He looked back at me. His eyes were wet. 'It's all right. Do you think I'd want you to have forgotten him?'

I sat in school, looking at the desk, thinking about Raf. I smelt that faint smell of the gas works and my

123

lips felt his, and the fuzz of new moustache on his upper lip. He was letting his moustache grow, because Jews weren't allowed shaving soap, but it was all soft and fair, you hardly noticed it. I'd had an extra meeting with him, Mum had given me a bag of groceries on the in-between Sunday and sent me off to Friedrich Street. That had been good.

Klotz was teaching us the geography of Nazi-dominated Europe, but in my head Raf was telling me about the model housing he was designing in his few spare moments.

'Air and light,' he'd said, 'that's what most Berliners don't have. Oh, I know there are those wonderful buildings in Siemensstadt, but most workers still live in tenements that are crawling with rats.'

I'd said, 'The Nazis did put up some model housing.'

'Poky little boxes.' I'd loved the contemptuous way he'd said that.

Paula looked at me and then scribbled on her rough book: *Are you thinking about Klaus-Heinrich?*

I nodded – it was almost true anyway – and she made a soppy, teasing face at me. I grinned back.

Neither of us paid any attention to Klotz. I might as well have left school for all the good it did me: the best teachers had been sacked or they'd gone of their own accord and we were getting the kind of education the Nazis thought was suitable for girls. Faith and Beauty and keeping ourselves for Aryan men – there was a lot more of that now we were fourteen.

Chapter Ten
1942–1943

One hot day Raf and I were kissing in a narrow alleyway. I'd been stroking his sides, feeling his ribs, and suddenly he put his hand on my breast. I stopped what I was doing; for a moment we stood quite still; then we kissed again and I felt his heart beating hard against me. Now the kissing was different, more intense than before.

Then we heard heavy footsteps turn into the mouth of the alley and walk towards us. We stiffened, both of us together. I looked towards the sound and saw a man in green uniform, a shako on his head with an eagle and swastika emblem. A policeman. My whole self was fizzing with terror, but Raf pulled me tight to him and started kissing me again, hard. I kissed him back, I guessed he was hoping the man would be embarrassed so he wouldn't disturb us. The footsteps came towards us, slowing down as he approached us. I felt Raf's tongue moving against mine, his heart and mine were thumping as if we only had one heart between us. I kept thinking: Raf's blond. I was red-haired, and some people thought that was a Jewish thing. That was the crazy, horrible thing, the policeman might arrest us because he thought Raf was the race-traitor and I was a Jew.

He was behind me. I thought I could feel him looking us over. Any minute now his hand would be on my arm, wrenching me away – then Raf lifted his head and I saw him grin and wink. Not at me, at the policeman. I heard the man clear his throat, I was sure he'd demand to see our identity cards. I kept still, close to Raf, waiting for the disaster to start happening.

Only I heard the heavy footsteps start to move away from us. Raf had got away with it again. I was hardly able to believe it, my mind didn't want to let go of the terror, but the footsteps kept getting quieter and in the end I couldn't hear them at all.

'He was young,' Raf whispered. 'He's probably got a girl himself.'

'What if it happens another time?' I whispered back, shuddering against him. 'Raf, you know they'd kill you for kissing me if they found out.' Then I made myself say the thing I didn't want to say. 'We shouldn't be doing this, Raf. We should stay away from each other.'

I'd said it. Now he might agree, and how would I live the rest of my life? I stared at his feet and the cobbles he was standing on. My throat went so tight I thought I'd suffocate.

But he said, 'I can't do that, Jenny. Can you?'

'No,' I said, knowing how much I hadn't meant it. 'I can't.'

Maybe it was the time after that that we were in a

back alley near City Hall, and Raf was touching my breast, caressing me so I went on fire with wanting him. I said, 'Raf! Let's find a park, somewhere, where we can lie down and no one can see us.'

'It's no good,' he said. 'We'd have to go to the woods to be really private, it's too far to walk, and they check identity cards on trains...' He took hold of me and pulled me right against him. 'I want you, Jenny,' he said. His voice was choked up with frustration. 'I want you so much.'

By the time we parted my new summer dress was all in creases. I was trying to smooth it out all the way home.

I rang the doorbell, hoping Mum wouldn't ask what had happened to my dress. She opened the door. She was holding a telegram. I thought: Dad. Karl. My mouth dried up and I felt sick.

'Mum—' I said.

'It's all right,' she said quickly. 'Karl's coming back, Jenny. For a training course in Frankfurt, and he'll have some home leave, too.'

Muffi went mad and wet the floor, she was so excited to see Karl. I stood there, hardly believing he was home, till he gave me a rough kind brotherly hug. Then I couldn't believe how brown he'd got.

I took him into my bedroom and showed him how I'd put all the desert sand he'd sent me into a glass jar. He laughed. 'Glad you like it,' he said. Mum came and hovered at the door because she didn't want me to steal him. We got the meal and he sat on the edge of the kitchen table and talked while I peeled the potatoes.

'God, I've been missing potatoes,' he said. 'We have terrible food out there. We get this Italian tinned meat. "Old Man", we call it.' He grimaced. 'We eat it, because there's no choice. We don't get vegetables, they're worried they'll go bad. When we capture a British unit, they have vegetables in tins, but we have to keep that to feed them. We're decent to the Tommies so they're decent to us. It's bad, though, we don't have enough equipment. So Rommel plays tricks to fool them. Once he put dummy tanks on top of a couple of Beetle cars.' He laughed. 'If anyone's short of anything, Rommel tells them to go and capture it from the British.'

I said, 'Norbert Mingers is home on leave too. From Russia.'

Karl frowned. 'Those are the boys who get all the supplies. We're just a sideshow as far as Army Command is concerned. I saw Dad, Mum. Last week. He sent you all his love, and this.' He handed Mum a letter. Uncensored. 'And one for you, Jenny. You've grown up, little sister, I hardly knew you!'

I opened the letter and read it quickly. Dad wrote: *I hate this war, not just because our nation is causing so many deaths and so much suffering to other people. I hate it because it's taking me away from you,*

Jenny, and Mum and Karl. I want to be there, talking to you, watching you grow up, but be sure, sweetheart, whatever you're doing, all my love goes with you all the time.

I missed him so much, too. I used to go into the sitting room and look at his photograph and he looked back at me out of his mild, clever eyes. Only I knew he couldn't really see me and that made me feel empty and sore inside.

Mum went white when Karl told us why he was home. His unit had almost been wiped out. 'Most of them were captured,' he said quickly. 'Captain Seebohm put most of the Circus – that's what we called it – too close to the front line. Fool thing to do. Only that day my platoon was with 90th Light Division – oh, never mind the names, Mum. So we escaped. Now the Tommies will be trying to get as much information as they can out of my mates. Poor beggars. Anyway, I'm being promoted to Lieutenant, and I've got to go and train with the new unit, in Frankfurt. Listen, it's a lovely day, can we go to the lake this afternoon? I never realised how lucky we are to have sandy beaches in the city till I went out to fight over desert sand where you can't swim.'

We went out to Wannsee. It was a weekday, so the beach wasn't full. We had a lovely afternoon. Afterwards Mum stayed on the train so she could go and pick up some thread from the haberdasher. When Karl and I got to our house we met Norbert and Willi Mingers putting up the shutters on their shop front.

'Heil Hitler!' Norbert greeted us nastily. 'Here's Afrika-Corps hero Friedemann all bronzed from stripping off in the sun – while the rest of us freeze among the subhumans in Russia.' He looked at Karl's and my wet hair. 'Been swimming today, have you? It's good to be doing so well you can afford to shut up shop for the afternoon.'

Karl just said, 'Hello, Norbert.' I didn't think I needed to say anything.

Norbert gave him a bad look because he hadn't said Heil Hitler. 'So what's it like down there?' he asked. 'With wonderful Rommel who everyone loves so much?'

'He's a good general,' Karl said shortly. 'Come on, Jenny, let's go upstairs.'

'Russia's fun, sometimes, though, isn't it, Norbert?' Willi asked, winking.

And Norbert walked out in front of Karl and demanded, 'Could you do what I've done, Afrika-Corps hero? Listen, one evening our Lieutenant comes out, he wants fifteen men with strong nerves for a job the next day. So a lot of us volunteer. The job's shooting vermin. Jews. We march them off to the nearest swamp.' He laughed, watching Karl's face. 'Cowardly lot, they were, clutching each other, men and women, young ones hanging on to their mothers' legs. We mowed them down. It was tough, but we were up to it. We got as much schnapps as we could drink afterwards.'

I felt dizzy and sick. Now I had to believe the stories. They were taking the Jews out to the East to kill them. And Norbert had pumped bullets into those ordinary families and afterwards he'd got drunk to celebrate. And it was so senseless, for all I knew how much the Nazis hated Jews, I still couldn't understand it.

Karl turned his head and glanced at me for a moment: easy now, his eyes were telling me, don't show *him* what you're feeling. I took a deep breath and shut my lips together.

Quite calmly, but coldly, Karl said, 'Sounds like you enjoyed yourself.'

'Yes,' Norbert said, still blocking our way, 'it beats sitting crouched over a radio set.'

'I've fought as well as decrypting radio signals,' Karl said, and he looked Norbert in the eye. Norbert was so close in front of us, if Karl had taken a step forward he'd have knocked into him – and suddenly I knew my brother *had* fought, there was something coming off him, something dangerous.

Norbert felt it. Norbert, the murderer, wavered and stepped back.

'Thanks,' Karl said, and we went upstairs. I cried once we were in the flat, and he put his arms round me, and held me while I sobbed out the things I'd thought, about not having wanted it to be true, and why? I thumped my fists on his chest the way I'd done when I was little.

'I know,' he said. 'It's shit. And swine like him call themselves good Germans – but I'm lucky, Jenny, there's nothing like that in North Africa.'

I was shocked then. I said, 'But Karl, you'd never volunteer to kill Jews.'

Almost as if he was talking to himself, he said, 'No, but you can bet the ones who don't are made to feel like cowards.'

All at once I was telling him how it had been when I'd seen Hitler. I think he was the only person I could ever have told. He said, 'It's powerful, that kind of thing,' so I knew he'd felt the same, sometimes, and I felt less lonely about it.

He patted me on the back. 'What matters is that you don't carry on feeling like that afterwards. But it makes you see why he's succeeded with a lot of people.' And then he said, 'It can't last forever, Jenny. It just can't.'

He came with me the next time I took the groceries to Raf. He said to Mum, 'We'll find a quiet place and have a little chat with him.' Mum started to shake her head, but Karl said, 'I know how to be careful, Mum.'

'All right,' she said, though I could see she wasn't happy.

We went to a café this time. Another useful noisy one. I couldn't touch Raf. That was hard. We sat down at a table in a corner. Karl wanted to know how bad things were for Raf and Aunty Edith. Raf played the badness down.

'People are kind sometimes,' he said. 'One night, Mum was on the tram back from work – you know, she's only allowed to use the tram because it's so far to the factory, and even then she's not allowed to sit down.'

Karl nodded grimly.

'Well, a workman stood up for her. "Come on, old lady," he said. "Rest your weary legs." And some smartly dressed fellow ticked the workman off, but the workman just bawled him out. "Look, mate, I do what I like with my own arse." And once a woman knocked into Mum and shouted, "Crud of a Jew!" but she shoved a packet of butter and meat into her hand.'

He smiled, but he looked really tired. I wanted to stroke his hand. I couldn't, though, not with Karl there.

I said, 'Why can't we join up with people like that and get rid of the Nazis?'

Karl frowned. 'I'd fight them if I could. Only there wouldn't be enough of us. It's not the little believers like the Mingers who are the problem, it's all the others who'd stay out of it because they didn't want to get involved.'

Raf shrugged his shoulders. 'One day the swine'll get what they deserve. I just hope I'm alive to see it happen.'

'You will be,' Karl said quickly. 'You'll be there, cheering when they string them up.'

Then we all knew we didn't want to talk about bad things any longer and we started joking around. We were almost like three kids again. Almost.

When we paid the bill and went out, Karl said, 'I'll leave you two to say goodbye.' I remember looking at his back view as he went away, strolling easily, good-naturedly.

'He knows,' Raf said. 'I suppose it's not hard to see.'

One evening Karl said, 'Jenny, Mum – you know we get trained in how to behave if we're captured. Because of course the Tommies'd want to get information out of us. We just have to give our name and number and then refuse to answer any more questions. But we have to shout at each other and try to get each other to give more stuff away. So we can keep quiet if it's ever for real. Well, you two ought to practise too, just in case . . . '

I got a bad feeling in my throat. I couldn't say anything.

'Just keep going through what you're prepared to say to them,' Karl went on. 'Do it over and over again so you know it by heart.'

Mum nodded, grim-faced.

'One thing I thought you could do,' he said, 'is make the most of Grandma's maiden name.'

'Montgomery,' Mum said, and she laughed suddenly. 'The man the British have sent to take on Rommel?'

'Our new second cousin,' Karl said, grinning. Then, seriously, 'Look, Mum, we're not doing well any longer in Africa. Nor anywhere, I reckon. Especially not now the Americans are in the war. Those swine in the Gestapo probably know that better than anyone and they'll be wondering what'll happen to them if we lose. They'll go easy on people with well-placed English relations. I know what, why don't we try it out on Uncle Hartmut and Aunt Grete?'

So when we paid our duty visit to the villa, in the middle of Uncle Hartmut's questions about Africa, Karl said, 'It's odd, though, fighting your own relation.'

Uncle Hartmut's eyes narrowed for a moment. 'Who's your relation?' he demanded.

Mum said, cool as you like, 'You know my mother's maiden name was Montgomery.'

She said it as if Uncle Hartmut and Aunt Grete ought to have known.

'You're related to General Montgomery?' Uncle Hartmut demanded, staring at her like a bull about to charge.

'My second cousin,' Mum said, as if she couldn't see why he was getting so interested.

'You never told us that before,' Uncle Hartmut said.

'Why should we have done?' Mum said. 'You've never asked.'

There was a silence. Then Uncle Hartmut said, 'You knew each other before the war?'

'I haven't seen him since we were in England,' Mum said, 'and that was a long time ago, but I kept in touch with my English cousins until the war started.'

He changed the subject, then. I wondered if she had convinced him.

'It doesn't matter,' Karl said afterwards, 'you practised. Now hold onto that story and work on it, get more details into it, imagine it as if it was really true. And think how you'd use Uncle Hartmut, too. He's really in with all of them. Who you know does count, Mum.'

I remembered the brush-headed man in the Café Kranzler. I said, 'Or who you pretend to know.'

It was November when the telegram came about Dad, after the battle of El Alamein, which Rommel lost to Montgomery and the Americans. Missing, believed captured.

'He's alive,' Mum said. 'I know it.'

I nodded. I wouldn't let it into my head that Dad might be dead. But I was terribly scared. I cried about him on Raf's shoulder and in bed at night. At last we got the first Red Cross letter from his prisoner-of-war camp in Africa. Twenty-five words, that was all we'd be allowed to write at a time from now on. But we were so glad. He was safe, and out of the war.

In early February even the German news broadcast had to admit that the entire Sixth German Army had surrendered after the battle of Stalingrad.

Raf said excitedly, 'This is the beginning of the end. If we can only hold out—'

Then the other telegram came, about Karl. He'd been killed in Tunisia. There was no doubt about it. The truck he'd been in had been blown up.

There are millions of people in the world, but if you lose one person who means as much to you as Karl did to us, nothing's ever the same again.

Part of me still can't really believe it.

Chapter Eleven

Raf held me, huddled against a house wall in the rain. We were both crying.

'Damn it,' he said. 'Curse it. Why did it have to be Karl?'

I said, 'We had to tell Dad in twenty-five words.' I had the Red Cross letter we'd sent by heart. 'Mum and I went over and over it, trying to get it right – but you can't get something like that right. And it hurt, doing it, Raf, I'm hurting all the time.'

Karl killed, we'd written in the end. *Deepest grief. If only we were together, we miss you so much. Try to find some comfort. We love you dearly. Sylvia. Jenny.*

I said to Raf, 'I wake up every morning and I feel all right, and then I remember about Karl and it starts. I don't want to get up, I want to hide in bed. Only I can't stay there. I can't stay anywhere for long.'

'I know,' he said, and his arms tightened on me. 'I felt like that when Dad died.'

'Of course, you must have done.' The rain came down harder and dripped off our foreheads into our faces. I didn't care, my face was already wet. I said, 'The filthy Nazis, making the war and stealing his life.'

Raf nodded. 'They don't care how many people they kill.'

I hadn't gone to school the day we got the telegram, so Mum had had to write a note, explaining why. Klotz was our class teacher that year, and when he read the note, he said, 'So your brother has made the ultimate sacrifice for his country.' He paused, looking at the note, then he raised his head and I saw anger in his little piggy eyes. He was angry with me, and I couldn't believe it, not even from Klotz, not at that moment. He said, 'And you can't even be bothered to join the German Girls' League and contribute to the war effort.'

Elfriede Griesweil muttered, 'Yes, I was making bandages all yesterday evening while Friedemann was sitting with her feet up.'

Paula spoke. 'Sitting crying for her brother, Griesweil. D'you think that was fun?' She put all the arrogance of her aristocratic ancestors in her voice – and she looked at Klotz, who hunched his shoulders, he was scared, suddenly. He didn't know how to handle Paula – he never did – but this was one of his worst moments. He put his hand on the edge of his jacket and clutched it tight, as if he was trying to stop it going up and touching his forelock to her. Then the bell was ringing, jangling through the air. It was time for our first lesson. Klotz picked the heavy register up and escaped. There was no other word for it.

I went to my desk and Paula put her arm round me.

'Swine,' she muttered. She stayed alongside me after that, all the time we were at school. She even went to the toilet when I did. I was so glad to have her there.

Muffi knew, I'm sure. She kept coming to Mum and me and whimpering. And Kattrin came to see us and wept. 'He was the best lad in the world,' she said. 'It's a wicked war, that's what it is.'

One day I burst out to Mum, 'I don't know what to do with myself!'

'I know,' she said, and her own voice was half-crazy with pain. 'Look, put Muffi on the lead and let's get out. Anywhere.'

It was Saturday lunchtime; even Frau Mingers had shut up shop. We took Muffi and started walking. It was when we reached the light railway station that we realised we were going to Wannsee, where we'd gone with Karl the summer before. Neither of us said anything, though, even when Mum bought the tickets. The train was full and we had to stand. I could feel Muffi leaning against my legs.

We went to the lake beach and trudged heavily across the fine sand. The spring sun spread a sheet of light on the lake. It made my eyes hurt.

I said, 'He's not here, Mum. Why did we come?'

Muffi nudged her nose against the back of my leg, but Mum strode away so I had to run to keep up with her. Then she turned round and said fiercely, 'I needed to know he's not here.'

We walked till we were really tired. It was a kind of relief.

As we rattled through Grunewald station on the way back a woman behind me said to her friend, 'This is where they load the Jews into the trains at night, at the freight depot. My brother works for the railway, he says they pack them in like sardines and they don't give them anything to eat or drink. It's terrible, some of them die on the journey.'

Maybe she was a little deaf. I don't think she knew how loudly she'd said it till she saw the woman opposite staring at her. Then she shut up. But I looked at Mum and saw her eyes wide and dark with the same fear I was feeling.

The SS were taking more and more Jews now, pouncing on them without notice at home or at their work so they couldn't escape. They had new forced labourers to replace them: French men and women, Hollanders, Russians sometimes.

My heart started to thump and it kept thumping horribly in my chest. It wouldn't stop.

Fuel was still short and we had all our meals in the kitchen nowadays to save heating the dining room. That night we ate early, about half past five – to get it out of the way, Mum said, and I nodded. There was less decent food about now, even though Kattrin was still doing shopping for us, but that wasn't what had taken our appetite away. Neither

141

of us had enjoyed eating since the news of Karl's death.

We'd just started on our thin beef stew when the yard bell rang; a very short ring, as if it was someone who didn't want to make a noise. Muffi wuffed.

'Muffi,' Mum said. 'Quiet!'

I opened the door to the back stairs and ran down. Mum came after me. Raf was there, filthy and stinking of the gas works.

I pulled him in and shut the door as quietly as I could behind him. We put our arms round each other. I felt his horror like a sick clutch round my own heart. 'What's happened?' I whispered.

He opened his mouth, but Mum hissed from halfway up the stairs, 'No! Don't talk here!'

I looked at her and saw that we'd given ourselves away to her. We went up the stairs holding hands, keeping our mouths shut till we were in the kitchen with that door shut as well.

'They came for us,' Raf said, keeping hold of my hand.

Mum's face was very pale, and her eyes were intent, with big shadows under them.

'Just before five. I hid behind the hoppers – where the coal's stored. I never thought I'd get away with it. They had a list of names, but when they called mine the foreman said I hadn't come in that day. And the officer said, 'Workshy Jews, eh? We'll pick him up at his place.' He said they were bringing a lot of

Hollanders in half an hour. Just like that. The foreman made a big fuss about training them and the SS man said they'd be experienced gas workers.' He stopped and brushed the back of his hand over his cheek, making it even dirtier. 'The foreman let them go away, then he came round behind the hoppers – he knew exactly where I'd gone – and he told me to pull my star off and get out at once. So I walked over here. I didn't dare take the tram in case someone checked my papers. And now—'

'You're worried about your mother,' Mum said.

His hand was trembling slightly. I squeezed it.

'If they're going to our place—' he said, biting his lip. 'I'd never get there soon enough.'

'You mustn't go,' Mum said. 'You don't want to risk them picking you up.'

I said, 'I'll go. If I find Aunty Edith I'll bring her back here.'

'Thanks, Jenny,' he said. His voice was hoarse and tired. He'd been working all day, he'd hidden in terror, now he was beside himself with fear for Aunty Edith.

I gave him one last hand-squeeze and then went to the hallway to get my outdoor things on. There wasn't any time to waste. Mum came out to me.

'If the SS don't find Edith or Raf, they might come here looking for them both. If they're here when you come back, get away till they've gone. I'll hide Raf.'

I knew where she'd hide him.

I ran towards the tram stop. There was a tram

143

coming, I could hear it in the darkness and I made myself run faster as it overtook me. It stood still for a few minutes, letting people out. I thought I'd get to it, but it pulled away just as I reached the door. I stood panting, furious with the driver. It seemed an age before the next tram came and when I got in, it crawled. The stout woman next to me yawned and said, 'Nice to be going home, isn't it?' I wanted to hit her.

It was properly dark by the time the driver called the name of my stop. I switched on my dim blackout torch and made my way to the shabby house.

I got to the front door and it opened. I saw a torch shining much brighter than mine, lighting a woman's legs in shoes I knew, and a pair of shiny boots beside them. A man's voice snapped, 'Hurry up, Jewish bitch! Do you think we've got all night?'

I felt winded, as if something enormous had slammed into me. I thought: If only I'd caught the first tram, why didn't the driver stop?

At the same moment, the SS man's torch caught my legs and feet and flicked upwards to my face, blinding me. I heard Aunty Edith catch her breath, she knew it was me – and I realised how much danger I was in. I was right outside the door, I had definitely been coming there, and the SS man might want to see my papers, to know what I was about. I had to have a story. Then I heard Raf's voice in my mind's ear: Play act, it said. I remembered him telling me that the

144

landlady's daughter, who was about my age, often came for the rent.

I put a bit of Berlin working girl's accent into my voice and spoke to the darkness above the boots.

'Heil Hitler, sir.' My throat was tight with horror and I was shaking, but that shouldn't look odd. Most people were scared of the SS. 'Is that Frau Jakoby you're taking away? Mum sent me to pick up the rent from her.'

He said, 'Your mother's her landlady, is she?'

'Yes,' I said. The torch was still too bright. I had to look down. 'M-maybe she's got the rent on her now?'

He turned round, letting the torch swing away from me, and shone it on Aunty Edith instead. I could barely see her at first for the blue dazzle-flecks in front of my eyes.

She said, 'I'm glad you came. I didn't want your mother to lose the money. I didn't expect to – leave – today.'

'Come on,' the SS man snapped. 'Give her the money.'

She reached into her pocket and pulled out her purse. In a hurried voice, she asked, 'And how's your brother, he was ill, wasn't he?'

I knew what she was really asking. Raf, she was saying, tell me about Raf!

'He's fine now,' I said, and I was so scared the SS man might guess what was behind the words, but he didn't seem to. 'He's at our house, finishing his dinner. But what about you, Frau Jakoby? Mum'll miss you, you've been a good tenant.'

'Cut it, girl,' the SS man said. 'Worrying about a filthy Jew, that's race-treachery. Your mother can get a good Aryan tenant now.'

And all of a sudden I was scared Aunty Edith hadn't really understood. I said to him, 'Sir, my brother wants to go to the SS himself, he's got blond hair and blue eyes, do you think he'd make it?'

The SS man let his torch dangle and said in a different, self-satisfied voice, 'He'd have to get through a tough set of tests.'

The torch beam went back and forth like a pendulum, lighting the SS man's dull leather coat and spit-and-polish shiny boots, but the top half of Aunty Edith and of me were in the dark, and that was when she reached out and squeezed my hand. I squeezed back. If only I could have put my arms round her and screamed at the SS man that he couldn't take her, if only the whole of Germany had been full of people putting their arms round Jews and protecting them from the SS when they came for them – but I was only one girl – and Aunty Edith's hand tightened on mine as if she was warning me.

'You're not to worry about me, child. Take care of yourself – and your brother. Here's the rent money.'

I said, 'Thanks, Frau Jakoby. I will.' I stroked her hand one last time to let her know how much I loved her.

She said, 'Greet your mother and brother from me. Wish them all the best.' I felt her hand tremble.

'I will,' I said again – and the SS man's torch beam

moved upwards, so I had to let go of Aunty Edith and pretend to be putting something away in my pocket. I almost couldn't bear it.

'That's enough, now,' he said to me. 'D'you think this is the only house call we've got to make? We're cleaning Berlin of Jews, they've all got to be out of here for the Führer's birthday.'

I said, 'Goodbye, Frau Jakoby. All the – all the best.' I couldn't make myself say Heil Hitler at that moment.

I stood there in the dark while she scrambled onto the truck. The man used his torch to light the step. I saw a huddle of anxious faces inside there.

I went back to the tram stop, thinking: I should have caught the first tram, why didn't I run faster, if I'd got here twenty minutes earlier I'd surely have got her out easily before the SS arrived. I kept thinking that, as if it could change what had happened.

Only it couldn't.

Mum said, 'He'll want to go after her, you know he will.' Tears were running down her face.

I said, 'I'll stop him. I can tell him she wanted him to stay with us.'

Mum wiped her face with the back of her hand, almost the way Raf had done earlier. She knew there was another reason why I wanted to go to Raf, but she only said, 'Jenny, in case *they* come – you'll have to have an explanation for being down there. I left my mending basket when I shut Raf in. You can say I had it in the shop this morning and forgot it. I sent you down for it. And take Muffi. She'll give you some warning, maybe. Though they'd probably come up here first, at this time of night. And take this pillow, I gave him a duvet but I couldn't carry a lot of stuff down there. There's a hole in the case, if they find you with it, say you needed to mend it. And if – if they arrest us—'

She threw her arms round me and we held each other, tight, for a moment. I felt her damp cheek against mine.

'I love you, Mum,' I said. It seemed desperately important to say it.

'I love you too,' she said. 'So very much. Take Muffi, she might bark if she hears someone.'

I used the back door that led into the shop from the yard. Muffi sniffed around, wanting to pee, but I said, 'Later, Muffi,' and she trotted inside after me.

'They've taken her,' Raf said. 'Haven't they?'

I nodded, feeling the pain round my heart. He was sitting on the bare floor, not on the duvet. It was crumpled up behind him, beside the pile of Uncle Markus's forbidden books in the corner. The light from the shop shone slantingly into the stock cupboard and shone on part of the outside staircase: it looked strange from underneath and it scared me, but everything was frightening that night.

I dropped the pillow. It wasn't the time to say

anything about it. He'd got it, that was what mattered. I hoped he'd use it later on.

'You've got to let me out,' he said. He stood up. 'I'll go and join her.'

'*No*,' I said, putting myself in front of him. 'Whisper, Raf. If anyone heard you—'

'I know where she'll be.' At least he did drop his voice. 'They take them to the Levetzow Street synagogue. I'll go there and—'

'*No*, Raf,' I said again, and took hold of his shoulders. He stared at me. His eyes were red-rimmed and wild in his dirty face.

'She didn't want you to,' I said. 'I saw her. I let her know where you are. She was glad.'

'How could you tell each other anything with the SS there?' He got hold of my hands and pushed them off his shoulders, we were struggling with each other and I careered into the door frame, knocking my shoulder. I gasped with the shock of it.

'Oh God,' he said. 'I've hurt you. Listen, though, Jenny, you've got to let me go.'

I said, 'No, Raf, *you've* got to listen to me.'

He stood still then and let me talk. He made me go through it three times. Then he just said, 'I can't let her go alone.'

'Raf,' I said, 'look, you stayed in Germany to be with her, I know that, but—'

I stopped, because he was looking at me as if I was his enemy.

'She needs me.'

'If you want to break her heart,' I said, 'go and find her.'

And then Muffi barked, sharply. There was a vehicle pulling up outside.

'It's them,' I said. 'Now I have to lock you in or we've all had it.'

He backed away from the door. I saw his drawn, miserable face even after I'd shut it.

I heard the booted feet running up the stairs, then the hammering on the apartment door and the shouting. 'Open up! Gestapo!' I was fiddling with the catches on the back wall of the theatre, telling myself it was a good thing the Gestapo had come, not the SS men who'd picked Aunty Edith up. They'd have recognised me.

I heard Mum open the door. I heard them tramp inside, and I thought about the fairytales I'd told the SS man and how easy it'd be for anyone to check up on Aunty Edith's landlady. She had a daughter my age, I knew that, and a son, but she'd tell them she hadn't sent her daughter off to collect the rent this evening. I felt cold inside. I remembered again how I'd missed the tram. I thought I'd made a mess of everything.

I had to go upstairs, I knew, it'd look suspicious if I didn't. And I didn't want to leave Mum on her own with the Gestapo. Then I was scared Muffi would bark at them and they'd shoot her.

I took hold of her head and pushed her hair back from her eyes. 'Muffi,' I said, 'it's terribly important for you not to bark. Do you hear?' She moved her head, trying to get free, but I said again, 'You've got to be nice to these people.'

It was what we said to her when workmen came to the house. It usually worked. I hoped desperately it'd work this time, too.

There was something I had to take with me, but I didn't know what for a moment, then I saw the mending basket and knew that was it.

I went up by way of the kitchen. I came into the hall and saw the officer holding Mum at gunpoint against the wall. And Muffi didn't bark, though she stiffened; she wanted to, but she'd understood what I'd told her. Well done, Muffi, I thought.

The officer shouted, 'Where've you been? Get against that wall now!'

'Downstairs,' I stammered, 'getting this for Mum.' I backed against the wall, dropping the mending basket. Muffi bent down and picked up a rolled-up pair of socks, which she held out to Mum, wagging her tail rather nervously, trying to be a good dog.

'I can't take that now, Muffi,' Mum said in an anguished voice.

The officer laughed. He had a raw-boned face with a scattering of freckles across it and his eyes were pale grey. He smelt of cigar smoke and proper coffee.

'The dog's a clown,' he said, 'is it?'

A man came out of my bedroom and clicked his heels. 'Nobody in there, sir!'

I stood rigid with my face to the wall, and listened to the creak of a wardrobe door being pulled open – Mum and Dad's, I thought. There was a clatter of clothes hangers and a swish of fabric as the man threw the clothes onto the floor and a screech as he moved the bed. I felt the wallpaper against my forehead and the palms of my hands. I felt helpless and defenceless, I so much wanted the wall behind my back.

When they'd ransacked every room, he said, 'There's the shop downstairs. We'll search that. You, girl' – he pointed to me. 'You can come down and let us in.'

I went cold and calm then. I felt strange, not quite real. I didn't look at Mum. I knew I mustn't.

Muffi came out of the door with me. I saw the officer make as if to kick her back, but she wagged her tail again under her cords of hair and he laughed again.

'All right, you comic dog, you can come too. And now, girl,' he turned on me – 'when did you last see your Jewish friends?'

And I knew how I had to be. Scared, but honest. We'd practised this. 'In January, the same year the war started, when they moved out.'

'Lies,' he said. 'I know you've seen them since then. Get down those stairs, you'll be sorry if you hold me up. You were thick as thieves with them, weren't you? We had to take your father in for trying to protect his Jewish crony.'

He was behind me on the stairs with his pistol. I couldn't see his face. I went down half the flight, then I muttered, 'What happened to Dad, then—'

'Taught you all a lesson, did it? Good.'

We got to the bottom. 'Come on,' he snapped. 'Open up that door.'

I put the shop door key in the lock. I said another of the things we'd practised with Karl. 'My uncle Herr Hansen talked to us about the Jews. He's close to the Führer. He made us understand—'

I'd reminded him about Uncle Hartmut – but he didn't say anything, so I had no idea if it had worked. He reached out and flicked the light switch down. His men began rummaging round the shop. I tried to believe, right inside myself, that there was nothing incriminating for them to find.

One of them went into the toilet, another flung open the wooden cupboard where Dad's tools were kept. There were only a few marionettes hanging from the rack, mainly the ones from the Pinocchio set, which wasn't for sale, but belonged to Karl and Raf and me. There were a lot of Mum's doll's clothes on little cardboard hangers. Mum was doing well with those, they were what made it worth while to keep opening the shop. Long-suffering old Geppetto watched us anxiously from the wall. I thought: His face is like Dad's. I'd never seen that before. Jiminy Cricket dangled unhappily beside him.

One of the men went to the marionette theatre and hammered on it.

Keep calm, I told myself. I was suddenly cold all through, I thought I was turning to ice.

'What's that?' the officer demanded.

I said, 'My father used it to demonstrate marionettes. It's got a place up there, for the puppeteer to sit. Then the audience don't see them. You see, if you sell a marionette, the puppeteers want to try it out—'

'What's behind it?' he interrupted.

'Just the wall.'

'It's hollow.'

I said, 'The back of the theatre's wooden, that's why it sounds hollow.'

One of the men reached inside and ran his hands all over the back. He wouldn't find any catches there. I stood still, trying to breathe normally.

The man climbed up and perched on the plank where the puppeteers sat. 'It holds,' he said, as if he'd expected to crash to the floor.

'Nice workmanship,' the officer said, still swinging his gun round his finger. He had a pair of fur-lined gauntlets hanging out of his pocket, and the motion made one of them fall out. Muffi trotted forward, picked it up and held it out to him.

He started to laugh again. The sound of it tore at my nerves like a wire brush.

'I can't find any door handles,' the Gestapo man said, but he was looking at Muffi. So was the other one, the thickset thug with greasy dark hair coming out from under his cap.

The officer took his glove from Muffi.

'Thanks,' he said, and patted her.

Muffi sat up and put her paw out. He crouched down and took it as if he was a normal human being. She wagged her tail and grinned at him.

'Where do you get a dog like that?' he asked, finding her chin and scratching it. I thought: I'm going to go mad, talking about dogs to the Gestapo with Raf hiding in the cupboard. Only I knew what he'd given me the chance to say.

'Herr Hansen has her mother. We got her from him.'

He stayed crouching there, playing with Muffi's cords of hair while she grinned and wriggled. She'd understood what I'd told her, all right; she was giving a brilliant performance. But my breath didn't want to come, I was scared I was going to suffocate.

'Your uncle, eh?' he said suddenly, standing up. 'All right, that's enough. You can go back to your apartment, girl. Heil Hitler!'

'Heil Hitler!' I said back, because I had to. He watched me all the way up the stairs, whistling a Nazi song.

I couldn't believe they'd finished.

As soon as I shut our front door, Muffi started to growl. She kept growling at the door and barking as if she was letting off all the anger she'd kept inside.

And I was shaking, I felt sick, I could only just stop myself vomiting. I bent down and started picking up the things they'd thrown out of the coat cupboard. Dad's winter boots were lying helter-skelter across Mum's everyday coat. I put them back where they belonged and hung Mum's coat up. It helped to do something. Muffi raced across the floor, threw herself on her back and rolled, still growling.

I gathered up Dad's good coat, the one he always wore to Meeting and Mum came out from the kitchen. She was holding the kettle. It had a dent in it.

She said, 'I remember Edith coming with Raf to see you when you were newborn. He was a little toddler with white curls, and he complained because you couldn't play with him. But Edith picked you up and held you and she cried because she'd lost Ursula, and then she kissed you, she said you were a blessing. Jenny, we've got to keep Raf safe for her.'

Chapter Twelve

'Mum,' I said, 'I love him.'

She looked at me rather sadly. 'Yes. I saw that.'

I asked, 'Are you angry?'

I thought she was, because she didn't say anything for a moment but then she shook her head. She said, 'You've always been in love, the pair of you, haven't you? Even when you were little things. Edith and I talked about it. It's just – it complicates matters. But we can deal with it.'

I said, 'I suppose you think I should have told you.'

'It would have been sensible,' she said, all severe suddenly, but then she put her arms round me and hugged me. 'Jenny. I was young once, too.'

Now – because she'd understood – I really did want to tell her everything. I said, 'When you sent me with the groceries, we wanted to talk, and then...'

She nodded, keeping her arms round me. I went on telling her things – I really needed to, now. I even told her about the Kranzler and meeting Uncle Hartmut and Aunt Grete. I felt her tense when she heard that.

'That was bad,' she said. 'But he didn't betray you. I wonder what's going on in his head.'

I said, 'Raf thought it was an insurance policy in case we lose the war.'

She nodded. Then she said, 'I'm sure you're tired, but I don't think I can sleep in the pigsty those' – she was shaking now, hot with fury and hurt – 'those *filthy* Gestapo have made.'

I looked round at the mess and imagined waking up to it the next morning.

I said, 'I'll help you clear up, Mum.'

They'd broken Mum's wedding-present Dresden shepherdess. Mum cried out when she saw that, but then she frowned. 'There was a lot more broken china in the Jakobys' apartment, that night.'

'Yes,' I said, then: 'They broke this on purpose, it's a way of kicking us.'

Mum pulled herself up straight. 'We won't stay kicked. Anyway, I think I can mend this. It's only in three pieces.'

It was midnight when we finished. It wasn't just the putting things back where they belonged, they'd made black boot marks on the floors, and we had to rub those away. It kept reminding me of cleaning Aunty Edith's home, and I imagined her in the Levetzow Street synagogue, frightened, longing for Raf. Would they give her something to eat there? Before they put her into one of those terrible waggons with nothing to eat and drink – and I was thinking no, they mustn't do that to Aunty Edith, not my Aunty Edith! And again I thought: Why didn't I catch the first tram?

When I did lie down it was ages before I got to sleep, then I kept dreaming they were coming back and finding Raf and dragging us all away. I woke up just as the hall clock was striking six. I hardly felt as if I'd slept at all.

I could hear Mum moving about. I got up and went out to her.

'Jenny,' she said, when she saw me. 'Did you and Raf whisper last night?'

'*Yes*,' I said, and I was annoyed – how stupid did she think I was? We were teetering on the edge of a quarrel, but Mum bit her lip. 'Jenny, don't. I've been waking up all through the night and worrying in case you'd forgotten, it wouldn't have been surprising, with the bad news you had to tell him.'

She hadn't slept much either. Her face was yellowish and her hair looked greyer than I remembered it looking yesterday.

She said, 'Listen, I've got to go to Raf straightaway, with some food, while it's still properly dark. And to take the night pot from him. Thank God we had the toilet put in down there. We won't have to lug a pot all the way upstairs.'

I was shocked, because I hadn't thought about that. But I said, 'I'll go, Mum.'

She shook her head. 'We'll take turns, Jenny. It looks less suspicious, me going to the shop in the morning.'

I had to admit she was right. I said, 'Supposing *they're* in the yard, watching?'

'I'll take Muffi down first, she has to go out any-

159

way. If they're watching us, she'll find them out. If not, I'll come back upstairs and get the food.'

The Gestapo weren't there, so Mum came quickly back for Raf's breakfast: four slices of bread and margarine – the butter had disappeared from the shops by then – with honey that Kattrin had got from under the counter, a bit of mousetrap cheese, a wrinkled apple and a bottle of water. And some chocolate. Kattrin always managed to lay her hands on chocolate for Raf.

I said, 'It'll be awful for him if he has to be in the dark all the time. There's a light in the stock cupboard, isn't there? Could we let him have that on?'

'Maybe,' she said. 'But there's a ventilation grille.'

'There's ivy all over it.'

'So there is, but I think we'll have to check if the light shows in the daytime. He can't have it on after dark, though. I used the shop light last night – I suppose you did, too.'

I nodded.

'We mustn't do that again. We'll have to use black-out torches to light him, and be sure we point them away from the grille. We'll have to be so careful, Jenny.'

I made thin porridge for Mum and me. There was enough honey left to drizzle on it. We'd need that, we both had to stay strong to look after Raf. I boiled the kettle and made cereal coffee and all the time I was on edge to know how he was and aching to go down to him.

I heard Muffi's paws scrabbling up the stairs, and

Mum's footsteps coming after her. I went quickly to the door and opened it.

Mum looked upset; that terrified me. I thought: Raf's managed to let himself out, he's gone off to Levetzow Street after all. I asked, 'Is everything—'

She shook her head at me. 'Wait till we're properly inside,' she hissed.

She came in and shut the door. 'I couldn't get a word out of him,' she said. 'He just sat there with his head on his knees. And I gave him my clock with the luminous dial – that is, I put it down and told him to switch the light on at nine and I'd have a look and see if it shone through the grille. I said if I could see it I'd knock three times on the back of the theatre and he should switch it off. Honestly, I don't know if he even heard me. He looked like a trapped animal in there, Jenny.' She put her hands over her face for a moment. 'It's his birthday next week. He'll be seventeen. Seventeen, and cooped up in a cupboard in the dark.'

I felt as if I was shut in there with him – only I wasn't there with him, that was what was so grim. He'd be alone there all day, brooding about Aunty Edith.

Mum said, 'Jenny, you'll have to keep Raf going. He'll need you, the state he's in.'

I nodded. Only there were so many hours before I could go to him.

'Let's have that porridge, anyway,' Mum said. 'I just hope Raf eats something.'

*

It came on to pour. I put on my coat and rain hat and took Muffi out for a quick walk round the block. When I came back there was a big Merc parked outside the house. The Gestapo, I thought, and my mouth dried up, but then I saw Brettmann, Uncle Hartmut's chauffeur, sitting behind the wheel reading the *People's Observer*. That was better than the Gestapo, but not much.

I tried not to look at the shop door on my way past. 'Seventeen, and cooped up like an animal,' Mum had said. It was awful, it shouldn't be happening.

There was a puddle in the entrance; maybe Aunt Grete had shaken her umbrella there. I told myself I had to go up to the apartment and be polite to Uncle Hartmut. After all, he'd kept his word and hadn't denounced me and Raf – and I'd used his name to help with the Gestapo last night. Staying on the right side of him was a way of looking after Raf. I started to climb the stairs, wondering what he and Aunt Grete were up to? Dropping in wasn't something they usually did. They waited to be invited.

Mum let me in.

'Aunt Grete's here,' she said, raising her eyebrows. No Uncle Hartmut, then, well, that was a relief – but my aunt had never dropped in on her own before, either.

She came out of the sitting room as I was pulling my wet waterproofs off. She was wearing a vile purple costume with a black velvet collar and a black velvet

162

hat decorated with an enormous black velvet rose.

'I'll get Muffi's towel,' Mum said and disappeared into the kitchen. I curtseyed like a well brought-up girl, though it felt stupid bobbing with rubber boots on.

'Uncle Hartmut's busy at his desk,' Aunt Grete said to me, 'but I came to see how you are.'

Mum came back and knelt down beside Muffi to rub her dry. She was wearing an everyday dress in dull turquoise, but the colour was just right for her, and the line and fall of it made her far more elegant than Aunt Grete in her expensive costume.

Mum said, 'Aunt Grete's brought us some treats, Jenny. Real coffee, and chocolate, and cake, and some lovely ham. And a bag of potatoes, and even half a dozen eggs!'

I had to say a nice thank you to Aunt Grete, of course, and I did, but my eyes met Mum's. She gave her head a tiny, bemused shake. Aunt Grete always brought coffee and cake when she and Uncle Hartmut honoured us with a visit – after all, fat cats like them, who were in cahoots with the high-ups, wouldn't lower themselves to eat the rusked stale bread and cereal coffee the rest of us had to put up with. But all the other stuff? It was like a miracle, now we had Raf to feed. Only there weren't any miracles. Or else the first tram would have stopped for me last night.

Mum had already ground up the coffee for this afternoon's drink, and every now and again the fragrance of it got through the stench from Aunt Grete's perfume.

My aunt had brought us apple and cinnamon crumble cake. I could smell the real butter in the crumble even before I bit into it.

Aunt Grete sat on the sofa and came out with the usual horrible stuff about Karl's 'noble sacrifice for the Fatherland'. Mum made herself say something tactful but I kept my mouth shut for fear I'd say what I was thinking, that her husband was making money out of the war that had killed Karl.

Aunt Grete sighed. 'Poor child, it's hard for her.' Then, in a buttery, wistful voice, she said, 'It does me good to see you, Jenny. I do so miss my little girls.'

Your horrible girls, I thought, who'd have been pleased to think of the Gestapo taking Aunty Edith away. Kunigunde would have laughed in our faces about it.

But Aunt Grete went on with the buttering-up. It was Muffi's turn now. She patted Muffi's head. Muffi let her do it. She tolerated Aunt Grete, though she always backed away from Uncle Hartmut. She knew what *he* thought of her.

'If it weren't for the white patch,' Aunt Grete said, patronising our mongrel dog, 'you'd think she was pure-bred.' Then she crossed her plump legs in their sheeny silk stockings and uncrossed them again. She peered at her fingernails and said, 'Sylvia, I don't know how much stock you've got left in the shop—'

'We're fine,' Mum said, looking prickly. 'And we've got Dietrich's pay, and I've got my clients.'

'Don't take offence, Sylvia,' Aunt Grete said, chewing her lips. 'It's just – the reason I've come to see you – my couturière's workshop has closed down so that her seamstresses can do war work – of course, in these times, she has to do what she can for the Fatherland – and I was wondering – you have such good taste and you're such a good seamstress...'

So that was it. The food was a bribe.

Mum started looking at Aunt Grete in a different way. The way she looked at me when she was considering what kind of frock or coat to make me. I knew what she was thinking. *Not purple*. It highlighted all the little red thread-veins in Aunt Grete's cheeks and washed her skin out. Only would Mum be able to make her see it? Maybe Mum thought that too, because she frowned.

'And we could send the car for you, when you came to do fittings,' Aunt Grete went on. 'And of course I would pay you well...'

She stopped and looked scared and embarrassed.

I looked at Mum, thinking: Do it! It'd mean more food parcels as well as money. Luxuries that we could share with Raf. And we need the Hansens on our side, you know we do. Our eyes met. I hoped she was thinking the same thing.

But she said, 'I've got a lot of work already, Grete, existing clients who depend on me.'

'But Sylvia,' Aunt Grete said beseechingly, 'there'd be fabric over.'

No textile rations for *her*, not with Uncle Hartmut in the business.

Mum sat silent, tapping her hand on the arm of her chair. Aunt Grete kept her eyes fixed on her like Muffi waiting to be given her dinner. I could practically see a tail anxiously wagging inside her dreadful purple skirt. It made me want to laugh hysterically.

Then Mum said, 'All right, Grete, I'll help you out.'

Aunt Grete sighed, crossed her legs again, leaned back and drank the rest of her coffee in one gulp.

'Thank you,' she said.

Frau Mingers came out of her door as soon as Mum opened ours to let Aunt Grete out. I thought: Has she been lying in wait? She stared at Aunt Grete so hard that Mum introduced them.

'Hei-'Itler, pleased to meet you,' she said, her eyes gobbling up Aunt Grete's Persian lamb coat. Her own coat was one of the cheap synthetic ones that you could get on coupons this season, and she'd got the buttons done up wrong, one side was higher than the other. For a moment she turned back towards her front door, then I saw her remember she was meant to be going out. She twitched and headed downstairs. She *had* only come out to see Aunt Grete. I could feel the mad laughter wanting to come out again. I bit the inside of my cheek.

She had the Mother Cross slung round her neck. As she went away, Aunt Grete looked at it and sighed.

'She's had four children,' she said. 'If my health had been better…'

Frau Mingers' back stiffened proudly. She'd heard. Now she was pleased as Punch with herself because the fine lady in her fur coat envied her the goblins she'd produced for the Fatherland.

When we were back in the apartment, I said to Mum, 'What happened to the Broomstick's fur collar?'

'She gave it away for the troops in Russia,' Mum said.

'I bet some Nazi fat-cat's wife's wearing it, right now. Mum, I thought you were going to turn Aunt Grete down.'

'Good God, no,' Mum said. 'I was just dragging it out to torment her a little. But Jenny, there must be other dressmakers in Berlin. She didn't have to come to me.'

'Do you think they've swallowed the thing about us being related to General Montgomery?'

'Maybe,' Mum said. 'Anyway, they saw you out with a Jew. Maybe Hartmut's even heard about our visitors coming last night. Through his contacts.'

Now I did have to laugh, but it was sour laughter, it hurt my throat. 'Our bad reputation in Nazi Germany makes us a good bet if the Tommies win? And I was using Uncle Hartmut's name to impress the Gestapo.' And suddenly I wanted to cry, but I swallowed the sob.

Mum smiled bitterly. 'He covers our back now, and

he's hoping we'll cover his if the Nazis lose the war. I wonder if we would?'

Later on I said, 'Supposing there's an air raid?'

'Raf'll have to stay put,' Mum said. 'I just hope the house doesn't get hit. If they found his body, it'd all come out.'

'If he was killed,' I said, 'I'd want to die too.'

'No, Jenny!' Mum said, reaching out and gripping my shoulder. 'Staying alive is what we have to think about. Listen, how can we make it look innocent when you go down to the shop tonight? And all the other nights, too.'

I said, 'I'll be letting Muffi out, won't I?'

'That's good. And then she can check the yard at the same time. So it'll be the same as when I went down this morning. If there's no one there, you come back for the food.'

I nodded.

She said, 'I've filled a bucket of water and put it in the shop. An extra air raid precaution, if anyone asks, but it's really for flushing the toilet when you've emptied the pot in there, and rinsing the pot out afterwards. I can pull the flush in the mornings, but you can't do that. It'd sound suspicious.'

I didn't know how I was going to cope with taking the pot from Raf, but I told myself it was part of taking care of him. Then I told myself again because it hadn't sunk in properly the first time.

*

168

All the same, I was desperate to go to him. I kept looking at the clock and getting angry with it for going so slowly.

My chest was tight with impatience all the while Muffi was sniffing round the yard and finding the right place to pee. She didn't find any Gestapo men, so I went back upstairs for the warm Kilner jar full of potato-ey stew and the water bottle. Clutching the Kilner jar inside my coat with my left elbow, I picked four squares of chocolate, a slice of Aunt Grete's ham and my torch off the table. I put them in my right hand pocket, took the water bottle in my right hand and went down again. It was hard to open the back door of the shop without dropping anything, but I managed it.

'Raf,' I whispered.

He lifted his head and looked at me. He was crouched in a corner of the stock cupboard. His face was still dirty and his eyes were red. His hair was all in a mess, as if he'd been pushing his fingers through it for hours.

I put the food down on the floor of the stockroom and climbed in there with him. It was narrow, but long, so there'd been room for him to lie down last night – if he had done. He looked as if he hadn't moved for hours. I crouched down beside him and tried to put my arms round him, but he went stiff and shrugged me off.

'Raf?' I whispered again.

'Here,' he said, pointing at the night pot. 'You need to take this.'

I cringed, but I reminded myself how much he must have wanted to get rid of it. I took it away and did all the stuff with the bucket, then I came back and opened up again. I thought: He'll let me comfort him in the end.

I said, 'I've brought your dinner, and here's a spoon to eat it with, and there's some ham, Raf, and more chocolate—'

'I don't want chocolate,' he said. 'I don't deserve it.'

'Yes, you do,' I said, then, 'Raf, I love you.'

'I'm sorry, Jenny,' he said. 'I – I can't – everything's changed.'

I felt as if something had sucked my insides out.

He said, 'I know you and Aunty Sylvia are being marvellous, having me here – but I want to go after Mum.'

I said, 'Raf, she doesn't want you to! Anyway, she might – she might be gone by now.'

'I've let her down,' he said.

'*No*,' I hissed. I didn't want to believe what he was saying. 'You haven't let her down. I told you, she was glad when she knew you were with us. She said to tell Mum to take care of you.'

He didn't answer. I said, 'Did you have the light on, today?'

'No,' he said.

'Do you want the light?'

He looked at the floor. 'I suppose so.'

So Mum would have to look at the ventilator again

tomorrow.   There was a howl building up in my throat, but I forced it down. 'Have you eaten anything today, Raf?'

'A bit,' he said. 'Not the chocolate. You can take that away.'

'No,' I said. 'You might want it later. Listen,' I made myself keep talking, 'put the light on tomorrow, then if it doesn't show, you can read. Karl's got a book about architecture—'

'Maybe,' he said in a dull voice. 'You'd better leave me, hadn't you? It'll be dangerous to have the door open too long.'

I managed to hold the tears back till I got up to the kitchen. Mum was standing there waiting for me with Muffi, who started licking me, but I ran off to my room and chucked myself down on the bed.

Then Mum was there, putting a hand on my shoulder. 'Jenny,' she said anxiously. 'Is Raf all right?'

I rolled over and looked at her. 'He doesn't want me. He's stopped loving me.'

'Oh, Jenny,' she said. She put both her arms round me. 'Oh, my darling, whatever he said, don't take it to heart. He's half-crazy with grief, and it's not surprising. When you think what he's been through . . .'

She stroked my hair. I knew how much she wanted to make it better for me, but she couldn't.

Chapter Thirteen

I had to go to school on Monday. I sat in class, while Emmerich the history teacher went on about the ancient Germans, but I was thinking about Raf. He'd washed in the basin in the shop toilet, and changed into some of Karl's old clothes that Mum had carried down in her mending basket, so at least he wouldn't smell of the gas works any more. I was hoping that was a good sign. And Mum had taken Karl's architecture book to him and he'd promised to switch the lamp on. I hoped it didn't show in daylight, so he could read.

I imagined the sounds he'd hear from inside the stock cupboard; Janke sweeping the cobbles in the yard with his long broom, whistling tunes no one ever recognised; the noise of the big bin lids clanging and the thud of rubbish landing in there – not much of that nowadays, though, so much was being recycled for the war effort. He'd hear the twitter of sparrows; Muffi being let out and running round, Mum calling her in again. But then other sounds started off inside my head: the big car pulling up, its doors slamming, the booted feet on the stairs, the voices. 'Open up! Gestapo!' My throat went tight and my belly cramped.

Supposing they went outside and worked out there was a space under the staircase?

They'd execute Mum for hiding a Jew. Probably me too. And I kept thinking about Aunty Edith. I could still feel her hand squeezing mine, her fingers when I'd stroked them. They'd been rough from the work at Uncle Hartmut's factory. I thought: If only I hadn't missed that first tram. We could have squeezed her into the stock cupboard with Raf. They could have kept each other company. Suddenly I was sure it was all my fault, and I knew why Raf didn't love me any longer. I didn't deserve to have anyone love me.

Desperately, I thought: Maybe she won't die on the train. Please let her escape somehow, and find someone who'll hide her. I tried to send my love towards her, wherever she was, to strengthen her.

'The Germans of old were mighty warriors,' Fräulein Emmerich said. 'They feared nobody.'

Paula scribbled on her rough book: *They didn't have a Gestapo, then.*

I just managed to make myself grin, but then life arranged a little torment for me. Some man walked past the classroom window singing raucously.

> *'When I look deep into your eyes*
> *My heart flies off to paradise –'*

The song from the Café Kranzler. All of a sudden tears were running out of my eyes and plopping onto the woody paper of my rough book. Emmerich bore down on me.

'Friedemann, what's this disgraceful exhibition?'

She was a raw-boned woman staring at me over the pince-nez she had perched on her bony nose. She had fishy eyes.

Paula slid her rough book neatly under her text book and said, 'Fräulein Emmerich, you know Jenny's brother was killed—'

'Well?' Emmerich demanded. 'The women of ancient Germany didn't weep for their fallen brothers, Friedemann. They were proud that they'd gone to Valhalla to drink mead with Wotan in his hall.'

I blew my nose and managed to stop crying. But I hated the idea of Karl in Valhalla. He'd rather have a glass of Pilsner than mead, and a friend to kick a ball around with, and some nice technical problem to solve. He'd want to meet up with Grandma, too, and Uncle Markus. I so much didn't want the Nazis to rule the afterlife as well as the present.

Emmerich picked up my rough book. 'You've soaked this,' she said indignantly. 'Don't you realise paper is a scarce and precious resource?'

I mumbled that I was sorry.

'Dry it carefully,' she said, 'then you'll still be able to use it.'

I felt sore inside from crying, but I thought: Paper. If Raf can design buildings, it'll give him something to do. Now where can I get him paper from?

'The ancient German women were thrifty,' Emmerich preached, standing over me. She stank of mothballs. I thought she must have been hoarding them, or maybe she had a secret supplier. Kattrin couldn't lay her hands on mothballs anywhere. 'They spun their own wool and wove it into cloth for their families.'

Envelopes, I thought. That's it. I can open them out and there'll be quite a lot of paper inside them. And then there are all the endpapers of books, some of them are blank at least on one side. It was a good idea to think about paper, it blocked out the other horrible thoughts.

There was something else I had to do. I told Paula Klaus-Heinrich's mother had taken him to the country to be with his grandmother, who was ill. In Baden, I said, deliberately making it as far from Berlin as possible.

'Will you write?' Paula asked, looking worried for me. 'You're going to miss him.'

'Of course I'll write,' I said, 'but it's not the same, is it?'

Mum agreed it was a good idea for Raf to have paper, so I spent half an hour opening out old envelopes and vandalising our books. I had quite a lot of paper in my pocket when I went down to him that evening.

'What's this?' he said.

'For you to draw on,' I said.

He kept his hands by his side. 'I don't need it.'

My throat went tight. I said, 'Are you angry with me for not saving Aunty Edith, Raf? Do you think I should have caught the earlier tram?'

'No,' he said sharply. 'This is nothing to do with you, Jenny.'

If he'd stabbed me, it might have hurt less. I swallowed hard and said, 'I've sharpened you some pencils, look. I'm going to put it all down here, Raf. It's up to you if you use it or not.'

Looking anxiously at me, Mum said, 'The thing about Raf is, he was so determined to stay with his parents, he wanted so much to look after them – and now he can't do that any more. That's what's tormenting him.'

She ladled me out a bowl of stew with Aunt Grete's potatoes in it. 'And even though he hated it at the gas works, he was *doing* something. Now he's just sitting there, he can't do anything, and he's got all the time in the world to brood—'

'Mum, if you're trying to make me feel better about – him and me – please stop. I don't want to talk about it.'

I didn't think she'd let me get away with that, but she stood up and went to the kitchen dresser.

'There's a letter from Dad.'

I said, 'Had he – had he heard – when he wrote it?'

She shook her head quickly and handed me the letter.

My darlings, Dad had written, *I think about you day and night. Conditions good here. I am in good health. Please always take care of yourselves. Dad, Dietrich.*

I said to Mum, 'He'd agree with what we're doing, wouldn't he?'

'Yes,' she said. 'Of course.' Then: 'I wonder when he'll hear? He'll be all on his own with it, Jenny—'

And then we howled in each other's arms. For Dad, for Karl, for Aunty Edith. For Raf. I suppose Mum was crying for me, too, though I didn't realise that then.

The next night the paper and pencils were still in the corner of the cupboard and Raf hadn't used them, but he did admit that he was reading.

Just before I left, he said, 'There was some woman having a spat with Janke in the yard. She was telling him the place was a disgrace, and he started yelling at her that if the Tommies hadn't shot half his leg off at Ypres he could be fighting Russians instead of facing harridans on the Home Front. And she started yelling back that it was her husband and her son who were fighting on the Russian Front, and he just marched off and left her.'

'Janke and Frau Mingers,' I said. 'They can't stand each other.'

'The woman who's living in our apartment?' Raf asked, and his face closed up. He wouldn't talk any more.

I went up the back stairs telling myself I didn't care. Kattrin had brought us some carrots, and with potatoes and some of Aunt Grete's ham, and some onions, we had a very good stew for wartime. We were just washing up when the doorbell rang. I went to open up, Muffi beside me, barking.

It was the Gestapo officer from the other night with his two men.

I felt ill with fear when I saw them standing there, but I went cold and calm too, as if there was something inside me that knew that was the best thing to do. And Muffi – thank God for her cleverness – started wagging her tail, which meant her whole self wagged inside her moppy coat.

He bent down to pat her, then said to me in quite an ordinary voice: 'Heil Hitler, I'm First Lieutenant Brenner. We met the other night. I want to have another look at your shop.'

He made Mum come downstairs too, this time. The men marched straight to the theatre – he must have briefed them in advance – and started trying to drag it away from the wall while Brenner watched Mum's face and mine.

They couldn't budge it. I stood there, forcing myself to think the thoughts I ought to be having, that it was unpleasant and scary having the Gestapo in the shop, but that was all it was, and I only hoped they wouldn't damage the theatre, it'd upset Dad, said the little actor I had become. Once I thought: They must have gone outside and thought about the staircase –

but then my heart thumped so hard that I made myself stop thinking at all.

'My husband screwed it to the wall,' Mum said to Brenner – she was putting on a good act. 'The theatre has to be stable when people are sitting on the ledge.'

'Has either of you got a screwdriver?' Brenner demanded, looking at his men.

They didn't, of course. Dad had several in his tool cupboard, but neither Mum nor I pointed that out to them.

The one with the scar looked at the screw heads and said, 'Lieutenant, these screws have been here for ages. There's unbroken paint round them.'

Brenner stepped up to the theatre, peered, and nodded. 'And no door at the back, I can see that.'

My heart felt as if mice were running races through it, but I stood still, trying to keep the innocent look on my face. There's nothing to hide, I kept repeating inside my head, while Brenner tapped his booted foot on the floor. And then the sirens started to wail.

'Air raid,' Brenner said. He frowned. 'We wouldn't have time to get back to Prince Albrecht Street, would we?'

'Not from here, sir,' the taller of his men said.

'All right,' Brenner said to us. 'Where's your shelter?'

'In the cellar,' Mum said, 'but we'll have to go upstairs and get our stuff and open the windows—'

'Yes, yes,' he snapped. 'Windeck, you go up and

keep an eye on them. I'll find the cellar. Does the dog come too?'

'Of course,' I said.

'Oh, well,' he said. 'At least that'll make it less boring.'

I heard the distant whack of the first bombs, and the wave of blast ran through the ground, shaking the foundations of the house. Muffi came to me and stuck her nose against my leg. She wanted to bark, but she knew that wasn't allowed.

'Berlin soil,' Brenner grunted once. 'Sand carries the blast a long way.'

The bare electric lightbulb shook on the end of its brown cord. I saw Frau Schmid scowling at us – we were bad news, always having the Gestapo round. Herr Tillmann kept his eyes on his shoes, and old Herr Berger from the top floor above us stared at the book of Schiller's poetry that he always brought down to the shelter, his lips moving as he read.

Frau Broomstick said in a fawning way to Brenner, 'My second son's doing his duty to the Fatherland on air raid protection duty.'

Thank heavens. It meant I didn't have Willi staring at me in the cellar any more.

'That's very proper,' Brenner said, smiling in a superior way – I saw how much he loved having people scared of him and licking his arse.

Frau Mingers clutched her Mother Cross, making

sure Brenner saw it. 'Our family are right-thinking people, we'll give our heart's blood for the Fatherland. But those two' – now she stopped fawning to snarl at us – 'with their English blood and their germ-laden foreign dog—'

She'd been furious when Janke, who was the house air-raid warden, had said Muffi was allowed to come to the cellar with us.

Brenner slapped her down. He said, 'The Führer loves dogs.'

I heard a little whine as she sucked her breath in, and at that moment the light went out.

It had never happened before. It felt – that first time – as if the darkness was a choking blanket that had fallen on us. And I thought about Raf. No, I felt him; felt his muscles tighten with every explosion and wave of blast and his fingers grip his bent knees as the stockroom wall shivered behind his back. I felt his stomach knotting itself up.

The light flickered on again. Frau Mingers was eyeing Brenner, anxious to know she hadn't blotted her copybook with him, but he wasn't interested in her. It was Mum's and my faces he was intent on, and I knew why. I pushed the thought of Raf away into the furthest parts of my mind.

At last the All Clear sounded and everyone went out onto the street to make sure nothing was on fire there. We knew it wasn't really, we'd have heard if any bombs had fallen in the neighbourhood, but we had to look, every time. There was a bright red glow in the sky.

'That's bad,' Brenner growled. 'They've hit the centre again, Jew-loving British skunks. Hope head-quarters is all right.' Then he turned round to Mum and me. 'That's why we have to make sure we find the Jews who are still skulking here.'

Mum glanced at him with an innocent, upset face, and said: 'Of course, but – First Lieutenant Brenner, there aren't any Jews in my house.'

'Maybe not,' Brenner said, heading for the car.

He came back again a week later. When I opened the door he was standing at ease, hands in the pockets of his leather coat. He was on his own, and he had a felt hat on instead of his uniform cap. If that was meant to make him look like a civvy it didn't work. Ordinary men didn't walk round in long leather coats and jackboots. He patted Muffi and she made up to him as if he was an old friend.

Brenner strolled round the apartment with us and opened all the wardrobe doors, but not as if he expected to find anything there. Again, he made us take him down to the shop, where he gave a token kick to the theatre, but not hard, you'd almost have thought he was worried in case we put in a claim for damages – and then he left. Afterwards, Muffi ran round in circles, growling furiously and showing her teeth.

Mum said, 'One day things will change, Muffi, and then you'll be able to bite him.'

'Better not,' I said, feeling savage. 'His blood might poison her.'

Three weeks after Brenner's last visit we decided to bring Raf upstairs. 'We can't leave him in that cupboard,' Mum said. 'It'd be enough to drive anyone out of their mind.' Only then she looked anxiously at me.

I said quickly, 'It's a risk trotting up and down stairs with things for him, anyway. I keep expecting Frau Broomstick to come out and start asking why I'm going to the shop at that time of night.'

When I went down to Raf for the last time, I felt for the untouched paper and pencils, found them by the door, and stuffed them into my pocket. I wasn't going to let him leave them in the stockroom.

In the whisper I'd got used to, talking to him, I asked him, 'Can you bring your duvet and pillow? Then when you come out I can shut the cupboard door and switch the light on in the shop. It's blacked out, so it's safe.'

When I switched the light on I saw him properly for the first time in a month. His eyes, dazzled and blinking, looked very blue in his thin white face, and his cheekbones stood out. There was a fuzz of hair on them, and a pale moustache on his upper lip. And I loved him again, and that hurt me as if someone was scouring my insides out.

I stiffened myself. 'Raf, Mum wants me to go through the rules with you again.'

He looked at me as if he wasn't quite sure who I was, but he recited them.

'I have to stay in Karl's room in the daytime. I can have the light on because you don't raise the blackout blinds in there, ever.'

Frau Mingers had asked Mum why Karl's window was always blacked out, and she'd burst into tears and said she didn't want to let the daylight in on her dead son's things. That had shut the Broomstick up.

'I can use the toilet, but I mustn't pull the flush, or run any water. I mustn't make a noise in the apartment when you're not there. Not any kind of noise. At least I'll be able to move about in the room. As long as I'm quiet. I can only come out at night when the blackout blinds are down. And I mustn't speak out loud. Ever.'

'It'll be better than being down here,' I said.

Suddenly, he was furious. He hissed, 'I'll still be cooped up, it's just a bigger coop.'

I just managed not to snap back at him. I said, 'I know it's hard for you, Raf – but listen, Karl's got that set of weights in his room. You can work with them, that'll give you some exercise—'

He shook himself. 'You must think I'm an ungrateful swine. I'm not, only...'

'It's all right,' I interrupted him. I was scared he'd start explaining why he'd stopped loving me, and I couldn't bear that. I said, 'Look, let's go up. Mum's got dinner ready for us.'

I switched the light off and opened the back door. It seemed a few kilometres through the dark yard to the bottom of the kitchen staircase. I cursed the stupid people who'd built the house. It was a good thing that we were the only floor to have back stairs, but why hadn't they made them open into the shop?

We didn't have much of a dinner. Aunt Grete's luxuries had run out. Kattrin was due to bring us another black-market parcel the next day, but even she wasn't able to rustle up as much stuff as she'd used to. There was a bit of turnip and a carrot chopped up small, potatoes that had gone wrinkly, a few grammes of pork and some haricot beans cooked in with them.

I couldn't enjoy my dinner anyway. With him sitting there I had to remember the things that were over and done with – and a voice in my head that I hated kept whining: Why, Raf, why? When we'd finished the stew, Raf started fishing bits of something out of his pocket. It was all the chocolate we'd given him over the last four weeks.

'We'll eat these together,' he said.

'They were for you,' Mum said quickly.

'What do you take me for?' he whispered, frowning.

'Aunty Sylvia, I don't really want any chocolate, but I'll have some if you'll share it with me. You need it.'

It was the first chocolate I'd had for over a year. I put it in my mouth, but it felt too sweet, sickly sweet. I ate all the pieces Raf gave me, though, to be polite to him.

After dinner he asked if we had any steel wool.

'Why?' Mum asked.

'I want to clean the cooker for you,' he said.

'You don't have to do that—' Mum began.

Almost desperately, he said, 'I need to *do* something.'

So Mum fetched him the tangle of steel wool and while she washed up and I dried, Raf scoured the cooker.

I put the plates away in the cupboard and said to him, 'It's a horrible job.'

'It's something to do,' was all he said, and he went on scouring. I could see the muscles moving on his arms and his back and I was furious with him, suddenly. I wanted to scream and throw something at him. Instead, I ran out of the kitchen to my room and slammed the door behind me.

Chapter Fourteen

I woke up and kept my eyes closed. I didn't want to open them, I didn't want to see the shining green hands and numbered face of my bedside table clock and the little pool of reflection on the glass that were all I could see inside my blacked-out bedroom. I didn't want to see how soon I'd have to start another day. Instead, I made myself believe I could hear Karl getting up in the next room, getting ready to go to his lectures at the university, where he was studying engineering. I told myself Kattrin was getting my breakfast ready and when I went to school the teachers wouldn't be Nazis, because there weren't any Nazis and so there wasn't a war either. After school I'd see Raf and we were in love and everyone was pleased, especially Aunty Edith; if she saw us kissing she'd shake her head but smilingly.

Only as soon as I thought of kissing Raf, I remembered he didn't want to kiss me now, so my dream world was wrecked. It was like the sandcastle I'd made with him when we'd been really little kids on holiday at the North Sea: we'd built the walls so high, we'd said, 'They'll keep the tide out, nothing will conquer our castle.' But the first wave washed the walls into humps of sand, and the second one flattened them altogether, and I cried and Raf kicked the waves, but the sea didn't care.

I opened my eyes and saw the alarm clock; it was five to six. I had five minutes before I had to get up into the real world where Dad was thousands of kilometres away in Africa and Karl was dead and they'd taken Aunty Edith away and killed her, maybe, and Raf didn't love me any more.

I started to cry. I dug my head into my pillow so nobody'd hear me, and then suddenly I was praying. I talked into my pillow as if there was a telephone receiver inside it that connected to God. 'Please, please,' I said, 'show me a way forward.' I could hear the words getting lost in the feathers, and I felt miserable, I might have known it was pointless saying prayers. Only suddenly I had a feeling of Dad, as if he was beside me there. I thought: Maybe he's thinking about me in Africa, whatever he's doing there at this time of the morning. And I remembered how I'd talked to him before the war and he'd said as long as we loved each other and held on to that we'd find the way forward. I thought: So maybe, I just have to keep loving Raf, even though he's stopped loving me. And then Muffi was scrabbling at the door and Mum was calling, 'Jenny, it's time to get up, you'll be late for school.'

*

We ate breakfast in the sitting room with the blinds down, so Raf could join us and listen to what the Nazis called 'Enemy broadcasting' on the BBC. We sat in a huddle, close to the wireless set, which had to be turned really quiet so the Tillmanns wouldn't hear from upstairs, though Raf said, 'They're probably too busy listening themselves to notice.' Luckily there was the width of the dining room between our sitting room and the Mingers' flat.

Mum always sat in the middle, so Raf and I weren't so near each other. And now I was in the room with him I couldn't believe loving him would make any kind of way forward. I just had the same feelings I always had when I was with him nowadays, I was miserable and angry and stupid – and guilty because I felt angry.

I didn't want to look at him, so I stared at the brown polished wooden sides of the wireless and the fan-pattern of the loudspeaker-front. I'd got to know it so well, I saw it when I shut my eyes at night and it gave me the same bad feelings I got in the mornings.

We listened to the BBC because that was where we always heard the first news of German defeats. The German programmes waited about a week before they told us about the Army's 'strategic withdrawals'. These were all supposed to be stages on the way to what they called 'The Final Victory'.

At school, Klotz said that the police had a special device that could tell who was listening to foreign broadcasts. Mum said that was nonsense. 'They'd have half Berlin in prison if that was true. Even Hartmut listens.'

'What?' I said.

'Grete let it out to me, at the last fitting.'

In April, Paula's mother decided to take her away to the country.

'Before Hitler's birthday on the twentieth,' Paula said. Everyone thought the Royal Air Force would mount a massive raid to spoil his day.

She and her mother were going to stay with her aunt in the Bavarian castle – the uncle was away at the war. 'You could visit me in the summer holidays,' she said, sitting on my bed. 'There's a wonderful park round the castle, and there are Haflinger ponies – you know the ones with white manes and tails and golden coats? You could learn to ride. And we can swim in the lake, and you can bring Muffi, Aunt Gertrud loves dogs, and we can go on the train to the mountains—' She saw my face and stopped.

'Oh,' she said. 'You've got your Jewish friends here. I did wonder. Don't look at me like that, Jenny, you're right to be cautious, but I'm safe, you know that. Mum's got connections, they'll never haul us in for questioning.'

I told her then. Maybe I shouldn't have done, but I told her everything. I really knew I could trust her. How I'd fallen in love with Raf – and told her lies –

how he'd come to us, and how I'd gone to fetch Aunty Edith but the SS had got there first. And how he'd stopped loving me.

She put an arm round me. 'Oh, Jenny,' she said. 'That's so tough, but listen, I bet he still loves you, really. One day he'll realise it and everything will be all right. And the Nazis will lose the war, it's only a matter of time, and then you and Raf will have your Final Victory.'

She made a face at me. There was always something about her that heartened me.

'Look what I've got in my handbag for you,' she said. 'You'll wear it for Raf one day, trust Aunty Paula.' It was a little Bohemian glass perfume bottle. She squeezed the bulb, smiling, and a mist of rose-scented drops landed on me. 'Mum's perfume. *Fantasia de Fleurs*. In memory of all the times we've helped ourselves to it off her dressing table. Only this is legit, Mum gave it to me for you. I bought the bottle, though.'

I gave her my musical box. It had an enamelled reproduction of a Degas ballet dancing scene on the lid. When you lifted the lid up it played the *Waltz of the Flowers*. Before she went she wagged a finger at me and said, 'And watch out for that boy downstairs. He was leering at me today. Always stay two metres away from him, do you hear?'

There were only nine girls left in my class after that. I got along with them, but they weren't my friends.

That was just as well, because visitors were nerve-wracking, but I missed Paula terribly.

Kattrin went before Hitler's birthday, too. Her cousins in Mecklenburg had invited her and her mother to stay till the war ended. The eldest son had gone to fight, so they could do with a good worker like Kattrin to help out.

'And you know,' she said to Mum, 'now they're calling women up to do war work, if I stayed here I'd have to go to a factory and work long hours away from Mother, but if I work on the farm, there'll be the whole family to keep an eye on her. It all seems right, only – this place is still my home, Frau Friedemann, and I can feel the others round me here, Herr Friedemann, and my darling Karl – would you mind if I went into his room for a few minutes? I used to go in there and complain at him for making it untidy, but now—'

'No!' Mum said, then her hand went up to her mouth.

Kattrin understood. A broad smile lit up her face.

She said, 'You mustn't try and make do with the rations, you'd never manage. I'll take you both and introduce you to my shopkeepers.'

The British only sent a few bombers to Berlin for Hitler's birthday, after all. The day afterwards I came home from school and found Willi Mingers cleaning the outside of the shop windows.

'Heil Hitler, Jenny,' he said, putting his cloth into the bucket of dark grey water.

'Hello, Willi,' I said as curtly as I could.

'I'm glad to see you,' he said, coming closer to me.

I moved away to keep the two metres between us. 'I've got to go up to lunch.'

'You can spare a few minutes,' he said. 'Can't you?' Then he eyed me up and down. 'You're pretty, Jenny. I – I think about you a lot.' He stopped and chewed his upper lip. He went on, 'You know, a German girl – there's no need for her to wait nowadays, with so many men getting killed at the Front we need to replenish the nation and—'

I felt sick, I didn't want to believe what he was saying to me. I looked at our shop door – if Mum was still in there I could escape to her – but the CLOSED sign was on it. She'd gone up already. I said, 'Mum's waiting for me, our lunch'll be getting cold,' and went into the passageway, towards the stairs, but he came after me, still talking.

'I've got good blood, you know. You should give yourself to a true Aryan. I might apply for the SS—'

I could feel his breath on the back of my neck. I thought: He's going to grab me, if he does I'll stamp on his foot. Only the shop door opposite opened and his mother came out of it. 'Shameless slut!' she screeched. 'Flaunting yourself, perverting my son – you're lucky I don't report you to the authorities, you are. As for you, Willi, what do you think you're

193

doing, wanting to soil yourself with *her*—'

I ran then, all the way upstairs.

'What was that about?' Mum asked, when the front door was closed behind me.

Raf had come out into the hall – we'd decided he could go there in the daytime, because it had no windows. I didn't want him to be there because he didn't want me and it seemed Willi did – it was all horrible and the last thing I wanted to do was talk about it.

I shook my head. 'Just that woman downstairs losing her rag. With Willi.' And then I looked at Mum and saw the strained look on her face. My throat went tight with fear.

'Mum, something's wrong, isn't it?'

'There's a letter from Dad,' she said. 'Nothing's wrong, only—'

Darlings, the letter said. By now we'd all learned to leave out any words that weren't strictly necessary in those short letters. *Transferring to America. Will be well treated. Only long distance away. Both always in my heart. Take care yourselves. Interesting see America. Dietrich. Dad.*

I put my arms round Mum, still holding the letter so that it crackled against her back. She gave me a quick, unhappy hug, then she let go of me and started to talk really quickly, saying Dad'd be safe in America, there was no fighting there, and he'd be well fed – and I knew she was being brave for Raf's sake, because we knew where Dad was, didn't we? Nobody knew where Aunty Edith was. I made myself be brave too, though I could see all those thousands of kilometres of grey choppy Atlantic that were going to separate us from Dad – maybe it wasn't any worse than Africa, but it felt worse. And then I thought about Aunty Edith and wondered where she was and if she was alive, and that was the worst thing of all.

Mum said, 'Raf's done all my accounts for me.'

'It wasn't much,' Raf said, shrugging his shoulders.

But it was quite a lot, because of the dressmaking. Not just for Aunt Grete. Several of my aunt's friends had admired her new clothes and wanted to use Mum, too. Women with high-up husbands who needed a supply of outfits for Nazi functions – and could lay their hands on plenty of fabric. It was useful in other ways, too. We knew why Mum had never been called up to help with the war effort.

We had bread and turnip jam for lunch. Aunt Grete was away on her monthly visit to Hildegarde and Kunigunde and our supplies were running low. Raf had his in his room. I ate in the kitchen with Mum. Food was supposed to be more filling if you didn't wolf it, so I ate slowly, difficult though that was. Then we had coffee – cereal coffee with a pinch of ground coffee from one of Aunt Grete's mercy packages – it was a real art, grinding coffee beans two at a time – and a few drops of evaporated milk.

'I'll have to go shopping,' I said as cheerfully as I could manage.

'Yes, please,' Mum said.

We left the washing up for Raf to do in the evening. He did it so thoroughly the pattern was coming off the china, but Mum and I didn't mention it.

As I put my outdoor clothes on, Raf stuck his head out of the door and whispered: 'Jenny, I don't suppose you could manage to find any paper, could you? Please.'

I hated it when he was polite to me, as if I was a stranger. And it was another chore.

I spoke sternly to myself. I ought to be glad he wanted paper. It might mean he was designing buildings again, as well as doing housework after dark and the accounts in the daytime and trying to lift heavier and heavier weights and catching up on his education from Karl's schoolbooks and scrubbing the roses off our china. He had all this cooped-up energy, he needed a lot of things to do.

I said, 'I'll try,' and he said, 'Thank you,' and at that moment I wanted desperately to touch him, but he shut his door – in my face, that was what it felt like. The helpless anger rushed up through me and I bit my lip hard. I put my arms round myself and squeezed myself, I felt my face girning up like a baby's. I didn't cry out loud. I couldn't bear Raf to know he'd made me cry.

*

The first queue, for the greengrocer's, was only twelve long, but the word was there wasn't anything there except turnips and swedes. I hoped for something better because I had Mum's and my unused cigarette coupons for him. I'd tried smoking with Paula, but I didn't like it, and now that was proving useful – though when I saw the young woman with red lipstick who was just in front of me, I wished I did smoke. It was the way she blew the smoke out of her mouth, it made her look knowing and able to take care of herself. If the man she cared about stopped loving her, I thought, she wouldn't be stupid like me, she'd shrug her shoulders and find another one.

She asked the old lady with the dented hat, 'D'you reckon the Tommies will be back to bomb us tonight?'

'I hope not,' the grandma said.

Another woman said, 'They're working on a secret weapon, I hear. Some huge gun that'll shoot missiles as far as London and wipe the whole city out.'

The grandma shifted from one tired foot to the other. 'Oh good,' she said in a flat voice, 'then all our troubles will be at an end.'

She didn't believe it. Neither did I, but I sometimes had nightmares about it.

When I got to the top of the queue Herr Dillmann lifted my bag over to his side of the counter, put the turnips into it and added a couple of potatoes. They were wrinkly and sprouting, but they plumped up if you soaked them in water. Then he gave me a lot of carrots, and three onions. I said thank you and slipped the cigarette coupons to him along with the money and the normal coupons.

Herr Gross the butcher needed a better barter than cigarette coupons, but we'd come up in the world now that Aunt Grete was giving lengths of fabric to Mum.

'Silk,' I whispered to him.

'How much?' he asked.

'Two metres.' That'd be worth extra meat for the next month. Nice meat, too. I passed my shopping bag over the counter to him, and he fished out the silk and packed me up an extra half kilo of beef and a bone. It glistened darkly through the paper he put round it and made me hungry even though it was raw. He whispered to me, 'I'll have chickens next week. I'll put one by for you.'

I got the bread, and some noodles at our grocer's. My arms were aching with the weight of it all, and for a moment I thought I'd just go home. I could tell Raf I'd been too tired to get his paper. Wouldn't that serve him right? Only all the time I was thinking that I kept walking in the opposite direction to home, to the street where Frau Grün the stationer lived. Maybe it was the same pride that hadn't wanted him to hear me crying. I'd fetch his paper, I'd smile when I gave it to him, I wouldn't let him know he'd broken my heart.

Or maybe – I don't know – I just wasn't eager to go back to the apartment where he was.

We'd always bought all our schoolbooks from Frau Grün, but never black market stuff, so I wasn't sure if she'd trust me. I'd have to try, though. I had the last of the coffee beans from the pantry for barter.

A bomb had fallen in her street; it had made a crater in the road, demolished a couple of houses on the right-hand side and blown the front walls off two houses opposite. I made my way along the narrow path that had been cleared through the rubble and stared up at what looked like giant children's doll's houses; I could see all the kitchens, the sitting rooms, and the bedrooms, a lot of them still with all their furniture, only it was all white with dust and there were chairs and bedside chests lying on their sides as if the little giant had been careless when she'd put them away. There were people up there, they were getting their stuff out, lowering it down on ropes from the upper storeys or schlepping it out from the ground floor and piling it up in the road. I tried not to imagine where Raf could go if that happened to our house.

The next house had only suffered a few broken windows and cracks in the facade and the grocer's on the ground floor had a good-sized queue in front of it. At the back of the queue, a little girl in a pushchair was crying to go home. Her mother turned round to her and snapped, 'Be quiet, Heidi, we've got to wait our turn and that's all there is to it!'

Frau Grün told me at first she didn't have any paper, but I showed her the little bag of coffee beans and she let me have an exercise book; thin rough paper, but quite a lot of pages in it. I got a pencil too. So now I had to go home. Little Heidi and her mother were still queueing up as I went down the street; the kid was sucking her thumb and her mother was talking to the woman behind her. There were only two people in front of them now.

I'd just got into the next street when the explosion happened.

One minute I was walking along with the bag-handles cutting into my fingers, the next I was flat against the wall with my hands over my head and the bags were on the ground at my feet. I didn't dare move for a few minutes, I wasn't even sure if I was still alive. Then I came away from the wall. I was shaking.

I heard someone screaming. My head felt light. A time-fuse, I thought. Sometimes bombs were set to go off hours or days after they'd been dropped. I picked my bags up – luckily there was nothing breakable in them, but two of the potatoes had escaped and I had to gather them up.

I went back to look. The pavement and the cobbles of the road were scattered with splinters of glass, wood, bits of brick and half a sofa – and there was a little arm lying in front of me. I thought: Theresia. No, that was five years ago. Then I noticed the seeping redness at the end of the arm.

Five years ago I'd looked at a doll's arm and thought it was a child's, now it was the other way round. I remembered the little girl crying in the pushchair. Heidi. I stared at the arm again; the blast had blown it about five hundred metres along the street. There was a ringing in my ears and a blankness in the middle of me, I didn't feel anything.

Then I saw something else, about a metre from me. Three tins lying close to each other. I bent down and snatched them all up without thinking what I was doing. I stuffed them in my bag, then I was off down the road, walking, not running. It'd have been suspicious to run. I was a looter now.

When I collected Muffi from the shop, Mum was setting a sleeve into a jacket and concentrating so hard she didn't even look at me. I went upstairs, put my shopping bags down by the front door and let myself in. There were patches of dust on the bags from when I'd dropped them. I heard Raf open his bedroom door and he came out into the hallway.

'You've got a nice lot of stuff!' he said. I heard him and I still didn't feel anything. I thought maybe this was the way to be, numb. I wasn't in love any more. The bomb had blown it all away.

He whistled softly when I showed him the beef. 'Well done!' he said. Muffi put her nose in the air and drew in rapturous breaths. Not that she got much meat nowadays, only a few scraps, but she'd have the bone after we'd boiled it for broth.

Then I brought the tins out.

'Yellow plums!' he said. 'That's a bit of a luxury, isn't it? And baby peas and carrots, what did you give for those?'

And suddenly I was hurling the tins across the floor so that Muffi yelped and ran away, her tail cowering between her legs, and Raf was standing there, staring at me, horrified. I thought he was scared of me, and I knew I'd wanted to frighten him, but that didn't make me feel better that I had done. I wasn't numb now. I screamed, the way I'd been wanting to for ages, and Raf took a step back from me. I threw the exercise book and the pencil down on the floor, too, so that the precious point of lead broke off, I saw it bounce on the parquet – and I ran to my room.

I slammed the door, threw myself on the bed and howled because I knew Raf wouldn't come after me. I was right, because I heard his bedroom door shut and Muffi's claws on the parquet as she went in with him. I dug my face into my pillow and clawed at the duvet, thinking that neither of them wanted me. And I wanted my big brother, if Karl had been there he'd have come to me, *he* wouldn't have left me to howl alone. I could maybe even have told Karl about the little girl's arm, but I couldn't tell Raf because he thought I was rubbish.

And then I was hating him, really badly; I talked into my pillow, frightening myself with what I was saying, but it came out. 'I should have let him go after Aunty Edith if he doesn't want us.'

Only I felt Aunty Edith's hand, gripping mine, as if I was back there with her on the dark street. I shuddered away from what I'd said. I rolled over and stared at the ceiling. It was getting a bit dingy, because you couldn't redecorate in wartime. I whimpered, really quietly, 'Aunty Edith, I want you so much.' Then I felt as if she was talking to me, she was being kind but firm, the way she'd been sometimes, when I was a naughty kid, telling me that I had to go on. I didn't think I'd be able to move, but I managed to get off the bed and go back into the hall, I picked the shopping bags up and I put everything away, even the tins. They were all dented; probably I'd made some of the dents myself.

I told Mum the grocer had given them to me because they were so knocked about. I never told anyone about the bomb going off and the child's arm.

Chapter Fifteen
May–October 1943

The butcher put a chicken into my bag and said, 'I'm letting you have all this extra meat and look how thin you are! You're not feeding it to that dog of yours, are you?'

I laughed it off, but it made me nervous, he wasn't stupid. When I came home I went to collect Muffi from the shop before I took the shopping upstairs. Frau Tillmann was there, talking to Mum, who was working on a dark blue suit jacket for Aunt Grete.

'It's the blast that frightens me,' she said. 'It'd only take a bomb to drop nearby and everything in our stockroom would be in splinters – mind you, it's a good business to be in these days, china. We don't carry so much of the high-quality porcelain as we used to, but people who've been bombed out need new crockery—'

There was a crash upstairs.

Frau Tillmann let out a little shriek. 'What's that? Frau Friedemann, you've got burglars!'

Mum put the jacket aside quickly and stood up. There was no need for either of us to pretend to look scared. We were terrified – and Frau Tillmann said, 'I'll get Tillmann, shall I? He can go upstairs with you and see – or maybe you should call the police—'

I stood there, I couldn't move with panic – then I was opening my mouth and saying – I even managed to smile while I said it:

'It's all right. I know what it is. I left the big atlas propping my window open.'

I couldn't believe I'd thought so fast, and Mum said, 'Oh!' nodding and looking as relieved as she really was.

'The latch is broken,' I explained to Frau Tillmann. 'And the wind must have blown, and so . . .'

'Fresh-air fiends,' Frau Tillmann said, shaking her head and laughing.

I knew I had to laugh too. I went up the back stairs with Muffi. I was relieved to get away because my mouth had dried up and I wasn't finding it easy to talk. I was jittering, wondering if Frau Tillmann had really believed us, and what might she do if she hadn't? Even if she was still friendly towards Raf, even if she didn't want to give us away, she might say something to her husband and that'd be two extra people who knew, that felt really dangerous. I thought: No, she did look as if she believed us. Only then I had the idea that she might just pretend, to set our minds at rest while she went to denounce us.

No, I told myself. She wouldn't do that. She came to help clean at the Jakobys' after Crystal Night. Then I thought: How could Raf? How could he? Why couldn't he be careful?

As soon as I got into the kitchen I heard him come out of his room into the hall. Muffi rushed out to greet him. I didn't. I took the kettle to the sink and started to fill it up. I didn't want to see him, I was scared I might scream at him again, and if I did that Frau Tillmann would definitely want to call the police.

Only I heard him call softly, 'Jenny.' I thought: I don't have to go out to him. I can stay here. But in the end I couldn't bear to ignore him. I put the kettle on the draining board and went into the hall, biting my lower lip to keep myself under control.

His face was white and tense. 'Was there someone in the shop?'

'Frau Tillmann,' I said.

Raf took a step towards me, then stopped himself. 'I'm sorry. I was trying to lift too much and I dropped the weights.'

I stared at him. I didn't know what to say, I'd been so afraid, my mouth still felt as if someone had dried it out with cotton wool.

He said, 'I'll be more careful from now on.'

I just nodded. I went back into the kitchen, I put the kettle on the cooker and lit the gas. The flame was hissing, it sounded too loud, I wanted to shush it. I heard Raf's bedroom door close, very quietly, that seemed too loud, too. I remembered how he'd moved towards me, as if he wanted to put his arms round me after all. Only he hadn't.

I took a whole teaspoonful of real coffee beans and

ground them up to put in the coffee. That was extravagant, but I didn't care. I thought I'd share it with Mum. I poured out a cupful for myself and drank it. It did make me feel a bit better and I even poured some out for Raf. I opened his door just enough to put it down where he could see it. Then I got away quickly.

Frau Tillmann had gone when I went downstairs. I was so glad.

'Coffee?' Mum said. 'Thanks, Jenny.' She reached up and kissed me. Then she shook her head and laughed angrily. 'I don't deserve it, I've been an idiot, look what I've done to this sleeve.' She held it up for me to see. I looked at the shoulder pad and the sleeve roll set in, all on the wrong side. It'd take her ages to undo it, time she couldn't really spare. I knew why she'd done it.

I said, 'That was bad, wasn't it?'

She nodded. Very quietly, she asked, 'Was it the weights?'

I nodded. 'He says he'll be more careful.'

She started to unpick the stitches with her small pointed needlework scissors. Then she said, even more quietly, 'I wish all this was over, Jenny.'

A couple of weeks later Raf knocked something down in his room when Uncle Hartmut and Aunt Grete were sitting with us. A book, I thought from the sound of it. Up till then he'd always been really quiet when we had visitors.

'What was that?' Aunt Grete said, half standing up.

My hands and feet turned cold as ice, but this time Mum thought of something.

'Sit down, Grete,' she said. 'It's the dog.'

Uncle Hartmut frowned and stared at me. I tried to make my face innocent and blank.

'Oh, the dog, of course,' Aunt Grete said, sinking back onto the sofa. 'Sylvia, I'm so nervous nowadays, anything makes me jump. I keep getting palpitations – I'd love to be able to find some war work to do, but the doctor says I mustn't think of it. Of course I go to my afternoons with the Women's League, we scrape lint for bandages, one has to do what one can to help with the Final Victory.' She peered at me. 'You're very slender, Jenny. Actually, you're both thin. It must be the worry of the bombing.'

Uncle Hartmut was looking us over as if he was calculating the calories in our rations and the food Aunt Grete was supplying us with, and comparing them with the amount of fat on us. I wished I could stop my heart thumping.

Mum said, 'I'm so busy, and Jenny's always on the go, shopping—'

'Well, at least you've got your health,' Aunt Grete said. 'Anyway, I've brought you plenty of food this time, that'll save Jenny's legs. There's asparagus and two pots of jam. Strawberry and raspberry. And Black Forest ham, and I'm in Berlin for the next three weeks. I was hoping you'd be able to make me a couple more evening dresses, Sylvia.'

Aunt Grete couldn't get enough evening dresses. She had to go to receptions, parties, dinners with high-up Nazis – 'and of course it wouldn't do to wear the same dress more than twice, I have to look smart, it's part of keeping morale up.'

Mum and she started talking about styles and fabrics, but Uncle Hartmut was running his eyes round the room as if he was looking for evidence of Raf's presence. He wasn't interested in clothes and he knew what we were capable of. He'd seen me with Raf at the Café Kranzler. Then our eyes met and this time I didn't drop mine, because I suddenly thought: He knows the war's going badly. He listens to the BBC. And he thinks we're related to Montgomery, and if he's guessed we're hiding Raf he'll think we might be useful to him one day when he's got the Allies to deal with.

He frowned again, at me this time, as if he'd heard my thoughts and disapproved of me having them.

When they'd left, Raf came out to say how sorry he was, but there was a wild look in his eyes. 'I can't stand this,' he said. 'And you must be sick of me doing stupid things and putting you in danger...'

'Please, Raf—' Mum said. 'You belong with us. You're part of our life. So don't say things like that. Just try and be careful.'

His hands went into fists, but he said, 'All right, Aunty Sylvia.'

Later, she said to me, 'Jenny, supposing he runs away?'

I came in once and the apartment felt so quiet and empty I was sure he'd gone. I stood there, thinking I wouldn't have to see him any longer and for a moment I felt blank and free – and then I was horribly afraid and knew I couldn't bear to lose him.

I dropped the shopping bags in the hall, I ran to his door and tapped on it. I didn't expect an answer, but a moment later the door opened and there he was.

'I'm sorry,' I said, feeling like a fool now.

But he said, 'No, it's all right. Do you want to come in?'

I hesitated. I thought I'd get hurt if I did. Then I went in anyway. Muffi came behind me, wagging her tail.

I looked round the room that had been Karl's when he'd been alive. Karl's cowboy books were still on the shelves, but there was a heap of his technical books on the desk. The one about architecture was on the top of the pile. Karl's cat marionette from the Pinocchio set was hanging from the ceiling. I remembered how we'd used to bring all the Pinocchio marionettes up from the shop and practise a scene to perform for the grown-ups at Christmas. Karl, Raf and me. I'd been right about getting hurt, it hurt to remember that.

There was a dip in the middle of the duvet. Raf had been lying there. I shut the door because I'd left the meat in the hall, in my shopping bag, and I didn't want Muffi to go out and get it.

Raf said, 'I've been watching that spider, there. Look at him.'

The spider had a body like a hyphen and long legs with tiny bulges where the joints were. It was going downwards, spinning its thread with dancing leg-movements as it went. Muffi went to snuffle at it, but Raf pushed her away.

The spider got to the floor and ran away at once. Raf shrugged his shoulders and sat down on the bed. Muffi jumped up beside him, turning round, making a nest for herself in the duvet. Abruptly, Raf said, 'Could I borrow Pinocchio?'

His thin, tense hands were playing with Muffi's locks now, deftly teasing them apart where they grew out of her skin, the way you had to, to stop her turning into a mat of hair. He said, 'I'm interested in the way marionettes move. You know when the Tokyo earthquake happened in 1923 the only building that was left standing was a really ancient pagoda, and it had moved with the earthquake. I've been looking at the cat, I thought I could extrapolate the principles to buildings, but I'd like to look at another marionette, for comparison ...'

Muffi stretched out her nose and sighed with pleasure – *she* was happy. I remembered how Raf had stroked my hands once and I was miserably jealous of my dog.

211

'All right,' I said. I got up to fetch Pinocchio, though I knew I'd miss the marionette, he was like a little bit of Dad in my room. Oh – I was so unhappy already, why would it matter if I was any unhappier?

But Raf said, 'Don't go yet. Listen – the other thing I'm doing is to design a kitchen.' He let go of Muffi and started to run his fingers through his own hair instead. 'Your kitchen's so badly designed, it assumes there's a maid who'll have hours and hours for cleaning, but she wouldn't have to if everything was built-in so there weren't any cracks to collect dirt. And the oven should be made easy to clean . . . ' and then he faltered. He got off the bed and walked across the room as if he was trying to get away from something. Muffi jumped down and went after him, wagging her tail.

He came to a halt in front of the blackout blind. He said, 'When I was still working at the gas works there were rumours – nobody wanted to hear them, mind you . . . '

I felt sick. I'd heard those rumours too and I hadn't wanted to hear about them either.

'There are supposed to be special camps in Poland, just for killing Jews. They've built a kind of death factory and the people come off the trains and they herd them into rooms and gas them there. They can kill a thousand people in a day. And they burn the bodies in ovens – they keep some of the Jews alive to shovel the corpses out.'

And I was imagining Aunty Edith being taken off

212

the train after a grim night with no food or water and being driven into one of those horrible rooms and the gas hissing out of the pipes, suffocating her—

'No, Raf,' I said. '*No.*'

Raf said, 'Why shouldn't it be true? They've been shooting the Jews in Poland and Russia, haven't they?' He looked at me.

'Yes,' I whispered. 'Norbert Mingers was boasting about it. This is worse, though.'

'Why?' Raf said. 'No, it is worse, I know. It's like a slaughterhouse.' And then he said, 'I want to be on my own now, Jenny.'

The British bombers flew a big raid on Berlin at the end of August. The Reich radio said they'd hardly managed to do any damage and went on about the Luftwaffe fighters who'd seen the Lancasters and Halifaxes off, but afterwards Goebbels, our scrawny Propaganda Minister and Governor of Berlin came on the air and urged non-essential workers and schoolchildren to leave Berlin. The city half-emptied itself. The Schmids, the Kohls, and the Kribses moved out of our house and old Herr Berger went off to stay with his brother and sister-in-law in Silesia. Frau Mingers stayed, worse luck. So many of the girls from my school went away that it closed down altogether.

I told Mum I didn't want to go to any other school – there were some still open, but I was fifteen, I could have left a year earlier, and I'd had enough of Nazi education.

Mum said, 'What are you going to do, if you're not at school? I know you go shopping, but that's not a full-time job, even nowadays. All right. You can help me with my work.' She sighed. 'God knows I'm busy enough.'

I knew I shouldn't stay upstairs all day with Raf, so I said yes.

The first morning she set me to pinning and tacking up the seams of a bottle-green cashmere and wool costume she was making for one of Aunt Grete's friends. I did my best, but she didn't explain properly what she wanted me to do and snapped at me when I got things wrong.

I snapped back, 'Mum, you're a useless teacher.'

'If you only tried—' she said angrily.

'I have been trying.' I put the garment down on Dad's work table and walked round the room. Gepetto looked resignedly at us. We had red hair, he knew we couldn't help it.

'Not hard enough—' then she stopped herself. She rubbed her hands over her face. I saw how tired she was.

I said, 'You don't want help, Mum, you just want to do the work yourself.'

She nodded unhappily. I said, 'Look, I could make rag dolls out of the scraps and we could sell them in the shop.'

She looked doubtful, but she said, 'All right. Make a rag doll and we'll see.'

I liked sewing if there was no one nagging at me. I made a rag witch with a long twisty nose. She was ready by dinner time. I took some twigs off the tree in the yard to make her broomstick.

Mum turned her over. I gritted my teeth while she inspected the sewing, but she smiled. 'She's got personality. Almost like one of your father's marionettes.'

I was pleased. I started thinking about all the other rag dolls I could make. I'd do a girl in a dirndl next. Mum had some scraps of green flowered fabric that'd be nice for the dress and I could embroider an apron; that was one useful skill my school had taught me.

I wasn't particularly scared when the siren went that night at half past seven. There'd been so few bombs on Charlottenburg, we'd got almost blasé about air raids. We opened the windows as usual, we left Raf, and trooped down to the cellar. I remember being annoyed because I'd have to spend an hour or so with Frau Mingers.

But the explosions started heading our way and every one of them rocked the cellar with more violence than we'd ever known. The light went out – I'd thought I'd got used to that, but now it felt really bad again. Muffi was on my lap, trembling, only just managing not to bark. Mum reached her hand out to me. I gripped it tight. I couldn't breathe properly. I

215

kept thinking about Raf up there all on his own. Mum squeezed my hand back. I could feel her wedding ring digging into my fingers. We sat there, sharing our terror in the dark.

There was a whine that sounded as if it was coming down on us. The floor heaved so I thought it'd erupt underneath me. Fragments of the cellar ceiling fell on my face and caught in my throat. I shrieked, 'The house has come down!'

'Not yet,' Janke said grimly. Mum made soothing noises at me but I'd imagined Raf dead and it was hard to come back from that. I was shaking. Muffi started nervously licking my face. Her breath smelt of fish, though she hadn't had any fish, or much meat at all lately. I pushed her away, feeling sick. An engine droned right overhead. Janke said, 'I reckon that's a Lancaster.'

'What does it matter what kind of plane it is?' Frau Broomstick burst out. For once I had some sympathy with her. It didn't last. 'Oh,' she said, 'maybe the *Friedemanns* are interested, maybe they told the British where to drop their bombs.'

Mum said, 'I don't want to be killed by British bombs any more than you do, Frau Mingers.'

But I was thinking: Why have we been listening to the BBC and wanting the British to win, when they're trying to kill us? And they killed Karl. And Raf's being attacked from the air, like the Jews in the Ghetto in Warsaw, and he hasn't even had a chance to fight.

Muffi sneezed and shook her head, still trembling. I clutched her with one hand and Mum with the other, and another bomb whined downwards. Everything jarred and shook, I couldn't believe the house would survive it and I hated the British so much.

When the All Clear sounded at last we switched our torches on and went shakily upstairs. The lobby was scattered with bits of broken plaster. Janke shone his torch through the dusty air, finding a wide crack in the wall zigzagging the dim beam after it all the way up to the ceiling.

'There'll be plenty more of those,' Herr Tillmann said, coughing.

'Let's go up,' Mum said to me.

Raf came out of Karl's room as soon as we'd shut the front door. Our feet crunched on more broken plaster.

'Are you all right?' Mum asked him.

He said, 'I got the kitchen colander and put it on my head. And I screamed and shouted as loudly as I could while the noise was going on. It was all right to make a row then, nobody could hear me.'

He sounded half-insane, but exhilarated, and suddenly I felt crazily happy too. I threw my arms round Mum.

'We're alive,' I said. 'We're all still alive!'

She hugged me tight. I turned to Raf, I was so beside myself I was almost ready to hug him, but I pulled myself up short. Muffi let out a wild bark and started running round in circles. We were all like lunatics. A moment later the light came on.

Mum took my rag dolls to show Aunt Grete and she showed them to her friends. Nazi fat-cat women who wanted presents to remind their evacuated children they loved them. They bought my work and asked for more. I started to make bigger dolls, boys and girls and dressed-up mice, rabbits and cats. By the time I turned sixteen in October I was a working girl with a business.

Mum made me a new winter dress in midnight blue cashmere – Aunt Grete had supplied the fabric, of course. On my birthday I put it on and came out into the hallway to show it to her and Raf. Mum walked round me, giving it a final once-over.

Raf stared at me for a long time without saying anything, then he pulled a leather jewellery case out of his pocket.

'I asked Aunty Sylvia to let me have this for you,' he said. 'I know Mum would – would want you to have it. Go on. Open it.'

He turned and disappeared into his room. I stood still. I didn't know what to do.

'Open it,' Mum said, making her voice encouraging.

Aunty Edith's aquamarine necklace and earrings lay shining on a dark blue velvet cushion. I stared at them, wondering if he'd given them to me to make me feel better about him not loving me.

I made to shut the case, but Mum said, 'Put them on, darling,' so I did, but when Raf came out five minutes later and saw me, he didn't say anything about it, even when I thanked him.

Uncle Hartmut and Aunt Grete arrived shortly after that, with a parcel. I opened it and found a cream silk dressing gown and nightdress.

'From Paris,' Aunt Grete said, smiling. 'A friend of mine brought it.'

The nightie had ribbon straps and a V-neck, and the dressing gown did up at the front with ribbons. I stroked its softness. Uncle Hartmut gave me a hard sideways stare. I prayed Raf wouldn't make any more noises.

Aunt Grete said, 'Where *did* you get those aquamarines? I love the white gold setting, so elegant. Can I see them better, Jenny?'

I had to let her come right up to me and inspect Aunty Edith's earrings and necklace, but I hated it. I wished I'd taken them off before she came. It felt so bad that I'd thanked Raf for them and he'd just stared at me.

'They used to belong to my mother,' Mum lied smoothly. 'She left them for Jenny to have when she was sixteen.'

Aunt Grete sighed, as if she'd been fond of Grandma. She hadn't. They'd always been prickly-polite whenever they met. 'Is there any word from Dietrich?'

'Yes,' Mum said. 'He's in Oklahoma.' We'd had the letter the day before. 'They've sent him to work in a hospital there, he likes that.'

'Treating Americans?' Aunt Grete asked, and she sighed again. 'Well, let's hope the Final Victory comes soon, then we can bring him home.'

Chapter Sixteen
22nd November 1943

I was late walking Muffi that evening. Mum and I were both terribly busy, she had ten evening dresses to make before Christmas, and I was working flat out on toys. And it had been pouring. The rain eased to a mizzle close to blackout time so I got Muffi on the lead and stuffed my torch into my pocket.

Muffi snuffled along the lampposts. The heavy rain earlier had washed most of the dog-pee bulletins away, but she found one now and again and then she squatted down and added her own. I went up to the Kurfürstendamm and took her round a good-sized block of streets to make up to her for being so late. I remember wondering if there'd be a raid tonight and thinking it wasn't likely. The bombers liked clear skies.

By the time I got back to our street it was really dark and I was using my torch. I was about ten metres away from our house when Willi Mingers grabbed me. I knew him at once by the stink of carbolic soap.

I should have screamed, but I couldn't, somehow. Suddenly everything was happening at once, and yet really, horribly slowly. He was pulling me against him, saying, 'Come on, Jenny, you know you really want me.' He pushed his groin against me and I felt the bulge there – *no*, I thought. He was forcing his mouth down on mine, I could feel his lips and taste his spittle, and it was disgusting. I didn't want it. I struggled, but he was strong, and now his tongue was coming into my mouth and I most of all didn't want that.

Muffi was snarling. I felt her angry body surging against me – and felt Willi's grip loosen. I stamped on his foot as hard as I could, dug my elbows into him – and thank God, I was free. Muffi was still growling ferociously, threatening to bite – but I didn't think she would, she was too sensible.

'You slut,' Willi yelped. 'You hurt me. Get that vicious dog away, will you?'

But I was backing away from him, pulling Muffi on the lead, glad to hear her still growling threats at him. I shouted, 'You deserved to be hurt, you filthy swine!'

Then I ran. I didn't stop till we'd reached the courtyard. I didn't want to go to Mum in the shop. I wanted to go straight up to the bathroom and wash my mouth out. I wanted to be alone more than anything else. I shone my torch on the cobbles, looking for the back door. At that moment I thought I heard Willi coming behind me. I whipped round, tilting my torch up into his face. But Muffi wuffed softly, happily, and I saw it was Raf.

I was horrified, then beside myself with anger, and it made me angrier that I couldn't say anything to him while we were in the yard. He went to the back door and I heard him unlock it. I followed him, feeling the rage boil inside me, I locked up behind us and we climbed the stairs.

Raf was surprised I didn't say anything as soon as I'd shut the kitchen door behind us. I saw his mouth half-open, making him look stupid. He could wait, I thought savagely. I could still feel Willi Minger's filthy slobber on my face and I was desperate to clean myself up. I ran to the bathroom and slammed the door behind me. I washed myself off and swilled my mouth out, glad I'd ignored Raf. I thought it served him right. Then I opened the bathroom door and went back to the kitchen to tell him what I thought of him. If he's gone to his room, I thought, I'll go after him, there's no lock on the door. But he was sitting at the table, fiddling with Muffi's hair. He looked up at me then, facing me out, as if *I* was in the wrong.

'Are you crazy?' I hissed. 'Where have you been?'

'Just down to Savigny Square and back,' Raf said, still giving me that defiant stare. 'It's always been all right.'

'Always? How long has this been going on?'

'Only since last week. Not every day.'

I breathed in hard. 'I don't believe this. You've been risking your life – and ours – just to go out for little strolls?'

'Little strolls? I was going crazy, cooped up in here. Jenny, you've no idea what it's like for me, I had to—'

I said, 'What you have to do is to hold out till the war's over.'

He flared up. 'Oh, yes? And how many years will that be? It's all right for you, you've got your business and you get to go out shopping, you can *move*, you can play the heroine and go and see my mother for the last time and come back and tell me what she's supposed to have said—'

I was shaking with fury now. 'Are you saying I told you lies about that?'

He got off the table. 'No. I'm sorry.' He bit his lip. 'I know you want to save me, Jenny. But I feel like a tame mouse the two of you are keeping in a box. You give me my feed every day and make sure my water bowl's full, you even give me something to exercise with, you've drilled nice little breathing holes in the side so I don't suffocate – only – I *am* suffocating.'

I said, 'Supposing you'd met someone? I know neither of the Mingers would recognise you, but they'd wonder who was coming out of our apartment, and then there are the Jankes, and the Tillmanns—'

'I've met Janke,' he said.

'What?' My mouth dried up all the way to my throat.

'He just said, "Don't worry, lad, I won't tell."'

I said, 'The Broomstick hates Janke, supposing she denounces him to the Gestapo? They'll get everything he knows out of him. Everything, Raf. And who else have you said hello to?'

'Only Frau Tillmann. She's all right. Anyway, she'd already guessed. That time I dropped the weight.'

I said, 'If one of the Mingers saw you, they'd guess too. Oh God, Raf, how could you? If Aunty Edith knew—'

He breathed in hard. 'My mother's probably dead. Gassed. And here I am, hiding like a coward, when – I'm going now. I've had enough, Jenny. Enough!'

He ran out through the kitchen door, which I hadn't locked, and down the stairs. He unlocked the bottom door and shut it again behind him.

My mouth opened of itself and I felt a howl rise in my throat like a baby's. Muffi whined, looking at the door, then at me, and pawed my leg. She wanted to go after Raf and bring him back. But I didn't think I could. I felt crippled by guilt all of a sudden. I should have realised what it was like for him, I shouldn't have been so angry. I thought: If only I could do it all over again. Then I knew I'd have to go and see if I could find him. I heard Mum's key in the front door. I looked at my watch. It was ten past six.

'Jenny,' she said, coming into the kitchen. 'I was getting worried—'

'Raf's gone. He says he's had enough.'

She put her hand to her cheek. 'Oh God.'

I said, 'Muffi wants to go after him, and I—'

'I'll come with you,' Mum said.

'You'd better not. If he comes back there has to be someone here to talk to him.'

'All right, Jenny,' Mum said. Her face was pale.

*

I let Muffi lead; her nose was all I had to rely on. She took me towards Kurfürstendamm. When we got there, she stood still, as if she was wondering which direction Raf might have taken. The rain came on. I thought it'd wash all the scent away, but she went to the wall and sniffed there. Maybe Raf had brushed against it. Then she turned firmly towards the city centre. He might have gone that way, towards his old flat maybe?

Just as long as he didn't march up to a policeman and say, 'I'm a Jew. Arrest me.' That would be the end of him. And we'd never know.

Ahead of me there was a woman shining her torch down on her bare, goose-pimpled legs and high-heeled shoes. It made you cold to look at them. A dark man-shape was going up to her. The dim torchlight showed me a pair of grey uniform trouser legs.

''Ei' 'Itler,' the soldier whispered. 'How much?'

Muffi pulled me away from them and I was glad. It seemed horrible that the soldier was picking his bit of skirt up while Raf was walking dangerously through the streets. A little way further up a couple pushed their way out through the hanging leather curtain that stopped the light coming out of a restaurant doorway. I smelt a steamy whiff of cabbage and a tiny trace of meat. Muffi pulled on her lead.

I said to her, 'Is he in there?'

She nudged her nose against my leg. I knew she was saying, 'There's food.' I pulled her away. 'Not for you,' I said. 'I thought you wanted to find Raf too, Muffi. Raf!'

She shook herself, splattering me with rain, and we went on. The darkness was full of people. I heard bits of chat, like a patchwork conversation.

'This blackout's a pain in the neck, having to wait till you're inside till you light a cigarette—'

'How the restaurants dare serve up that kind of stuff, it's outrageous—'

'You want to live where I do, old chap. My brother has a farm, lets me have—'

'Are you crazy? Shut your mouth, you don't know who's listening.'

Yes, I thought, why don't you all shut up? Their talk was a distraction, a fog of stupidity between me and Raf. I heard the clock on the tower of the Kaiser Wilhelm Memorial Church chiming the three quarters. A quarter to seven. We'd been out half an hour already.

'You don't mind the rain so much, do you?' I heard a woman say to her friend. 'Not when you know it'll keep the bombers away.' I wanted to slap her.

I went on, staring at all the figures and none of them were Raf and I hated them all. Once I saw a policeman and a figure beside him that I thought he was frogmarching along. I went tight and raw with shock but then the figure moved away from him down a side street. I walked on, still rattled, imagining another policeman arresting Raf somewhere else, maybe half an hour ago, maybe just outside our house.

When the clock struck seven I leaned against a house wall and cried. Muffi came and nosed me. I said to her, 'It's hopeless, Muffi. We'll never find him.'

But she stuck her nose in the air, sniffed suddenly, wuffed, and set off at a run. She took me up towards the zoo. I wasn't sure she was really following Raf's scent, maybe someone was up ahead with some black-market beef, but I went anyway. Once she started tugging me across the road, but a tram came and we had to wait. When we did get across she cast about, uncertain of the scent now. Then she stiffened, headed back towards Café Kranzler, doubled towards the zoo again.

The big church clock chimed the quarter. I wondered how long we could stay out? I heard a man say, 'If there is a raid, it'll be half past seven, that's when they always come nowadays. Good time-keepers, the British.'

Muffi lapped water out of a puddle, shook herself again and came up close to me. I put my hand down and caressed her wet head. She sat on the pavement and looked up at me. She'd given up, and she was hungry.

'We'd better go home,' I said, 'hadn't we?'

We'd got as far as the Memorial Church when the sirens started howling.

Oh God, I thought. This on top of everything else. Only Muffi stiffened. She'd scented something. She pulled me into the stream of people heading for the underground station.

It wasn't far down to the lit-up platform and that was when I saw Raf. He was a good way away, and there was a dense mill of people between us. He'd sat down, hugging his legs up against his chest. His face was tense but alive, somehow, almost glad. I thought: That's it. He's happy because he's got away from us.

Chapter Seventeen

I was right next to a pillar and I sat down so I'd have a back rest during the raid. Muffi came into my lap at once. Other people, who were obviously used to public shelters, were taking cushions out of their bags. There was a train in the station; a few really lucky ones had got seats on it.

I could still see Raf across the heads and bodies. Muffi knew he was there, too, she pulled on the lead and whined. He must have heard her because he glanced over and saw us. He stared at me, then he looked away. Muffi whined harder.

'No, Muffi!' I said.

I'd had the idea that if I caught up with him I could say I was sorry and we'd make it up. But now I thought how he'd been pushing me away ever since he'd come to our house and I realised nothing was any good, it had all been wrong for months and then I thought it was all my fault, I should have got to Aunty Edith before the SS did. I wanted to cry.

There was a thin elderly man sitting on a faded brocade cushion next to me, he had tufts of hair sticking out either side of his head and a briefcase in his lap. He introduced himself – Herr Hildebrand, he was called. I told him my name.

'What kind of dog is that?' he asked.

'A cross-bred Puli,' I said automatically.

The floor was really hard underneath me. I looked quickly at Raf again. He didn't notice this time. He was talking to a man next to him. I heard his voice in my head, saying, 'I'm suffocating.'

'Maybe it's a false alarm,' Herr Hildebrand said, taking his glasses off and polishing them on his handkerchief. 'I hope so, my wife'll have my dinner in the oven.'

But there was a booming noise. 'Drat it!' Herr Hildebrand said. 'It is a raid, those are the anti-aircraft guns at the flak tower by the zoo.'

I'd never heard them from so close. A moment later, a bomb came yowling down and everything shook.

'All right, Tommy,' Herr Hildebrand muttered, 'drop your bombs and leave, so I can go back to my wife.'

You'd have thought Tommy had heard him. A second bomb fell at once, then another and another, they were coming down like hailstones, and the floor was shuddering under my feet and the pillar behind my back was shaking so hard I thought it was going to fall on me. It didn't stop. It was worse than any raid we'd ever had. I cowered there and realised what it was like in Cologne and the Ruhr, in the cities the British had been pounding since last year, sending hundreds of bombers, a thousand even – it sounded as if there were a thousand of them attacking us tonight.

And the underground tunnels weren't very deep, but neither was our cellar – and I was in anguish about Mum. I didn't want to be so far away from her, not knowing what was happening to her and she'd be frantic about me. Everything was wrong, wrong, wrong, and I was so frightened.

The people around me were staring at the floor or shutting their eyes. I'd read somewhere that you could smell fear. I hadn't believed it, but I smelt it now, the air was so sour it made my eyes blink. Probably I smelt sour too. Muffi shoved her nose under my arm and kept it there.

Herr Hildebrand put his briefcase on top of his head to shield it from anything that might fall down from above. Then he frowned, took it off again, and opened it up. He brought a file out and offered it to me. 'Just be careful,' he yelled against the noise of the bombing. 'It's an important document.'

I held the file on top of my head with one hand and clutched Muffi with the other one. There was a bomb-howl really close and a massive explosion seemed to jolt the world apart. Now everything was black: I'm killed, I thought. Muffi was shrieking like a terrified puppy. I guessed I was still alive if I'd heard her, and a moment later someone switched a torch on, then another came on, and another. Muffi's hair was full of bits of plaster and sharp fragments of tile. A woman was sobbing close by but the next bomb drowned her voice out.

I bent double over Muffi, my hand clamped to the thing – whatever it was, I'd forgotten – that was protecting my head. My ears were ringing and I felt sick.

In a short lull between explosions Herr Hildebrand gasped, 'My wife, she's in the house all on her own.'

'Aren't there other people in the cellar with her?' I asked.

'We live in a house,' he said, 'not an apartment. Out at Dahlem.'

I said, 'I'm worried about my mum—' and another bomb shrieked downwards, drowning me out.

The raid went on and on.

At last there was a gap between bombs that seemed to be lasting for a very long time, then I realised the raid was over.

Mum, I thought at once. I've got to get to Mum. Only there's Raf, what shall I do about him?

I remembered what the thing I'd been clutching to my head was and reached it back to Hildebrand. He took it as if he wasn't sure what it was.

'Why don't they sound the All Clear?' he demanded. 'I've got to go home.'

Then it sounded, and all at once there was a getting up, a shuffling of feet, a dim muddle of light-specks from the torches that were moving impatiently to and fro. I carried Muffi, I didn't want anyone treading on her in the dark. I couldn't see where Raf was, but it wouldn't have mattered if I had. I could only go with the crowd. My mouth was dry with fear of what I'd find outside.

I heard the fire before I saw it, a howling and roaring at the entrance to the station. The smoke caught in my throat.

Muffi shrieked again, jumped down and tried to go back into the underground. Luckily I still had hold of the end of her lead, otherwise she'd have caused God knows what chaos in that crowd. I dragged her back. She went between my legs and stayed there, coughing. I remembered I had a scarf in my pocket, pulled it out and tied it round my mouth and nose. I picked Muffi up and tried to put my handkerchief over her nose, but she wouldn't let me. She shoved it under my arm again instead. I hoped that'd protect her.

She wasn't struggling any longer, thank heaven.

There were flames blowing like orange curtains out of the windows of the Kaiser Wilhelm church, and everything was lit by the red glare of the fire. A billow of black smoke surged towards me. The stench of it got to me even through my silk scarf.

'We've got to go home,' I said desperately to Muffi. Suddenly, Raf was beside me, wrapping a handkerchief round his face, staring at the burning street. He didn't notice me till Muffi let out a high-pitched bark under my arm. He heard that and turned.

'Jenny,' he said, 'did you come after me?'

'Yes,' I said. 'I know you didn't want me to.'

He didn't answer. I said, 'I've got to go and see if Mum's alive.'

My head was reeling with the shock and the smoke and heat. I thought: Even if Raf doesn't want me, Mum does.

I walked away from the entrance. A cold blast blew a cloud of embers towards me. I had to brush them off me, and off Muffi and now I was shivering, but it felt unreal that there was any cold air in all this heat.

I saw a man in front of me with a suitcase in his hand. He seemed to have materialised out of the smoke.

I asked him, 'Do you know what it's like near Savigny Square?'

The man shook his head like a crazed person. 'Fire-storms everywhere. There can't be a soul left alive.'

I burst into tears. Furiously, I said, 'It can't be. Stop telling me lies.'

I started to run, but I had to slow down because of the chunks of rubble lying around. There was splintered glass everywhere, too, so it was a good thing I was carrying Muffi. I walked on down a Kurfürstendamm I barely recognised, trying to forget what the man had said. Once I thought I heard Raf saying, 'Jenny!' but I didn't think I could have done, because he wanted to be free, didn't he? He wouldn't follow me.

The silk scarf clung round my nose and mouth, it was wet with my tears, or maybe sweat, because the

235

flames kept blowing gusts of scorching heat towards me. And other stumbling people came through the smoke with makeshift masks over the lower halves of their faces, they were coughing and weeping, pushing prams loaded with stuff, carrying suitcases, holding children in their arms, going God knew where, everywhere seemed just as bad as everywhere else. There was a burned-out tram in the middle of the road, its metal twisted and torn.

All at once there was a huge crashing and heaving and the next thing I knew I was lying flat on my face in the dark.

I couldn't feel anything at all for a moment, but I tried my arms and legs and they moved. My knees and elbows stung. I knew I'd grazed them. I thought: If that's the only pain I can feel I must be all right. I saw a little ragged-edged red hole in the darkness. It was just about as big as my head. The fire was roaring nearby as if it wanted to catch me and eat me.

A warm tongue licked my face. Muffi.

I put my hand out and found her forehead. I reached out to her back and her four legs and her paws. She let me touch them without crying, so I guessed she wasn't injured either. I felt around us. My hands found rubble on one side, a rough metal beam above me, and beyond that what seemed to be a section of mortared bricks. We'd been lucky. So far.

I wriggled forward and started to try and make the hole bigger. I managed to shift some bricks, but three more beams had fallen down there, wooden ones this time, and they barred my way. I pushed at the nearest one, but it wouldn't give way. I tried to get up on all fours to push, I thought I might be stronger that way, but my back hit the metal beam, jarring me badly. That was when I started screaming. I didn't scream words. I just let out sounds, desperate for help.

Suddenly Muffi wriggled away from me and just went out of the hole. I couldn't believe it, she'd abandoned me. 'Muffi!' I yelled. 'Come back!'

I heard her barking. The next moment Raf was shouting into the hole. 'Jenny. Jenny!' He'd followed me after all, I wasn't abandoned – and Muffi had only gone out to get his attention.

'I'm trapped,' I shouted. 'I'm not hurt.'

'It'll be all right,' he yelled through the hole. 'I'm going to find someone to help me shift all this stuff. But call Muffi, she's better off with you.'

I thought about her paws, and the glass on the street. 'Muffi!' I called out. She was there in a moment, in my small underworld with me.

I lay there on my face with her beside me. I was crying for joy because Raf had come after me, because he was going for help for me. Then I was frightened someone might guess he was Jewish. No, I thought, they'd never guess from his looks and surely nobody's going to ask to see his papers tonight.

I was uncomfortable on my front, so I rolled onto my side, there was just space for that. My hands pushed against something hard and smooth as I turned. It was an oblong tin. I pulled the lid off and found a soft spice cake. I crammed it into my mouth – it tasted so good – and gave the next one to Muffi. There were six spice cakes in the tin: I had four and Muffi gobbled up two. I thought that was fair because she was so much littler than I was.

It felt hotter now. I tried to think I was imagining it. A minute later I was thinking about burning to death, would it be quick, or – *no*, I told myself. No. Raf knows where you are, and he's bringing help. I was getting thirsty, but that had to be because of the spice cake. And the smoke, and the dust.

I heard Raf again, 'It's all right, Jenny, I've got help.'

Thank God, I thought. Thank God.

There was the sound of shovels scraping against brick and stone. A few bricks bounced down in front of me and there was a slide of gritty stuff that made my head swim with fear for a moment, but it stopped.

'Slowly!' Raf yelled. 'You're not digging in a sand-pit, you know. You'll bring the whole lot down on her the way you're going.'

Whoever it was started taking the bricks away one by one and throwing them down. But I'd heard the fear in Raf's voice and a little mad spark of delight flashed in my heart because it was me he was afraid for. I wished they didn't have to go so slowly, though.

It was torment to lie still in there.

I saw gaps of red light appear around the wooden beams, and a moment later, a hoarse lad's voice said, 'I think we could try and lift that beam now, Lieutenant.'

Lieutenant? I thought. What?

'All right,' Raf said. 'Just be very careful.'

There were dark shapes in front of me, heaving the beam upwards.

'Can you manage on your own, Jenny?' Raf asked.

I crawled forward. My grazed knees hurt, but I didn't care. I was getting out. I was out, scrambling shakily to my feet. Muffi came too. I picked her up again, to save her paws, while Raf and his helpers lowered the beam slowly down onto the ground. I thought they were all boys, they were wearing tin hats, but you couldn't see their faces, because they had their gas masks on.

'Are you all right?' Raf asked anxiously, turning to me.

'Yes,' I said. But I was shaking, clutching Muffi with one hand and feeling for my scarf with the other. It had fallen inside my coat collar. Raf took the ends of it and tied it round my mouth and nose again. It was filthy now.

'Well done, lads,' he said, saluting. 'Heil Hitler!'

They all saluted back. One of them lifted his gas mask up and said, 'Glad to help, Lieutenant, sir.' Then they ran off.

'Not so bad,' Raf said to me, 'the young lads nowadays.' I heard the grin in his voice, coming right through the handkerchief. 'They're air-raid helpers, they got separated from their officer. They're off to find him now.'

'Lieutenant, sir,' I said. 'And what's your surname?'

'Lieutenant Frey,' he said. 'I'm on leave from the Italian Front. You get it, don't you? Frey? Free?'

That made me laugh. I stood there laughing crazily on the glass-littered Kurfürstendamm, with the fire raging behind the empty window holes of the building opposite.

'Why did you run away from me?' Raf said. 'I want to see if Aunty Sylvia's all right, too, you know.'

'Mum!' I said. 'Let's get moving again, Raf.'

He walked beside me, saying, 'Jenny, I want to tell you. When I thought you were dead, I—'

Only the sirens were howling again, there was going to be another raid already, and a policeman appeared out of a fog of smoke and pulled his gas mask away from his mouth.

'Get to shelter!' he bawled. 'Get underground now!' He was really scared, I could hear it in his voice.

'No,' I said. 'We've got to go home!'

Raf said, 'Jenny, we won't do Aunty Sylvia any good by staying out when the bombs are coming down.'

'That way!' the policeman shouted. 'The hotel over there!'

He was pointing at a dark building that looked strange because it wasn't ruined or on fire. He hurried round, waving his arms and screaming at everyone else on the street to take shelter under the hotel. I didn't want to go, but Raf put an arm round me and dragged me stumbling across the mess that had been the Kurfürstendamm, into the hotel doorway.

We were in a big smart lobby with a wrought-iron cage lift in gilt-painted wrought-iron housing to the left of it. There were palm trees in pots and a subdued elegant lamp shining on an empty mahogany reception desk. I blinked in the light, I hadn't expected it. Then I saw two figures coming towards us, ashy-haired, with a fur of grey ash shrouding their clothes. The one on the right was carrying a dog who looked like a filthy mop.

'What?' I said, then realised I was looking into a mirror. Beside me, Raf had thick ashy eyebrows and a splinter of wood sticking out of his hair. I saw a queue of other ashen people behind us, treading filth into the expensive crimson carpet.

'Come on!' Raf said. 'It doesn't matter what we look like.'

I was still aching to see Mum, but I followed him and we found the stairs down to the cellar behind the lift. They were covered with linoleum, not carpet, but it was nice linoleum. There were tidy plain lights on the walls. We went down the stairs and came into a large room with sofas and arm chairs and shaded lights hanging from the ceiling. There was a billiard table in the corner and a wind-up gramophone with a fluted trumpet.

The smart people who were sheltering there were dressed in fur and cashmere overcoats and shiny shoes and they stared at us with horror-struck eyes; we weren't the right kind of customers for this shelter. A woman's voice behind me said defiantly, 'The police sent us here.'

A woman in a neat coat who must be the manageress said, 'You're all welcome, madam. Come and rest yourselves.'

We'd just sat down on a nice smart sofa when an explosion almost burst my eardrums. The lights went out. People shrieked, and a man said aloud, 'But I didn't hear any planes!'

'Can't have been a bomb, then,' a Berlin worker's voice said with heavy sarcasm.

'A time-fuse,' another man said. 'That's why we didn't hear it coming down.' There was a sound like a gust of wind and then a roaring above our heads.

Quite calmly, Raf said to me, 'The hotel's on fire.'

Chapter Eighteen

A torch shone a metre or so away from me. The manageress's voice called out, 'I need someone to help put the fire out.'

She had to shout to be heard above the roaring, but she still sounded as calm as Raf had done. People were getting up, I could just hear them.

'I'll go,' Raf said. He put his hand on my shoulder. 'You stay here with Muffi.'

I wanted to beg him not to go, I didn't want him to leave me, even for a second, but I knew I daren't try to stop him. He needed to prove himself, make up for all the months he'd spent hiding. And he was off, pushing towards the manageress. I reached my hand behind me and felt the edge of the sofa. I sat down on it, holding Muffi tight.

I saw the manageress's torch shining round a lot of male and female faces.

'Thank you all,' she shouted. 'I'd like this gentleman, and you, sir, and you, and you.'

Three of the men she'd chosen looked like soldiers on leave. The fourth was Raf.

'There are buckets of water and sand in the lobby,' she told them. 'And four stirrup pumps. Don't use the

243

sand unless the water gives out. We can bring the buckets down here to refill them, there's a tap...' She pointed her torch to the wall just beside me. I shut my eyes then, I didn't want to see Raf going into danger.

An elderly woman with a white lace-edged apron showing between the open edges of her coat fetched candles out and handed them round. I didn't take one. I didn't want Muffi moving suddenly and knocking it. I stared at the little flames lighting the cellar like Christmas and thought about the huge fire blazing overhead. It seemed so crazy, my mind went completely blank, the way it had done when the bomb had gone off in the street and I'd seen the child's arm. I sat down on the sofa. I could hear the water hissing as it fell on the flames, but the fire roared louder. Muffi stuck her head under my arm again.

I saw Raf coming down with an empty bucket.

'It's blazing Hell up there,' he said to me. 'I don't know if—'

He turned the tap on. A dribble of water fell out, then there was a sputter and nothing. I knew the water main had fractured and I still didn't feel anything.

'Curse it!' Raf said, and ran back up the stairs.

A man beside me said, 'They've got sand—'

'What good is that?' another man said, and his voice was shrill. I thought: They're scared, really scared, why aren't I? A moment later Raf and the others came running back into the cellar. It was getting hotter, and smoke was creeping into the air. It made me cough; suddenly terror ran all through me.

'Very well,' the manageress said. She was covered in ash and soot like me now, but she'd shut the cellar door as softly as she'd have done any time when she didn't want to disturb the ladies and gentlemen. She shone her torch across the room and picked out the door-shaped patch of roughly mortared-in bricks. She called to one of the soldiers, 'Will you break open our escape hatch, Captain Brixen?'

The escape hatch, I thought. It's all right. We're not trapped.

The Captain shouldered his way across the cellar, seized the mattock that was standing ready there, swung it back and heaved it forward at the bricks. They came tumbling away. I could just see the wooden door behind them. He reached out to it and pushed. It didn't give.

That was a bad moment. Nobody said anything but Muffi whined softly in my arms. Raf put his hand on my shoulder again and squeezed it hard. Captain Brixen picked the mattock up and battered the wooden door with it. It fell apart in a mess of splinters and rubble that rolled loudly down onto the cellar floor.

'Blocked!' he yelled. 'Try the other one!'

It was only a metre or so away from Raf and me, and Raf stepped over to break it open, but as he reached it, the door, which was visible on this side, swung open towards us.

'Can we come this way?' a man asked. 'There's no way through on the other side.'

'It's blocked here too,' Raf said. The man stood still, his jaw open. I knew he didn't want to believe he was trapped any more than I did.

Muffi pressed herself against me and whined again. A woman started to scream, then I heard a sharp slap and she stopped. It was getting hotter, but the cellar door was holding the worst of the smoke off.

'I think we'd all better have something to drink,' the manageress said. Her voice was still really calm. She walked over to a metal cage in an alcove, unlocked it and swung it open. I thought: We can't be going to die, she's not worried.

The woman who'd handed out the candles didn't like what the manageress was doing. 'Frau Kaiser,' she scolded, 'the best champagne—'

'Frau Leffler,' Frau Kaiser said. 'The champagne's going to burn anyway. This heat is drying my mouth out and I'm sure our guests are thirsty.'

'Stuff the bubbly,' a rough voice bawled across the room, 'get us out of here!'

Raf shouted, 'We've got to clear the rubble away from that hatch.'

Frau Kaiser, holding a champagne bottle, smiled – I saw her – and said charmingly, 'Thank you, sir. It's worth trying.'

I felt beads of sweat burst out of all my pores and start dribbling down me. The heat was drying my mouth out, too. I did want a drink.

Raf was already at the escape hatch, he was hacking into the blockage with the mattock. I saw chunks of parquet flooring fly backwards. The soldiers came to join him, Captain Brixen brought the second mattock and the other men started scooping the mess to one side. Only the more Raf and the Captain cleared, the more seemed to come, parquet, splinters, plaster, and bits of a table and chairs.

'The whole of next door's in that cellar,' the man beside me said. His voice was grim.

A champagne cork flew through the air. Frau Kaiser took the bottle to the woman who'd screamed and held it to her lips. The froth went creaming over the woman's face and Frau Kaiser's hands.

'Ladies and gentlemen,' Frau Kaiser called, going back to the champagne rack. 'Come and get refreshments.'

Frau Leffler didn't protest again. I put Muffi down, keeping her lead slung round my wrist, joined the crowd round the cupboard and took my bottle of champagne. I noticed how sore my grazed hands were when I started untwisting the wire stopper-guard. There were already corks popping everywhere.

'Cheers!' an elderly man with a moustache shouted,

tossing a glass back, and I recognised him. He was a film star, Kattrin was really keen on him. I couldn't remember his name, though.

My cork went off like a bullet and the bottle smoked like a gun. I poured the fizz into a tumbler and let the foam settle before I drank. I didn't feel as if bubbles would quench my thirst.

Muffi whimpered and pushed against my leg. She was thirsty, too, but I didn't like to give her alcohol. I looked at the empty tap, there was a little puddle of water underneath it. I led her to it and she lapped it up.

Raf was working away at the hatch. I watched the muscles moving on his back; he was putting nine months of frustrated energy into it. Lieutenant Frey, I thought. Saving me again. I took another swig of champagne and my head swam.

The film star went to the gramophone and started winding it up. 'Music for our rescue workers!' he shouted.

One of the soldiers tapped Raf on the shoulder, then Captain Brixen. 'Take a break, mates!' he bawled. 'There are plenty of us who're fresh, we'll get out sooner that way.'

Raf gave him the mattock and made his way across the room to me, wiping the sweat off his face with his sleeve. Someone handed him a champagne bottle and he took a long drink out of it.

The music started off from the gramophone.

I'm dancing in your arms
And forgetting grief and harm
When I look deep into your eyes
My heart flies off to paradise—

Raf was beside me, filthier than ever. He wiped the froth off his mouth, he looked questioningly at me, just as he'd done in the Café Kranzler – and joy flew up in my heart like a wild, mad bird.

'Jenny?' he said.

The old film star pulled an old lady to her feet.

'Let's dance,' he said to her, and they were off, cheek to cheek. Another couple got up, and another. I couldn't believe this was happening.

Raf said, 'Jenny. Dance with me. Please?'

We had to dance in a very small space, with Muffi treading bemused half-circles round us on the end of her lead. Raf held me tight, as if I was the most important person in the world.

'I've got to tell you,' he said. 'These last months – Jenny, I've been foul to you, I know. I didn't think I deserved you.' His fingers tightened on mine.

'You didn't deserve me?' I asked. Something caught in my throat, setting me coughing. There was a haze of smoke in the room. It stank. I thought: Don't let us suffocate before we've talked. Please. Please.

'Ladies and gentlemen!' Frau Kaiser shouted, but her voice was breaking up into coughs. 'Gas masks!'

she managed to get out. 'Or some other means of . . . ' She gave up then. She'd got her point over, anyway.

I dragged my scarf up over my face. Raf fumbled for his handkerchief, and I picked Muffi up. She hid her nose inside my arm again. The gramophone stopped playing the schlocky, beautiful song, but Raf put his mouth to my ear and talked on behind his handkerchief.

He said, 'I couldn't let myself be happy because they'd taken Mum away and I was safe. Maybe it doesn't make sense, but that's how I felt.'

I found his ear and talked into it. 'But it was my fault, Raf, I ought to have got that first tram.'

'It's *not* your fault, Jenny. You might as well say it was your fault you couldn't fly to Moabit. Listen, when the building fell back there, I thought I'd lost you, too, and I realised . . . ' He couldn't go on for coughing.

The smoke was getting in behind my scarf, making me cough too. And then we heard Frau Kaiser croaking:

'The hatch is clear! Please, pass through in an orderly way!'

I was desperate to escape, but Raf and I were nearly at the back of the queue. The air was filling up with smoke, you couldn't see the hatchway, only the dim light of the torches people had got out and switched on to light their escape. Raf had his arm round me; I held onto Muffi and we were all still coughing, everyone was.

The film star and his dance partner were just in front of us. They were both carrying smart pigskin suitcases and the old lady had her mink coat slung over one arm.

Raf put his handkerchief-masked face to my ear and croaked, 'I realised how much I love you.'

'I love you too, Raf,' I managed to answer, then I was coughing myself sick. The fire was roaring louder than ever overhead, I couldn't believe that the floor was holding it off from the cellar. Now I was thinking: Let us get out. Please. Please. I so much wanted to stay alive, it wasn't enough that we'd managed to talk, after all.

Raf pulled me closer and kissed my cheek through his handkerchief and my scarf. We were still moving forwards, small step by small step. At last we were close enough to the escape hatch to see it in the light from Frau Kaiser's torch. A woman was heaving her suitcase through, bumping it against the rough opening. Go on, I thought. Hurry up! Then a middle-aged woman scrambled through, helping a frail old man to stumble over the rubble, then the film star's partner. The film star went after her; he was pretty agile, old as he was. And it was our turn. For the first time I wondered what dangers we'd find on the other side of the hatch.

I remembered my own torch and fumbled it out of

my pocket for Raf to take. He switched it on as we went through and we saw that the nextdoor cellar's ceiling had come down at an angle, its broken beams were still leaning against the far wall. There were trailing electricity cables as well.

'Don't touch them!' Raf said to me. I all but fell over the roller of a fallen blackout blind, but he reached out and steadied me. Muffi struggled – I just managed to keep hold of her. The red light of the fires outside shone in through the empty window frames and lay in patches on the littered floor. There was a gap between two beams, that was where the film star and his partner were going. We went into the dark underneath a section of the ceiling that was still intact, following the little torch beams. I could see the next escape hatch gaping ahead of us and the people going through it. The cellar after that was unharmed.

We clambered through one opening after another. When we got to the fifth there was a man complaining loudly about all the crowds coming through. 'Be quiet, Manfred!' his wife scolded. 'What do you think the escape hatches are for?'

Frau Kaiser, who'd come through behind us, actually apologised for the intrusion.

Three cellars later we heard the All Clear sounding and came up only a short way away from home.

I stood looking down our street and the houses were quiet and dark, as if the raid had never happened.

'Mum's safe!' I said to Raf. I was mad with joy. He put his hands round my waist, lifted me right off my feet and swung me round. Muffi wriggled and barked wildly under my arm. He set me down again; the next moment I'd pushed my scarf away and he'd got his handkerchief round his neck and we were kissing. I was still holding Muffi, that didn't make it easy for us, but we managed. There were bits of ash and grit between our lips and when I put my free arm up and stroked his hair I could feel it stiff with ash. There was a crazy, wonderful sweetness running through me – only Muffi struggled harder and harder till we had to let each other go.

Raf kept his arm round me as we hurried towards home, away from the red firelight into a kind of sunset light, towards the wonderful safe darkness, towards Mum. There were two women just in front of us with three children and a pram. I saw a toddler in the pram, peering over a pillow, a cooking pot handle, and the edge of a photograph frame.

'She lives at number thirty-seven,' the woman pushing the pram said to the other, 'my cousin Ulrike.'

'Are you sure she'll have room for me and the girls?' the other one said.

'It's a huge apartment—' the first one reassured her.

Another troop of uniformed air-raid helpers, lads and men this time, were hurrying up the street behind their officer. One of them stared at me walking with Raf. His mates shouted at him and he moved on. I felt a jab of fear.

'Who was that?' Raf asked.

'Willi Mingers,' I said.

Raf said, 'He doesn't know who I am. All the same, I think we'd better split up now, Jenny. Nobody'll think twice about me going into our building on my own, even if they see me, not with all these people wandering about on the streets. But if they see me with you—'

I didn't want to leave him, even for a few minutes, but I knew he was right. I even agreed to go first.

I went up the stairs and opened the front door with my key. Mum's bedroom door opened and she came up the hallway in a rush. She was holding the oil lamp we'd got for power cuts. She'd been crying.

'Jenny! Thank God. But Raf—'

'I found him,' I said. 'He's coming. Oh, Mum, I'm so glad you're safe!'

She put her arms round me and sobbed with relief while Muffi jumped up at us and barked.

Ten minutes later Raf was at the back door.

Aunt Grete had brought us some nice stuff not too long ago, and we sat there in our dirt and ate with Mum – she'd had nothing to eat till then, she'd been so worried – liver sausage and bread and apples and chocolate and some beer that I'd managed to get hold of the week before. Muffi got stale bread crusts and a chunk of liver sausage. We gave her our apple cores, too, and she wolfed them happily.

'What happened?' Mum asked.

Raf and I looked at each other.

She said, 'I want to hear everything. It can't be worse than the things I've been imagining.'

So we told her. She shuddered, and sat silent for a moment, then she shook herself.

'You're safe, anyway,' she said, 'only Jenny, you'll have to think up a story if Willi's chattered about seeing you with a boy. And' – sounding more like herself – 'look at the state of you both, you're filthy and I can't get water out of the taps up here. I had the kettle full, and we'll need to save that for drinking. There's water in the fire buckets, but we need that, in case the Tommies come back.'

Raf grinned at Mum. 'We can wash in one of the fire buckets, can't we, Aunty Sylvia? Dirty water'll put a fire out as easily as clean water.'

Raf fetched the bucket that lived on the back stairs. Mum got towels and dressing gowns for each of us – a warm one for me, not the flimsy silk negligée Aunt Grete had given me. And a hairbrush. Raf and I took turns to wash.

It was easier to get clean than I'd thought it would be, because most of the filth was on my clothes. I took them off and washed my hands and my face, shivering in the cold. When I'd finished I took the kitchen sieve and skimmed the floating dirt off the top of the water to make it cleaner for Raf. I dried myself off and brushed my hair till all the dust was out of it.

Raf smiled at me with his dirty face as he went in for his turn, and I smiled back with my clean one. He put out his hand and touched mine briefly. A dart of delight went through me. Mum saw that and she frowned slightly. But she should have been pleased Raf and I had made it up. She ought to be happy for me.

She looked at her watch. 'I'll have to take a turn on the roof,' she said to me. 'Janke's set up a rota to watch for firestorms. If they get going, he says, they can set a whole street on fire in minutes. If that happens, Raf will have to use the back stairs – let's hope it doesn't.'

I said, 'Shall I come up with you?'

I wanted her to say no, and she heard that in my voice. She frowned again, but she shook her head. 'You need sleep, after what you've been through.' She took hold of my shoulders. 'Make sure you *do* sleep, Jenny.'

I didn't ask her what she meant. I knew.

I tried to be the good girl she wanted me to be. I put on my warm nightdress and huddled up underneath my duvet. I heard Raf come out of the kitchen, and Mum telling him to go to bed, too. 'It's past two in the morning.'

I heard him say goodnight to her, and shut his bedroom door. I lay in the dark and every bit of my body fought sleep.

The clock in the hall struck the half hour. I heard Mum open the front door and go out. I heard her key turning in the lock from outside, heard her footsteps start up the stairs and go out of earshot.

It was hopeless. I got up.

I groped in my drawer and fetched out the silk nightie and negligée. I didn't put the warm dressing gown on, though I was shivering, and I was in such a hurry all of a sudden that I didn't put slippers on either, but I did stop to dab on some of the perfume Paula had given me. I went out into the dark, feeling my way past the door frame, through the hall and into Raf's room.

I heard the springs creak as he sat up in bed, and the rasp of a match on the side of the box. The next minute he was holding the lighted match to the emergency candle by his bedside. The small yellow flame grew up from the wick, pointing straight at the ceiling, and I could see his face in the light, all soft, and a little bewildered, as if he'd just been dozing off. Suddenly I was scared; what'd he think of me, coming in to him like this? I looked at the floor. I was ready to run out of the room.

'Oh, Jenny,' Raf said. 'You're so beautiful.'

Chapter Nineteen

The silk negligée and nightie didn't stay on me long.

I felt shy and thrilled to have him look at me naked. He said again, 'You're so beautiful.' His voice shook. 'Jenny,' he said. 'I want you.'

I pulled his nightshirt off. Now it was my turn to look at him. All of him. Then we were close against each other, his hands had found my breasts, and we were kissing each other, crazy for each other.

Only he drew away for a moment. No, I thought, reaching out to pull him back.

He said, 'Jenny, are you sure?'

'Yes.'

'Even if – if you had a baby?'

I said, 'I don't care.'

He was worried about hurting me. It did hurt, but I wanted him so much I didn't care about that either. It was over rather quickly, and he said, 'Sorry, Jenny – are you disappointed?'

'Disappointed?' I said. 'I love you.' I stroked his hair and he kissed me, but he was still worried. I had to let him know how happy I felt. I said, 'It was lovely. I belong to you now. Properly.'

'Thank you, Jenny,' he said, kissing my face very gently. '*Thank you.*'

I loved those gentle kisses. I put my head on his shoulder and peace crept over me, it felt as if I was slipping into warm water. I fell asleep like that, close to him.

It was dark in the room when we woke up, because of the blackout blind, but it felt late. Raf stirred beside me and yawned.

'Jenny,' he said. 'I didn't dream you. Oh, my God, what time is it?'

I looked at the luminous dial on Karl's alarm clock.

'Eleven o'clock. I'd better get up.' I put on my nightie and negligée.

Raf said, 'What are we going to tell your mother?'

'I don't know,' I said.

It was worse than I'd thought. I opened the door and there she was in the hallway.

'Jenny.' I was shocked to see she was almost in tears. 'I need to come in there. I want to talk to you both.'

Raf lit his candle and put on his dressing gown that had been Karl's. I perched on the desk – I didn't want to sit on the bed – and shivered in the chill morning air. I was curling up with horror at what she might say.

Mum said, 'Have either of you thought about the risks you're running?'

I thought: No! Don't talk about it! But what I said was, 'I don't think it's a risk, Mum. I'd be happy if I had Raf's baby.'

She sighed impatiently. 'And who'll we say is the father if you get pregnant?'

I said, 'Lieutenant Frey?'

'What?'

I said, 'That's who Raf told the air-raid helpers he was last night.'

'So you'll say you just went out and met this soldier and in the middle of the bombing, you – Jenny, how's anyone going to believe that?' She got up and went out of the room. A few moments later she came back with two small packets and threw them down on the bed. 'If it's not too late . . .' she said.

I felt my cheeks flush red. I didn't know where to look. And I didn't want to think about the reason why Mum had those packets. I ran away to my own room, where it was still dark, and buried myself under the bedclothes. I never wanted anyone to see me again.

Then I heard the door open.

'Go away,' I said.

It was Raf, and he didn't go away. He sat down next to me on the bed and put his hand on my side. That made it hard for me to stay still, but I wouldn't move. I couldn't believe that Mum had talked about me and Raf, that she knew. It was dreadful.

He said, 'Your mother's right, Jenny.'

I said, 'She's spoiled everything.'

Patiently, he said, 'I can't hear you when you're in there.'

I pulled the duvet away from my face. He'd brought

his candle in, so I could see his worried expression. I could feel my anger melting, but I hung onto the last dregs of it.

'It was so lovely last night, not thinking about anything – and it's probably really complicated, using those things . . .'

He gave me the grin. 'We can learn a new skill.' He made me laugh then, the way he always could when he wanted to. 'Come out of that duvet so I can kiss you properly.'

The grown-up, reasonable part of me knew he and Mum were right, so I did the sensible thing, but I really, secretly, hoped his baby was already growing inside me.

Janke came and told us there was water in the cellar. The pressure wasn't high enough to get it upstairs, but we could go down with buckets. I met Frau Tillmann there.

'Thank God you're safe!' She shook her head. 'Your mother didn't say much, but I could see she was suffering, not knowing what had happened to you.'

When I'd finally got myself to face Mum again and have breakfast she'd told me how she'd explained my absence – and her worry – to the other people in the cellar. She'd said I'd been taking an order to a customer near the Botanical Gardens. We spent about half an hour working out what my story of the evening was going to be. And even though Frau

Tillmann and Janke had seen Raf, we weren't going to mention him to them.

Frau Tillmann picked up her bucket and sighed at the weight of it. 'It was very inconsiderate of those people, expecting you to go home in the blackout.'

I put my bucket down and turned the tap on. 'Mum wanted me to wait till today, but I thought it'd be fine if I took Muffi. And I didn't expect a raid.'

'Young people.' She shook her head again. 'They never think anything can happen to them. So where were you when the bombs started falling?'

'I was on the underground,' I said, 'coming home.' We'd decided to stick as closely to the truth as possible. 'The train stopped at Kurfürstendamm when the sirens went off and we sheltered there. Getting back was awful. I don't want to think about it.'

She nodded darkly. 'They say there was a train on fire going round the outside of the city. It didn't stop till it ran out of coal and all the time the driver was dead and so were all the passengers.'

Frau Janke came down with *her* bucket and I said the same things to her. Frau Tillmann talked about the trainload of corpses again and Frau Janke said the zoo had been hit and the elephants had all been killed. But the lions had escaped and they'd been seen roaming the streets.

Frau Tillmann shivered. 'We're back to the Dark Ages, having to carry water about and wild animals lying in wait to kill us. Well, I'd better get moving.

We've opened the shop up as usual. We've already had customers looking for new china.'

I took the bucket of water upstairs and told Raf about the zoo.

Raf said, 'We used to go and see the elephants washing themselves, do you remember? I suppose it's the same elephants, they live a long time, don't they?'

I said, 'Poor things, what had they done?'

Raf put his arms round me and held me close. 'You be careful if you go out. I don't want you ending up as a lion's breakfast.'

I did go out later, in case there were any shops left standing. I put my trousers on because I'd have to climb over the rubble, and a pair of walking shoes. The burned smell hanging in the air was worse than anything I'd ever imagined. I wrapped my scarf round my mouth so I wouldn't throw up, and joined the crowd of Berliners picking their way through the remains of the city. Some of them had shopping bags, like me, others were pushing handcarts with furniture on them, or carrying suitcases.

The baker was only a few doors away, and he was open. I joined the queue just behind Frau Mattes from up the road. Gaby Mattes had been in my class.

'All last night,' Frau Mattes said to me through her flowered scarf, 'however bad it was, I was so glad I'd sent Gaby to the country. Your mother should have sent you. It'd be a weight off her mind to know you were safe, especially since your brother—' but she saw I didn't want her to talk about Karl. 'Have you heard? There are crocodiles swimming in the river, escaped from the zoo, and lions and tigers on the loose.' She looked nervously around her.

An elderly man laughed harshly and said, 'They won't need to hunt fresh meat. There are enough bodies around, ready cooked for them.'

'For shame!' Frau Mattes said. 'A bit of respect wouldn't do any harm.'

'Too late for that,' the man said, and hit the pavement viciously with his stick.

The butcher and the greengrocer were a block away, close to each other. If they were still there.

I turned the corner and saw a row of burned-out houses, their chimneys pointing up to the sky as if they wanted to show everyone where the fire had come from. I saw blackened tiled stoves hanging on the walls. Down below, the end of a bath reared out of a heap of rubble beside the front half of a piano whose keys spilled out among the bricks like broken teeth. The people had written on the ruins: *Zimmermann, first floor. We are still alive. Moved to Zehlendorf* – and then they'd written up their new address. The Essers, the Westenbergs, and the Knapsteins who'd lived there were still alive too, and I was glad for them, even though I didn't know them.

Further on, there wasn't any writing, just a heap of

rubble and rearing beams. The stench there got in through my scarf, and I retched, but I stood still and stared at the ruin. Monika Schroeder from my class had lived there. She'd been a shy, mousy girl who jumped if the teachers shouted. Now maybe she was dead.

There were men digging in the rubble, terribly thin, scared men in striped uniforms, they had to shovel bricks into wheelbarrows and heave beams free while a well-fed guard strolled to and fro with a gun in his hand. Prisoners from somewhere, a concentration camp maybe. One of them tripped and fell over the debris and a guard stepped over to him and kicked him. I hated to see that, but he staggered up and went to his work again. Then the guard saw me.

'What are you gawping at?' he yelled. And I knew it'd be dangerous for me to get into trouble; I walked on. In my head, the guard was kicking the poor convict the way they'd kicked Dad that time, but I went carefully, making a detour round the loops of fallen overhead cables and a mess of ash and black branches that had once been a tree. I got to the block where the butcher's and the greengrocer's were, and it was still intact, another island in the middle of the destruction, like our block. Both shops were closed, but the butcher had a sign saying:

MEAT TOMORROW.

I read it and then the door opened. Gross nodded at me.

'Fräulein Friedemann. I'm glad you're still with us. And your mother?'

'She's fine. Where are you getting your meat from?'

Gross scratched his chin. He hadn't shaved today. 'You're not squeamish, are you?' I stared, horrible ideas coming into my head. He said, 'The people at the zoo are selling the dead animals. I'm on my way there now.'

I went back, wondering whether I'd be able to eat elephant meat.

The men in the striped uniforms were carrying a figure out of the rubble. I saw black legs and arms, stiffly bent at right angles, sticking out from underneath an embroidered tablecloth that the rescuers had put over the head and body. The worst thing was what looked like white claws at the fingertips. They weren't claws, they were ends of bone.

I was retching, my breakfast shot into my throat in a slurry of sourness. Two women came in the opposite direction. They glanced at me, but a girl being sick on the street was nothing to them. I heard one say, 'And the phosphorus from the incendiaries, it comes down in flakes, and if that so much as touches you it burns you right down to the bone.'

I didn't see any big cats.

We ate at five thirty as usual; we did the washing up; we sat down; and Mum, who'd finished a dress for

Aunt Grete that day, fell asleep in the armchair Raf had carried into the kitchen for her. I needed to keep up with my work, so I sat at the table and stitched away at a brown-faced dwarf with a green jacket and a red pointed cap. He was the biggest in a set of seven. I had Snow White to do as well. We hadn't got the electricity back but the oil lamp gave enough light for me to work by.

I looked at Raf. He was drawing a building and it had all his attention. I knew architects usually drew on huge sheets of paper, but Raf had to fit his designs onto the exercise book I'd got him. They were tiny, like houses for fleas to live in. He looked up suddenly, riffling his hair with his hand, then our eyes met and his face lit up. I knew he was remembering last night. I wanted to creep over to him and kiss him, only Mum woke up, and a moment later the sirens started.

I put my work down, Raf put down his notebook. We were in each other's arms, clutching each other. Mum just went and began opening the windows. The cold air and the howling siren noise came into the room together.

I swallowed hard. 'I'll stay up here with Raf.'

'Are you out of your mind?' Mum demanded. 'How would I explain that? It was bad enough last night.'

'But I can't leave him behind.' I was crying.

'Cheer up,' Raf said. His heart was thumping against me, but he grinned. 'I'll be all right, I've got my tin hat.'

'What?' I asked stupidly.

'The colander. And I'll crawl under the table.'

I had to let go of him. I had to help Mum with the windows. Raf couldn't, in case someone shone a torch up there and saw him.

We went down to the cellar with our suitcases in one hand and our torches in the other. Mum was carrying the oil lamp. I felt as if my heart was tearing apart.

Frau Tillmann came down the steps after us, saying we had to hold onto our ribs when the bombs went off so the blast wouldn't rupture our lungs. I hadn't done that yesterday and my lungs were all right, but I still started worrying about Raf, who didn't know it. And how could I hold onto Muffi's ribs?

'The best thing,' Frau Mingers said – she was just in front of us – 'is to sit with your back against an outside wall.' She scuttled to the wall that ran along the street and plonked herself down there.

We sat with our oil lamps and candles, waiting for the bombers to arrive. I saw Janke rub his jaw and realised how tight mine was. I thought: I want us to make love again, at least once more. I felt the first shock of blast from far away.

I bit my lip and started twisting Muffi's locks round and round. She turned her head and licked my hand. I could feel her heart racing inside her narrow ribcage. I thought: They mustn't kill Raf, they mustn't.

Frau Tillmann was looking at Muffi. 'Poor little beast, she doesn't understand.'

Frau Mingers snorted. 'She should be upstairs.'

Janke said grimly, 'They shouldn't need to drop their Christmas-tree flares tonight, the city's still lit up with all the fires they left behind them yesterday.'

I imagined the magnesium flares drifting down, sparking prettily over the red glare of the fires and the plumes of smoke. I imagined the searchlights moving through the sky, trying to catch the bombers so that the guns in the flak towers could shoot them down. And I was thinking: Get them all, so they can't kill Raf.

An explosion shook the walls and made the useless light bulb dance. And Raf was upstairs, crouched under the kitchen table, he'd have the cream colander with its green rim sitting ridiculously on his head. I tried to send a message to him: I love you, Raf, I love you. I thought I felt his message coming back: I love you too, Jenny.

Something came down hard and the whole house seemed to heave.

'God,' Janke muttered. 'That was close.'

Then Frau Mingers opened her mouth and started on a Nazi song:

'*Clear the street for the brown batallions marching*
Clear the street for the gallant brownshirt man
The yearning millions at our flag are gazing –

'Aren't you going to join in?' she demanded, staring threateningly round at us.

269

So we had to sing the whole thing for fear she might denounce us, and I wanted to stop singing and yell at her, 'I'm sleeping with the boy I love, and he's a Jew, do you hear? I'm contaminating the race with him, that's what you call it. And I'd really like to have a baby, a sweet little half-Jewish baby and if I do he'll be so much prettier than your horrible Aryan goblins—'

It came to me that everyone in that cellar – except Frau Mingers – might know that Raf was up there on his own in our apartment. If Janke had told his wife and Frau Tillmann had told Herr Tillmann they'd all be hoping he'd survive. They were fond of him, they'd known him from childhood up. That made me feel a tiny bit better.

The All Clear sounded and our house was still standing, but I couldn't go back to Raf. It was my turn to go up on the roof to fire-watch with Janke. My feet crunched on fallen lumps of plaster as I followed him through the attic. The bombs had shaken the cobwebs loose and they were hanging in rags from the wooden beams.

Janke said suddenly, 'When you were little mites you used to come and play here on rainy days, the three of you.'

'Yes,' I said cautiously.

'Proper little brats you were,' he said. 'I was always having to bawl you out.' But he sounded sad. 'Bad times,' he added. 'There's a tile off there, I'll have to get that fixed. All right, up we go.'

He went awkwardly up the steep flight of stairs – it was almost a ladder and tough going for him, with his artificial leg.

I'd never been on the roof. Karl had said he'd been, but Raf and I didn't believe him. The trap door had always been firmly locked when we'd tried.

I put my scarf round my face.

'Can't bear a gas mask, eh?' Janke asked, from behind his own scarf. I nodded. He laughed harshly. 'If there ever was a gas attack, we'd suffocate in those things, anyway.' We came out of the trap door. We were right beside the chimney. 'Do you like my crow's nest?' Janke asked. 'Neat, isn't it? Made it ages ago.'

He'd rigged up a rough wooden platform with a rail round it. We stood there with our backs to the chimney. I couldn't see anything because of the smoke blowing across the roof. Then it cleared.

On our side of the street and opposite there was a dark mass of untouched houses that reached about fifty metres to the next street down and about fifty more to the last street before the Kurfürstendamm. Beyond that there were houses burning like bonfires.

'Dear God,' muttered Janke, and then, 'We'll have bombed-out families quartered on us, Fräulein, you can be sure of that, with four big apartments standing empty. People we don't know.' He paused and looked at me. What's coming? I wondered.

He said, 'Tell the lad to stay indoors from now on. It's not safe, what he's been doing.'

He didn't say anything else. I didn't answer. We stayed up there for two hours, watching Berlin burn.

I washed my face and hands before I went to join Raf in bed. He was awake.

'I was worried about you,' he said. 'Is it bad out there?'

'Yes.' He put his arms round me and we kissed. I was already forgetting everything except him, but I said, 'Was it awful up here, in the raid?'

'You get used to it,' he said, then, 'Yes. But I shouted again. And I thought about you, that cheered me up.'

His hands ran down my body. I knew what he meant.

Afterwards, he said, 'Was that better than last night?'

I gave him a sleepy kiss. '*Even* better.'

I slept with my back against his front, held in the warm curve of his body. I don't think either of us moved all night, we were so tired.

Chapter Twenty

The butcher was still there the next day, and he had his zoo meat. The greengrocer's was still shuttered up.

'Antelope,' Herr Gross said to me, wrapping the meat up in newspaper. 'Tastes just like venison. A nice treat for you, only will you be able to cook it?'

I said, 'Janke's building an oven in the yard for everyone to use. We're all bringing coal down.'

'Plenty of firewood about,' the butcher said, grimacing. 'Thanks to the Tommies, though they seem to have put ladies' legs out of fashion.' He grimaced again at my trousers. I laughed, and he laughed back. He was a good sort.

The baker wasn't open, he'd run out of flour, but I'd already heard from Frau Tillmann that the Nazi welfare women were handing out black bread. I went to join the queue at one of their stalls. They had big oblong loaves that they were cutting in half with mechanical slicers, raising the blade and thumping it down. When it was my turn and I got my half-loaf, the woman smiled at me. 'Keep your pecker up, my girl,' she said, 'we're going to win through.'

She reminded me of Kattrin. It was the way she talked, and something about her square, straightforward face.

I had to smile back, as if she was Kattrin, and I was grateful for the bread anyway. The bread the Nazis had given me to feed a Jew in hiding.

I thought, how can she be so nice and be one of them? Then I was thinking: But we're all in this together. Whoever we are, we're all being bombed, aren't we? And I wondered if that was a really clever thing to think, or a really stupid one, and I couldn't decide which.

When I got to our landing my belly cramped up with horror because there was Willi Mingers. I took the bread in my hand and held it firmly. It was a good solid rye loaf, it'd knock him out cold if I hit him with it.

He hissed, 'Who were you with the night before last?'

I'd practised this moment several times in my head, but it was still a shock to hear the question. But I gave him the answer I had ready.

'Why should I tell *you?*' I fetched my key out with the hand that wasn't holding the loaf. I kept my eyes on him in case he tried anything.

He stared back at me and I had a bad feeling in my belly. 'Slut,' he said.

The electricity had come back, but there was still no gas so we took turns to cook our zoo meat in Janke's outdoor oven. Frau Tillmann was before me on the rota: she was standing there in a pair of red ski trousers, cooking crocodile tail.

274

'It smells good,' she said. 'I never thought it would, but have a sniff for yourself, Jenny.' She pulled the lid of her pot sideways and I sniffed. It did.

The Broomstick came down early for her turn, flying the flag of Nazi womanliness with a saggy skirt and a pair of woollen stockings that were knobbled with darns. She looked at my trousers and clicked her tongue before she came out with her 'Heil Hitler!'

'Good morning,' I said.

She clicked her tongue again. 'I suppose I should be glad we're living in a house with mongrel traitors. There's no need to wonder why this place is still standing. Frau Friedemann has told the British where she lives.'

I started to laugh, I couldn't help it. It was so crazy, the idea that the British bombers could organise their targeting accurately enough to miss our house every time. She hissed at me, 'One day you'll be laughing on the other side of your face, you filthy little bitch.'

Frau Janke, who'd come down to the bin, turned on Frau Mingers. She said, 'The Friedemanns are good people. If God's protecting them, we should be thankful.'

I knew Janke had told her about Raf.

I said to Raf, 'I wonder what Willi Mingers would have been like if there'd been a better government?'

Raf said, 'He'd never have been anything but a swine. I wonder what I'd have been like if the Nazis had never come? More irresponsible, probably. I'd have liked that.'

'You wouldn't be in bed with me,' I said. I didn't say he'd been irresponsible enough, now that three, probably four outside people knew where he was hiding. Mum had told him that at dinner. 'You'd be living next door and we'd be seeing each other like a good boy and girl from nice families.'

Raf grinned at me. 'Aunty Sylvia would have liked that.'

I said, 'Maybe we'd have been so used to each other, we'd never have fallen in love.'

'Oh, no,' Raf said, and he kissed me. 'I was always in love with you.'

I remembered what Mum had said, but I teased him. 'Even when you used to pull my hair?'

'That was just my way of showing it. I'm better at it now.'

He was. We were both getting better at lovemaking all the time.

Once he said to me, 'I used to wonder why I was still alive after Mum – went – but now I know. It's not just for her sake, or yours, or even my own. It's to bear witness. Who knows how many German Jews are left?' He shuddered. 'People will need to know what happened. And I've got to find out more about being Jewish. If the Nazis hadn't come to power, I might have gone on just being German and forgotten I was different. Now—'

I said, 'When all this is over, if the Allies do win, I wonder what it'll mean to be German. They'll call us a nation of murderers.' I felt desolate and hopeless all of a sudden. I started to shiver. 'The Nazis have killed so many good people.' I thought about Uncle Markus and Karl – and there was Aunty Edith – and the rabbi, and the men who'd helped to carry Uncle Markus's coffin. Where were they all now?

Raf pulled me close to him, putting his face against mine, and then we were both crying. I was still shivering, too, even though his body was warm against mine. But he brought the duvet cover up to my face and wiped the tears off with it. 'Come on,' he said. 'You wouldn't let me give up and run after Mum, remember? We've got to keep hoping. Dad would have said that, you know.'

'And my dad,' I said, remembering how he'd told the rabbi about an ocean of light. 'Only with Dad, that's religion. I wonder what he's doing for religion in America? I don't suppose there are any other Quakers in the camp.'

'Uncle Dietrich will manage,' Raf said. Then he went quiet.

'What are you thinking about?'

'I wonder – would you and Aunty Sylvia do Shabbat with me tomorrow?'

Of course we did.

*

Mum bought some extra black-market candles for Raf to light. He said a blessing over them, then over us. He'd told us beforehand that it was usually parents who said blessings over their children, but he wanted to thank God for Mum and me. Then he prayed for Dad and Aunty Edith and said the Kaddish prayer for Uncle Markus and Karl. It was good, having a special time where we could make a ceremony out of our feelings and hopes – and cry. Even though I didn't know what I really thought about God.

Raf said another blessing over some beer we'd still got which had to stand in for wine, and over the bread – it was from the baker, who'd just managed to get flour again. We should have had special rich egg-bread called *challah*, but the baker's black bread tasted pretty good when we ate it.

He said afterwards, 'I'm not going to start demanding kosher food, though, Aunty Sylvia.' He grinned. 'It's a huge amount of trouble. The orthodox boys at the Jewish school told me all about it. Anyway, the Commandments are to live for, not to die for, I learned that at school, too. If pig or crocodile tail are all there is to eat, I've got to eat them. Anyway,' he grinned, 'I love sausage.'

'Is crocodile tail forbidden?' Mum asked.

'Reptile flesh is,' Raf said. 'Never mind. And I'll do the washing up and help with the cooking just the same, even if it is Shabbat. I'm not going to land you with them, that wouldn't be a good way of being Jewish.'

Aunt Grete and Uncle Hartmut appeared the next day, in their Merc. I was coming home from shopping, so I saw it crawling along the narrow carriageway that had been cleared through the rubble further up the street, where the houses had all been destroyed. There was only just room for it to pass.

'It's taken us two hours,' Aunt Grete said. She kept her fur coat on. Mum and I were wearing two sweaters each, warm trousers, and woolly socks inside our slippers. 'You can't imagine the detours we've taken. But we had to come and see if you were all right. It's like a miracle! I'm not coming about the dress, Sylvia, I can well imagine—'

'I've finished it,' Mum said. Aunt Grete exclaimed, but Mum only said, 'I'd have brought it to you if you hadn't come.'

'You'd have had a job,' Uncle Hartmut said darkly. 'And God knows how much more damage those terrorists are going to inflict on us. At least the moon's waxing – and the British are too cowardly to fly here at full moon, they know the Luftwaffe will pick them off. Do you know their Air Marshal Harris is planning to flatten Berlin the way he did Hamburg? God help us.'

Mum looked at Uncle Hartmut and said, 'I don't suppose the Londoners like being bombed either. Or Coventry, or any of the other cities.'

There was a long silence. I held my breath. Uncle Hartmut shook his head suddenly. 'I hope you haven't said that to anyone else, Sylvia.'

'No, Hartmut,' Mum told him. 'I haven't.'

There was another, strange silence, then Mum asked, 'Is your factory all right?'

'Only superficial damage,' Uncle Hartmut said.

'And your house?' Mum asked.

'It's fine,' Aunt Grete said. Like someone rescuing the situation, she went on in a determinedly bright voice, 'But you're a heroine, Sylvia, I can't believe you've finished my dress.'

They'd brought incredible amounts of food. Bread, potatoes, ham, eggs, sausage, more butter, and vegetables in jars and tins. 'Because I wasn't sure if you had gas,' Aunt Grete said.

'It's just come back,' Mum said, picking up a jar of gherkins and smiling at me across its top. We hadn't had gherkins for ages. There were some rollmops, too, that'd be a treat for Raf. He loved them.

When they'd gone, I said to Mum, 'Do they know, or do they just suspect?'

'I'm sure Hartmut knows,' Mum said. 'Grete – maybe, maybe not.' She unscrewed the top of the gherkin jar and fished one out with a fork. She cut it in half and passed half to me. I bit into it, loving the sharp taste.

She said, 'Whatever happens, his sort will be there, running things. And Grete's sort with their hands tucked into the rich men's arms, living off them.'

I said, 'Have they always got on your nerves?'

'Right from the moment I married your father. They've always patronised us. And we have to act grateful for all this food. I'm not grateful, though. I'm just glad to have it.'

'Me too,' I said. I picked up the jar of rollmops and got a plate and another fork. 'I'm taking this to Raf.'

That night the British attacked again, but we got off lightly. I suppose they thought they'd more or less demolished Charlottenburg, anyway.

Janke met me on the stairs the next day. 'Have you heard about Willi Mingers?'

There was a note in his voice that stopped me asking if Willi had been given the Iron Cross to go with his mother's brood mare decoration.

I said, 'What's happened to him?'

Janke said, 'Him and three other lads. They'd just left the Air-Raid Protection office this morning and a house wall came smashing down on top of them. They're all dead.'

'Oh God,' I said, starting to shake, because I remembered the crash and heave as the building toppled onto me on the Kurfürstendamm. Only there'd been no beam to save Willi Mingers.

Janke said, 'Their officer had to come here this morning and break the news. He stopped in to tell me.' Then he said quietly, 'You have to pity her, unpleasant as she is.'

Mum felt the same. She wrote a note of condolence and slipped it under Frau Mingers's door. 'I lost my son, too,' she said to me.

I gave her a hug. We both cried. Because of Willi Mingers. It was crazy.

'I don't understand,' I said to Raf. 'I really loathed him. If you'd asked me if I wanted him dead, I'd have said yes, only now I'm not glad.'

Raf frowned. 'You'd be glad if you knew Hitler was dead, wouldn't you?'

'*Yes.*'

Raf said, 'Hitler would only have been a silly man with a moustache on a soap box if it hadn't been for all those people who shouted for him and voted for him. And spat at me and Mum on the street because we were wearing a yellow star. And the Mingers boy was thrilled with his brother for murdering Jews in Russia.' He bit his lip. 'You know in that cellar. I felt good, working with those soldiers to get us out, but maybe they'd been in the murder squads. Maybe one of them killed Mum, even.'

That was a horrible thought. But I said, 'You did it to get yourself out, and me and Muffi.'

'Yes,' Raf said. 'I did, didn't I?'

Frau Mingers put a photograph in the shop window: Willi in his Hitler Youth uniform. There was a drape of black fabric round it, and a large piece of card, saying:

OUR SON. MURDERED BY THE BRITISH TERROR BOMBERS.

She shoved Mum's note back under our door. She'd scrawled across it: *Spare me your hypocritical sympathy, you stinking British bitch.*

A few days later she wasn't there. She'd gone to Bavaria to be with the goblins. Janke came to the apartment to tell us.

'The boys are on a farm there, and the farmer's wife invited her down, when she heard. Though whether she'll regret her kindness—' He made a face. 'Frau Friedemann, the Mingers has been saying the wildest things about you. And the baker told my old lady she'd been asking him questions about the Jakobys.'

My breath caught in my throat. 'What sort of questions?' Mum asked, keeping her voice calm.

'What they'd looked like. Did they all have dark hair? "I couldn't help her," the baker says. "I don't remember that kind of thing." That was lucky, but there are other people she can ask. I reckon she saw young Raf when he was out on one of his little strolls.'

I knew, though. Willi had told her about seeing me with a fair-haired boy.

I said, 'How long's she away for?'

'She's spending Christmas down there. She'll be back on the twenty-seventh.'

I looked at the calendar that hung in the kitchen. It was the first of December. Just under four weeks before she came back.

Janke said, 'We'd offer to take the lad, but if the Gestapo came, chances are they'd turn our place over too, you know what she thinks of me. If there's anyone else he could go to, someone who doesn't live in this house—'

Something inside me screamed: 'No!' I pushed my lips together to keep it in.

Mum said, 'Thanks, Janke.'

'The other thing is,' Janke went on, 'we're having a lot of bombed-out people quartered on us soon. I've had a notice about it, with the apartments standing empty, upstairs – and I don't know what kind of folk they'll be. Enough said, Frau Friedemann. Good day to you.'

I was in a panic.

I said, 'I don't want him to go away!' I expected Mum to tell me I was being selfish, to say I had to think of his life. She didn't. She just sat there. Then she said, 'I don't want to send him away either, Jenny. Only—'

I remembered the hammering on the door, the shouting: 'Open up! Gestapo!' And the Gestapo could check Raf's details in a file, they wouldn't need to ask the baker what colour his hair had been. As soon as they heard I'd been seen with a blond boy and wouldn't say who he was, they'd be along.

I could hardly make myself say it, but I did. 'I know. We've got to think about it.' I forced myself to

284

ask, 'Could he go to Kattrin's cousins' farm? Would that be safe?'

'No,' Mum said. 'Kattrin's connected to us, it's another obvious place they might look. If the worst comes to the worst, there's always the stockroom. Only we might not get away with that this time. Not when you've been seen with him.'

I hated Willi Mingers now. Alive or dead, he was a menace to us.

'We've got time,' Mum said, trying to reassure me. 'We can think.'

I said, 'Why does it have to be like this? It's not fair, Mum—'

I was struggling not to cry; I didn't want Raf to hear me. Mum reached out across the kitchen table and took my hand. Then she got up and came round to me. I leaned against her front and muffled my sobs in it, while she stroked my hair. Her belly felt so familiar inside the cotton apron and her trousers, I'd cried against it so many times when I'd been a little kid.

I'd been inside it, once. I felt the thin cotton all wet from my tears, and the gathers of her trousers against my cheek and I thought: Maybe I've got Raf's baby inside me, now. That made me feel a tiny bit better and I stopped crying. I straightened up and wiped my eyes.

Mum looked anxiously at me. 'I wish—' she said, then she bit her lip. I knew what she'd stopped herself saying. She wished Raf and I had never fallen in love. I didn't wish that. Whatever happened.

I don't think it occurred to either of us that Frau Mingers might denounce us in Bavaria. Probably it was a good thing we didn't have that to worry about.

There was a postcard from Paula. *Are you all right? We've heard terrible things about Berlin. Please write at once and tell me you're not dead. I miss you.*

I sent her a postcard by return of post and hoped it'd arrive. You never knew, nowadays.

Sometimes I dreamed I was at the lake with her and Raf, and another nice boy for her. We were swimming and playing about and ducking each other and it was all right, nobody minded that Raf was a Jew. Even while it happened I knew it was only a dream.

The new people moved in, and put their cards tidily on the letter boxes. Mum and I met the ones above the Tillmanns: Frau Steffens with her mother Frau Hanselmann and her six children, all under ten. The children had been evacuated, but they'd been miserable, so Frau Steffens had brought them back again.

'If we're going to die,' she said, 'we might as well all go together.'

Frau Hanselmann was a stout woman with white hair and red cheeks. She looked after the children while Frau Steffens worked long hours for the

Berlin Transport Company. Frau Steffens didn't wear a Mother Cross. I was glad to see that.

Herr Steffens was a prisoner-of-war in America, like Dad, but in Minnesota, not Oklahoma.

We kept trying to think of a safe place for Raf to go, and we couldn't.

Chapter Twenty-one

And then one morning I found out I wasn't pregnant.

Raf was still asleep: I thought I'd muffle my tears in the pillow and he'd never know about it, but he woke, and I had to tell him.

'But we agreed,' he said. 'It wouldn't have been safe.'

'You don't understand,' I said, still lying on my front and crumpling the wet pillowcase with my fingers, 'I wanted to have your baby!'

'Jenny,' Raf said. 'Look at me.'

I turned to him, even though I really didn't want to.

He said, 'After the war, when the Nazis have gone, we will have a baby. It'll be safe then. We'll walk down the street together pushing the pram and the Mingers woman will gnash her teeth at us.'

I had to laugh, and he put his hands round my face. 'It's going to be all right in the end, Jenny, believe me.' He started playing with my hair, combing it with his fingers, smiling at me. 'It's like silk,' he said.

The water came back on upstairs. That felt like luxury.

We had thirteen long, raid-free nights from the fourth of December onwards. When I took Muffi into the yard at night I looked up at the moon and blessed it for getting fatter and keeping the British bombers away. I wished they'd stay away for ever, I wished the Broomstick would stay in Bavaria forever. But the moon started to thin, and we got closer to the time when Frau Broomstick would come back and probably denounce us – and we still didn't have anywhere to send Raf.

Every night we made love and fell asleep and he lay curled round my back till morning, his legs still mixed up with mine, his hand resting on my hip. In the daytime we'd run to each other and kiss, holding each other as tight as we could. I remember his eyes all intent and loving, looking down at me – and we were both so scared of losing each other.

On the evening of the sixth of December, Raf and I set out our shoes like little kids and Saint Nicholas filled them up. Luckily he'd had Aunt Grete to provision his sack. We had an orange each, half a bar of chocolate and two spice cakes, walnuts, hazelnuts and almonds in their shells. We shared it all with Mum, of course. The three of us sat there cracking nuts and eating sweet stuff, with the tangy smell of torn orange peel filling the air in the kitchen.

When we went to bed there was another little present; three new packets of contraceptives lying on the duvet.

Raf said, 'How did she get those?'

I knew. 'The pharmacy round the corner got hit by

a bomb. Mum must have done some looting. I hope she was careful.'

He grinned at me. 'Shall we thank her nicely?'

'No,' I said. 'If she'd wanted us to thank her, she'd have handed them over in person.'

On the sixteenth, the bombers came back and we went down to the cellar with our new neighbours. The waves of blast shook our building like a dog shaking a rat. Frau Tillmann muttered, 'I hope I put enough straw round the china in the shop.'

I thought: Why can't I stay with Raf? No, why can't he come down here?

It was crazy, wicked, that he had to be up there on his own. It made me furious to see all the new people, even the six pretty little Steffens children huddling up to their mother and grandmother. I knew it was unfair, but if they hadn't all come to live in our house we could have brought Raf to the cellar for as long as Frau Mingers was away.

The bombers did a lot of damage to the city centre and hurt the railway system badly, but they spared Charlottenburg again. We even kept our water supply.

Mum and I kept working in our shop. I'd finished most of my toys; I only had one last order to deliver on the twentieth, to Herr von Himmelrein, an aristocratic old newspaper editor who lived in Dahlem. Mum's work wasn't done. She had orders for New Year's party dresses to keep her busy right up to Christmas Eve.

The Von Himmelrein grandchildren were getting my Snow White, the Seven Dwarfs, the Witch and the Prince. I'd taken a lot of trouble to give each dwarf a different expression, some cheerful, some dour, some a bit sad, and they all had different clothes, darned and patched in bright colours. I finished them on the eighteenth and took them upstairs to Raf. I put them on the bed. He looked at them and the grin spread over his face.

'They're wonderful, Jenny,' he said.

Everything I did was for Raf, really, and he showed me all his designs: he was imagining a new Berlin. All white stone and balconies and airiness and clean, rational lines.

He said, 'They'll need architects after the war,' but I saw an anxious muscle tighten in his cheek.

On Sunday the nineteenth we went to my uncle and aunt's – they were off to Heidelberg the next day, to spend Christmas with Hildegarde and Kunigunde. I didn't want to go, I hated leaving Raf. I had to, though. I got into Uncle Hartmut's car with Mum and Brettmann drove us between heaped-up rubble along street after street of hollow, burned-out houses that had been people's homes once. I thought about London and Coventry; probably they looked just as bad, and I felt miserable, I couldn't understand why things had to be this way.

It wasn't quite so bad out towards Wannsee, a lot

of the streets hadn't been touched, but there was a burned-out villa three doors up from the Hansens' house. The trees in the garden had been knocked over; their black trunks lay there with their root-balls splaying out in the air. I thought: But Uncle Hartmut and Aunt Grete won't get *their* house bombed, they'll have made sure it's safe, somehow. It was a crazy thought, but I believed it.

Mum handed over the dresses she'd made for Aunt Grete, and gave her the blouse she'd made her for free as a Christmas present. I gave Uncle Hartmut the tie I'd crocheted for him. I'd wrapped the parcels in some tissue paper that was left in the shop, tied them up with coloured wool and made red and green wool bobbles to attach to them. They looked nice. I'd made cards for Hildegarde and Kunigunde.

Aunt Grete gave Mum and me bottles of eau de Cologne. That was nice, though I'd only used half the bottle of *Fantasia de Fleurs*. And there was a big bag of food with extra Christmas treats. We sat down and had coffee and cake.

And then Uncle Hartmut said, 'I'm going to a funeral on Monday. My friend at the Interior Ministry. His plane was shot down over the North Sea.' He paused and gave us a significant look. He'd been careful not to mention his friend's name, but he didn't need to. The man who'd got Dad out of prison, and had maybe been shielding us from the Gestapo.

'You'll have to be really careful now,' Uncle Hartmut

said, looking straight at Mum. Mum kept her mouth shut. I stared at the floor. It was a strange, scary moment.

Aunt Grete immediately started to tell us about the concert Hildegarde and Kunigunde were performing in: they'd be dressed as Valkyries and singing German patriotic songs. 'The battle-maidens, you know,' she said in an anxious voice, 'the ones who used to gather up the dead heroes and take them to Valhalla.' Then she looked out of the window, as if she was hoping to see a flight of them winging over on their way to the Russian front.

'They definitely know,' Mum told Raf, when we got home. 'Both of them. Anyway, Hartmut's friend being dead makes it more dangerous for us.'

'Maybe I could go to see Kattrin after all,' I said. 'Let me get some coffee, Mum, it'll help us think.' I put the kettle on and fetched Aunt Grete's beans out of the bag. They lay in my fingers, brown and shiny. I put them in the mill and turned the handle and the good smell came out and filled the whole kitchen.

'There's probably no train service out there,' Mum said, running her fingers through her hair. So much of it was grey now, it made me sad to see it. 'Even if you did get there – how do you find out if we could trust her cousins?'

'I could just go out at night and find some hole in among the rubble,' Raf said, 'so I could live there. You could bring me food . . .'

Mum shook her head. 'Too dangerous. Too cold at night. You'd freeze.'

I said, 'If only Paula hadn't gone away. I think she and her mother would have helped.'

'Yes,' Raf said, 'but they're your friends. That's one reason why it wouldn't be any good me going to Kattrin. There's a clear trail from you to them, do you think the Gestapo wouldn't follow it? I wish I knew where the foreman from the gas works lives, he might know someone.'

Mum said, 'I could go to the Quaker House, maybe? If it's still standing. I could say I was going to give them news of Dad. I wrote a note to them when he was taken prisoner.' She smiled sadly. 'A way forward, that's what we need.'

I thought of Dad, and wanted him even worse than I usually did, I was sure he'd know which Quakers might help us. Or was I just thinking like a kid? It was up to us now.

'It's a lot to ask of anyone,' Raf said, chewing his lip.

I put my arms round him.

'You're worth it. I wish Frau Broomstick would drown in a river in Bavaria, though, that'd solve everything.'

Raf said, 'It's my fault for going out, that night.'

'Water under the bridge, Raf,' Mum said sharply. 'Don't blame yourself.'

I lay in bed with Raf holding me. Neither of us was

asleep but we didn't talk. I thought: Maybe we're panicking about nothing. Maybe it'll be all right if he stays. Only then I was thinking about what would happen if we were caught. They'd put Raf into a cattle truck and deliver him to one of those places where they gassed Jews. Aunt Grete would send Dad a letter telling him what had happened. How many words would that be? *Jenny and Sylvia executed. Hiding a Jew. Jew transported.* Nine. She'd have room to add: *Deepest regrets that your family so stupid, now who'll speak for us when war ends?* I started to shiver, Raf held me tighter, but we still didn't say anything.

I took the Snow White set to Herr von Himmelrein's house the next day. He lived in a grand villa near Dahlem Village underground station. It should have been easy to find his place, but I turned right instead of left out of the station. The first side street I came to was Fountain Lane, and I stared at the sign, thinking: Somebody told me they lived there, once. Only I'd no idea who it was. I went on walking, but I saw none of the things Herr von Himmelrein had told me to look out for, so I realised I was going in the wrong direction. I hurried back, worried I'd be late for him, and noticed the turn-off to Fountain Lane again. I thought: It was somebody with a dog, and my mind went on prodding at the name, trying to nudge the meaning out of it.

Then I found Herr von Himmelrein's villa. The house next door had been destroyed and the next two were so knocked-about nobody could live in them. There were the usual helpless, splay-rooted trees in their gardens. But the von Himmelrein villa was immaculate, cream-stuccoed with ivy growing over it – the leaves flashed in the winter sunlight – with a pillared portico and pillars supporting the balconies on the first and second floors and an onion tower above the balconies. I liked it.

The maid let me in and conducted me to a big sitting room that was full of elegant pale gold wooden furniture and papered with Chinese wallpaper. Herr von Himmelrein came in, opened the parcel, smiled, said, 'My grandchildren will be delighted,' and gave me the money at once. He had stiff white hair and a tidily-trimmed beard and moustache. His wife was friendly with Aunt Grete, but he'd said, 'Good morning' to me, not 'Heil Hitler', so I didn't think he was a real Nazi. I was thinking that I liked him, and suddenly it came to me who the person was who lived in Fountain Lane. The Quaker woman with the two rough-haired dachshunds and the secateurs in her coat. Agnes Hummel.

There are some things that decide themselves in your mind before you've had time to discuss them with yourself. I knew I'd found the way forward. She was it.

The maid came back with coffee for us both – good coffee, I reckoned a hundred per cent real – and I made myself chat to Herr von Himmelrein about air raids and my business and his grandchildren. He wanted to give me a lift home in his car. I said it was really kind of him, but I wanted a walk. Maybe he was relieved I said no, because of the petrol coupons, but he was a gentleman, so he had one more try at persuading me before he gave up. He kissed my hand when he said goodbye to me.

I walked back past the half-timbered underground station. I remember seeing a newspaper flapping around in the gutter just ahead of me, and an old lady bending to tidy it up and giving me a bad look – maybe she thought I'd dropped it there? I only shrugged my shoulders so she called out, 'Modern morals, you young people don't care about order, do you?'

I didn't see why I should answer that, I wouldn't drop newspaper, even a page from a Nazi one. I'd take it home for kindling. I saw the turn off to Fountain Lane and walked quickly down there, leaving her behind.

There were only four houses in Fountain Lane and they were roomy, not huge like Herr von Himmelrein's villa, but they had big gardens and were set well back from the road. I didn't know the number of Agnes Hummel's house, but that wouldn't matter if her name was on the letter box at the gate. There hadn't been any bombs down here and birch trees stood straight in the gardens, but they shivered in the wind, as if they were scared. The first house was half-timbered like Uncle Hartmut's, and there was a name on the letter box. Hubertius. The next one, diagonally across the road, was all shuttered up. The owners must have left Berlin because of the bombing. There was no name on this box. The third house wasn't shuttered up but the garden was neglected and I remembered the secateurs in Agnes Hummel's pocket, so I didn't think it was hers, though here again there was only a number, not a name, on the box. The last house looked most promising. It had yellowish walls and an orange-red roof and there was a rose growing up the front of it, just bare thorny stems at this time of year. I saw fruit bushes at the side of the house and there were several lovely blue firs with huge cones. Even in winter, the garden had a nice shape, and the name on the letter box was Hummel.

The gate opened without a squeak, someone kept it well oiled. I went to the front door, rapped on the door – the knocker was made like a dachshund – and listened. I expected dogs barking, but nothing happened inside the house. I could hear a clock ticking, that was all, then it struck twelve times. I thought: If only I had something to write on, I could leave her a note – no, that was a bad idea, I shouldn't put anything in writing. The wind blew again and a cloud came over the sun. Everything was grey now.

I was shutting the gate behind me when I saw her coming down the road with a shopping bag. She was wearing the same coat she'd worn at the Quaker

Meeting four years ago and a headscarf. She put her head on one side and looked at me, frowning slightly the way people do who know you from somewhere and can't remember where.

I said, 'I'm Jenny Friedemann.'

'Ah,' was all she said. 'Come in.'

She led me into a wood-panelled hallway and then into her sitting room. 'Sit down,' she said. I sat down on a leather armchair. I watched her face, especially those kindly grey eyes – they had tired shadows under them now – wondering if I could trust her, and what I'd say to her if I thought I couldn't.

There was a wariness behind her smile, and I realised with a shock that she was sizing me up too. She asked, 'How's your father getting on?'

I said, 'He's fine, but we miss him.'

'And the rest of your family?'

'Mum's well, but my brother was killed in Africa.' I bit my lip. I hated telling people that.

'I'm sorry,' she said. She hesitated for a moment, and I knew she'd decided to say something dangerous, to try me out. She said it, very quietly. 'What a terrible waste of his life.'

'*Yes,*' I said, just as quietly. Our eyes met. I saw her eyebrows twitch slightly. I took the leap. 'The Nazis killed him. I hate them.'

She nodded. Then she went outside into the hallway. I knew she was putting something over the telephone. I noticed the thick lace curtains in the windows, it'd be

299

hard for anyone to look in and see who was with her. She came back into the room.

'Why have you come here, Jenny?'

I said, 'We need help.'

'What can I do?' she asked.

I said, 'I don't know if you can do anything, but we're hiding a Jewish boy, from the family who used to live next door to us. Only the woman opposite is a real Nazi and she's getting suspicious. She's away till after Christmas, but then—'

She nodded. 'You're in a lot of danger,' she said. 'I'll see what I can do. We'll have to meet again, but it's better if we avoid each other's houses. Listen, there's a little café still standing in Savigny Square. Café Wagner. Do you know it?'

I nodded.

'Meet me there on the twenty-third, at four o'clock. If it's been wrecked, we'll meet in front of it. Now I'll make us some tea. You stay here and rest yourself.'

I thought if I was going to have tea on top of Herr von Himmelrein's coffee I'd better go to the toilet. She escorted me upstairs to the bathroom and showed me it, as if she was making sure I didn't open the wrong door. I was sure then that she was hiding someone herself, but I knew better than to ask.

I remembered the dachshunds when I was back in the sitting room, because now I was alone there I looked round and saw a photograph on a side table of a girl with the two of them. They were likeable-looking animals with bristly faces and grins. Agnes Hummel came back with a silver pot and two cups and saucers with roses on them, like Aunty Edith's had used to be.

I said, 'Your dogs look nice.'

'I miss them,' she said. 'They were old, they both died. I think maybe the air raids had something to do with it, though it's not as bad out here as it is in the centre, of course.' She passed me a teacup. It was peppermint tea.

I said, 'Is that your daughter with them?'

'Johanna,' she agreed. 'She lives in Heidelberg. They haven't had any raids there. I'm glad. And she's got a baby who's walking now, such a pity my husband isn't alive. He'd have been so thrilled with his granddaughter.'

I was sure, as I walked away from her house, that I'd done the right thing, but when I sat down on the underground train and rattled away towards home the doubts began. Agnes Hummel might be a Gestapo stool pigeon. She could have been that right from the start, planted on the Quakers to catch naïve idealists like the Friedemanns. Maybe the person she'd had in her house had been a Gestapo agent, not a Jew, and he'd listened in to all our conversations. The further I went, the more certain I got that I'd just betrayed us all.

I came out of the underground at Kurfürstendamm and went through the burned-out, rough-tidied streets. Someone had strung up a Government poster saying: OUR WALLS HAVE BROKEN BUT NOT OUR HEARTS. There was a lad picking bits of wood from the wreckage, and stowing them in a sack for kindling. He was whistling, keeping an eye out for the police. Everyone was doing that, though it counted as looting.

I caught the revolting smell of dead bodies rotting under the ruins. I'd be sick if I breathed that in. I put my handkerchief over my nose. I'd dripped *Fantasia de Fleurs* on it on purpose. I couldn't stop wondering what was going to happen to us.

Mum said, 'Your father thought she was a good woman.'

'I hope he was right,' I said.

Raf said, 'You'll have to trust your judgement, Jenny. I think you probably were right.' But his voice was flat and unhappy, as unhappy as I was now. We were going to be separated. I felt as if I was wandering in a grey country, everything was grey, sky, buildings, people, earth.

'If the Gestapo do come,' Raf said, 'I'll go down the back stairs and out into the yard. Maybe they won't guard that door. It's a chance, anyway. I'll go to ground in the bike shed, there's a little space at the back there – *you* remember, Jenny.'

I said to Mum, 'It's like a tunnel that reaches round the corner behind Janke's tool shed. It was always our secret hiding place. We didn't even tell Karl.'

She looked at me, halfway between smiling and crying. 'Was that the place that used to make you so filthy?' she asked.

'Yes,' I said.

She laughed shakily. 'I love you both so much.'

When Raf and I made love that night, we held each other as tight as we could, as if we could fuse with each other so we'd never really be parted, whatever happened to us. If only, I thought.

I was still spending time in the shop with Mum, but I wasn't making toys now. I was knitting my Christmas present for Raf. I'd managed to get enough wool to make a sweater, but in three different shades of dark blue, so it had to be striped. I was taking so much trouble over it, I felt as if I was making it to keep him safe, somehow. If anyone asked who it was for, I was going to say it was a commission. But though neighbours and Mum's friends came in to leave cards and say thank God we were still there, none of them asked.

'After all,' Mum said, 'you might be knitting it for yourself.' Then she sighed. 'I've forgotten what it was like when we didn't have to be careful all the time.'

The Gestapo didn't come so we guessed Agnes Hummel was genuine.

Chapter Twenty-two

There was the sound of the alarm ringing in my ear. I woke up and felt Raf's hands holding onto me. His fingers felt hard and anxious. He said, 'It's the twenty-third, Jenny.'

My throat tightened.

Raf said, 'Supposing she wants me to go away tonight?'

I hadn't thought of that. I turned round and we found each other by feel in the dark. I ran my hands over his sides and his back, found the corrugations of his ribcage, his shoulder blades, the muscles in his arms. I touched his face, loving his cheekbones, his bumpy nose, the tiny movements of his eyes under the closed lids, while his warm hands ran over my head and face, my back, my breasts. Then we were kissing, that was good, because suddenly I forgot everything except being there with him.

Mum didn't complain about us getting up late.

I ate breakfast, I finished the sweater for Raf, I went shopping. The greengrocer was open again and he'd got carrots and turnips – and a red cabbage for me, apples and onions.

'Marvellous!' I said, fetching out the cigarette coupons. 'That'll do us for Christmas.'

'So abstemious,' he said, 'not smoking. How do you manage to keep your nerves calm? No, you just live on your nerves, don't you? That's why you're so slender.'

He said he'd have a tree for us on Christmas Eve. I hoped we'd still be all together to enjoy it.

After lunch I sat on the bed in Raf's room and hemmed Mum's Christmas present; I was making her a scarf from a bit of silk chiffon that Aunt Grete had slipped me. We had the electricity back so there was plenty of light. Raf was next to me, busy with a picture frame he was making for Mum with pieces of wood that had been in the shop. I'd brought tools and sandpaper up for him. Now he was varnishing it. He wouldn't tell me what he was putting inside it. And I was on edge, clinging to every moment of this time together, dreading the days that were coming when he'd be gone.

Our parcel for Dad had gone off a long time ago; home-made spice cake, a witch rag doll from me because I wanted him to see what I'd been doing, a set of hemmed handkerchiefs from Mum. He was such a long way away. We'd looked Oklahoma up in Karl's geography encyclopaedia: it produced a lot of oil and gas and its fields had been reduced to a dust bowl a few years ago. Dad was still working in the hospital. I could imagine him going from white bed to white bed, patient, kind, generous, the way he always was. Then he'd go outside and see the dust whirling off the dead fields. He'd miss us terribly, the way I missed him, the way part of me, horribly, was already missing Raf.

I pulled the thread too fast and it slipped out of my needle. It was quite short, I'd need a new one soon, but thread was too precious not to use the last centimetre of it. I tried to remember what Dad had said to me before the war – about us finding the way forward if we held onto how much we loved each other. I licked the thread's end, smoothed it to a point and tried to put it back through the eye, but it went beside the eye, and I sat there holding it like a fool. I thought: But it's loving people that really hurts.

'What's wrong?' Raf asked.

'I can't thread this needle,' I said. He knew it wasn't that, though. He set his work down and moved close to me, putting his arm round me. I huddled against him and he stroked my hair.

The clock struck two. Two thirty. I was halfway round the scarf.

'What time are you going out?' Raf asked.

I said, 'A quarter to four. That'll give me loads of time to get there.'

Someone seemed to have speeded the clock up, how could time be going so fast? I finished the scarf at twenty-five past three, and put it down. I wrapped it up in Christmas paper that we'd smoothed out carefully last year and put away to use again.

I stood up, so did Raf. We went into each other's arms.

The hall clock struck the three quarters. I got up and went to get my coat and hat and outdoor shoes on. Raf came after me.

'Take care,' he said anxiously.

'Yes. I will.'

We kissed goodbye and he went back into his room so that if anyone was coming down the stairs they wouldn't see him.

Café Wagner was a come-down place with a stopped gilt clock hanging on the wall next to one of the huge cracks that were part of everyone's décor nowadays. It was quite full. Agnes Hummel must have known it would be, that was why she'd chosen it. I saw her sitting in the corner of the café. She saw me and she stood up.

'So glad to see you,' she said, 'and how's your dear mother?'

I realised we had to play-act. She called the waitress and ordered a pot of coffee. Then we went over to the counter and looked at the miserable cakes they had there. The poppy-seed cake looked more or less edible, so I chose that. So did she.

When it came, it was dry. I could hardly eat it. I washed it down with the cereal coffee. The milk in it was skimmed and tasted sourish – the cream had probably gone to Party bigwigs and the likes of Uncle Hartmut and Aunt Grete.

I talked about Mum and her Christmas orders, and how I'd finished mine. Agnes said, 'You've got quite a business, then!' and I said yes, and she made me tell her the kind of things I'd been making. She said she'd like a rag doll for her granddaughter's birthday, only she'd have to ask her daughter what kind of doll – and I knew her talk was camouflage, only when was she going to tell me if she could do anything for Raf?

It all felt unreal, like a film I was watching. I wished I hadn't thought about camouflage, because it made me think of Karl in North Africa, and wish he was still alive. If only he'd been taken prisoner like Dad, why hadn't he been?

My mouth was dry. I drank some more cereal coffee; it was obviously made from scraped burned toast. Agnes Hummel was talking about someone called Dorothea. I pretended, as I had to, to know about this woman and be fascinated by her move out to Potsdam to live with her sister.

'And you're still living in the same place,' she said, as if she was checking. 'That's good.'

In the end she got up and said, 'Well, I must get back home. It's been so lovely to see you again and I'm so sorry your mother was too busy to come.'

I got up, too, frantic because nothing had happened. Maybe she hadn't been able to find a place for Raf, after all. I knocked against the next person's chair and he muttered something about it was bad enough with the bombers coming so often, now a man couldn't sit and eat terrible cake in a café without being barged into.

Agnes Hummel fumbled in her shopping bag. 'I almost forgot. Here's a Christmas present for you both.'

She handed me a parcel that looked as if there was a small book inside. It was wrapped up in red cloth and tied with raffia.

'I'm sorry it's so little,' she said. 'Don't open it now.' She looked hard at me. I knew the parcel was something to do with Raf. I put it in my pocket and went out of the café with her. She gave me a hug and whispered, 'You'll have a caller on the twenty-sixth, around five o'clock. Get your friend ready to go with her. She'll quote this play. Page one hundred and sixteen. Rub out the pencil mark beside the line when you've read it.' Then she held me away from her and kissed my cheek. 'Don't worry, my dear,' she said. 'We're living through bad times, but we'll win in the end, I'm quite sure we will.'

It sounded like patriotic stuff about the war, but I knew what she meant.

Mum was upstairs when I came back. We opened the parcel in Raf's room. Inside it there was a softback copy of Schiller's play *Don Carlos*. I opened it and started to turn the pages.

'I know what it'll be,' Raf said. 'We did the play at

school. Have you found the page? Right. It's the Marquis of Posa asking the King of Spain to give his subjects freedom of thought. Isn't it?'

His eyes met mine, triumphant. 'Yes,' I said. The triumph faded.

'I don't want to leave you,' he said. 'I know I've got to, but . . .'

Mum went out of the room and left us alone together. After a while, he said, 'We'll have Christmas, anyway.'

There was another air raid that night, not a bad one. And then it was Christmas Eve.

When I appeared at the butcher's – with Mum, this time, because there'd been the tree to carry as well as the groceries – Herr Gross called his wife through and she appeared carrying a dress made of the silk I'd given her husband for meat. Her red face shone like a setting sun. Mum and I both admired the dress and then Herr Gross produced a goose for us – off-ration – and a carp for Christmas Eve. I could hardly believe it.

'You'd know Frau Gross was a butcher's wife,' Mum said later, peeling an onion and sniffing, 'the pig's ear she made of that dress.'

I said, 'But she was pleased with it.'

'Yes,' Mum said, 'but why couldn't she make a straight hem, for goodness' sake? And the way the sleeves were set in—'

I was annoyed with her for being so superior. I opened my mouth to remind her that not everyone had been couture-trained, but she said, 'I think it's time to do the blackout now, Jenny.'

I ran round the apartment, pulling the blinds down. Then I called to Raf and he came out of his bedroom carrying a saucepan full of sliced red cabbage, apple and onions. He'd been doing it at his desk.

'Dear God!' Mum said, looking into the pan. 'Even Kattrin never got it cut as fine as that.'

Raf grinned, delighted with himself. 'Nothing thicker than a millimetre,' he said. 'Shall I stoke up the sitting-room stove now?'

He picked up the coal bucket and almost danced off to the sitting room. It didn't matter how much coal it took, we weren't going to have Christmas in the kitchen. I went after him, holding the box with the tree ornaments in it. Mum and I had set up the tree in the room; we were going to decorate it together. Aunt Grete had popped a lot of red candles in with the food.

I was wearing two jumpers, but I was still shivering. I'd got my fingerless gloves on. Raf laid the fire in the green tiled stove, newspaper first, then the bits of wood that I'd filched from bombed-out buildings. The flames shot up, sinking and hissing when he set the first pieces of coal in on top of them. I crouched down and put my hands out to the tiny, growing heat.

'There,' he said. 'We'll let that get going.' He turned round to kiss me, holding his dirty hands away from me as he did so. After the kiss he brought them forwards and waved them in front of my face. They were purple from the red cabbage and covered in brown specks from the coal.

He said, 'Our stove was just the same as this one. I suppose it's still there.' He grinned. 'We could break into the place and see what the Mingers have made of it. No, I know. It'd be too dangerous. Anyway, I can imagine. Swastika-patterned wallpaper and pictures of Hitler everywhere.'

'Even in the toilet, probably.'

'With a notice,' Raf said savagely. 'We thank our Führer that we are able to crap in this bowl.'

And then we were both laughing till we forgot to be angry. Raf laughed into my hair. It tickled. I loved that.

It was getting a bit warmer. Raf put some more coal into the stove and went to clean his hands off. Then we started decorating the tree. We hung it with the silver and gold bells and baubles and put the wax-headed angel on the top. We squabbled about the gold baubles with the glittery snowflakes on their fronts. Raf wanted them at the side, I wanted them at the front because they were my favourites. In the end he gave in to me. 'As long as I get a kiss,' he said.

We hung up the long silver strands of foil. Then we fastened the candles onto the blue-green branches, fiddling the holders round to get them level. The warmth from the stove was unlocking the scent of the tree.

Raf said, 'Now we're safe inside Christmas.'

312

I knew what he meant. The bombers were back at their bases, looking forward to their English Christmas Day and turkey. Even the Gestapo must have trees to decorate and carp to eat.

I went to get my presents and Raf went to his room and came out with two little packages. We put them under the tree. Mum's parcels for us weren't there yet.

Raf said, 'Dad and Uncle Dietrich used to take it in turns to be Father Christmas. There was always a whole heap of presents.'

I said, 'It took me ages to work out why one of them was never there and Father Christmas was there instead. You know, I think it's always most exciting when the presents are still in their wrappings. They could be anything then.'

It was Christmas, but it was Friday night as well, so we had the meal and did Shabbat before the presents. Raf and I carried the dining table and three chairs into the sitting room and we lit the candles there.

Raf said the blessings over us, and we remembered Dad and Aunty Edith – 'And Karl and my dad,' he said suddenly. Then he blessed the wine – it was real wine this time, Aunt Grete had given us some – and the Christmas stollen she'd given us. After that we feasted on carp stuffed with potatoes and red cabbage, with its complicated delicious sweet and sour taste from the apple and onion and sugar and vinegar it was stewed with. We finished off with the buttery stollen and shared an orange between us and ate Christmas spice cakes from Nuremberg. And then we couldn't eat anything else. It was incredible, being so full.

Raf said, 'Do you think Uncle Dietrich will be having Christmas in Oklahoma?'

'Yes,' Mum said. 'But they might not get a proper tree. I don't know what kind of trees grow over there.' She took a sip of her wine and I saw she was crying. I put my hand out to her and held her wrist. That made her cry harder, but through her sobs, she said, 'Raf – your mother. She's alive. I'm sure she is. I can *feel* her.'

'What?' Raf asked. 'Here with us now?'

'She's my best friend, you know,' Mum said.

A piece of coal fell inside the stove and there was a flare of flame at its window. I thought: Please let her be right, please let Aunty Edith be alive.

Very quietly, Raf said, 'I've been feeling her too. I only hope it's not her ghost.'

We lit the candles and switched the lights out the way we'd always done on Christmas Eve. There was nothing to see in the room but the tree, its branches dark and gleaming slightly, the apricot-coloured candlelight reflecting in all the shiny decorations and the long trailing bits of foil.

Raf breathed in hard through his nose, smiling. 'That tree scent. It's the same every year but it always surprises me. Listen, shall I be Father Christmas?'

Mum said, 'We've got the costume, if you want it. It's in my room.'

So Raf went out with her while I sat looking at the lit-up tree and the presents that were still all mysterious inside their wrapping and all different colours. I thought about Aunty Edith again, knowing how much I loved her. For a moment I thought I felt her hand stroke my cheek and then – just for a moment – I was certain Mum was right and she was alive. Only where was she? In some hideous concentration camp, freezing and hungry? I said a prayer that she was all right and hoped there was someone out there who could make it come true.

Father Christmas arrived, walking into the room in his red robe and white curly beard. Only Raf was a bit taller than Dad and Uncle Markus, so I could see his shoes and the bottoms of his trousers. He went to the tree and handed our presents out to Mum and me.

Mum had made me a grey jacket, really smart, fitted and single-breasted. On the lapel she'd pinned a silver filigree brooch that had really come from Grandma. When I opened the little package from Raf, I knew Mum and he were in league with each other, because he'd given me a black onyx pendant set in silver filigree on a chain, with a pair of matching earrings. That was a present from Aunty Edith too, because it had been hers.

Raf had put a photograph of me inside his frame

for Mum. While she was turning it round and telling him how good the workmanship was, he asked her if he could have a photograph of both of us to take away with him.

'Of course,' she said, and her voice trembled for a moment. But that was the only time that evening that we talked about Raf going away.

When Mum opened my present I thought: Please don't let her inspect the hemming, or else I'll get annoyed, even though it's Christmas. For a moment, she looked as if she was going to, then she put it round her neck and ran out to the hall to look at herself in the mirror.

'Lovely, Jenny,' was all she said when she came back.

Then Raf went to open his own presents.

I said, 'Take the Father Christmas outfit off.'

He looked at me. 'Why?'

'I want to see your face properly when you look at them.'

He took it off and laid it in a red and white heap on the sofa. Then he picked up his presents. He opened mine first and his eyes shone. 'It's really good,' he said. 'I'll love wearing it.' Mum had knitted him a pair of gloves, a hat and a scarf, and bought him another book about architecture. He loved those, too.

The candles burned down and we had to put them out to stop the tree catching fire. We had more to light again the next day. Mum sat back in an armchair and listened to the record of Christmas music that the grown-ups had always listened to at that point in the evening. Raf and I washed up and then we came back and did a marionette performance for her; Pinocchio being cheated out of his money by the greedy cat – Raf's fox marionette had been smashed by the storm troopers on Crystal Night. We'd used to go down to the theatre to do the plays, that wouldn't have been safe now, but it didn't matter. For a little while I felt like a kid, safe and happy, manipulating Pinocchio, talking in his squeaky voice, and Raf opposite me, making his voice slimy and shifty, saying, 'All you have to do is to bury those four coins in the Field of Miracles and in the morning you'll have a thousand.'

At half past eleven, when we were already in bed, I heard the faint noise of bells from some church that hadn't been bombed. We got up and I reached behind the blackout blind and opened the window. We held each other tight to keep warm and listened to the sound ringing across the battered city – and then another set of bells chimed in from a different direction, and the ringing of yet another set came from a long way away.

'They'll be going to church now,' Raf said, 'for midnight service.'

I said, 'We've unwrapped Christmas. It's over.'

He said, 'I'll be wrapped in you every time I wear that sweater.' He kissed me. 'Jenny, we've still got tomorrow.'

Chapter Twenty-three

As soon as I got up the next morning I smelt sausage. I went into the kitchen to see what Mum was doing. Muffi was there, hanging round Mum's legs with her nose in the air, snuffling longingly.

'I'm stuffing the neck,' Mum said. 'You know Aunty Edith used to do that.'

I nodded. She'd always stuffed it with sausage. It had been delicious. I took our breakfast and went back to Raf.

When I went to get our lunch, Mum was back in the kitchen, sitting with a cup of coffee and the photograph album. It was open at the picture of her and Dad's wedding.

'Let me see,' I said.

She pushed it over to me. There was Dad, with all his hair and not a bit of grey in it, holding a top hat in his hand. He was beaming at the camera. Mum had a wreath of flowers on her head and a long veil embroidered at the edges with more flowers. She looked shy and happy. Of course I'd seen the photograph plenty of times, but now I really noticed how happy they both looked. They were so young, and looking forward to living together and having a family – only now Karl was dead and Dad was a prisoner in America. The usual stab of grief dug into me, but I pushed it away, it was too much when Raf was going away tomorrow. Instead I thought about Mum and Dad being two lovers like me and Raf. It sounds silly, but I'd never properly realised before that they were people as well as my parents.

I found myself saying, 'Mum – did you and Dad wait till you were married?'

She knew what I meant. 'Yes,' she said, sounding severe. Then she softened. 'My parents made sure we didn't have the opportunity to do anything else.' She smiled. 'Your father had just set up his marionette-making business, and I was learning dressmaking at Frau Winselberg's. My father thought that was all wrong, he wanted me to study, but I only wanted to make clothes. And then suddenly marrying your father seemed more important than anything else. But I finished my apprenticeship. Anyway, we couldn't have afforded to get married quickly.'

I cut slices of bread and spread Aunt Grete's butter on it. She'd given us cheese, too. I said, 'And Grandmother Friedemann didn't approve of you.'

'Your father's father had been very nationalistic, very royalist. Your grandmother felt just the same as he had. She thought it was an outrage, your father marrying a girl who was half English.' She hesitated, then she said, 'Your grandfather Friedemann was a hard man altogether. He used to thrash Dad and Aunt Grete, and sometimes he hit his wife.'

I was shaken. 'What?' I said.

Mum said, 'That's why Dad never smacked you or Karl and he never let me smack you either.' She made a face. 'You might have been a bit more obedient if I had done.'

I made a face back. 'I might have turned out like Hildegarde and Kunigunde.'

'Heaven forbid,' Mum said, laughing. Then she looked thoughtful. 'Do you know why your father ended up in the medical corps?'

'No,' I said. 'Tell me.'

'He volunteered with all the other lads in his class and when they started training they had to bayonet a sack stuffed with straw, as if it was an enemy soldier. They had to jab the bayonet in really savagely, and twist it in the sack to disembowel it.' I winced at the thought, and she nodded. 'Your father kept thinking about doing that to a real person and he couldn't bring himself to stab the sack properly. In the end they decided he'd be better off looking after the wounded. Your grandfather was ashamed of him.' She smiled sadly. 'Dad's a brave man, though.'

'Yes,' I said. Then I remembered Karl saying, 'We fight' to Norbert Mingers. 'Karl must have killed people,' I said. 'I'm sure Dad minded that.'

'Of course he did, but he never expected Karl to be the same as him. That's why I love him, Jenny. He's generous.'

320

I said, 'There's no one like him.'

We hugged each other and tried not to cry. I said, 'Aren't you bringing your lunch into Raf's room?'

'Don't the two of you want to be alone?' she asked.

'Come on,' I said, and she came.

Just before five o'clock I was terrified in case the note had said the 25th, not the 26th, and we'd all misread it. But nobody came that evening to take Raf from us.

We had a wonderful dinner of goose and red cabbage and potatoes and more stollen afterwards. We drank wine and laughed and joked. But Mum kept the stuffed goose neck back. I knew why. She was going to give it to Raf for his journey, wherever he was going. No, I thought, I've got to forget about that, it's still today, isn't it? I almost persuaded myself the war would end and the Nazis vanish overnight. The wine helped with that, I guess.

Only I couldn't get to sleep after we'd made love. The wind got up and I heard it growling and woofing round the house. Something fell off the roof and smashed. Another tile, probably, more work for Janke. There was a strange scuttering noise along the street. I didn't know what that was.

When I did fall asleep, I dreamed of Karl. He was in the room with us, shaking his head at us and saying, 'What are you doing in my bed?'

I said, 'But you're dead, Karl.'

'No, I'm not,' he said. 'Who told you that?'

I woke up. It was morning and Karl really was dead. And Raf had to go away.

Mum said, 'You'd better take Karl's rucksack.'

The one he'd always slung on his back when he'd gone off for weekends rambling with Fritz. Fritz was dead, too, killed in the Ukraine. His mother had come to tell Mum about it.

Raf put a change of clothes inside it, the two books about architecture, and the photographs of me and Mum that she'd given him. And all his drawings. He said, 'There's something in the desk drawer, Jenny. Read it when – when I'm gone.'

He was wearing the sweater I'd made him.

I ran into my bedroom and fetched the little wooden pig that Dad had made me for my fifth birthday. It lived on my desk. I'd always fiddled with it when my homework was difficult.

'There,' I said. 'Take that with you.'

'Thanks,' he said. Then we were in each other's arms again.

'I don't want to go!' he said.

The front door bell rang. We both jumped. He said, 'Not already, surely?'

'It's too early,' I said angrily. 'It can't be – that person.'

*

It was Frau Steffens. 'I'm sorry to disturb you,' she said.

'It's good to see you,' Mum said, though I knew that wasn't what she was thinking. 'Come into the kitchen, it's warm there.'

Frau Steffens followed her and sat down in Raf's chair. She was a thin woman now, but she must have been plump before the war. Her skin hung loose under her chin and I could see where her dress had been taken in. Mum could see it too, her nose was wrinkling at the botched darts. I wondered if she'd come to ask Mum to make something for her. Then I saw her face crumpling up.

'I miss my husband,' she said, gasping. 'And – I didn't want to break down in front of the children, and I thought you'd – you'd understand, because of Herr Friedemann being in America too, even though he's in Oklahoma, not Minnesota – and I know they'll have Christmas out there, but – a prisoner, you know – they've got him cutting trees down, maybe they make the Germans do all the most dangerous jobs, and—'

Mum patted her back. Frau Steffens went on sobbing and having her back patted, and I thought: I should be sorry for her, it's hard for her – only why did she have to come today?

She made an effort and stopped crying. She said to me, 'Do you remember your father at all?'

'Of course,' I said. I was furious. What did she think I was?

She noticed that. 'I'm sorry. It's just that my children

are younger, and they don't, not even Marlene. They're just used to being with me and their grandmother. Oh—'

She was off again, and I couldn't be sorry for her. I thought: How many hours is she going to stay? I couldn't go off to Raf, we didn't think that was safe when people came to visit. I thought she was never going to leave. And suddenly I was crying with rage and frustration.

She thought I was crying for Dad. She stood up and started apologising for upsetting me – that took another five minutes, with Mum telling her she mustn't feel bad.

Yes, you must, I thought. But at last she went out. I remember how she said, 'We have so much to cry about, these days.'

Mum closed the door behind her. 'Yes. More than she knows.'

It was lunch time. Mum and I ate with Raf in his bedroom. Cold goose and the last of the red cabbage. After lunch she said, 'I'm taking Muffi out for a good long walk.'

We made love fiercely, desperately, holding each other as tightly as possible, kissing as hard as we could. Afterwards he lay with his head on my shoulder and I kissed his hair and stroked his shoulders and all the other parts of him I could reach. I spent a lot of time running my fingers round his ears. I thought he had the most beautifully shaped ears I'd ever seen. Then he pushed himself up and started kissing me, my face, my body, my hands, looking at me, the way he'd done that first night, eating me up with his eyes.

'I love you,' he kept saying, and I kept saying, 'I love you too, Raf.' Over and over again.

There was a key in the front door. Mum was back. I heard Muffi running around. She came to our door and put her nose to it, snuffling; she knew where we were. I heard Mum go into the kitchen. I got dressed and went out to her. I could smell the coffee she was grinding from the hallway.

'We might as well,' she said. 'I'll bring it in to Raf's room.'

I got the coffee down, but I couldn't swallow the bits of stollen and the spice cake that Mum had brought in on the best cake plate, nor could Raf. We talked about the Christmases when we'd been little, we'd all gone out for walks in the Tiergarten or to Wannsee, and Raf and Karl and I had run round and played chase. I sat on the bed, huddled up to Raf – and the clock struck three, then four, and then suddenly it was half past four.

'Blackout time,' Mum said, standing up. 'I'll do it.'

She was being so kind, but I had a horrible feeling in my throat. Every moment hurt.

When Mum had finished she called us into the kitchen. 'I've got food for you, Raf,' she said. She gave him a couple of parcels. 'Stuffed goose neck, and there's the last orange, and the end of the stollen.'

'Thanks, Aunty Sylvia,' he said. His voice was hoarse.

I remembered how he'd refused to go on a Kindertransport to strangers and now he *was* going to strangers. I wanted to howl but I knew I mustn't.

The clock struck the three quarters.

Raf said, 'I want to say a blessing again. As if it was Shabbat.'

We sat down, and he said the blessing over the goose neck and the stollen, and over us. Then he hugged Mum and kissed her, and said, 'Thank you, Aunty Sylvia. Thank you.'

'The goose neck has pork in it,' Mum said, as if she'd only just thought of that.

He shook his head. 'It's what we always had at home.' He got hold of my hand and held it tight.

We kept trying to think of things to say after that, but we couldn't. It was torment, like on a railway station when you almost want people to go because the waiting's such a strain – and yet I thought I'd die when he was gone. Muffi came up to Raf and whimpered, so he took her onto his lap and tipped her onto her back and rubbed her belly. She licked his hand and grinned.

The clock struck five. I was somehow expecting whoever it was to appear at once, like a djinn in the *Arabian Nights*. They didn't, though.

We sat there, still waiting. My hands were clenched tight. Raf put Muffi down and took hold of me again just as the doorbell rang.

Mum answered it. There was a pause. I knew the person was saying the password. Then Mum brought her into the kitchen. She was wearing a shabby light-brown hat and coat; she was neither old nor young, the kind of woman you'd walk past on the street. The right woman for this job – she'd be hard to describe to the Gestapo.

She said, 'We can't go yet. I need to stay a while, or it'll look suspicious. Do you have a back entrance there?'

'Yes.'

'Good. After I've left,' she said to Raf, 'you go down the back stairs, turn towards the Kurfürsten-damm and meet me a few doors down. I'll be waiting for you.'

Mum said, 'Do you want some coffee?'

She sniffed the air. 'You've been making real, haven't you? I don't want that. I'll have cereal coffee. Don't want to draw attention to myself with the smell.'

Mum put the water on to boil.

I said, 'Where are you taking him?'

She said, 'My dear, it's better if you don't know.'

I felt put in my place, like a little kid, even though I knew she was right. I stared at the floor.

'We'll be together when it's all over, Jenny,' Raf said. 'I'll come and find you. I promise.'

I swallowed hard. 'Yes, of course.'

The woman looked at us, and I saw she understood. 'We'll do our best for him,' she said, and her voice was kind. She drank her coffee. 'Now I'll go,' she said. She turned to Raf. 'Count to fifty and then follow me.'

Mum took her to the front door. Raf held me in his arms for the last time, starting the count. Mum came back just as he was opening the back door. I went down with him. He unlocked the yard door, turned, gave me a brief, fierce kiss, and went away. I locked the door behind him.

I held the tears in till I got upstairs. Mum was crying, too. But she wiped her eyes.

'Now,' she said. 'We've got work to do, Jenny.'

'What?' I said.

'We've got to clear Raf's room.' I wanted to say no, but I knew she was right. So we stripped the bed together. There wasn't a laundry any longer. We'd have to wash the sheets ourselves later on.

'If anyone asks,' she said, 'they're your sheets.'

I realised she'd been thinking how to make us safe while he and I were still wrapped up in each other and our parting. We put the uncovered duvet and pillow neatly back on the striped mattress. All the time I was hurting so badly, I felt as if I was bleeding to death inside.

We didn't have to tidy the books back onto the shelves. Raf had already done that. Mum picked up the rubbish bin with his pencil sharpenings in it.

'You take Pinocchio back,' she said as she left the room.

I'd been waiting for her to leave me alone. I opened the desk drawer, fished out the piece of paper Raf had left for me, folded it up and put it in my pocket. Then I unhooked Pinocchio and took him back to my own room.

I hadn't slept there for weeks.

I went back to Raf's room. 'That's it, isn't it?' I said.

'I'll open the window,' Mum said. 'We need to air the room so it doesn't smell slept in.'

Mum went downstairs to the shop and came up with a fat misshapen envelope. The photographs of the Jakobys. They'd been in the stockroom all this time. I wondered if Raf had looked at them when he was down there.

'What are you going to do with them?'

'Burn them.'

'No!' I said. I felt as if she was tormenting me on purpose.

'Jenny,' Mum said. 'If the Gestapo come and smash open the theatre and find these, we've had it. They've all got to go.'

I said, 'Mum, I've got to have a photo of Raf at least. You can't burn them all, Mum . . .'

She bit her lip. 'I've got to, Jenny. There'd be no safe hiding place for it, don't you see? If you kept a photograph of him – well, you might as well confess.'

329

I was furious. 'He's got photographs of us.'

'Yes,' she said, 'and I shouldn't have let him have those. I've realised that. And there's another thing. Did he leave you a letter?'

I stared at her. 'Were you listening?'

'*No,*' she said. 'I just guessed. But you'll have to burn it.'

'I hate you,' I said.

She winced, but I saw her face set hard. 'You can read it first.'

I hissed, 'That's kind of you. You think you know best about everything, don't you, you must think I'm so stupid, and you don't care, *you've* got letters from Dad, and photographs of him, but that's different, of course—'

'Jenny—' she said. I just ran away to the scullery and started running hot water into the sink. I wasn't going to let her wash Raf's and my sheets.

I got the bottle of dissolved soap-ends that we used for laundry and poured the oozy liquid into the water, stirring it with my hands. I put the pillowcase to my cheek one last time. It smelt of Raf, but I wasn't allowed to have anything of him now. I plunged it into the water and started washing it. I was too angry to cry.

Mum was there. 'Jenny,' she said. 'I'm sorry.'

I said, 'I'm not burning Raf's letter!'

She didn't answer that. She said, 'Call me when it needs mangling. I'll help you turn the handle.'

I told myself I wasn't going to call her, and I tried to do it on my own, but it made my arms ache horribly. Raf had been doing it for us, he'd said it was another kind of training.

Mum came back. 'Jenny love,' she said, really gently, 'let me help you.'

Suddenly I couldn't be angry any longer. We both laid hold of the handle and turned it. The suds creamed out from between the rollers and the bed linen came out all flat and defeated-looking. I ran clear cold water into the sink and rinsed it, and then we mangled it again. You couldn't talk while you were mangling, you could only try and get your breath.

When we'd hung the washing up I went to my room and lay down on the bed. Mum didn't try to stop me going away. I took the piece of paper out of my pocket and unfolded it. It was a drawing. I thought: Is that all? Then I realised what it was.

He'd drawn the house he was going to build for us, after the war. It was in the same style as his other drawings, light and airy with a balcony that he'd sketched geraniums on. But it was a single house, not an apartment. There was a garden for Muffi to run in, and in the plans he'd put: *Jenny's workroom. Raf's workroom.* And: *Our children's room.* He'd designed a streamlined kitchen '*so that you don't have to skivvy, my darling*'. And our house was going to have a big sitting room and dining room combined, with

French windows opening onto the garden – and an old-fashioned tiled stove like the one in our apartment.

Mum came in to me with another cup of real coffee. She sat down beside me while I drank it.

She said, 'I do understand how you feel. I haven't got Dad, you know.'

I said, 'That's not the same—'

'Only because we've been living together longer. Do you think it hurts less if there's a lot of time to look back on? It hurts worse.' She laughed suddenly. 'I know you don't believe me, but it's true, Jenny. Anyway, we've got more important things to do than quarrel.'

I stared at her.

'We've got to practise,' she said. 'You know, how Karl told us to?'

So we questioned each other, we told each other when we gave unconvincing answers. Karl had said, 'Never tell the same story over and over again in the same words. That looks really suspicious. You've got to vary it, that's the way someone does when they're really remembering.'

Mum said, 'You don't know anything about the stockroom behind the theatre, do you understand? I do, because Dad told me. I've got my own story about that, but you don't need to know that. That way, if you're there when I tell it you can look surprised.'

I went to bed. I was cold and miserable without Raf. After a while I stopped trying to sleep and I switched the light on. I fetched Raf's design for our house and I looked at it over and over again till I had it off by heart. Then I got up and went to the kitchen. Muffi rose from her bed, stretched, and followed me in there. I burned the paper on the embers in the tiled heating stove.

I gave Muffi a few scraps of goose out of the pantry and thought: I've got it inside me now, the home we're going to have one day. Nobody can take that away.

Chapter Twenty-four
December 1943–March 1944

I pulled the duvet tight round me and tried to pretend it was Raf. I started to talk to him under my breath, as if he was there. 'We're ready for the Gestapo to visit, Raf, we've done everything. Only maybe they won't come, then we'll have sent you away for nothing.' Now I was crying. 'And I won't get you back, Raf, not till the Nazis have gone, and why are they still in power, everyone must know we can't win the war, why doesn't someone do something to get rid of them?'

I knew what he'd say to that. 'We've got to keep on hoping.'

'All right,' I whispered. 'I will, Raf, however bad things get. Even if the Gestapo take us away for questioning.' Then I thought of Muffi. We weren't ready for the Gestapo after all.

I ran into Mum's room as soon as her alarm went off the next morning. I said, 'Mum, if the Gestapo arrested us, what'd happen to Muffi?'

Mum sat up in bed, frowning. 'Oh God,' she said. 'How could I forget about her?'

I said, 'What'll we do?'

Mum stared at the picture of Dad that hung beside the bed. 'Grete,' she said after a minute. 'Muffi likes her nowadays.' That was true, though it was probably only because of the food Aunt Grete brought.

But I said, 'Uncle Hartmut doesn't like Muffi.'

'Grete will keep her away from Hartmut,' Mum said calmly. 'It's not forever, anyway. If a month goes by and nothing's happened, we'll bring her back.'

So when Aunt Grete came to collect the dress Mum had made her for a New Year's function, Mum said Muffi was going distracted with the bombing, and since they weren't getting so many bombs out at Wannsee, would Aunt Grete consider taking her for a while till she'd calmed down? Mum said we'd come over every weekend to take her for walks.

'Yes, of course,' Aunt Grete said at once. 'The poor thing.' She called Muffi to her. Muffi came and wagged her tail. Aunt Grete rubbed her under the chin and we hoped it'd be all right.

Only when we put her in the car she looked round, expecting us to come too. I shut the door on her, and saw her jump up at the window with her mouth open as the chauffeur drove off.

'Oh God,' Mum said. 'She must feel we've betrayed her.' She started to cry and cry. She'd been so strong all this time, I'd never have thought parting from Muffi would upset her so much.

'It's not for ever,' she said at last, and I knew she wasn't just thinking about Muffi.

So now we really were ready for the Gestapo – and Frau Mingers came back.

I met her on the landing and she walked past me as if I didn't exist. That was all right by me, but that evening there was an air raid and she sat opposite Mum and me in the cellar. She looked at me then, pressing her lips together and narrowing her eyes. I saw her fingers crook round as if she wanted to scratch my face to shreds. I thought I could hear her thoughts. 'You'll get what's coming to you, just you wait, you filthy Jew's whore.'

'She's denounced us today,' I said to Mum when we got upstairs. 'You can see she has.'

I went to bed with Mum that night. Neither of us got much rest, we were both tossing and turning. And then they were hammering at the door.

Mum put the bedside light on. I saw her face, she was white, blinking in the sudden brightness. 'We'll put our dressing gowns on,' she said, 'and our slippers. I'm not going out there barefoot, even if it means they break the door down.'

I took her hand as we went to open the door, and she held it tight and said to me, 'Think of Dad.'

They burst in, made us stand against the wall and started to search the apartment, just like the first time they'd come. The officer didn't bother to introduce himself. They were rougher with the apartment than Brenner's men had been. I saw Mum wince when they smashed something. I thought: This'll take hours to clear up, and we're both so tired.

When they'd ripped the guts out of the place and still found nothing, they marched us downstairs and smashed the back of the theatre. It was a good thing it was a long time since Raf had been there. It was all dusty and cobwebby inside now.

'So!' the officer said coldly to me, when he saw the entrance to the stockroom, 'There's nothing behind that thing but bare wall, is there?'

I stared at it. I knew I had to be astonished.

Mum said, 'She didn't know anything about it. I did, but we haven't used it for years. My husband did it to hide our cash eleven years ago, when a lot of shops were burgled round here.'

'So why didn't you tell Lieutenant Brenner about it?' the Gestapo officer demanded.

'I'd forgotten how to open it and I didn't want you to break it open and destroy it. My husband put so much work into it—'

He slapped her face so hard she staggered. I tried to go to her, but one of the men grabbed me and pulled me back.

The officer snarled, 'What does your husband's work matter, you bitch? All right, you're coming with us. Both of you.'

I was terrified then. I couldn't help it, a little whimper came out of my throat.

Mum shot a glance at me, and she faced up to the

officer, though she was trembling herself. 'May I ask why? You haven't found any evidence—'

'Evidence?' he said. 'Insolent bitch. Who do you think you are? Jew-lover. And your husband's a Quaker, a filthy pacifist traitor. As for your slut of a daughter...'

We had to get dressed with one of them standing in the room. Mum told him to turn his back, and I was scared he'd slap her face too, but he grunted and did as she said. It felt awful, all the same. I huddled my things on inside my nightdress. Then I tried to hug Mum, but he whipped round and threatened us with his gun.

'None of that.'

They pushed us out of our home. I saw Frau Mingers' door shut quickly. She'd been listening on the landing, gloating over what she'd done. I really hated her.

There were two wardresses waiting for us inside the prison. One hustled me away, the other took Mum in charge. Mum turned round and shouted, 'Jenny, I love you!'

'I love you too, Mum!' I shouted. The wardress clouted my head.

'That's enough bad behaviour from you,' she snapped.

She took me to a bare room, made me take my clothes

off and searched them. I hated being naked in front of her and she saw it.

'Gone all coy now, have you?' she demanded, laughing harshly. 'Jew's whore?'

'I'm not a whore,' I said. She punched me so hard I fell over. I lay on the floor, hurting, gasping for breath, and she laughed at me again. I felt small, humiliated, alone, and so scared. I thought: Are they hitting Mum, too?

'Get dressed,' the wardress said.

She allowed me to wear both the jumpers I'd put on, but she confiscated my coat and hat and my shoelaces. Then she marched me along a lot of corridors – to my cell, I guessed. It was hard to walk in my loose shoes. She opened a door in the last corridor, pushed me through it and turned the key on me.

There was a dim electric bulb dangling on a dusty flex from the ceiling, a narrow plank bed with a straw mattress on it and a blanket. No pillow. The place stank of chlorine. It took me a moment to realise the smell was coming from the bucket in the corner of the cell, and another moment to realise it was the toilet. I saw the spyhole in the door and realised they could watch me any time they liked. And I was terrified all through me. I'd never been so afraid in my life.

I lay down on the mattress and pulled the blanket over me so nobody could peer in and see my face. I shivered and wept, that went on for a long time. Then suddenly I thought I heard Mum saying, 'Jenny, we've got work to do.' It was so real I pulled the blanket off my head and looked for her. When I didn't see her I was sure I'd heard her thought.

I went through all the lies we'd practised together – only I mustn't think they were lies. I had to believe they were the truth. It was bad that I had to forget Raf, but I made myself do it. It was for his life as well as mine. Then I thought of Dad, they'd had him in prison too, maybe in the men's section of this one. I imagined him saying, 'Jennychen, I love you.' It heartened me a bit.

The next thing was to sleep so I was strong and could stick to my story. I got up and looked for the switch to turn the light off. There wasn't one. When I lay down again the bugs started to bite. They wouldn't leave me alone. It was crazy, but it felt as if Frau Broomstick was egging them on. I imagined her standing there laughing like the wardress when she'd punched me. And the fear came back and shook me like a fever.

The same wardress bullied me out of my cell in the morning and marched me to the prison yard. I had to go into a closed truck along with three other grey-faced women. They had bruises on their faces and blood on their clothes. One had a broken nose, and I knew how it had got broken. I started to shake when I saw it, but I made myself think about what I had to say, muttering it inside my head as the truck jolted along. I knew where we were going. The Gestapo headquarters in Prince Albrecht Street.

They pushed me into a room where a bright light shone in my eyes. I tried to look away from it, but there was a Gestapo man beside me and he cuffed me and shouted at me to face forward. There was another man behind the light, I could hear his voice yelling questions at me, but I couldn't see his face.

'How often did you see Rafael Jakoby after his family moved away?'

'I didn't see him.'

'You're lying, you did see him.'

I said, 'I didn't. Truly.'

'You did. You had meetings with him. We know all about it, you might as well tell us.'

'I didn't. I was just going to school and getting on with my life.'

'Why didn't you join the German Girls' League?'

There was a black splodge in front of my eyes from staring at the light. I felt giddy. I said, 'I was too busy.'

The man laughed. 'Oh, yes, we know you were. You were working the streets, weren't you?'

I didn't realise what he meant at first. 'What?' I said.

There was a brutal, jeering note in his voice. 'You went out in the blackout and picked up men. You brought them back to your apartment and gave them sex for money.'

I felt as if he'd pulled my clothes off. '*No*,' I said. 'I didn't.'

'If you weren't a prostitute, why did you pick up a man on the twenty-second of November?'

This was something I'd practised with Mum. I said, 'I was coming home after the air raid and a building collapsed on top of me. He saw it happen and he got me dug out. Then I took him home to Mum because he had nowhere to stay.'

'Why were you out at all?'

Mum and I had expected this too, and we knew the story she'd cooked up on the night wouldn't do. It was too easy to check up on.

'Mum and I had a row. I ran out of the apartment.'

'But she told your neighbours you were delivering something to a client.'

'She didn't want to say about the row. Frau Mingers would have said she wasn't bringing me up properly.'

'She wasn't, was she?' He laughed. 'Letting you go out and work the Kurfürstendamm. Or maybe she thought that was a good thing to do.' He paused for a moment, then snapped, 'Who was the fair-haired man you were seen with?'

'He was called Lieutenant Frey. He was on leave from the Italian Front.'

'Lieutenant Frey? It was Rafael Jakoby. Wasn't it?'

'No. I don't know what happened to the Jakobys. I suppose they were sent to Poland.'

'All right, the man you were with was Lieutenant Frey. He was one of your johns and you took him back to the apartment and gave him sex.'

It wasn't hard to guess what a john was.

I said, 'I kissed him; that was all. He'd been so kind, and he'd saved my life.'

The voice behind the lights said, 'You gave him sex, you little slut. Don't pretend you're a virgin.' He laughed. 'As for that, I think I'll have a look for myself, right now.'

'No!' I shrieked, and I clutched my arms tight round me to protect myself. I was sobbing. I can't stand it, I thought.

'Come on,' the voice said, 'don't bawl, talk! It'll be better for you in the end.'

I put the back of my hand up to my nose and wiped it. I felt hopeless, weak, I didn't know what to say – but there was something inside me, some survival instinct, that told me the right thing.

'All right. I did – when I brought Lieutenant Frey home. He didn't have anywhere to go, the hotel he'd been staying in had been bombed and he'd saved my life. Mum was grateful to him. And she had to go up fire watching, and – well, we liked each other. Things got out of hand.'

The Gestapo man came out from behind the bright light and slapped my face hard. I saw him then. It was Brenner.

'Drop all these lies,' he said. 'You went to bed with

343

Jakoby. With the shit-Jew you had hidden behind your shit-theatre.'

I said, 'Just be careful how you treat me, Lieutenant Brenner.' My voice was too high, and shaking, I sounded stupid to myself. 'I'm related to General Montgomery, you know. He's my mother's cousin.'

'As if I cared about some Englishman,' Brenner said. 'And don't spin me the line about your uncle Hartmut Hansen. He won't stick his neck out for a Jew's slut.'

He went behind the light and started shouting questions at me again. The same ones, over and over. And it was the same the next day, and the next.

I couldn't sleep at night. It was too cold. If I did drift off, the light and the bugs saw to it that I woke up again. I cried in my cell. I wailed to the straw mattress and the stinking air that it wasn't fair. I was so tired, I needed just a few hours' rest, why couldn't I have it? I even begged the bugs to go away. And I kept thinking about Mum, though I learned quickly not to imagine her being interrogated in Prince Albrecht Street, because I had enough to do coping with being interrogated myself, without imagining it happening to Mum. Every now and again I brooded about Frau Mingers, sharpening my hatred like a knife, trying to direct it at her in her bed. This is the truth, I wished it could kill her.

We got left in our cells when the air-raid sirens

sounded but first the wardresses made us open the windows to save them from blast, just as we would at home. That was the only time they switched the lights out. I went to the window, pulled the blackout blind up and watched the raid. Every time a bomb fell the woman in the next cell shrieked: 'Oh my God, oh my God!' But I stood there, cold and still, watching the flares we called Christmas trees float downwards and the red glow spreading in the sky as the incendiaries set the broken buildings on fire. I went beyond fear during the air raids, it was crazy, but I felt as if nothing could happen to me. I was the watcher, that was all.

The food they gave me tasted vile, but I was starving hungry, so I ate it up.

Then Brenner told me Mum had confessed, so I might as well give in.

'If you let us know where Jakoby's gone you won't be executed,' he said.

For a moment I believed him but then I heard Karl's voice inside my head. 'They'll tell you someone else has confessed everything. It's standard practice. It sounds stupid when you're not in prison, but apparently it's powerful if you are.'

I thought: They're probably telling her *I've* confessed.

Karl had said, 'Remind yourself, if they know everything, why are they so keen to get it out of you? You'll be fighting, each of you. For the other's life, as well as for your own.'

345

Mum's life, I thought, and in my head a tiny voice whispered: And Raf's. No, I told myself, you mustn't think that.

I said, 'I haven't seen him for years. How can I tell you where he is?'

'Come on,' Brenner said, almost coaxingly. 'If you tell us it'll count in your favour. You're young, maybe we won't execute you.' And then, 'Think about your father. Do you want him to lose *all* his family?'

I was half-crazy with tiredness, suddenly my head swam and I thought I heard Dad talking about the ocean of light. It was all around me, I thought, the ocean of light from the lamps. I was floating away on it and everything was all right, Dad was there now and I was a little kid, drifting into sleep in his arms.

I was on the floor, I was soaking wet, cold and shaking with shock. I saw the man beside me holding a bucket. I realised I'd passed out and they'd thrown the water on me to bring me round.

'You won't get out of it that way,' Brenner's voice said.

I started to cry. 'I want my dad,' I said.

He said, 'You know, we can get in touch with the people in his prisoner-of-war camp, loyal Germans who'll punish him if you keep on being stubborn.'

He's lying, I insisted to myself. The Americans won't let the Nazis hurt Dad.

Then one evening, after a whole day's interrogation I

got back to my cell and found another prisoner there.

She said, 'You're Jenny Friedemann, aren't you?'

'Yes.'

'I saw your mother taken away to be executed this morning.'

'Oh God,' I said. My head swam. Then I thought I heard Karl again. 'They sometimes put someone else in with you and try to get you to talk to them.' But I was rigid with fear that it was true.

'She sent a message for you.'

I didn't answer. I could feel the tears ready to come. But I thought: This woman didn't just come strolling into my cell. They brought her.

The woman looked at me out of hollow haunted eyes. 'Don't you want to hear it?'

I couldn't have said I didn't want to hear. 'All right. Tell me.'

'She said you've got to confess where Jakoby is and save yourself. She said you're her own flesh and blood and she wants you to live.'

I said, 'I don't believe you.'

For a moment, something lit up in her eyes, then it went away again. She carried on trying to persuade me, but I said, 'My mother knows I've got nothing to tell.'

I wonder who she was, and what they'd threatened her with if she didn't get me to own up?

There were always women in the truck going back to prison who were groaning and crying, screaming sometimes, because they'd been tortured. You couldn't comfort them because the wardress was there with her truncheon. They smelt of blood and shit and urine. One day one of them went quiet and then it was the wardress who was making a noise. 'Stay alive,' she screeched, 'you cursed bitch, you don't think you'll get free of us that way – just wait till we get back, I'll have the doctor to you, you scum . . . ' She thumped on the window to get the driver to speed up and he did, but the woman died before we reached the prison.

I kept wondering when they'd start torturing me, but they never did worse to me than clout me round the face or tip cold water over me if I keeled over. So I thought the Montgomery story must carry some weight. Or maybe it was something to do with Uncle Hartmut, even though his friend was dead.

It was bad, though, standing there with that dazzling light searing my eyes. Getting tireder all the time, silly with lack of sleep. I'd slur my words and they'd trip over each other and get in a muddle. I toppled over again and again they woke me up with a bucket of freezing water. I felt as if my body belonged to them, it wasn't mine, I had nothing to do with it at all.

And then one day they didn't come for me, or the next day either. They left me in the cell for God knew how long, with only the bedbugs and the air raids and the rotten food to think about.

When they opened the door and fetched me out I thought they were taking me back to Prince Albrecht

Street, but they put me in the back of an open truck with a lot of other girls and drove me away from Berlin.

I met Luise and Erna in the truck, they sat wedged against me and when it jolted we held onto each other. We comforted each other because we were all three scared, not knowing where we were going, leaving the people we loved behind. We talked. Luise had been a munitions worker, she'd worked in the same factory as her mother. She didn't have a father, he'd beaten them both up too much and her mother had thrown him out. She'd been arrested for giving food to Russian slave-labourers – having sex with them, the police said.

'If only,' Luise said, blowing on her hands and shoving them into the front of her coat to warm them. 'I never got the chance, and one of them was really good looking.'

Erna raised her plucked eyebrows when she heard the Gestapo had accused me of being a prostitute, because she really had been on the game, along with a bit of black-marketeering to help out.

'You!' she said. 'Anyone could tell you've no idea.'

Luise said, 'Well, of course, they wanted you to say: "No, I'm not a prostitute, I kissed that Jew and confusion to all you Nazis, now execute me, please!" Pity Lieutenant Frey hopped off so quickly. Did you love him?'

'Yes,' I said.

Erna took her cold hand out of her coat and squeezed mine. 'Shitty life, isn't it? As for that woman who denounced you, you get that kind of old bat everywhere, ugly as sin themselves, so they can't bear pretty girls.'

We came to a gateway: WORK MAKES YOU FREE was written over the top. They took us to a long ugly building where they bawled at us to strip. A brute of a woman hacked my hair off. I stood there naked with bits of my hair dropping past my eyes and falling on the floor at my bare feet. When she'd finished with me I put my hand to my head. It was horrible, I was almost bald. Then they shoved us into a freezing cold shower and out again. I had to stand damp and naked while an SS doctor stared at me and put his hands all over me – and inside me.

'Not a virgin,' he said coldly. I gritted my teeth together and tried not to let him see how bad he'd made me feel.

'They were enjoying themselves,' Erna said afterwards. 'They're arseholes, Jenny. Don't let them make you cry.'

We were in the women's concentration camp at Ravensbrück. After ten days they brought us to Uckermark. They took our names and our clothes away and gave us numbers instead. And forbade us to speak to each other, though we found ways of getting round that, Erna and Luise and I. You had to be careful though, some of the girls were informers. I didn't know what they got out of it, they didn't seem any fatter than the rest of us.

We were supposed to be learning self-discipline and hard work. Self-discipline meant physical jerks every morning. We had to do them barefoot even though it was freezing cold. If we didn't move fast enough for Grendel and Kerner they hit us with their rubber truncheons. When we shivered under the ice-cold showers every night before bedtime, I could see how we were all covered in bruises.

The hard work was sewing uniforms for soldiers. Your fingers got stiff with cold, chapped and bleeding. If you ran your needle into them, that made it worse. There was a stove. It was beside the guard. It kept her warm and just stopped us freezing into blocks of ice.

Then one night, Grendel came up to me at bedtime. I thought she was going to take me away and punish me for something I'd done wrong. My teeth started chattering and she laughed at me for a moment, she loved scaring people.

'We've been sent some marionettes to keep our morale up,' she said. 'I used to do puppeteering when I was a German Girls' League leader, so I know how to work them, but I need someone else. Your father used to be a marionette-maker, didn't he? Have you learned puppeteering?'

It was hard to get my head round the idea of them needing their morale kept up, but I nodded. Then, instead of going to my bunk, I had to go outside the wire with them, to their common room. I thought about trying to run, but I heard the SS dogs baying and I knew they'd track me down.

The marionettes weren't anything like as good as Dad's, but I wouldn't want SS guards to have Dad's work. There was a witch, a young girl with hair that came off when you worked a lever at the back of her head. A man and a woman, a prince. Rapunzel. I don't think any of them saw how crazily funny it was that they were keeping a lot of young girls locked up away from men, just like the witch – even cutting our hair off – and now they were going to amuse themselves with that story out of all the ones the Brothers Grimm wrote up. Maybe the person who'd sent the marionettes had a sense of black humour.

I was let off work one Sunday to rehearse with Grendel. In her quarters. And she smiled at me, scarily friendly all of a sudden.

She said, 'So your grandmother was English? What was she called?'

She was working the Rapunzel marionette, making her walk across the floor. She'd said she wanted to be the heroine, and Rapunzel's mother. I had to do the witch, and the prince, and Rapunzel's father. Every time my witch locked Grendel's marionette up in the tower, I had to bite my cheek to stop myself laughing insanely.

I said, 'Montgomery.'

She nodded, as if she'd heard this already and was just checking. She looked expectantly at me, and I told her General Montgomery was my cousin. I didn't have anything to lose, after all.

She said, 'That's interesting.' Then we went on rehearsing. She was a clever puppeteer and I thought that was odd at first – Dad always said a good puppeteer had to have sympathy with people – but then I realised that a person who didn't give a shit for other people might pay a lot of attention to them, so they could manipulate them and use them.

It was strange, though, you couldn't work with someone without seeing that they were a human being. I actually started to believe Grendel was human.

One day she said, 'We have to do as we're told, here in the camp. But maybe there's something I could help you with?'

I saw her glance at the picture of her brother in his SS uniform. He'd been killed last year at Stalingrad. There wasn't any point in Grendel being a pure Nazi now. I knew the Russians had crossed the Polish border, it was one of the last things we'd heard on the BBC before they'd arrested us. I was sure the Germans hadn't pushed them back again, we'd have heard about it if they had. The guards always made a big song and dance about what they called German successes. Probably the Russians had got quite a lot further by now, and the SS hero's sister needed to look after herself. And if she thought I might be able to help her after the Allied victory that everyone really knew was coming, I decided to chance it. 'I'd like to get a letter to my Aunt Grete, in Berlin.'

'I could do that,' she said. 'I'm going to Berlin next weekend.'

I wrote the letter that afternoon, on her writing paper, with her pen. I told Aunt Grete about the camp, the beatings, the cold, the starvation, and about the girl they'd tied to the post to die, and how she'd called out for her mother. I said I knew Uncle Hartmut's friend had been killed, but surely he could find someone to help us. I said I might die in this camp, and probably Mum was somewhere that was just as bad.

Grendel took the letter and put it away. Ten days later we had the marionette show. It went down well, but afterwards she brought me back to the block and locked me in with the others. The next morning she was cold with me. So probably she'd just been stringing me along – manipulating me like a marionette. No, she'd been treating me the way a cat treats a mouse it's caught, fooling me that I might escape so that she could have the fun of pinning me down. And now I was locked in a cell waiting for the Director to come back and deal with me.

How long had I been here, anyway? It felt like hours.

Chapter Twenty-five

Someone was unlocking the door. I was on my feet before I knew I'd got up. I saw a big-chinned guard who looked like a man with breasts. The secretary woman was behind her and she passed a bowl and spoon to the guard.

'Take it, girl!' the guard said sharply. I took it from her. It was hot. I didn't believe it, I'd had nothing but lukewarm food since I'd been arrested.

The guard slammed the door shut. I heard the key turn. I was alone with a bowl of food. I sat down, feeling the warmth of it against my cold fingers, smelling the good things before I saw them, pieces of real meat, bits of leek, carrot rings, little squares of potato, pearl barley.

I felt the saliva run in my mouth, but I didn't dare eat it. I was trying to work out why they'd brought it. Maybe they were watching through the spyhole in the door, as soon as I put a spoonful to my mouth they'd burst in and beat the living daylights out of me for daring to touch it. Or maybe it was poisoned. When I was spitting blood and screaming with agony, they'd drag me out and march the girls past me to show them what had happened to me.

I put it down on the bench and turned my head away from it, but I knew it was there. I was trembling violently with all the fear and the hunger – and suddenly I picked it up and spooned it down me. It tasted more heavenly than I could ever describe. And it put hope into me. I couldn't believe it was poison now, and they'd let me eat it. That had to be a good sign.

After a while I heard the door being unlocked again. 'Have you finished eating?' the secretary said. No guard this time. 'You're to come through to the Director.'

That sent me witless with fear. I stood up and my left clog went over sideways, hurting my ankle. I whimpered when that happened, I'd learned not to cry out when I was hit, but this was different.

'Don't damage yourself!' the secretary said, frowning over the top of her brown-rimmed glasses. On the edge of my panic a tiny, rational voice said: If they were going to kill you they wouldn't have cared how much you were damaged.

I dropped a curtsey to the Director and Heil-Hitler-ed at her, but I couldn't look her in the face. I stared downwards, at the legs of her desk and her shiny, knee-length boots planted flat on the floor. I was shivering.

'Sit down, Friedemann,' she said.

It took me a moment to realise that she'd used my name, not a number. I felt as if my mind was still stumbling around in the cell. My head swam. I almost fell onto the wooden chair and felt a cushion under my behind for the first time in two months. The secretary sat down in the corner of the room.

I looked at Frau Director then. I saw her light blue eyes in her square, fleshy face. She started to talk and I tried to listen. I heard her say: 'unfortunate error,' and 'released'. I thought: Did she really say that? Are they letting me go, or am I having hallucinations?

She was smiling, showing all her big white teeth. What was she saying? 'But I hope you won't regret the time you've spent here. Our aim is to build character, and that should do nobody any harm.'

I stared at her. I'd no idea what kind of expression my face ought to be wearing. Only it seemed likely now that I had heard right. They were going to let me go.

She said, 'You've seen what a hard job we have with the degraded girls who come here. How we shirk no effort to reform them. Firm, but just, that's my policy.'

I managed to nod. I was thinking about Luise and Erna. Luise had come here because she'd been kind, and yes, Erna was a prostitute, but did that make her worse than the Director? I didn't think so.

The Director was talking to the secretary. 'She's been fed, Frau Schmidt?'

'Yes, Frau Director. Just a small meal, as you said.'

'Good, we don't want her eating too much and making herself ill. How long ago was it?'

'An hour.'

'There's a car coming for her in another hour. We can give her a little more in the meantime.' She turned to me and said, 'If you fell on the first meal your uncle gives you he might get some misconception.'

My uncle. Grendel had taken the letter after all. I should have been so happy, but everything still felt unreal. And I was still thinking about Luise and Erna, I was getting out of this hell-hole and they weren't. It wasn't fair.

While I was sitting there in a daze, the Director had been talking to the secretary. Something about my clothes, and getting them from the store. Well, it would hardly do to present myself to Uncle Hartmut and Aunt Grete in the camp uniform. The secretary went out of the room.

The Director looked straight at me, still frowning. She said, 'Friedemann. I might need someone to speak for me in the future.' She said it hurriedly, in a secretive voice as if she didn't want to let herself know she was saying it. There I was with my shorn head and my filthy feet and she was currying favour with me. I knew Grendel had told her about my cousin the British general.

Her face twitched. 'I hope I can count on you.'

I thought: Oh, yes, you can count on me to tell anyone who asks all about this hell-hole you've made. But I nodded. I knew I had to.

The secretary came back with my clothes. Someone

had washed them, that was just as well, they'd got pretty filthy in prison. *I* was still filthy, though. The Director was saying:

'You'd like a shower, I expect, Friedemann. Schmidt, take her to my bathroom. You can change there, too. Schmidt, bring her some – bread and margarine, I think. And a small piece of cheese, and some coffee. Some of mine.'

I got real coffee. And the water in the shower was hot and there was shampoo and soap and a proper, thick towel. I could still hardly believe what was happening.

The sun came out as I left and gleamed on Uncle Hartmut's shiny black Merc as it sat outside the office. The Director had come out with me to say goodbye.

'Remember,' she said, 'you've been fairly treated here.' There was a bit of buttering-up in her voice and a grating edge of threat. I nodded again.

Brettmann was there, opening the door for me, I couldn't believe it was him, in his smart uniform, in this place with the watchtowers and the high wire fence. 'Heil Hitler, Fräulein Jenny,' he said. 'Please get in.'

He spoke to me as if I was a film star, or some high-up Nazi woman. I'm sure he was shocked at the way I looked, but he didn't show it. I slid into the leather-smelling back of the car. Then I saw who else was sitting there.

'Mum!' I said, and I started to cry. 'Oh, Mum.'

Brettmann put the key in the ignition and started the engine. The car swept away from Uckermark.

Mum held out her arms to me. I went into them, wanting comfort from her, but when she put her face against mine it was hot. At once I was terrified again. I pulled back and looked at her. Her face was too flushed and her eyes were glassy, and now she began coughing as if she'd bring her lungs up. She was as thin as I was. They hadn't cut her hair off, but that didn't make me happy because I was worrying she might have tuberculosis or pneumonia.

'Mum,' I said. 'You've got a fever, you'll have to see a doctor.'

She shook her head. 'It's nothing. Just a cold. Jenny, your hair! My poor love.'

From the driver's seat, Brettmann said, 'We keep aspirin in the car, madam, if it'd help. For Frau Hansen's headaches. The box in between the seats. There's a bottle of mineral water there, too, and some biscuits, if you'd like some.'

'I'd like some aspirin, please,' Mum said, coughing again.

'I'll get it for you,' I said. I opened the mahogany box. Inside there were four cut-crystal glasses, a silver pillbox, and two little bottles of mineral water. There was a small bottle of cognac, too, but I didn't think that'd do Mum much good. The biscuits were in another little silver box, little sugar-coated pretzels for Aunt Grete to nibble.

Mum didn't want a biscuit, but when I'd given her the aspirins and a glass of water I ate one. Then I had to have another, and another till I'd wolfed them all down.

I said, 'Mum, where have you come from?'

She shuddered. 'I was at Ravensbrück.'

She'd been just next door.

She asked, 'Herr Brettmann? Are you taking us home?'

'No, Frau Friedemann,' he said. 'To Herr Hansen's.'

Good, I thought, because we didn't have a ration book and there certainly wouldn't be any food in the cupboard. And I'd no idea if our house was still standing.

Mum fell asleep after she'd taken the aspirins. I was tired, but I sat up in my seat, thinking how ill she seemed, thinking bad thoughts. I'd seen girls with coughs in the camp, they'd got worse quickly, then they'd been taken away and they'd never come back. We knew they must have died. I couldn't bear it if Mum had got out of Ravensbrück too late.

Then I felt sick. I had to ask Brettmann to stop the car, and I got out and vomited on the brown winter grass at the road's edge. I saw all the biscuits in my sick, and the bread and cheese I'd had before I'd left Uckermark. Brettmann looked really upset when he opened the door to let me back in. I knew it was my fault, the Director had talked about eating too much and making myself ill, now I'd done it.

I was glad there were curtains in the back of the car. I didn't want people looking in at us and knowing we'd been in concentration camp.

There was the Hansens' house, black and white and bogus, just as it had stood in front of me when I'd come in my best clothes on so many Sundays. Minna opened the front door to us, and she curtseyed, but I winced away from the shocked pity in her eyes.

There was someone else there. Muffi, squealing and moaning with joy, wagging her whole self, panting, and making a puddle on the parquet floor.

I bent down and hugged her, feeling her warm smelly dog-breath on my face. Mum reached down and patted her back. Muffi wiggled round to her and started to bustle anxiously: she knew Mum was ill.

Uncle Hartmut came down the corridor. 'You look terrible,' he said, shuddering. 'Both of you. Sylvia, you'd better get straight to bed.'

I said, 'Where's Aunt Grete?'

'I persuaded her to go and stay with the girls,' he said. 'The bombing was affecting her nerves. She knows you're here. I rang her this morning and told her you were coming. Jenny, go and see your mother settled, then I want to talk to you. You can come to my study.'

Minna led us upstairs to the guest room. There was a big double bed with two mattresses and plump, white-covered pillows and duvets. The wooden floor was so well polished it looked like liquid honey. Muffi went between Mum and me, turning her head round to lick whatever parts of us she could reach.

'The guest bathroom's through here,' Minna said, opening a door.

The bath, sink and toilet were white and heavy with shiny chrome taps and handles. There was a crystal jar full of bath salts, there were fluffy white towels, far nicer than the Director's. I saw a towelling bathrobe hanging on the back of the door. I felt too bedraggled for all this luxury.

When I went back into the bedroom, Minna was laying out a nightdress for each of us – borrowed from Aunt Grete, I supposed. She bobbed a curtsey and said, 'I'll get some lime-blossom tea for you, Frau Friedemann. And a bowl of chicken broth with noodles.'

Those were the things an ill person ought to have. I told myself: If Mum has chicken broth, that'll help her, the girls in the camp didn't have chicken broth. And I'll see Uncle Hartmut and tell him he's got to call a doctor for her.

'I just want to sleep, Minna,' Mum said.

As if Mum was a child, Minna said, '*When* you've got some goodness inside you, Frau Friedemann.'

She'd always been in the background when we'd come to visit, a plump efficient middle-aged woman with an immaculate white apron over her black dress. Now I realised she was really kind. I was so grateful.

Mum fell asleep as soon as she was in bed and we had to wake her for the tea and the broth. She drank them both obediently, then lay back and slept again.

It was getting dark when I went to Uncle Hartmut's study. Minna pulled the blackout blinds down, drew the crimson brocade curtains, and slipped out of the room.

I sat facing him across his desk. 'Mum ought to have a doctor. Can you call one for her?'

He said, 'Let's see how she is in the morning. No, don't argue, Jenny! I don't think you appreciate the situation we're in.' He shifted in his chair and tapped his fingers edgily on his pink blotting pad. Muffi put her paws on my knees and I lifted her into my lap.

I said, 'Uncle Hartmut, I'm really grateful to you for—'

He interrupted. 'I had to buy you out, you know. Of course I did what I could with the Interior Ministry as soon as you were arrested.'

I wonder, I thought.

He shoved his chin forward. 'I used your fairy tale about Montgomery. Oh, I know that's a lie. You never pulled the wool over *my* eyes. But it made them go easy on you.'

Maybe, I thought. After all, they hadn't tortured me. I supposed I ought to thank him again, but he didn't seem to want my thanks and the way he was talking didn't make me feel like repeating them. I said, 'They weren't exactly nice to me, all the same. And the concentration camp was no picnic.'

'It's no use thinking I should have kept you out of there,' he said, irritably. 'That kind of negotiation takes time. Even before your letter came—'

I interrupted him. 'What did we cost you, Uncle Hartmut?'

'A lot of diamonds,' he said. 'Nobody wants Reichsmarks nowadays. You're a cheeky girl, do you know that, Jenny? Your father should have given you a few good hidings. And your brother, it'd have taught you both manners.'

I was furious. 'Don't talk to me about Karl. Anyway, I know why you got us out. So we can speak up for you after the war.'

He didn't answer that. 'You don't realise how delicate things are. That officer, Brenner – the one who interrogated you – he's got a real spite against you because he never realised what was behind that theatre of your father's. You cost him a promotion, did you realise that? He'd have beaten you to a pulp if he'd been allowed to. He could still get you rearrested – things are complicated in the Interior Ministry, you know. You're sitting ducks in my house. You'll have to leave tomorrow. And don't go home. They'd find you there, too.'

'Leave?' I said. I was terrified and even angrier than

before. 'And we can't go home? Where do you expect us to go with Mum ill?'

He just said, 'I know you've got contacts.'

Agnes Hummel. Of course. I wondered why I hadn't thought of her at once. 'There is someone,' I said, hating him. 'If they're still alive.'

'Where do they live?' He was drumming his fingers on the blotting pad.

'In Dahlem.' I knew he wouldn't want to be told any more than that, and I didn't want to tell him.

He looked relieved, as if his troubles were over. 'Brettmann will drive you there before sunrise tomorrow. Better if you go before it's light. I'll give you money to take away with you—'

I interrupted. 'The house might have been bombed, I don't suppose you care about that, though. As long as we're off your hands.'

He let out a heavy sigh. 'Jenny,' he said. 'Can you get it into your head that I don't want the Gestapo to know where you are? This is for your sake. If this person's not available, of course you can come back and we'll try to think of something else.'

'Oh,' I said, loading my voice with sarcasm. 'I'm sorry, I should have realised you were protecting your investment.'

He opened his mouth to answer, but Minna came in. 'Dinner is served, Herr Hansen.'

I sat with him at the heavy walnut table in the dining

room. The tablecloth was white and spotless. We ate with silver cutlery off blue and white Meissen china and I remembered the metal plate and cup and grey pocked spoon I'd used for my breakfast. When Minna brought Muffi meat in a white porcelain bowl, I thought how Erna and Luise would be gulping down watery soup with stale bread for *their* dinner. The thought of them kept catching at me, hurting me. They'd been good friends.

I asked Minna not to give me dumplings in the chicken soup, and I ate one small piece of potato and half a bread-crumbed schnitzel. I had a tablespoonful of red cabbage and two dessertspoons of rice pudding. It was really hard to hold off, the food was all so good, but I'd learned my lesson. Uncle Hartmut didn't say anything about me eating so little, maybe Brettmann had told him about my bad behaviour in the car.

There was real coffee at the end of the meal. Uncle Hartmut lit a cigar and smoked it as if he needed it. Poor man, I thought savagely.

Abruptly, he asked, 'Why did you do it?'

I knew exactly what he meant, but I asked, 'Why did I do what?'

He said, 'Hiding the Jakoby boy. Look what it's brought you to.'

I could have said, 'It's brought me to being someone who might be useful to you,' but I wasn't going to start letting things out to an uncle who was a Nazi, never mind how many diamonds he'd spent on us. I started tracing the patterns on the damask tablecloth with my fingertip. My skin was rough from the work at Uckermark and it caught on the delicate fibres.

'Jenny?' Uncle Hartmut said, and his voice sounded puzzled, confused even. I looked up, our eyes met, and I thought I would try and say something to him after all – only I couldn't. In the end I shook my head.

Uncle Hartmut's eyes narrowed and he gave his shoulders a little shake. 'You'd better go to bed,' he said. 'If there's a raid, Minna will come and take you down to the shelter. It's not just at night now, mind. The Americans have started bombing us in broad daylight.'

That must have been another reason for helping us. It made the Final Victory seem even less likely.

I went to bed. Muffi seemed to understand that she mustn't disturb Mum, and she curled up against me under the duvet. In the middle of the night I woke up suddenly, and knew Mum was awake, too. I put my hand out to touch her. She was really hot.

'Switch the light on, please, Jenny,' she said. 'Sweetheart, there's aspirin in the bathroom. Could you get it for me?'

When I brought her the tablets, she said, 'I can't believe you're not a dream.'

I didn't tell her about going in the morning, I didn't want her lying awake worrying. I said, 'I am here, Mum,' and I kissed her burning face. Minna had put a thermos flask of chicken broth on the dressing table. I lifted it off its silver tray and poured

Mum a cup full. She was glad to drink it, then she fell asleep again.

Minna woke us at four thirty. Mum's skin was cooler, I was so relieved. When I told her what Uncle Hartmut had said and where we were going, she grimaced, shrugged her shoulders and said, 'Well, then, we mustn't frighten him by staying on the premises.'

She managed to eat a roll and butter for breakfast, and drink more chicken broth. I thought: Maybe it is just a cold. But I so much wanted her to stay in bed and have the doctor.

Minna found us a warm hat each from the ranks of hats in Aunt Grete's dressing room. Mine covered my convict crop. And she handed me a shopping bag that I knew was full of food.

'It's a disgrace,' she said fiercely. 'Turning you out like this. When the mistress hears about it, she'll give him what for, Fräulein Jenny.'

I wondered, but I was too worried to be angry with Uncle Hartmut now. I said, 'Thank you, Minna. For everything.' I gave her a kiss, the way I used to kiss Kattrin, and she hugged me back.

'You're a sweet girl,' she said.

At half past five Brettmann drove us over to Dahlem. I was careful to make him put us down a few streets away from Agnes Hummel's house – and – to be extra safe – nowhere near Herr von Himmelrein's villa, either. I didn't want to meet him taking an early morning walk. Uncle Hartmut had told Brettmann to wait, in case we didn't find anyone at home. I told him to give us three quarters of an hour. We walked along through a misty twilight, I had Mum leaning on one arm, I was carrying the bag of food on the other, Muffi's lead in my fist.

When we got to Fountain Lane I saw that the end house had been bombed. I bit my lip, trying not to be afraid. I couldn't see Agnes Hummel's house, the mist fuzzed my sight. We walked further down and I saw the blue fir trees, and beyond them the house, still standing. I was a little bit relieved, but then I started to worry in case she'd been arrested herself, or was just out.

The wooden gate opened as quietly as it had done the last time I'd been there. I closed it carefully, and Mum, Muffi and I walked to the front door. There were snowdrops there now, their white bell-heads hanging over the edge of the path.

I knocked quietly. Nobody came. I heard the clock ticking again. I remembered her daughter and grand-daughter in Heidelberg. Supposing she'd gone away to visit them? Then I heard footsteps in the hall and the door opened as discreetly as the gate had done.

'Come inside,' Agnes Hummel said.

Chapter Twenty-six

All at once I was wild with hope. I looked round the hallway in case a door might open and Raf might come out of it. Agnes Hummel shook her head at me. My heart sank, and I was scared she might think we'd come looking for him even though the other woman had said it was better we didn't know where he was. Maybe she was annoyed with us.

Mum started coughing again.

'You're not well,' Agnes Hummel said to her. She wasn't annoyed. Her voice was really warm and concerned. That set me shaking, I don't know why. I pulled my hat off and saw her eyes widen. She said, 'What's been happening to you, Jenny?'

I told her about our arrest and the camp, and Uncle Hartmut bringing us to Berlin and then throwing us out.

'I'm glad you came to me,' she said.

She took us into the kitchen this time. It had the same thick lace curtains as the sitting room, and there was a girl of about seven years old standing beside the scrubbed table clutching the end of one of her brown plaits. Her eyes were eager and hopeful till she saw us, then her face fell.

'These are some friends of mine, Emmi,' Agnes Hummel said.

The girl said, 'I thought it was Mama—'

Agnes Hummel put a hand on her shoulder. 'I know,' she said.

She made lime-blossom tea for both of us in the silver teapot and poured it out into the rose-patterned cups that were like Aunty Edith's. The tea was warm and fragrant and it calmed me down. She said she'd get a doctor to come and see Mum – only it'd have to be later, she'd arrange it when she went out shopping. She introduced us to Emmi, who was Jewish – but I'd already guessed that.

Emmi said, 'We've been living here for six months, only Mama went out shopping for her lady and she didn't come back.'

Agnes Hummel explained, 'Emmi's mother has been cleaning for a good friend of mine.'

'But there was an air raid,' Emmi said miserably. She had green-grey eyes quite like mine and Mum's. At the moment that I noticed that, I saw Agnes Hummel take stock of it, too, but she didn't say anything.

Muffi went to Emmi and nosed her. Emmi bent down and stroked her, looking a tiny bit happier.

'Where are his eyes?' she said.

'She's a girl,' I said. 'If you push her hair aside you'll find her eyes.'

Mum put her teacup down. 'Agnes Hummel,' she croaked, 'what are we going to do?'

'Just call me Agnes. You're going to stay here with me. You're going to rest yourselves and get better. And not worry, either of you.'

I said, 'We've no ration cards, but there's food in the bag.'

We unpacked it. Minna had given us cheese, butter, eggs, a loaf of nice bread, a good length of sausage and a bottle of apple purée. And a packet of coffee beans and a bone for Muffi.

'A feast,' Agnes Hummel said, smiling. 'Have you had breakfast?'

'Yes.' I didn't want to eat too much of her food. I'd no idea how long we'd be here.

But she said she had a good black-market racket going. I gave her Reichsmarks from Uncle Hartmut's farewell tip and thought how lucky it had been for him that we'd had someone to go to. Mum kept coughing. Agnes put her to bed and showed me where the lime-blossom tea was kept. She'd gathered it herself from the tree in her garden last May. She made Mum and me have apple purée before she went out.

'You have to build up your strength,' she said.

Muffi was a godsend for Emmi, who had a lovely time dropping things for her to pick up and throwing a ball for her to fetch. In the end, Muffi lay down and ignored her. I had to explain to Emmi that dogs got tired just as she would. So then Emmi wanted to give Muffi the bone to chew, but I said we'd wait till Muffi was really hungry. Minna had given her a good meal that morning. It seemed incredible to be sitting chatting to a child instead of slaving my guts out in the camp. I imagined Luise and Erna spending a second day in the cow byre, wondering what had happened to me. Maybe they thought the Gestapo had got me in for more questioning. Grendel and Kerner would never tell them I'd been released. I wished so much I could have done something to get them set free, too.

'Let's play Ludo,' Emmi said. I opened my mouth to say I was too tired, but the wind blew outside and something rattled. I saw her whip round, staring towards the door, hoping it was her mother. I saw the hope drain away, leaving a lost look on her face. I said quickly, 'Yes, I'd like to play.'

When we'd played for a while I asked her how long she'd been there.

'A year,' she said, rolling the dice. 'Agnes is really kind.'

I said, 'Did a blond boy come here after Christmas?' I knew I shouldn't ask but I couldn't help it.

She shook her head. Then, in a tiny voice, she asked, 'Jenny. Do you think they've caught Mama?'

'I don't know,' I said.

She said, 'It's horrible when you keep wondering—'

'Yes,' I said. 'It must be.'

Agnes came back with a heavy shopping basket. As

she unpacked it, she said, 'Dr Fink will come after dark. How is your mother?'

'She's been asleep.'

She made me sleep after lunch – vegetable soup and Minna's bread. I was really tired. I lay down beside Mum and slept like the dead.

Dr Fink was a woman, brisk and impersonally kind. She said Mum had a chest infection and told her to rest and drink plenty of fluids. She insisted on examining me, too 'after what you've been through'. She said I was fine, but I needed building up. 'Not too much food at once,' she said. 'Little and often. That goes for both of you.'

I nodded. Mum wanted to pay her, but she shook her head. 'It's the least I can do.' Downstairs, she said to me and Agnes, 'I'll be back to see Frau Friedemann tomorrow.' She closed her bag and left.

I said to Agnes, 'She didn't say Mum was going to be all right. Supposing she gets pneumonia?' My own chest felt tight with fear and I didn't seem to be able to breathe properly.

Agnes put her arms round me and hugged me. She said: 'She's a good doctor, she'll make sure your mother's all right. Don't worry.'

Two days after that, in the afternoon, Agnes came back from one of her trips out. 'I want to talk to you all,' she said.

She put the kettle on and made Mum's lime-blossom tea. Then we went upstairs to the bedroom. Mum still had to rest, but Dr Fink was pleased with her progress, she said the cough was in her throat now. I kept going up to see her, to remind myself she was really there. We'd hug each other and she'd stroke my hair.

Agnes gave Mum her tisane. Then Emmi and I sat down on the bed and Agnes sat on the bedroom chair. Agnes said, 'It was like a gift, seeing the two of you turning up.'

'And Muffi,' Emmi said. Muffi was on the floor at her knee.

'Yes.' Agnes smiled at her. 'The three of you. Emmi, I haven't given up hope for your mother, but you need to leave Germany and wait for her in Sweden. I hope Jenny will agree to go out with you.'

'But I can't—' Emmi said.

'Emmi,' said Agnes, 'your mother will be happy if you're safe.'

She went still and quiet, burying her fingers in Muffi's hair. But I was suddenly breathless with panic.

'Just me?' I said. 'What about Mum?'

Agnes said, 'I'm afraid Sylvia can't travel with you, Jenny. For one thing, you'll be flying, and she's not fit to fly—'

I said, 'Leave Mum on her own here? I couldn't.'

'Yes, you can,' Mum said quickly.

'Jenny,' Agnes said, 'let me explain, please. You've got the same eye colour as Emmi, you can pass for her sister. Your father was a Swedish businessman who lived in Berlin and you've got Swedish nationality. Your mother died when Emmi was born, and your father got killed a month ago, in an air raid. Now you're going to your relations in Sweden – you've really got relations in Sweden, Emmi, haven't you?'

Emmi nodded. 'My cousins. They used to live in Copenhagen, but they had to leave.'

Agnes said, 'You've got an elder brother, and he's going with you, too. He's got fair hair and blue eyes. If anyone asks, he takes after his father, you take after your mother, the two of you. You're flying from Tempelhof tomorrow.'

'Tomorrow!' I said. I'd had enough of all this planning that I'd never agreed to. 'Agnes, I can't do this. Anyway, I haven't got a passport.'

I thought that'd finish the idea, but Agnes said, 'Emmi, go and play in your room.'

Emmi went, taking Muffi with her.

Agnes said, 'You've got to know this, so you don't show any surprise tomorrow. Your Rafael's going with you. He's going to be acting your elder brother. He had a photograph of you that we've used for a passport. It's a good thing the photograph's black and white, because you'll need to dye your hair brown, like Emmi's. The story is that your mother had brown hair, too.'

'Raf,' I said stupidly. I'd see Raf? We'd go to Sweden together? For a moment my heart sang. Only – how could I leave Mum behind? I felt as if I was being pulled in half.

'You've got to go, Jenny,' Mum said in a voice that shook. 'Jenny, I'm – I'm ordering you to go.'

I dug my fingernails into my palm. Agnes was still talking.

'You'll go to a house tonight. You'll get clothes and luggage and Rafael will be there. I don't want Emmi to know too much about him, that's why I sent her outside. And Muffi can fly with you. She'll have to go into a special cage on the journey, but she'll travel in the cabin, so you can reassure her. And about Rafael' – she looked emphatically at me – 'remember you mustn't let Emmi suspect you already know him. Not till you're in Sweden. When you get to Stockholm, there'll be people looking out for you. They'll take care of you.'

I said, 'But surely, it could wait till Mum's better, then she could be our mother.'

Agnes shook her head. 'We match the people we send out to the records of Swedish people who were baptised by their church in Berlin. There are entries for a family with three children who were about the same age as you three. That means we can send you and Rafael out with Emmi. But the mother's death is recorded for 1937. We can't resurrect her. Jenny, I'll take care of Sylvia for you. I promise.'

Anxiously, Mum said, 'How risky is it? Where are the family now?'

'They left Berlin before the war, but the German authorities don't know that. And the police station where the record of them would have been held was hit by a bomb.'

I said, 'Mum's not well, and there are bombs, and there's the Gestapo—'

Mum bit her lip. 'Nothing's safe, Jenny. I know that, but we just have to hope. And do what we can.'

I moved up the bed and put my arms round Mum. She stroked my back.

'Go with Raf,' she said. 'Dad would want you to go. And Aunty Edith.'

I remembered Aunty Edith telling us to take care of Raf. I knew Mum was right. I'd have to go. And my heart sang again: Raf. I'll be seeing Raf – and at once I was furious with myself – heartless, another voice said inside me, that's what you are.

I thought of something else. 'My hair, with it cropped the way it is, the police at the airport will know I've been in a camp.'

'I've got a wig for you,' Agnes said. 'Nice quality, too. If anyone notices that, tell them your hair got burned in the air raid when your father was killed. That's why you need to have brown hair underneath it.'

'All right,' I said. 'I'll go.'

Mum's arms went round me and tightened. 'Thank God,' she said. 'Thank God.'

Agnes got up to go out and leave us, but Mum asked, quietly, 'Agnes, what do you think has happened to Emmi's mother?'

'Christine?' Agnes said, just as quietly. 'I'm afraid she might have been killed in the air raid. Or they've taken her. She'd sooner have died than tell them where Emmi is, you know.'

Agnes took me into the bathroom and dyed my hair, then I sat in the bedroom with Mum and we talked till it was time to go. She kept saying nothing would stop her joining us in Sweden and I said, 'Yes, Mum. I know.' Only both of us knew – even though we didn't say it – there were so many things that could.

When I took one last look at her, sitting in the bed putting a brave face on, I had a horrible tearing feeling inside me.

'Look after her,' I said to Agnes as we went out of the door.

'I will,' she said.

I told myself Mum was as safe as anyone could be these days. And Agnes had a cellar for air raids and a little hiding place where Mum could go if the police came. Emmi and her mother had hidden there once. And Dr Fink was a good doctor, and she'd said Mum was on the mend.

Agnes took my hands and said, 'You're doing the best thing for her. Believe me, I'm a mother, I know.'

I couldn't speak. I went off down the path and I kept thinking: It's wrong, it oughtn't to be like this. Muffi whined and kept tugging backwards on the lead.

We had ten blocks to walk till we came to Clover Road, where Agnes had told us to ring the bell at number sixty. We didn't have any luggage, but I was carrying some of Uncle Hartmut's Reichsmarks. Some of them had paid for my air ticket – Mum had insisted – and Mum had kept the rest. Emmi was clutching the teddy bear she took to bed at night. He was a serious-looking animal who growled when you tilted him – it was more like a sheep baaing, actually. Bernhard, he was called. She put her other hand in mine and walked nervously along the darkening street. Muffi stopped trying to go back and crouched to pee beside a lamppost.

'I haven't been outside for a whole year,' Emmi whispered to me.

'Emmi,' I whispered back, 'you mustn't say things like that.'

'Sorry.'

But I felt strange too, out in the open with nobody giving me orders. I thought: I'm always getting out and other people get left behind. First of all it was Erna and Luise, now it's Mum.

The new house was as big as Uncle Hartmut's. It had no gates, though, they must have been melted down for the war effort. We went up the path and rang the doorbell. A stout white-haired lady answered it. Frau Ulrich, who was putting us up for the night. She smiled and put her arms round me. 'Welcome,' she said.

We went into a sitting room full of antique furniture. The blackout blinds were already down and the curtains drawn. And Raf was there.

He was wearing the sweater I'd knitted him. That was all I had time to notice before Muffi went mad. I stood there watching her jump up at him and squeal and lie on her back to have her tummy rubbed, thinking: We should have known she'd behave like that. And his eyes met mine and I knew he was half-crazy with joy, just like me. He picked Muffi up. He said, 'What a friendly dog.'

Frau Ulrich smiled blandly. 'She's your dog,' she said, wrapping Muffi and Raf in the story we were going to tell about ourselves. And I saw Emmi look at Raf holding Muffi in his arms, then at Frau Ulrich, and her mouth closed tight. She knew not to ask questions. But I had to keep watching Raf's hands stroking Muffi and I seemed to feel them on me, and when he bent and kissed Muffi's head I felt his lips on my hair, and I knew he was kissing Muffi the way he wanted to kiss me, only he couldn't.

'Now,' Frau Ulrich said, 'remember who you are?'

'Axel Andersen,' Raf said, putting Muffi down. She stood beside him, panting and wagging her tail.

'Helga Andersen,' I said.

Emmi said, 'Inga Andersen.'

'It's nice to have younger sisters,' Raf said, and he shook hands with both of us, but he held onto my hand for a moment longer than he needed to. 'You're very thin, Helga Andersen. And who's cut your hair?' His voice was worried.

'I'm all right,' I said, trying to reassure him.

'Come and have dinner,' said Frau Ulrich, 'that'll put some flesh on you.'

Her food was good, but nothing like as rich as Uncle Hartmut's. She told us to invent memories from our childhood together. 'Not just because of the police, you'll need to talk on the plane, and that's still German territory, you're flying Lufthansa, you know.'

'When you were really little,' Raf told Emmi, 'you used to call me Attel.'

'It's a good thing for her you're so much older,' I said to him, 'or you'd have cut her bear's hair off the way you did my doll's.'

'Heidi,' Raf said, and grinned, remembering my doll Heidi who'd really had to go to the toys' hospital to get new hair after he'd finished with her. Only then I remembered the woman hacking my hair off at Ravensbrück. I felt as if a pit had opened up inside me and I stopped talking.

Raf noticed and I saw him frown, but he started to tell stories about our maid Anna, and the cakes she always made for our birthdays, chocolate-covered with almond nibs sticking up to make the cake look

383

like a hedgehog. We'd really had those birthday cakes when we were kids, Karl, Raf and I. Raf was smiling at me, raising one eyebrow, anxious to make me feel better. I smiled back, to reassure *him*. I wished I could go into his arms.

Instead, I got us working out the story of the air raid – our house had started to burn, and we'd been getting furniture out, only the stairs had collapsed and killed our father and a burning ember had set my hair alight. Axel had put it out, but it had been so badly damaged most of it had to be cut off.

'Anna died in the raid too, didn't she?' Frau Ulrich prompted us.

I realised it was better if she had done. Just in case anyone tried to track her down. Our story had to stay watertight even after we'd left Berlin, because of the people who were still there, who'd helped us.

We were German-speakers, for all we were Swedish nationals. We'd been to a German school in Berlin. Our father had tried to teach us Swedish, but we'd never really made the effort.

'I can remember a few words,' Raf said, 'but not much.'

I guessed he really knew some Swedish but I didn't ask where he'd learned it. That could come later.

After dinner, Frau Ulrich showed Emmi and me our suitcases. They weren't new, but they were smart – best quality pigskin. Aunt Grete wouldn't have scorned them. They were full of our new clothes. Emmi and I stood in the bedroom where I was going to sleep and we dressed up in front of the big wardrobe with the mirror inside the door. Most of the clothes fitted. There were just two skirts that were too wide around the waist for me. 'But keep them,' Frau Ulrich said, 'because I hope you'll put on weight.' There was just one dress that Emmi would have to leave behind because it was too small for her.

We had coats, too, good thick wool and cashmere ones, warm enough for Sweden, and warm hats. We had to leave all the clothes we'd come with. Emmi was allowed to keep Bernhard, that was all.

I didn't ask where the clothes had come from, that'd be another secret.

Frau Ulrich sent Emmi to bed after that, and took me downstairs to have coffee with her and Raf in the sitting room. She wanted us to carry on with the game of inventing our past, but I was really tired. I felt sore inside because of leaving Mum, I was longing to be in Raf's arms, I wanted to stop pretending I was his sister. I dried up. Frau Ulrich didn't push me. I drank my coffee and Raf talked to Frau Ulrich about architecture – it seemed Axel Andersen wanted to be an architect too.

Then Frau Ulrich said she had to talk to the maid and she left the room. Raf and I stood up, ran together and kissed, lips first, then I began kissing the side of his neck and his ear and he started running his hands down my sides, but he stopped before he could reach my breasts. He held me away from him and looked into my face. 'Jenny,' he said, 'I can feel all your ribs, what's been happening to you? And what about Aunty Sylvia?'

I whispered, 'The Broomstick did denounce us, but they didn't find anything and we didn't talk. They sent Mum and me to a camp. Uncle Hartmut got us out.'

Raf went quiet and I felt the tenseness in his hands. 'That filthy hag,' he said. 'Jenny, as God is my witness, one day I'll make sure she gets what she deserves.' It made me shiver, the way he said it, but I was glad, because I felt the same way. I'd never thought I could hate anyone so much.

'How did you get out?' he asked.

I told him. I explained how Uncle Hartmut had sent us to Agnes Hummel. He knew the rest. I told him how bad I felt about leaving Mum. I cried in his arms and he kissed my hair, and we went on kissing till I heard Frau Ulrich opening the sitting-room door. She'd been gone a good while: I did wonder if she'd left us alone on purpose.

Chapter Twenty-seven

We were booked onto a plane at one in the afternoon, and the flight was supposed to take just over three hours – though you couldn't rely on timetables in wartime. Frau Ulrich was going to drive us to the airport in her car and she got us out to it at ten in the morning, because she was worried about holdups on the way.

'You can end up having to make enormous detours because of bomb damage,' she said. 'Or there might be a raid.'

Her car was smart and sporty-looking, grey and black with a hood, not at all the kind of thing I'd have expected her to drive.

'A DKW,' Raf said, and whistled.

Her face was sad and amused at the same time. 'It was my late husband's pride and joy.'

'Was he killed in action?' I asked.

She shook her head. 'He died of cancer.' I said something sympathetic and she sighed. 'Life isn't always easy.'

We loaded everything into the boot and got in ourselves, Raf in the front, Emmi and I in the back. Frau Ulrich turned the key in the ignition. Nothing happened. Raf said, 'Shall I try the crank handle?' so he got out and found it in the boot, put it into the front of the car and turned it round. The car coughed a few times but refused to get going. Frau Ulrich said, 'Drat!' She got out and looked under the bonnet, muttering something about spark plugs. Raf went too. I was surprised she knew how to fix a car – I wasn't sure how much Raf knew about it, either, but he was a boy, he'd never leave a piece of machinery alone. I sat there with Emmi while the two of them fiddled around and talked car engine language, and then Frau Ulrich said, 'Can you try and start her now?' and Raf wiped his hands off on a cloth she had in the garage and got in and turned the ignition key.

This time the engine didn't even cough and the two of them went back to fiddling with it.

Emmi said, 'Helga.' She was being very good, using my alias.

'Yes, Inga?'

'Are we going to miss the plane?'

'No,' I said, wanting to reassure her.

She said, 'If we couldn't go, maybe Mama would come back after all.'

I didn't know what to answer. I knew too well how she was feeling.

Frau Ulrich straightened up, putting one blackened hand to her back so I knew it was aching from bending down. 'It's no good,' she said. 'You'll have to go by the underground. At least we left plenty of time.

The underground will take half an hour if things go smoothly – it might be longer, of course, there are power cuts – but I'm sure you'll get there on time.' She was trying to sound encouraging, but I could tell she was worried.

'Are you coming with us?' Emmi asked, clutching her bear to her.

'I'm sorry,' she said. 'I would come, but I don't walk very fast. I'd hold you up, my dears, that's the truth.'

We walked down the street towards the underground station at half past ten. Raf had a new well-cut overcoat on top of the sweater I'd given him for Christmas. He had a pigskin suitcase full of new clothes too, it matched ours and we looked the part, a young lady and gentleman with their nice little kid sister and their dog, and Raf's rucksack – he'd kept that too – full of the picnic Frau Ulrich's maid had packed for us. Raf was carrying Emmi's suitcase as well as his own.

Frau Ulrich had said, 'If you do miss the plane, come back here.' I thought about the money Mum had given for the tickets, even for Muffi, so she could go with me. It'd be wasted if that happened. I felt the tension building up inside me, tightening all the muscles in my jaw and neck and shoulders.

But the first leg of the journey went well. We were on the line that led to the airport at Tempelhof, I was even beginning to wonder what we'd do while we waited for hours for our plane. Then the train pulled in to Mehringdamm station and I heard the sirens sounding.

Emmi shrank together and clutched my hand. 'Another air raid,' she whispered.

'It's all right,' Raf said to her. 'It's only ten to eleven. Anyway, the raid will hold the plane schedule up too.'

She said, 'Maybe the American planes will bomb the airport.' I thought she was right there. It was amazing they hadn't done it already.

'We'll worry about that if it happens,' Raf said. 'Cheer up!' But she looked at him with wide miserable eyes. She was trembling. She'd been terrified too much in her life.

I sat between her and Raf, Muffi on my lap. Muffi was trembling too, and I thought how good it'd be for her to live somewhere without air raids. A grey-haired man got into the train and asked if he could sit on my suitcase. Raf stood up for him and sat on Emmi's bag. A woman with a small boy came in, plonked herself down on Raf's case, then remembered herself and asked for permission. Raf told Emmi to come and sit on his lap so the woman could have a proper seat.

'Don't you get up,' he said to me, then, to the woman, 'My sister's been ill.'

That was a new story, but it was a good one, it explained my skinniness. Only the woman wasn't interested in my health.

'Day and night,' she muttered, shifting her son to

find a comfortable position, 'when are we supposed to rest?'

The grey-haired man twitched beside me and said, 'They want to wear us down, that's the whole point. But you ought to send that child out of Berlin.'

The mother stroked the boy's hair and said, 'I'm not sending my darling to strangers, who knows what they'd do to him.'

I was on edge, thinking about Mum. It wasn't just now, it was all the time ahead – God knew how long – when I'd have no idea if she was safe. Even if I got a letter from her in Sweden it'd only tell me she'd been alive when Agnes had left the house to post it. The Americans might drop a bomb on the house the moment Agnes had gone round the corner and no cellar could survive a direct hit.

I felt Raf's hand on my shoulder. 'Stay calm, sis,' he said. I looked at him and he raised his eyebrows at me. 'You've got to hope for the best,' he said. 'Remember what Dad always said.'

I thought: Hoping for the best didn't help Uncle Markus.

The man said, 'You're on leave, are you, young fellow?'

'We're Swedish,' Raf explained. 'We're supposed to be flying home this afternoon.'

'Lucky you,' the mother said.

The air was getting stuffy, with so many people sheltering in the station.

The man said, 'You're foreigners? I'd never know, your German's so good.'

'We were all born in Berlin,' Raf said, and we went into our routine. I told them how our mother had died when Emmi was born. Raf said our father had been killed in an air raid, and I shuddered and said, 'Don't talk about that!'

Raf said, 'So now we're going back to our grandparents. They live just outside Stockholm.'

The earth shook with bomb-blast and nobody felt like talking any longer.

It wasn't a long raid, not quite an hour, but towards the end the lights went out. People lit their torches – Frau Ulrich had made sure Raf and I had one each – and we sat in the dimness waiting. I'd been through so many bad air raids, you'd have thought I'd have got used to it, but I wasn't ever, not really. I held Muffi and now and again Raf stretched his hand out and grasped mine. Emmi huddled against him, clutching her bear and sucking hard on her thumb.

The All Clear sounded. The people who'd come in to shelter picked themselves up and made their way out of the station. I said to Raf, 'Do you think the power will come back?'

'Maybe not,' Raf said, looking at his watch by the light of his torch. 'It's twenty to twelve. I'm sure the planes will be delayed, but it's only one stop to the airport, after all. Shall we just walk?'

I said, 'Yes. Only I hope the road isn't blocked.'

'If it is,' he said, 'we can come back down again. We're taking a chance either way.' Our eyes met for a moment. It felt like a kiss, but I felt how strung up he was, just as much as me.

So we schlepped our suitcases up the steps. I was a bit nervous about what we'd find, though nobody was coming back downstairs and that seemed like a good sign. When we got out the street looked quite normal. We asked a man with his arm in a sling which was the best way to Tempelhof.

'Just straight down there,' he said. 'Mehringdamm turns into Tempelhofdamm. I hope the Amis haven't bombed it for you.'

We'd only gone about three hundred metres when someone stepped in front of us and a hard hand gripped my arm. 'Jenny Friedemann,' a voice said. 'And is this the famous Lieutenant Frey?'

Brenner's voice. I knew it at once. My arms and hands prickled and my heart started to thump as if it was going to explode inside me.

Brenner wasn't in uniform. He was wearing a brown striped suit, but he had a gun in his hand. 'I'm off duty,' he said, 'but a good Gestapo man's alert, all the time. You're under arrest, all of you. There are a lot of questions I want to ask you. And don't bleat about having been released from the camp, Friedemann. We don't care about that.'

I saw a man cross the road to keep away from us.

That was almost as frightening as the gun. Muffi growled.

'Quiet, Muffi!' I said, terrified he'd shoot her.

'The mutt's turned vicious, I see,' Brenner said, giving her a bad look. 'You should have left it behind, by the way. It made me notice you.'

I took Emmi's hand. It was cold and still.

'Let go of the brat!' Brenner snapped. 'I haven't got a car here.' He stopped to think, keeping his gun aimed at me. 'I suppose the phone lines are down if the electricity is. You can walk. The police station's close enough. And bring that luggage. I'll want to see what's inside it.' He laughed.

He herded us on up Mehringdamm, between the usual lines of rubble and shells of buildings. The odd untouched houses looked wrong among the ruins, but that wasn't important. The only thing that was important was Brenner and his gun.

Muffi walked anxiously alongside me. I was afraid she'd growl at him again and he'd shoot her.

Raf turned his head towards me. His eyes were full of horror. I looked back at him, taking notice of his mouth that I'd kissed so often, his nose that still looked a bit too big for his face. Raf, I mouthed, hoping Brenner wouldn't notice what I was doing. I love you so much. I saw his lips move. I love you too, he was saying.

They were going to drag us apart the way they'd dragged Mum and me apart. I wouldn't even get to kiss him goodbye. They'd send him to Poland and gas him.

I kept thinking: Why didn't Frau Ulrich's car start? And we were almost at the airport.

'Turn left!' Brenner commanded. We went round the corner and found a barricade of beams and rubble across the street. Dust was rising from it.

Brenner swore. 'Shit-Ami bombs. I wonder how many Germans are dead inside there.' He snarled at us, 'I suppose you're pleased to see it, are you?'

None of us answered. Brenner shrugged his shoulders. 'Well, we'll have to make a little detour. First on the right, look sharp.'

The suitcase was dragging at my arm and shoulder, hurting them and the air was full of dust, making us all cough, but Brenner's gun didn't waver.

The next street had been destroyed some time ago. The usual track had been cleared through the rubble, but it was littered with bricks and bits of masonry. The empty windows seemed to be watching us as we walked. I stumbled over something, I'd have fallen if Raf hadn't caught my arm, but Brenner shouted at him.

'Don't fumble your slut, Jewish swine.'

'Jenny's exhausted,' Raf said angrily. 'She needs a rest or you'll end up having to carry her to the police station.' He stared at Brenner with his blue, Aryan-looking eyes. Maybe that was what carried the point, because Brenner gave way.

'All right,' he snarled. 'A few minutes, that's all.'

I sat down on the suitcase. Muffi came and huddled against me. I saw Emmi rubbing Bernhard against her face, mopping up the tears that were streaming down.

Brenner said, 'So here's Rafael Jakoby at last. You had him in your stockroom when I searched your place last year, didn't you, Friedemann? And you thought you were so clever, making a fool of me. And holding out on me when I was questioning you. Your joke's backfired on you now, though. Were you on your way to the airport, the three of you? Your friends the Americans put a stop to that.'

He came right up to me, pushing his gun into my face, and that feeling came over me again, that my body belonged to him, not me. The most I could hope to hold onto was a tiny place in my head. I felt my muscles tightening, as if they wanted to barricade my real self inside that corner.

He said, 'The brat's a Jew, too. Isn't she? I don't understand scum like you and your family – why don't you go down to the sewers and get cosy with the rats?'

When he said rats, I noticed the rotting-corpse smell, all mixed up with the smoke. It made me retch, but I didn't throw up.

'Where's your mother, by the way, Friedemann?' Brenner demanded. 'No, don't make anything up, we'll get it out of you soon enough.'

Muffi's body was vibrating, she was growling again, but under her breath. I tapped her sharply, so

Brenner wouldn't notice. My throat kept heaving, wanting to be sick because of the corpse smell.

He said, 'I had to go soft on you last time, Friedemann, because of your filthy-rich uncle, but I don't think he'll stick his neck out for a criminal we've caught red-handed. Now I'll get everything out of you. Exactly who's been helping you, for one thing – what? I thought the raid had finished.'

The sirens were starting up again.

'All right,' Brenner said angrily. 'We'll find a cellar and carry on when the All Clear sounds.'

And I heard myself wailing. 'I won't go.'

Raf said sharply, 'Jenny!' I just heard his fear, but what sounded louder in my head was the girl who'd cried out for her mother when she was dying in the camp, she seemed closer than Raf or Emmi or the barrel of Brenner's gun that was swimming into two in front of my eyes. I could just hear what Brenner was saying.

'You'll go, or I'll splash your brains all over the cobbles.'

Then I saw something else: Hitler's face that time, smiling kindly at all of us cheering girls. I saw it really clearly and I remembered how I'd shouted 'Heil!' at him. I threw up, suddenly and horribly, all the way down Brenner's shoes and his trousers.

'Filthy bitch!' he shouted at me and he clouted my face hard, knocking me backwards, but as I struggled for balance I heard something hit the ground. I saw

Raf duck down and the next minute he was holding a gun, threatening Brenner. I thought: Where did that come from? Then I realised it was Brenner's own gun. He'd lost hold of it when he slapped me. At the same moment I heard the bomber engines. Already? I thought. They must have turned round and come back. I ought to have been scared of them, but I wasn't. Everything in me was focused on Raf and Brenner and the gun.

We were the ones with a weapon now, and the street was empty. Nobody was going to come out from behind those blackened walls to go to a shelter and there weren't going to be any air-raid wardens, either. Brenner opened his mouth and yelled for help, but he must have known it was useless.

'Whose brains will be all over the cobbles?' Raf taunted. I looked at Brenner and saw the fear and shock on his face.

'You'll never get away with this,' he said, but not as if he believed it. 'Put the gun down, it'll be easier for you if you do.'

'Forget that,' Raf said. 'You murdering swine.' He actually grinned. The bomber engines were getting louder, though they weren't overhead. I just noticed them, quite coldly.

'Put your hands up,' Raf said to Brenner. Brenner did as he was told.

'Turn round,' Raf said. Brenner turned round. Raf

put the gun against his back and forced him forward. It was hard for him to walk with his hands in the air, especially since Raf was making him go up the skirt of rubble that had been cleared at the side of the street, towards a gap in what had once been a house wall. But I saw his eyes scurrying from side to side, trying to work out a way of saving himself. He was still dangerous.

Emmi let out a sob. 'Jenny, I don't like this.'

And I didn't have time to be sorry for her. I had to go with Raf in case Brenner started anything. I said, 'Stay with Bernhard.' Then I was scrambling away from her. Muffi ran with me. I left little Emmi on her own with the bombers in the sky and only a teddy bear to protect her.

The floor of the ruined building was a mess of broken bricks, girders, charred wood and sections of plastered wall. Raf was making Brenner walk over them towards the corner of the building. I went after him. I didn't ask what he was going to do. I knew. Then a bomb fell somewhere, not nearby, but the floor shook. Suddenly there was a dark hole a few metres away from us, with a small landslide of rubble and grit slithering into it. The sky darkened.

Brenner whirled round and punched at Raf. Raf dodged and he lost the gun. I saw it go flying and land almost at the edge of the hole. Now Raf and Brenner were struggling beside the wall. Muffi bounded to them. Brenner's mouth opened. The noise of the raid drowned his yell out, but I knew Muffi had bitten him. I saw Raf grab hold of Brenner's head and knock it hard against the blackened plaster. Brenner tottered.

The gun, I thought. I've got to get the gun. I took a few steps, only I was scared of the ground giving way and hurtling me into the cellar. I stopped. I got down on my belly, my back prickling in case Brenner came up behind me, I stretched out and grasped the handle. Then I crawled backwards and stood up as fast as I could manage.

Raf had knocked Brenner down onto the floor. He was kneeling on his back, pulling his arm up behind him. Muffi stood guard, baring her teeth, snarling. Brenner was still struggling. Raf hadn't hit his head hard enough.

Raf was yelling at me. The bomber engines swallowed what he was saying, but I knew what he wanted. He wanted me to shoot Brenner. And it had to happen quickly, because Brenner was trying to push himself upwards with his other arm and roll Raf over. I wasn't sure if Muffi would bite again, it went against all her instincts to bite any person, even Brenner. I had time to think all those things because time seemed to have slowed down. Feeling sick again because of what I was going to do, I bent down and aimed the gun at Brenner's head.

Raf was still fighting Brenner, but he managed to shake his head. I understood. He didn't want Brenner's brains all over us. I'd have to shoot him in the back.

I crouched down, pressed the gun between Brenner's heaving shoulder blades – the barrel was almost touching Raf's knee – and then, in that slowness that seemed to make everything go quiet, even the American planes, I thought: I can't do this. I can't kill a person. Even after all the things Brenner had done to me, when I felt his muscles, felt his life that I had the power to end, it seemed too horrible.

But I saw Raf's face, saw the veins stand out on his forehead, and then Brenner was pushing harder, Raf couldn't hold him any longer. In that muddled moment my finger seemed to go down onto the trigger all of itself, and the gunshot shook me. I felt his last struggle and the way he went limp as the life went from him.

Raf got up. There was blood staining the back of Brenner's brown striped suit and more blood running from his mouth, spreading out and spilling over a broken brick like a little red waterfall, then it splashed onto a section of wall, staining the curls of charred wallpaper that were sticking to it. Muffi backed away from the body, still growling. Raf put his mouth to my ear and said, 'Come on, let's get away from here.'

I knew I had to get rid of the gun. I chucked it at the hole in the floor. It fell on its handle about ten centimetres from the edge, toppled over and and was gone, into the darkness. Raf took my hand and pulled me away.

We were climbing through the gap in the house wall again when I remembered there might be blood on me. I looked at myself, but there wasn't. Raf turned his head and raised his eyebrows at me. I said in his ear. 'I've got to check you for blood.' He nodded. There was just a little splash on his hand. I mopped it up with my handkerchief and threw the handkerchief away. I had a nightmare feeling in my head as if I wasn't a real person at all.

Emmi was sitting on one of the suitcases, rocking herself, hugging Bernhard, and still crying. I knew I had to comfort her now, so I put my arm round her. 'It's all right,' I yelled. 'He's gone.'

She got up. She didn't try to ask any questions. We got our bags – Raf carried both this time, and I held onto Emmi. We went back the way we'd come, heading through the air raid towards the underground station. No bombs fell right near us, but the ground was shaking, and ahead of us a wall crashed down into the street – and even that didn't scare me. When we got to Mehringdamm, I heard the All Clear sound. It must just have been a few planes who'd turned round and dropped more bombs, maybe to make themselves lighter so they could get away from the Luftwaffe fighters who were after them.

We turned back towards the airport. Almost as if we'd managed to make a loop in the day, as if Brenner wasn't lying just up the street with a bullet in his back that I'd put there. Almost. I was still feeling unreal.

We reached Tempelhof at twenty-five past one. The airport was all right, but there was a long delay on our flight because of the raid, so we were in plenty of time. There was a bar in the terminal building. Raf went there and got some unconvincing apple juice for the three of us, and schnapps for him and me.

'We need it,' he said.

I felt a bit better when I'd got the schnapps down, though it burned in my throat. The fake apple juice tasted better after that, too. I even managed to eat some of the picnic Frau Ulrich had given us.

Chapter Twenty-eight

At a quarter to three they called us through. I went to the passport desk first of the three of us.

My heart started to race again as I handed my forged passport over. I told myself: You've got nothing to worry about. You're the Swedish girl on the document. You're just nervous about the flight, and going to live with grandparents you hardly know. But nobody could feel comfortable being stared at the way the policeman was staring at me. Supposing there was blood on me after all?

At last he went on to scrutinise the document itself. He looked minutely and lengthily at the different stamps and ran his thumb over the perforations at the bottom. I hoped it was a good forgery. If not – no, I wouldn't think about that. He had a black bruise on his nail, it was shaped like a map of some country I didn't know.

I was almost shocked when he handed me my passport back with a routine-sounding Heil Hitler. I opened my mouth to Heil Hitler back, then remembered I was meant to be a Swede. 'Thank you,' I said, and went to wait while Emmi and then Raf went through the same inspection.

It was all right. They got through. Neither of them said 'Heil Hitler' either. The policeman didn't seem to care. After that we had our bags searched. The official who was going through Raf's bag found his notebook and took a long time leafing through it. He asked Raf, 'Architect, are you?'

'I want to become one,' Raf said.

'Is this the kind of thing you'll be designing?' the official asked. 'It's a good thing you're going to work in Sweden.' He laughed a gruff Berlin laugh.

We gave our suitcases up to go into the hold and went up the steps to the plane. I smelt the mixture of smoke and decaying unburied corpses again, blowing off the city. Brenner was one of those corpses now. I wondered how long it'd be before anyone went inside that building and found him. Maybe it'd never happen, maybe another bomb would bury him. And I'd killed him. I wondered whether Dad would still love me if he knew I'd done that? Only I remembered Karl saying: 'I've fought.' Karl would have pulled the trigger and killed Brenner. So maybe Dad would forgive me, too.

We were in the plane, strapping ourselves in and pushing Muffi into the cage the airline provided for dogs. She didn't like that at all.

We had to sit at the back where there was room for the cage, but there was a window on either side of us. The plane was about half full, so Raf had a seat to himself on the opposite side to me and Emmi. We'd let

Emmi have the window seat, like a good brother and sister.

We were taxiing and the propellers were whirling and we were racing up the tarmac and leaving the ground. We flew over our battered city, climbing steadily. Berlin was a grid-pattern of streets, blurred where they were ruined, as if someone had been roughly over the picture with a rubber.

Somewhere down there was Mum. I felt as if I was joined to her by a rubber band, and the higher we climbed, the tighter it pulled, hurting my chest. I thought about Aunty Edith and reminded myself I was lucky to know where Mum was, only it didn't work, I don't think that kind of thought ever does. I just felt bad because of Aunty Edith. Raf reached over and put his hand on my shoulder, like a brother. I looked at him and he whispered, 'She'll be all right, Jenny.'

'Thanks,' I whispered back and I did feel a tiny bit happier, but when I saw the edges of Berlin, the woods and lakes of Brandenburg, I started wondering if we'd fly over the camp. I thought about Erna and Luise being yelled at and starved and hit with truncheons, I thought about Grendel and Kerner and the Director and I wondered if they'd always been cruel, just waiting for the opportunity to show it? I felt terribly tired all of a sudden.

A lot of fuzzy cloud was coming between the plane and the land. We began to bump and shudder. Muffi started barking inside her cage.

'What's happening?' Emmi asked, almost in tears again.

The stewardess leaned forward from her seat just behind us and said reassuringly, 'Only a bit of turbulence, nothing to worry about. It's always like this when we climb through cloud.'

I told Muffi to stop barking and she lay down with her nose on the floor, showing us how patient she was with our bad behaviour to her.

The stewardess got up to serve us food and more ersatz apple juice, tea and coffee. I drank the drinks but I couldn't face the food. I leaned back in my seat and closed my eyes. The next moment I was asleep.

When I woke up, I knew a long time had passed.

'Feeling better?' Raf asked from across the aisle.

I nodded. 'You've been asleep for two hours,' he said. Emmi was beside him now.

'I lifted her over,' he said, 'so she wouldn't disturb you. You never stirred.' He gave me a brotherly pat on the shoulder. I wanted to be in his arms.

I said, 'Where are we?'

'We're over Sweden already. Look, there's no cloud. You can see everything.'

I looked out of the window, and saw a dusky indistinct landscape and a redness on the horizon that was the setting sun. There were little lights twinkling down there on the earth.

'They're not blacked out,' Raf said as if he couldn't believe it. 'No air raids to worry about.'

When we came down over Stockholm the whole city was like a Christmas tree with lights. It felt unsafe, naked somehow.

We went through Swedish passport control and the official inspected our passports, handed them back, and said, '*Välkomna hem*.' His voice was really friendly. I understood what he was saying, too, it sounded like English. 'Welcome home.'

I didn't know what the Swedish for thank you was, so I just smiled and nodded. I didn't feel as if I was at home, but then Raf put his arm round me.

'Jenny,' he said. 'We're free.'

Afterword

In his book, *The Righteous,* Martin Gilbert estimates that though a hundred and seventy thousand of Berlin's pre-war Jewish population either emigrated of were killed, about two thousand survived in hiding in the city. One of them wrote, 'We will never know how many Berliners had the decency and courage to save their Jewish co-citizens from the Nazis – twenty thousand, thirty thousand? We don't need to know the number in order to pay homage to this untypical, admirable minority.' The characters in this novel are all invented, but I wrote it as a little piece of homage to those people's bravery.

Raf, Jenny and Emmi were helped to evacuate from Berlin by the Swedish Lutheran church, who hid Jews in the church and in the houses of sympathisers in the city, and smuggled a lot of them out of Germany. I found out about their activities in Leonard Gross's book *The Last Jews in Berlin.* Agnes Hummel is an invented character, but many German Quakers did help and hide Jews. One of them was called Elisabeth Abegg: she turned her little apartment into a temporary shelter and assembly point for Jews who'd gone underground. She shared her rations with them and got forged papers for them. She has been honoured by the Jewish Holocaust memorial organisation Yad Vashem and the City of Berlin has put a plaque in her honour on the house where she lived. One of the people she helped called her 'A light in the darkness of Nazi Germany.'